TALES FROM CENTRALIA

WHISPERS OF WAR

C.L Gill

SILVER PINES
PRESS

Dedication

To all the incredible people from my server, past and present, This book exists because of your support, creativity, and continued stay on the server. Our stories inspired this book, making it what it is today. I couldn't have done it without you. Thank you for being an integral part of this journey, for sharing your ideas, and for always believing in me.
This one is for all of you.

-C.L Gill

CONTENTS

KINGDOM OF DRAYGVOR
EMPIRE OF CESAR
WINTMORIAN EMPIRE
CENTRALIAN EMPIRE
FAR WESTERN BARBARIANS
KINGDOM OF VICER
FAR WEST KINGDOMS
KINGDOM OF KILNOR
THE FAR ISLES

N
W
E
S
KINGDOM OF NOBLE
Duskfall Shores
Ashwing Isle
Stormhaven Isle
KINGDOM OF CALSENTIA
BARBARIC TRIBES
Tribes of Kaloina Plains
Tribes of Ecraldis
ASTARI EMPIRE
Tribes of Thaebrin
MALDOR KINGDOM
KINGDOM OF FROVIL

PROLOGUE

In the year 1259 of the Imperial Calendar, the skies above Wintmore burned with smoke and fire, the cries of the dying carried on the wind as the kingdom tore itself apart, fractured under the weight of a brutal civil war that had bled the kingdom dry. Once clear and radiant, the skies were now clouded with the smoke of warfare as two houses—the House of Lumordum and the House of Winsoria—fought for dominion over the throne. The ancient House of Winstoria, proud and unyielding, clashed against the House of Lumordum. The fields that had once fed the people turned into wastelands, desolate and barren, and cities turned into graveyards. Neither side would concede even a single step. In the smoldering chaos of Wintmore, a child scavenged for bread among the ashes, her cries drowned by the crackling of distant flames and the howls of the dying.

Amidst the chaos, the neighboring Centralian Empire, ever watchful and opportunistic, saw the weakening of their neighbor as a chance to strike. The small but resource-rich village of Edenthal, nestled at the very edge of the border, stood vulnerable. Its fortifications, once strong, had crumbled under the strain of the Wintmorian civil war. The Centralian army descended upon it swiftly, capturing the land and annexing it without challenge. The Wintmorian factions, embroiled in their own struggle for power, could not spare the strength to contest the invasion. They were too fractured, too consumed by their own bloodshed.

The civil war dragged on, until at last in 1265, House of Winsoria emerged victorious, exiling the remnants of House Lumordum, but the cost was immense; endless grief, empty villages, and an empire stretched thin. Wintmore sought stability, but resentment had festered. Deep in the hearts of those who had lost sons, daughters, and fathers to the endless tide of war, a new fury grew—one that burned hot and unyielding. Among the embittered were Wintmorian extremists, deeply scarred by the conflict and filled with a burning hatred for the Centralian Empire, whom they saw as opportunistic invaders. For they could not forget the role the Centralian Empire had played in their land's downfall.

Nine years passed after the civil war in fragile peace, when this simmering anger exploded into violence. The Centralian Crown Prince sent on a diplomatic mission to Edenthal, became the target of an audacious assassination at the hands of the Wintmorian extremists. His blood stained the city's cobblestones, and with it, the beginning of a new war was written in fire and blood. The spark ignited by that single act plunged the two empires into a brutal confrontation—a war that would shape the very future of their lands. Amidst this brewing storm, there were those who lived simply, far removed from the thrones and battlefields, tending to their lands and families. In villages like Elsenburg, where the air smelled of freshly tilled soil and woodsmoke, the village folk wished to be spared from bloodshed. The storm still gathered, threatening to pull them into its fury. One such villager was Kaelan of Elsenburg, a young man whose fate would soon be entangled in the rising tide of conflict. His world was about to be shattered by forces far beyond his control. He didn't know the extent yet, but his life would soon be swept into the currents of the conflict and survival would demand something of him he wasn't sure he had.

CHAPTER
1

The sun hung high above us, casting a soft light over the rolling fields that seemed to stretch endlessly in every direction. I could feel the clouds gathering, like the whispers of something waiting, something watching. I paused for a moment, resting my weight on the handle of the scythe, and looked out at the waves of golden wheat swaying gently in the breeze.

The crops looked almost alive, shifting and shimmering under the sun. My older brother Eamon, was a few rows over. I could hear the whistle of the scythe as he worked rhythmically, like cicadas singing in the afternoon heat. He joked about rain coming, about the rains kissing the blazing sun. But to me, it felt like the land itself held its breath, as if even the hills knew a storm was brewing somewhere beyond our quiet fields.

I wiped the sweat from my brow with the back of my hand, looking over at Eamon. He looked content, focused on the work in front of him. Eamon always took to fieldwork like he was born to it. I'd always admired that about him, how he seemed to understand the rhythm of the earth better than anyone else. For me, it took a little more effort, but I couldn't deny the satisfaction that came with each swing of the scythe, each weed pulled and tossed aside.

The day was warm, the kind of warmth that settled into your bones and made you feel alive. I could feel the heat on my skin, the sweat running down my back, soaking into my tunic. My hands were rough from the work and my muscles ached, but it was a good kind of ache—the kind that reminded you that you were doing something worthwhile, something that mattered. I glanced over at the rolling hills again. The tall grass rolled in the wind, and I could see Elsenburg's silhouette, the old bell tower standing. It was calming.

"You day-dreaming again, Kaelan?" Eamon called out, a grin spreading across his face as he straightened up, shading his eyes with one hand to look at me. I chuckled, shaking my head.

"Just admiring the view," I said, gesturing out towards the horizon where the fields met the sky, the boundary between earth and heaven almost indistinguishable under the evening sun. Eamon gave a short laugh, nodding.

"Fair enough," he said, his soft grin turning into a wide smile. "It is a good day, isn't it?"

I nodded. It was a good day.

The wind picked up for a moment, rustling the wheat and carrying with it the scent of the earth—rich and fertile. I closed my eyes for a second, breathing it in, letting the scent fill my lungs. It was the smell of growth, of life.

"Remember last summer?" Eamon said, his voice cutting through my thoughts. He was smiling again, a far-off look in his eyes. "When the great flood came and the fields were swallowed by the floodwater?"

I laughed, nodding. "How could I forget? We were out here for days afterwards, trying to save what we could. I swear I still have blisters from that week."

Eamon chuckled, shaking his head. "Yeah, but we pulled through. The fields look better than ever this year, don't they?"

He was right. Despite everything, despite the storms and the heat and the endless hours of work, the fields were thriving. The wheat stood tall, the stalks strong and healthy, with heads heavy with grain.

"Alright, back to it then," I said, lifting my scythe again and setting my feet. Eamon gave a mock salute and turned back to his row, the grin still on his face. I could hear the steady rhythm of his work start up again, blending in with the sounds of the fields.

I took a deep breath, letting the warmth of the sun and the gentle rustle of the crops wash over me before I started in on my own row once more. There was still a lot to do, but somehow, it didn't feel so daunting. Not today. Today, it just felt right.

Eamon and I worked in silence for a while, the only sounds being the steady crunch of our feet on the dry earth and the occasional scrape of the scythe against the ground. It was a companionable silence, one that spoke of years of shared work and understanding. We didn't need words to fill the time—the fields, the sun, the work, all of it was enough.

As the sun dipped lower, the sky began to change, the bright light fading into shades of orange and pink, with streaks of colored clouds painting the horizon. I straightened up, leaning on the fence my great-grandfather had built so long ago and taking it all in.

There was something almost magical about this time of day, the way the light softened, and the world seemed to slow down, as if the earth itself was taking a breath.

"You ever wonder what's out there?" Eamon asked suddenly, his voice breaking the stillness of the sunset. He didn't look up from his work, but I could hear the curiosity in his voice, the way it lifted, as if he was asking more than just a simple question.

"Out where?" I asked, even though I knew what he meant. I kept my gaze on the ground in front of me, moving the scythe with deliberate care, trying to keep my focus on the task at hand.

"Beyond Elsenburg. Beyond the hills and the fields and… all of this," Eamon said, finally pausing and looking up, his eyes catching the rays of the sun. He rested his scythe on his shoulder, his face thoughtful. "You hear stories, you know? Stories of a whole different world out there, with cities that never sleep; about Central, Wintmore and the other kingdoms. About the war and what's going on out there." He paused, a flicker of something intense crossing his face. Don't you ever wonder what it's all like? What else is out there?" I stopped, glancing over at him. There was a spark in his eyes, a glint of excitement and longing that stirred something uneasy in me. I shrugged. "I don't know, Eamon. The stories I hear aren't exactly the kind that make me want to leave. Wars and soldiers and people dying. Doesn't sound like much of an adventure."

Eamon sighed, "Yeah, I know. But still… I mean, there's got to be more out there than just war, right? Opportunities. Things we've never even imagined. His gaze drifted back to the hills as if they held some hidden promise only he could see, "I can't help but wonder what it'd be like to see it all for myself. To go to Central, maybe even further, like to Kilnor. To see what lies beyond the life we know here."

I shook my head, turning my gaze back to the field. "What's wrong with the life we have here? It's good, isn't it? We've got the farm, Ma and Pa, the fields… everything we need. I don't see the point in going off to chase something we don't even know is out there. Besides, the world's a dangerous place. Especially with the war."

Eamon looked at me for a long moment, his expression unreadable. Then he smiled, a softer, almost wistful smile. "I know you're right, Kaelan. I just I can't help it. He shrugged, his eyes drifting back to the horizon, where the sun was now almost completely gone, the sky darkening into deeper shades of purple and blue. "Maybe it's silly. But sometimes, I just wonder."

I let out a sigh, giving him a small, tired smile. "It's not silly, Eamon. I get it. I do. But this farm – it's enough for me. Besides, Ma and Pa need someone looking out for them."

Eamon smiled, and he reached over, clapping a hand on my shoulder. "I know, Kaelan. And that's why I've got you—to keep my head on straight. I nodded. "Good. Now, let's pack it up. It's getting dark, and Ma will be wondering where we've gotten to."

Eamon glanced at me, his mischievous grin returning. "Aye, aye, Captain. Let's get these tools in before Ma sends a search party."

As light faded, we gathered up our scythes and other tools, the sounds of metal clinking softly as we piled them into the wheelbarrow. The walk back to the farmhouse was quiet, the kind of quiet that wasn't awkward or strained, but comfortable, filled with the knowledge that we'd done our work and done it well. The sky was dark now, the first stars just beginning to peek out, and the air had cooled; the warmth of the day giving way to the gentle chill of the twilight.

Eamon walked beside me, his gaze occasionally drifting towards the horizon as if he could see something out there that I couldn't. I knew he probably would always have that part of him—that curiosity, that longing to see more, to do more. And maybe one day, he'd follow it. But for now, he was here, and that was enough.

At the farmhouse, the warm glow of the lamps welcomed us, casting flickering shadows on the walls. The comforting scent of stew filled the air, as Ma bustled about in the kitchen. Pa was already seated at the table, his eyes lighting up as we entered.

"There they are! Thought you boys might've gotten lost in those fields," he said, grinning. He gestured to the empty chairs at the table. "Sit down before the food gets cold."

"Sorry, Pa. We just wanted to make sure we got everything done before calling it a day," Eamon said as he plopped down in his chair, his usual grin in place. I slid into my seat.

Ma brought over a pot of steaming stew, setting it in the center of the table before taking her seat. She looked at both of us, her eyes brimming with affection. "You boys work too hard. But I suppose that's the way we taught you." She smiled. "Now, Dig. You deserve a good meal."

We didn't need to be told twice. The first spoonful was rich and hearty, just what I needed after the long day. For a while, the only sounds were those of spoons clinking against the old wooden bowls and the satisfied hums of a family at peace.

After a few minutes, Eamon broke the silence, leaning back in his chair. "We were talking about the war earlier," he said, his voice casual, "What do you think, Pa? You reckon things will calm down soon?"

Pa's face grew serious, his gaze drifting. "Hard to say, son. It has been going on for about a year or so, and the war was brewing for a while. Wars don't end as quickly as they start," he said, his voice serious. "And we're lucky to be here, far from it."

I nodded in agreement, glancing at Eamon. "I can't imagine leaving the farm to fight," I said, "I'd rather stay here, work the fields, and help the family."

Eamon chuckled, but his eyes held the same spark they had earlier. "Oh, I'm with you there, Kaelan. No way am I meant for the army either. But you know," he added, a mischievous twinkle in his eyes, "I could be a spy instead; slipping through the shadows unseen..."

Ma laughed, shaking her head. "Eamon, you'd barely last five minutes before someone caught you. You're far too loud to be creeping anywhere unseen."

"Hey, I can be quiet when I want to," Eamon protested, though his grin gave him away. We laughed. He laughed along, but then, his face grew more thoughtful. "Actually," he hesitated glancing at each of us, "I've been hearing about an opening with the Crimson Merchant Alliance. They're looking for people to join a caravan headed to distant kingdoms for trade." He paused, his voice suddenly serious, "I've been thinking – maybe, I'll join."

CHAPTER 2

The words hung in the air, as the room went quiet. Ma and Pa exchanged glances, their faces a mix of surprise and worry. I looked at Eamon. I could see the resolve in his eyes; this was no fleeting idea. He meant it.

Pa cleared his throat, his brow furrowing. "Eamon, joining up with the Crimson Merchant Alliance… that's a big step. It's dangerous out there, son, with the war and all the unrest. You might think it's just trading, but there's risk involved. More than you know."

Ma nodded, her brow lined with concern. "We just want you safe, love. Maybe we should all take a breath and think about this some more."

Eamon opened his mouth to respond, but Pa held up a hand. "No more tonight. Let's leave the talk of politics and trading for another day. We've had a long day. Tomorrow, we'll talk about it when we're fresh." He gave Eamon a thin smile, though I could see the unease lingering in his eyes. "Alright?"

Eamon hesitated, then nodded, his shoulders relaxing slightly. "Alright, Pa. Tomorrow."

The strain in the room eased a little. We all turned back to our bowls, the warmth of the stew filling the silence that had settled over us. For now, at least, the talk of leaving, the world beyond our fields, would have to wait.

After dinner, Ma cleared the dishes, and Pa went to stoke the fire in the hearth. Eamon and I helped tidy up, the routine tasks filling the silence that had fallen. The warmth of the fire soon filled the room as Pa settled into his chair, with Ma joining him, her knitting in hand. The quiet of the night returned, and despite Eamon's announcement, there was a fleeting sense of calm that settled over the house.

Eamon gave me a small smile as we finished up, a silent reassurance. I nodded back, and we both headed to our room, the tiredness of the day finally catching up with us. Though we didn't talk much as we got ready for bed, the weight of the earlier conversation still hung in the air, unspoken but present. I lay in my bed, staring at the ceiling, listening to the gentle crackle of the fire from the other room. Eventually, sleep took hold, and the worries of the day drifted away.

***

The morning came with the soft light of the dawn filtering through the curtains, washing over the room and waking me slowly. I blinked against it, stretching out the stiffness from the previous day's work. In the kitchen, I could hear Ma moving about, the clink of pots and pans as she prepared breakfast. The scent of freshly baked bread reached my nose, and I took a deep breath, letting it steady me. It was a new day, and with it, the promise of fresh conversations.

I quickly got dressed and made my way to the kitchen when Eamon caught up with me, Ma was setting out plates on the table. The bread was fresh out of the oven, the crust golden and steaming. She smiled at us as we entered. "Good morning, boys,"

"Morning, Ma," we both replied in unison, sitting down for a quick meal. We tore into the bread, savoring the warmth and comfort. It wasn't long before we were finished, and I could hear Pa outside already—the familiar clinking of metal and shuffle of tools being moved around. He was always up early, always working on something.

"Best get moving now, boys," Ma said, giving us both a nod as she cleared the dishes. "Your father could use some help today, I'm sure."

I nodded and we headed out into the morning light. Eamon seemed distracted, and I knew what was on his mind. The air was cool and crisp and Pa was by the barn working on repairs to an old plow. He inspected the blade, his hands moving with the practiced ease of someone who had done this a thousand times. A pile of tools lay at his feet—some needed sharpening, others waiting for their turn.

"Morning, Pa," I called out, and he looked up, giving us both a nod.

"Morning, boys," he replied. "Kaelan, why don't you start over there with the west field? Eamon, come give me a hand here for a bit."

I nodded, grabbing a hoe and heading out towards the west field. As I moved away, Eamon joined Pa by the barn, his voice low. I couldn't catch every word, but the mention of "Crimson Merchant Alliance" and "Central" reached my ears, and my heart tightened. I kept my head down, focusing on the rows ahead of me, but my ears were still tuned to their conversation.

Pa set the plow blade aside, his brow furrowing as he looked at Eamon. "You have given this much thought, have you not?" he asked, his voice low, but firm enough for me to catch it from where I stood. Eamon nodded, his expression earnest.

"I have, Pa. There's a meeting in Central next week. They said they could take me on as part of the caravan… It'll be three months. Just three months, and I'll be back. I'll be able to see more of the world learn more about trade. It's an opportunity I can't pass up." Pa sighed, rubbing a hand over his face. He was silent for a moment, then spoke again, his voice heavy. "Three months is a long time, Eamon. And Central… it's not close by. Things are uncertain with the war. It's not just about trading— there's a risk, and I need you to understand that."

Eamon nodded, his eyes steady. "I know, Pa. But I'm willing to take that risk. I've thought about it a lot. I need to do this… for myself."

I gripped the hoe tight, my mind racing. Three months. He's always the one with grand dreams, looking beyond our fields and village. Hearing it spoken aloud made it real in a way that I wasn't ready for.

After a tense silence, Pa placed a steadying hand on Eamon's shoulder, his gaze filled with a quiet plea. "Alright, Eamon. We'll talk more tonight. But just… promise me you'll mind yourself."

Eamon smiled, his face lighting up. "I promise, Pa." He looked toward the horizon with that familiar far-off look. I took a deep breath, turning back to my own work. No matter what happened, I had to trust Eamon knew what he was doing.

***

Midday finally arrived, and the sun hung high in the sky, casting a bright, almost blinding light over the fields. My muscles ached from the morning's work, and I was grateful when Pa called out for us to take a break. Eamon flashed me a grin, and I knew he had been waiting for this. We set down our tools, dusting off our hands before making our way towards the village.

Elsenburg was only a short walk from our farm, and as we approached, the sounds of the village met us —the chatter of people, the occasional bark of a dog, and the clatter of carts rolling over cobblestone streets. It was vibrant and full of life, and everyone knew everyone else. Children ran through the narrow streets, their laughter ringing as they chased each other. A group of women stood near a well, chatting animatedly as they filled their buckets, while a man led a stubborn goat down the road, muttering under his breath as the animal resisted every step.

Eamon and I wove our way through the lively streets. We passed the blacksmith's shop, the clang of hammer on metal echoing. The smell of freshly baked bread wafted from the bakery, and I caught sight of a cluster of villagers gathered outside, waiting for their turn to buy a loaf. The village was alive with movement, with people going about their daily routines, and it was comforting to be a part of it—to see familiar faces and hear familiar voices

"It's busy today," I remarked glancing at Eamon as we walked on.

Eamon nodded, his eyes scanning the crowd, a small smile playing on his lips.

"Aye. It always feels different coming here after a morning in the fields. It's as if the whole world's bustling along while we're there working the land," he said, his tone thoughtful. I knew what he meant—there was a kind of energy to the village, a sense of community that was comforting. Out in the fields, it was just us and the land, but here, we felt like part of something bigger.

Eamon nudged me with his elbow, nodding towards one of the stalls where a group had gathered. "Come on, let's see what they've got today," he said, his eyes bright.

The market was alive with colors and scents, each offering something different. One stall had bright fabrics hung up, swaying in the breeze, another had baskets overflowing with fresh vegetables—leeks, cabbages, onions, all arranged neatly. A little further down, a vendor called out, advertising jars of honey, the sunlight catching the golden liquid inside. The square bustled, with people moving from stall to stall, bartering and chatting. The air was filled with the mixed scents of herbs, leather, and livestock.

Eamon seemed fascinated as if seeing everything for the first time, stopping here and there to inspect a piece of carved wood or a bundle of dried herbs. I let him explore while I made my way toward the butcher's stall. The smell of smoked meats wafted toward me as I approached, and I waited in line for a moment before stepping up to the counter.

"Hey, Kaelan," the burly butcher greeted me with a nod. "What can I get you today?"

"A pound of pork, please," I replied, glancing at the slabs of meat laid out on the counter. The butcher nodded, wrapping a portion and setting it on the scale.

I pulled out a few Emerul coins from my pouch, my fingers brushing against the edges of the coins as I counted them. I noticed, with a frown, that the price had gone up again. It was more than it had been just a few weeks prior—another reminder of the war and its impact on everything, even here in

Elsenburg. The butcher caught my expression and gave me an apologetic shrug.

"Prices are rising, lad. Nothing I can do about it," he said, his voice tinged with regret. I nodded, offering him a small smile.

"I understand," I said, handing over the coins. He took them and gave me the wrapped pork, and I slipped it into my satchel before turning back to find Eamon.

He stood by a stall where a pale old man with a big hat sold small trinkets—rings, necklaces, and little carved animals. A silver chain with a green pendant caught his eye. His fingers brushed over it, lingering.

"Ready to go?" I nudged him gently and he looked up, giving me a grin.

"Aye, let's go," he said, casting one last glance at the pendant before turning away from the stall. Then we made our way toward the market's edge. Once we left the bustle behind, Eamon grew quiet, his gaze became distant, and I knew he had something on his mind. After a few moments, he glanced at me, his gaze solemn.

"Kaelan," he began, hesitantly, "Tomorrow, I'm heading to Central. The capital."

I stopped, staring at Eamon. "Tomorrow?" The word felt heavy. Eamon nodded.

"Aye. All has been arranged already. The Crimson Merchant Alliance is meeting there. It'll be three months, Kaelan. Three months of traveling with them, learning the trade…"

I felt a tightness in my chest, "Why didn't you tell me sooner?" I asked, my voice shaky. Eamon sighed, running a hand through his hair.

"I knew you'd try to talk me out of it," he said, a wistful smile on his face. "And maybe I'd have let you. I know it's sudden, but this is something I must do, Kaelan," he said, his voice sure.

I saw the earnestness in his eyes, the way his gaze shifted as if focused on something far beyond our village, our fields. It was the same look he'd had when we were boys when he'd talk about the world beyond Elsenburg, about all the places he wanted to see. And I knew there was nothing I could say to change his mind.

I nodded slowly, swallowing down my worry. "Alright," I shrugged, my voice steady. "Just… come back soon, will you?"

Eamon's face softened, and he clapped a hand on my shoulder. "I will, Kaelan. You'll see me back here before long. And when I return, I shall have stories to share with you—about Central, and the places we journey to. You'll see."

CHAPTER 3

The next day arrived quicker than I wanted it to, with the early morning sun casting a soft glow over our home. The air curled with excitement and sadness as we prepared for Eamon's departure. Ma insisted on throwing a little goodbye feast.

It wasn't anything grand—just a simple gathering with family and food, enough to make the day special. The kitchen table was covered with Ma's best cooking—fresh bread, roasted vegetables, a pot of stew, and even a small cake that she'd baked just for the occasion. Pa had brought out a jug of cider, pouring each of us a glass as we gathered around the table. The mood was light, though there was an underlying tension that none of us spoke about—the knowledge that after today, Eamon would be gone for a while, off to a place we'd never seen, doing things we could only imagine.

Eamon was all smiles, his eyes alight with excitement as he spoke about the journey ahead. He talked about the caravan, the traders he'd be traveling with, and the places they'd pass through on the way to Central. Ma's gaze lingered on him as if memorizing every detail of his face from, his light brown hair to his amber eyes, to even the tiny scar on his cheek from when we were kids, her eyes filled with worry.

"You make sure to write to us, Eamon," she said, her voice gentle but firm. "I want to hear all about these adventures of yours."

"I will, Ma," Eamon promised, reaching over to squeeze her hand. "I'll write as often as I can. And I'll be back before you know it."

Pa raised his glass, his expression proud but serious. "To Eamon," he said, his voice hoarse. "Keep yourself safe out there, and come back in one piece."

Eamon grinned, but I caught the flicker in his eyes, just for a second, as he looked at Ma and Pa. There was light laughter as we raised our glasses, echoing the toast. "To Eamon."

The rest of the morning passed in a blur of laughter and stories. We ate, we talked, and for a little while, it almost felt like any other day. But as the sun climbed higher in the sky, the time came for Eamon to leave. He had his pack ready, slung over one shoulder, and stood at the edge of the yard, looking back at us with a smile that was both excited and sad.

"Well, I guess this is it," he said, his voice wavering just a little. He looked at each of us in turn—Pa, Ma, and then me. "I'll miss you all."

When it was Ma's turn to hug him, she held him tight. "You take care of yourself, Eamon," she whispered, "and remember, no matter where you go, this will always be your home." She held on for a moment longer as if her grip might somehow keep him with us a little longer. Eamon hugged her back, his eyes glistering. "I know Ma. I'll be back soon. I promise."

Pa shook his hand, pulling him into a quick, firm embrace. "Be safe, son," he said, his voice gruff. "We're proud of you."

Finally, Eamon turned to me, and for a moment, we just looked at each other. There were so many things I wanted to say, but none of the words felt right. Instead, I reached out, pulling him into a hug. "Take care, Eamon," I murmured, my voice rasping. "I'll be here when you get back."

Eamon patted my back, his grip strong. "I know you will, Kaelan." He pulled away and looked into my face. "Look after Ma and Pa, Kaelan," he said. "Don't let them worry too much." His words left a weight in my chest, one that lingered as I watched him walk away, his figure growing smaller and smaller until he was just a speck in the distance, heading towards the unknown.

***

It felt strange, the way time passed after Eamon left. At first, I'd expect to hear his laughter somewhere in the house, only to remember he was miles away on the road to Central. Days in the fields blurred into each other, but each day held a spark of anticipation. Each time I saw the messenger, I felt a pull in my chest, hoping there'd be a word for us.

Finally, one afternoon, I saw Ma waving a parchment as she called my name. I dropped the hoe I'd been using, hurrying inside to hear Eamon's news. We gathered around the kitchen table—Ma, Pa, and I—as she carefully unfolded the letter. Her fingers trembled just a little, and I could see the excitement in her eyes. She began to read, her voice soft but clear, filling the quiet room with Eamon's words.

"Ma, Pa, and Kaelan," she began, her smile widening as she continued. "I hope you're all doing well. I miss you all every day, but I'm happy to say that I've officially become part of the

Crimson Merchant Alliance. I'm serving under the Centralian branch, and it's been everything I hoped it would be."

Ma paused for a moment, glancing up at us, her eyes glimmering. Pa gave her a nod, his expression proud, and she continued reading.

"I'll be staying in central and the surrounding towns for a few months trading locally before my last mission heading off to the Empire of Cesar and we'll be passing through Wintmore. I know you've all heard about the conflict there, but please don't worry. The Alliance takes every precaution to keep us safe, and I'll make sure to keep writing. You'll be hearing from me every chance I get, I promise."

Ma's voice trembled slightly as she read the next part, and I could feel the mixture of emotions that we all shared—pride, concern, and unspoken hope. "The journey will be long, but I'm excited to see more of the world. I think about you every day, and I carry your love with me wherever I go. Take care of each other, and I'll be back before you know it. With all my heart, Eamon."

Ma carefully folded the letter again, her eyes damp but her smile unwavering. "He fares well," she said, her voice full of pride. "He's truly making his way."

Pa nodded, his expression softening as he looked at the letter. "He's always been the adventurous one. I just hope he knows we're here, waiting for him."

I nodded, swallowing against the tightness in my throat. "He knows, Pa. And he'll be back."

By the time the third letter arrived, Eamon had been gone for almost two months. His letters had started to become a part of our routine, little glimpses of his world beyond Elsenburg, each one a lifeline to my brother, a glimpse into the adventures he was living beyond the boundaries of our village. His tone was effervescent as he spoke of the places he'd seen, the people he'd met, and the thrill of travel with the Crimson Merchant Alliance.

"Another letter, Kaelan!" Ma's voice rang out from the doorway one morning, as she waved a fresh parchment. I quickly brushed off my hands and joined her by the table, her face glowing with excitement as she unfolded the letter.

This one spoke of Central—the bustling streets, the market square filled with traders from distant lands, the caravan winding its way through mountains and valleys near central. He wrote about the sprawling beauty of cities near Central, where ancient stone walls seemed to rise from the earth itself, and about the camaraderie he'd found with the merchants he traveled with; the thrill of being part of something bigger than anything he'd known. The details were vivid, almost enough to make me feel I was there beside him, though each letter reminded me more and more how far away he was.

Seasons changed, and life on the farm resumed its familiar rhythm. The fields demanded tending, the animals needed feeding, and the work didn't care that a part of my mind was always somewhere else, waiting. It was a quiet kind of hope that grew in me—each evening, as we gathered around the hearth, I'd find myself glancing at the shelf where we kept Eamon's letters.

And, for a while, those letters came steadily, filling our home with stories of a world beyond our reach. As I read his words aloud, I'd catch Ma's proud smile, and Pa's nod of approval, feeling a mixture of pride and envy stirring inside me.

Whenever a letter arrived, I'd take it inside, and we'd sit together by the hearth. The fire crackled warmly, its soft glow lighting up the room as I read Eamon's words aloud. Ma would sit with her knitting, her eyes focused on me, listening intently to every word, while Pa would lean back in his chair, a smile playing at his lips as he listened. It was as if, for those moments, Eamon was right there with us, sharing in our lives even though he was far away.

One letter spoke of a grand festival in Central—the streets alive with music, bright banners draped from building to building, and people dancing late into the night.

Another told of a storm that had caught the caravan on their way to Wintmore, the rain pouring in sheets as they hurried to find shelter.

Eamon's words painted vivid pictures, his excitement leaping off the page, and I could see the twinkle in Ma and Pa's eyes as I read.

One evening, as I unfolded a new letter, I noticed something different in Eamon's words. He had reached Wintmore, he wrote. But the vibrant descriptions he used to send us had been replaced with phrases that felt clipped, cautious. "The people here are friendly but tense," he wrote. "It's different from Centralia. There are soldiers on every corner, and talk of unrest to the north and east. But don't worry—the Alliance keeps us well away from any trouble." There were whispers of unrest, he said, of soldiers and extremists moving through the countryside, of the conflict that had scarred this land not so long ago. I read his words aloud, but they felt heavy. Even as he tried to keep his letters light, to fill them with the same cheerfulness that had always been his way, I could sense the guardedness creeping in, an unease he couldn't quite hide. Ma and Pa didn't say anything, but as I read, I could feel the tension.

Later, I sat again by the fire, the latest letter in my hands. Ma and Pa watched as I read it aloud, my voice steady, but the words themselves betrayed a different story. "The roads aren't as safe as they once were," Eamon had written. "The Caravan Guards are on edge, and there are rumors of skirmishes to the East. But don't worry—I shall tread with care. The Alliance is keeping us well away from any trouble."

I glanced up at Ma, seeing the way her brow furrowed, the worry etched into her features. Pa's expression was unreadable, his gaze fixed on the fire, but I could tell he felt it too—the sense that things were changing, that Eamon's journey was no longer just an adventure.

And then, the letters stopped.

***

Days turned into weeks, and the silence grew heavier with each passing day. I'd go down the road, waiting for a messenger to arrive with news or the familiar parchment from Eamon. But each time, I returned empty-handed. Ma's face grew more withdrawn, her hands tightening around her knitting each time I came back empty, her shoulders just a little more slumped.

Pa tried to reassure us. He would say, "The roads are rough. The Alliance might be moving through rough country. Getting messages through is difficult when you're out there." But the worry was there, hidden in his steady voice. I saw the way he'd sit by the fire at night, staring into the flames, lost in thought.

I told myself the same thing too, that he perhaps couldn't get word across to us because of the unsafe roads, fighting back the thoughts that something had gone wrong. I kept myself busy—there was always work to be done. I threw myself into it, hoping that the rhythm of the fields would somehow quiet the worry that gnawed at me. But it was always there, just beneath the surface—the fear that Eamon was out there somewhere, in trouble, and I couldn't help him. The silence was a boulder in my chest.

One night, as we sat together in the dim light of the hearth, Ma spoke up, her voice subdued. "Do you think he's all right?" Her eyes brimmed with unshed tears. I looked at her, my heart aching, and then at Pa, who met my gaze with a steady, though weary, look.

"He's strong," Pa said, his voice firm. "He knows how to take care of himself. We must trust that he'll find his way back to us."

I nodded, swallowing the lump in my throat. "He'll be all right, Ma," I said, trying to sound more certain than I felt. "He promised he'd come back, and Eamon's never broken a promise."

Two months passed, and still, no letters came from Eamon. The silence settled around me, thick and suffocating, pressing down harder with each passing day. And in that silence, my fear turned into something else—purpose.

I had to find out what had happened to Eamon.

CHAPTER 4

The decision wasn't made lightly, but each day, it grew more certain as I watched the world around me change. There was tension in the air, a feeling of unease that seemed to hang over everything. Elsenburg was no longer the haven it once was. With the shadow of war looming, and young men speaking of joining the fighting, I knew I couldn't sit idly by while Eamon was out there. It was those talks that finally spurred me to make up my mind. I couldn't just sit by and wait any longer. Whether Eamon was in trouble or unable to reach us, I had to know. I couldn't let him face the dangers alone.

One evening, as the sun dipped below the horizon and the first stars began to appear in the sky, I sat down with Ma and Pa by the hearth. The fire crackled softly, filling the room with its warmth, but the atmosphere was heavy with the unspoken worries that had lingered for weeks. The words gnawed at me, but as I looked into their worried eyes, they finally spilled out.

"I'm going to find Eamon," I said. Ma's hands shook and the blanket she was knitting fell to the floor.

"Kaelan..."

I reached out and gripped her hands, "I have to Ma. He would have done the same for me."

Her eyes brimmed with tears, and she shook her head, her lips trembling. "Kaelan, please. The world is rife with danger. The war, the unrest… I can't bear the thought of you going into that."

Pa was quiet for a long time, his gaze fixed on the fire as Ma sobbed. Finally, his gaze met mine; pride and worry etched on his face. "You're certain about this?" he finally asked, his voice thick with emotion. I nodded, feeling my resolve calcify within me. Pa let out a long breath and nodded slowly. "Alright, then," he said, resigning, "If this is what you need to do, then we won't stop you. Just promise me you'll be careful."

Ma wiped at her eyes, her voice breaking as she spoke. "Promise you'll come back to us, Kaelan. Whatever happens, you come back home."

I squeezed her hand and my lips moved in a pale smile. "I promise, Ma. I'll find Eamon, and I'll come back. Both of us will."

The morning dawned too soon, and I was up as soon as the first light of dawn touched the horizon. Inside the house, everything felt quieter than usual. Even the walls seemed to hold their breath. I moved through the small space, gathering my belongings, each item a reminder of what I would leave behind.

I packed carefully: a sturdy pair of boots, my thickest coat, and a set of warm gloves. The weather could turn unpredictable, and I wanted to be ready for anything. I rolled up two spare shirts and a pair of trousers, tucking them into the bottom of my pack, alongside a simple tin cup and a small pot for cooking. I added some dried meat and bread Ma had prepared for me, knowing it would have to last until I found more along the way.

I took a dagger from Pa's workbench—the blade was old but sharp, and I knew it would serve me well.

But it wasn't all just practical things. I found myself lingering over a few small items, the things that meant more to me than I could ever put into words. A small, carved wooden horse that Eamon had made for me when we were just boys—I held it in my hand for a while, tracing the worn edges before slipping it into my pocket. A piece of cloth, embroidered with a simple pattern by Ma's hands, the fabric soft from years of use. I folded it carefully and tucked it into my bag.

Once everything was packed, I stood in the middle of our small kitchen, the weight of my pack resting heavily on my shoulders. I glanced around, taking in the familiar sight—the worn table where we'd shared countless meals, the hearth where I'd read Eamon's letters aloud, the chairs that Pa had built with his own hands. Every inch of this place held a memory, and I could feel the ache in my chest as I thought about leaving it all behind.

Ma stood by the doorway, her face streaming with tears. She reached up, cupping my face in her hands. "Kaelan, my boy," she whispered, her voice breaking. "Promise me, you'll stay safe. Promise you'll come back."

I nodded, the ache in my chest unbearable, "I will."

She pulled me into a tight hug, holding on as if she could somehow keep me there just by sheer will. I closed my eyes, breathing in the familiar scent of her, the scent of home. When she finally let go, I turned to Pa, who stood a few feet away, his expression stoic. He stepped forward, resting a hand on my shoulder. "You're a good son, Kaelan. And a good brother. Remember what I taught you—mind your wits, boy, and don't take unnecessary risks." He paused, his voice growing softer. "You bring him back to us."

I swallowed hard, nodding.

Pa pulled me into a quick hug, patting my back before stepping away. I looked at them both one last time—Ma with her eyes glistening, Pa standing tall, trying to be strong for all of us. I tried to commit the sight of them to memory, to carry it with me as I stepped out of the house and into the world beyond.

The village was already waking up, the early morning light casting long shadows as people began their day. I walked down the path that led from our home towards the square, the weight of my pack settling into my shoulders.

The other young men from the village were already gathered, bags slung over their backs, faces awash with determination tinged with dread. They stood in uneasy clusters, murmuring in low tones, casting wary glances toward the road ahead. The older men, who'd seen wars past, watched from the edges, eyes narrowed, speaking in hushed voices about "the front," "Centralia's lines," and "Wintmore's advance." Elsenburg was once a carefree village of Centralia— laughter had bounced off the walls and children roamed free. But now, it was shrouded in a thick tension. Every day, young men took up arms. Some returned, hollow-eyed and haunted. Others never returned at all.

I watched these sapling young men who would travel with me. I wasn't joining them in their cause, but our paths were intertwined. We would travel together, and then I'd break off to find Eamon.

Finally, I turned back once, looking down the road towards home. I could just make out the shape of our house in the distance. The door was still open, and Ma and Pa stood in the doorway. I raised a hand— a silent goodbye—and they waved back. I held onto that image for as long as I could.

CHAPTER
5

The morning mist clung to the fields, curling around the stalks of grain like ghostly tendrils. From the edge of the village, I looked out over Elsenburg, the familiar sights stretching unchanged before me. The distant chatter of the village markets, the smell of fresh bread from the bakery, the sight of farmers tending to their crops— everything appeared as it always had. Yet today, it felt like an entirely different place; everything seemed more vivid, more precious. This was home, the only place I had ever known. And now, I had to leave it behind.

I adjusted the leather strap of my pack, filled with meager supplies for the journey ahead and the few Emerul coins my father had pressed into my hands. My heart hung heavy with the weight of unspoken goodbyes, but the fire burned in my chest. I had to find Eamon. I had to bring my brother home.

A handful of young men from Elsenburg had also gathered near the edge of the village, their faces awash with excitement. They were bound for Central, united by a shared purpose: to serve in the Centralian Imperial Army and fight in the war that loomed over our land. I recognized most of them—boys I had grown up with, played with and worked alongside. But standing there now, we seemed like strangers, each of us at the threshold of a life unimaginable just a year ago. I scanned the group, picking out familiar faces. There was Cedric, the blacksmith's son, a tall, broad-shouldered, gregarious lad with hands as rough as iron but a grin that could light up any room. Beside him stood Jarin, one of the village shepherds, a quiet and wiry boy with sharp green eyes that missed nothing. On the other side of the group, Silas, the miller's youngest son, nervously adjusted his belt, his freckled face pale beneath his mess of auburn hair. None of us had ever ventured beyond Elsenburg, yet here we stood, ready to leave it all behind.

Each of us carried our own reason for stepping onto this path. My reason stood above all else: Eamon. My brother was out there, and I had to find him.

My plan was simple enough: I would travel with these young men who had chosen to enlist in the Centralian Imperial Army. I hadn't signed up, but I'd hoped to blend in, travel with them to Central, and use the opportunity to get information on where Eamon may be. It was a gamble, risky as Pa had said, but I had no choice. We waited impatiently for the village elder, Thoren, to give his customary farewell speech. The sun had begun to rise, casting a pale light over the rooftops. Suddenly, the sound of hoofbeats tore into the quiet sounds of our conversations. A group of riders emerged from the woods, their armor gleaming in the morning light—Centralian soldiers. They were four. And though their steeds looked travel-worn, they sat tall in their saddles, their backs as straight as ramrods, and their sharp gazes scrutinizing us closely.

I stiffened. Soldiers meant authority, and authority meant questions.

"Well, well. What do we have here?" one of them called out as they reined in their horses. He was a towering figure, broad-shouldered, with a dented breastplate that had clearly seen battle. His eyes swept over us, measuring, weighing in silence.

"A fine crop of recruits for the Empire, I see."

The boys around me exchanged uneasy glances. Cedric, ever the boldest among us, stepped forward. "We're heading to Central to enlist," he said, his voice steady.

The soldier's gaze rested upon Cedric for a moment before shifting to me. "All of you?"

My heart raced, but I forced myself to nod along with the others. The soldier's sharp eyes narrowed slightly, as though he could hear the sharp intake of my breath.

The other soldier dismounted, a thin man with a severe face; an ugly scar running from his temple to his jaw. He walked toward us, his boots crunching on the dirt. "Names," he barked, pulling out a small parchment.

One by one, the boys gave their names, some with pride, others with apprehension. When his attention turned toward me, I stalled for a heartbeat too long.

"Kaelan,"

The scarred soldier grunted and scowled at me for a while before scribbling my name on the parchment. Then, he turned to face us, his fiery glare piercing us all.

"From here on, you're all property of the Centralian Army. You shall travel under our watch and train before being sent forth to the Central then to Wintmore. "

A ripple of excitement went through the group. Silas shifted on his feet, his freckled face pale. "We thought we'd just train and then await…"

The soldier's glare silenced him. "You thought wrong, lad. War doesn't wait for no man." He turned to the rest of us, "Consider this your conscription. Anyone who doesn't like it can take it up with the marshal."

My stomach twisted. This wasn't part of the plan. I wasn't supposed to join the Army. I had only planned to travel with them until I could slip away and search for Eamon.

Amidst the excitement, the village elder, Thoren who had just arrived shuffled forward. His weathered face was marked by old scars and deep lines etched from years of toil. His skin was rough and sun-darkened, like the earth itself. His hair, long and streaked with silver, brushed against his tattered robe. He conferred with the soldiers in hushed tones. Fragments of their conversations drifted to my ears. They were passing through, the soldiers said, heading back to Central. Their timing, they claimed, was a stroke of luck. They would escort us to the army camp themselves before continuing to Central.

A thought insinuated itself into my head. If I played along, I could feign my place among them, blend into their ranks, and vanish when the time was right.

"You've got until we leave to say your goodbyes," the lead soldier announced, tearing into my jumbled thoughts. "Make it quick. We ride in an half hour."

They dismounted and hovered around us, their presence, a grim shadow over what I already felt was a solemn departure. The boys muttered among themselves and shuffled around eyeing the armed men warily. I heard a chuckle behind me and turned to see Cedric, his usual grin subdued but still present.

"Looks like you'd be a proper soldier too now, Kaelan," he said, his tone spirited. "You ready for this?"

I heaved a sigh, the burden of my mother's promise weighing heavily on my chest. "I don't know."

Cedric inclined his head, his expression softening. "None of us do. But we'll make it through."

Feathery fingers touched my back. I turned. It was old Thoren. His eyes held a weary wisdom as they looked over me.

"You don't want to be in the war, child?"

I let out a panicked sigh. "You must not let them take me," I said, my voice unsteady. "I need to find my brother."

Old Thoren shook his head. He placed a hand on my shoulder, his gaze heavy with pity.

"Kaelan, if you want to find Eamon, joining the army would be your best chance," he said. "The roads to Wintmore aren't safe for a traveler, especially for one without companions. As a soldier, you shall have a uniform, comrades, and access to places you could never reach on your own."

My eyes narrowed as I thought of it. If I fled now, I'd be branded a deserter—or worse. The notion of being a Centralian soldier swirled in my mind. It wasn't the path I'd chosen, but perhaps it was the one I was meant to walk. If joining the army was the only way to venture through the war-torn lands and find Eamon, then so be it. I heaved a resigned sigh. Finally, I made my decision: My brother was out there somewhere, caught in the chaos of battle. I would become a soldier. For his sake.

***

As I finally took my place among the group, Thoren stepped forward. "You lads," he began, his voice rough but steady, "are walking into a new world. A world far beyond these fields and forests. A world where the wind smells, not of fresh bread, but of blood and steel; where the only sounds you hear are the clashing of swords and the cries of men. But remember, no matter how far you go, you carry Elsenburg with you."

I swallowed hard, my gaze fixed on the old man's face while his words sank into me. This was no grand farewell, no sugar-coated blessing. This was the truth.

"Fight with honor," Thoren continued, "and return home. For those who fall… know that we shall remember your names here, in this village, for as long as these fields stand."

The elder's words hung in the air like a shadow as we gathered our belongings and made ready to leave. The soldiers came forward and rounded us up. One by one, we took our final steps out of the village edge, toward the dirt path that wound through the hills and into the unknown. My heart tightened as I caught one last glimpse of our farmhouse in the distance. For a moment, I imagined Ma still standing by the front door, her eyes filled with sorrow, but her chin lifted with pride.

"I'll find him," I had promised the night before as I stood before the fire with her. "I'll bring Eamon home."

She had smiled faintly, her hand cupping my cheek. "Bring yourself home too, Kaelan."

The half hour passed too quickly. Gradually, the village faded behind us, swallowed by dense woods. With every step that took me farther from Elsenburg, my hopes wavered. I looked into the skies of Elsenburg and for a fleeting moment, I wondered if I would ever see it again.

***

The training camp was located in the mountains between Elsenburg and Central, and the journey there began with quiet murmurs and awkward exchanges. None of us were soldiers—just farmers, shepherds, and smiths who had traded their tools for swords. Cedric, always loud and gregarious, broke the silence first.

"So, Kaelan," he said with a grin, walking up beside me. "You think they'll make soldiers out of us, eh?"

I chuckled despite the heaviness in my heart. "If they can turn you into a soldier, Cedric, they can do anything."

The others laughed, and for a moment, the uneasiness lifted. It was a small comfort, but I welcomed it. Cedric had always been good at keeping spirits high. Even when the work was hard and the days long, his easy smile and booming laughter were infectious, and I couldn't help but feel a little lighter.

As the day wore on, we found our rhythm, marching in step with the dusty road beneath our feet. The landscape changed slowly as we moved away from Elsenburg, the rolling hills growing steeper, the woods thicker and darker. I found myself walking beside Jarin, whose quiet demeanor had always intrigued me.

"What do you think it'll be like?" I asked, more to fill the silence than out of genuine curiosity.

Jarin glanced at me, his eyes thoughtful. "I think... it'll be different from what we imagine. We've heard stories of war, but none of us really knows what it's like until we're in it."

I nodded, my stomach churning with uncertainty. "You're right. I hope I find answers about Eamon too."

"You will," Jarin said quietly, his gaze fixed ahead. "We'll all find something out there, whether it's what we're looking for or not."

The road stretched on for hours, and by midday, the heat of the sun bore down on us, turning the dirt beneath our boots into a powdery haze. We stopped briefly by a stream to rest and refill our waterskins, the cool water a welcome relief from the heat. The banter between the young men slowed as the miles dragged on, each of us sinking into our thoughts. Some spoke of the glory they imagined awaiting them in battle; others wondered aloud what the training would be like.

I stayed quiet as the group pressed on, my mind spinning. I thought of Eamon; his face, the image of the two of us racing through the fields of Elsenburg, and the sound of his laughter. That laughter, so full of life and childlike joy had always seemed like a constant—a sound that filled the house, the fields, the entire village. But now, it was but a memory, fading with each passing day.

As we walked along the dusty road that wound its way out of the hills surrounding Elsenburg, I found myself falling to the back of the group, letting the conversations and laughter of the others fade into the background. I was used to hard work—used to days spent in the fields, hands blistered and back sore—but this journey felt different. The road ahead was long, and with it came uncertainty. I didn't know what awaited us at the end of this march, or what the war would truly demand of me. All I knew was that I had to find my brother, no matter what it took.

The first day of travel was exhausting. The sun beat down on us relentlessly, the once-cool morning air quickly giving way to a sticky, oppressive heat. The road was dry and rough, and as we walked, we kicked up clouds of dust that coated our boots and clung to our skin. I kept my eyes on the horizon, where the green hills gave way to the more rugged, unfamiliar lands beyond Elsenburg. I had never ventured this far from the village before. Few had. The hills we called home were giving way to a new, harsher landscape, one of jagged rocks and sparse trees. It was the kind of land that matched the hard lives we were about to enter.

Cedric kept the group's spirits high for most of the day. He joked about what we might find at the camp—gruel for every meal, marshals who never smiled, and enough grueling work to make us wish we had never been born. The young men laughed, some nervously, others more earnestly, as they tried to picture what awaited us.

I smiled faintly at their banter, but my heart wasn't in it. My mind drifted back to Eamon. I wondered where my brother had been when the fighting became worse—had he seen the violence firsthand? Had he been caught in one of the raids? The thought of him alone, lost in the chaos, sent a chill down my spine. I quickened my pace, trying to shake off the feeling.

By the time the sun began to sink toward the horizon, casting long shadows over the road, we had covered a good distance, though our bodies were weary. We found a small clearing off the road, sheltered by a few tall trees and the remnants of an old stone wall—likely the remains of a long-forgotten farmstead. We collapsed onto the ground, grateful for a chance to rest our aching legs and sore backs.

Jarin, always quiet and observant, sat next to me as we shared a meal of dried meat and bread. "You seem distracted," Jarin said, his voice low and thoughtful.

I looked up, surprised that anyone had noticed. "I'm thinking about my brother," I admitted. "I haven't heard from him since he left for Wintmore. I don't even know if he's... alive."

Jarin nodded, his eyes darkening. "I think we're all thinking of someone we left behind. It's part of why we're here, isn't it? To protect them, or... find them." I didn't answer, but his words struck a chord. I hadn't thought about it in those terms before, but I realized it was true. Each of us was marching toward war for our own reasons—some for glory, some for duty, and some for the ones we loved.

***

The second day was harder.

We awoke at dawn, stiff and sore from the previous day's march, and set out once more. The road grew narrower and less traveled, and the trees became sparser. The air was cooler, but the ground beneath our feet was rocky and uneven, making the march more difficult. As we walked, I fell in step with Silas, the miller's son. He had been quieter than usual, his freckled face drawn with fatigue and uncertainty. I hadn't spoken much to him during the march, but I could see the weight of the journey beginning to wear on him.

"How are you holding up?" I asked, breaking the silence.

Silas looked at me, his brow furrowed. "I'm... alright. It's just... I didn't think it'd feel so... real. You know? We've talked about this war for months. But now that we're actually going to fight in it, I'm starting to wonder if perchance I've made the right choice."

I nodded. I understood the feeling all too well. "I think we're all wondering that."

Silas sighed, kicking at a loose stone in the road. "I just keep thinking about my family. My father's too old to run the mill on his own. And my little sister... she's still so young. What if something happens to me? What'll happen to them?"

I didn't have an answer, but I clapped a hand on his shoulder, "We're all going to make it through this," I said, though the words felt hollow in my mouth. "We'll get through the training, and we'll come back stronger. Our families are counting on us."

Silas nodded, his eyes far away.

We continued in silence for most of the day, the weight of our own thoughts making the march feel longer than it was. By the time we stopped for the night, exhaustion had taken hold of us all. I found a spot beneath an old oak tree and lay down, staring up at the stars as they blinked into view. My body ached from the day's travel, but my mind refused to rest.

The thoughts of Eamon again descended on me. I pictured him sitting by a campfire like this one, maybe surrounded by fellow merchants or soldiers, telling one of his vibrant stories. Or perhaps he was alone, hidden away somewhere, waiting for a chance to return home. The alternative was too fearful to contemplate.

"Where are you, Eamon?" I whispered to the night, but there was no answer, only the distant rustling of leaves in the breeze.

CHAPTER
6

On the third day, our spirits began to lift as we neared our destination. The road had grown wider again, and more frequently we passed other groups of travelers—farmers with carts of produce, traders with their wares, and even the occasional soldier or two, their armor gleaming in the morning sun. Each new sight brought with it a reminder that the world beyond Elsenburg was vast and that our small village was just one piece of a much larger puzzle.

As we marched, Cedric began to talk about the training camp again, spinning wild tales of what we might face. He cracked jokes that kept the men howling with laughter, but I was only half-present. I found myself staring at the horizon again. The camp was close now—I could feel it. This was where our journey truly began.

By midday, we crested a small hill and caught our first glimpse of the camp in the distance with mountains towering behind. It wasn't what I had imagined. It was bigger. Much bigger. Rows of tents stretched out as far as the eye could see, their faded fabric flapping in the wind. Between them stood ancient wooden barracks, their weathered beams a testimony of centuries of use. In the distance, the training ground bustled with activity, recruits and soldiers alike moving like a relentless tide. Smoke rose in thin wisps from cooking fires, and the faint sound of hammers on metal drifted up to us.

"This is it," Silas said softly, his voice filled with awe.

My heart raced as I stared at the camp, the red and gold colors of the Centralian banners waving in the breeze like sentinels in this place where boyhood ended and manhood began. "You ready?" Cedric asked, nudging me with a wide grin.

I took a deep breath, gripping the strap of my pack a little tighter. "As ready as I shall ever be."

And with that, we started our descent toward the camp, where our lives would be forever changed.

As our group of young recruits crossed the threshold of the Imperial training camp, the energy around us shifted. The sounds of soldiers' drills, clanging hammers, and barking orders filled the air, casting a new weight upon our small band of fresh-faced youths. A thick scent of sweat, dirt, and smoldering wood-fires lingered as we passed the rows of tents and barracks, all arranged in neat lines across the dusty ground.

I glanced around, my heart heavy with anticipation. This was no longer the idyllic village life of Elsenburg. The camp had a harshness to it—both in its setting and in the faces of the seasoned soldiers who moved with practiced efficiency, barely sparing a glance at the newcomers. Tired, ragged banners flapped in the wind, their once-vibrant colors dulled by the sun, but they still stood as proud symbols of Centralia's might.

"Welcome to your new life," Cedric muttered under his breath as soon as our soldier companions had left us at the main training grounds. I nodded silently and glanced around the camp.

We didn't have long to marvel before a large, broad-shouldered man approached, his presence impossible to ignore. His face was rugged, with deep lines etched from years of battle, and his heavy dark brown beard bristled like the fur of a bear. He wore the dark, weathered armor of a Centralian general, his cloak and fur draped over one shoulder, swaying with each purposeful step. His eyes, sharp and unyielding, seemed to pierce through every recruit standing there.

This was Kyder, the Iron Bear, the Lord General of Centralia, known throughout the army for his ferocity in battle and even greater ruthlessness when it came to training new soldiers. His name had become a legend whispered with both reverence and fear.

"New blood," he growled, his voice like gravel. "You're here to fight for Centralia, but I wonder—how many of you will survive the training, let alone the battlefield?"

We stiffened, all eyes on Lord General Kyder as he loomed before us. "Listen, because I won't repeat myself," he continued, pacing in front of the group. "Some of you think carrying a sword makes you soldiers. You left your villages behind, and suddenly think you are warriors? You're nothing! Not yet. You're raw. Unformed. Let me tell you about the recruits who came before you—boys with bright eyes and foolish dreams, much like yourselves.

I remember a lad named Richard. Thought he'd seen enough fights in his village to take on the world. The first week out, he froze when the enemy charged. They cut him down before he could even raise his blade. And Jon—fierce as fire, that one. But he thought heart alone was enough. He didn't last a month. I tell you, lads, you're not soldiers yet. You're kindling, waiting to see if the flames will forge you into steel—or consume you entirely." I felt a chill run down my spine. There was an intensity in Kyder's eyes, a fire born from years of war. He was a soldier who had seen countless battles, and who had lost more men than I could ever imagine.

"For now, you're nothing to me," Kyder said, a slight sneer curling his lips. "You'll be assigned to barracks, and your training starts at dawn. But first—eat." He turned and motioned to a nearby soldier, who began distributing rations to the recruits.

I took my portion—a small, rock-hard loaf of stale bread and a bowl of dried meat soup that smelled faintly of old leather. It was far from the warm meals Ma used to prepare in Elsenburg, but hunger left little room for complaints.

I sat with Cedric and Silas on a rough wooden bench, and the three of us stared at our food in silence. Finally, I put a piece of bread in my mouth. It was near impossible to chew, each bite needing more effort than I anticipated. And the soup was more salt and water than any real nourishment. We ate in silence, knowing that this was the first of many such meals in the days to come.

"Could be worse, I suppose," Cedric said, trying to sound optimistic as he gnawed on his bread.

"I'm not sure about that," Silas muttered, wrinkling his nose at the soup. "How are we supposed to survive on this?"

"Survive?" I said with a half-smile that didn't quite reach my eyes. "If we're lucky, we'll just get through the night."

The banter continued, but a quiet tension hung in the air. The reality of our situation gradually settled in. No more carefree days in the village. No more warm beds or laughter around the hearth. From this point on, we were soldiers—recruits in the service of Centralia—and our lives would be shaped by whatever Kyder demanded of us.

That night, we found our way to the cramped barracks, nothing more than rows of rough wooden cots set under a tent. The air inside was stifling, thick with the smell of unwashed bodies and damp straw. Exhaustion from the long journey weighed on me, but sleep didn't come easy. I lay there, staring at the low canvas ceiling, listening to the sounds of the camp outside—the distant clang of metal, the murmured conversations of other soldiers, and the occasional barking of orders from the officers.

Tomorrow, the real training would begin, and I had no illusions about what lay ahead. General Kyder had made that clear. This camp was not just a place to become a soldier—it was a crucible, and only the strongest would survive the fire.

The first day of training dawned harsh and cold. The sun had barely crept over the horizon when the deep blare of a horn echoed through the camp, jerking me from a restless sleep. My body ached from the long march to the camp, and the hard cot offered little comfort. Groaning, I rolled out of bed and pulled on my gear, eyes heavy with exhaustion. Around me, the other recruits were doing the same, moving sluggishly but with a nervous energy that crackled in the air.

The camp was already bustling when we gathered in the training yard. My breath clouded in the chilly morning air as I adjusted my pack, trying to prepare myself for whatever lay ahead. General Kyder stood on the platform overlooking us, arms crossed, his sharp gaze watching everything.

"Today, we see if you have what it takes to march with an army!" Kyder's voice boomed across the yard. "We'll start with a ten-mile march. You'll carry your packs, weapons, and armor. No one stops until we return."

I felt the weight of my pack pressing down on my shoulders, already heavier than it had been the day before. I exchanged a glance with Cedric and Silas, both of whom looked just as apprehensive.

"Move out!" Kyder barked.

We fell into line, our boots crunching on the dry earth as we began the march. At first, the movement wasn't so bad— A surge of strength drove me forward, my body falling into a rhythm as we marched out of the camp and onto the dirt roads that cut through the surrounding fields. The pack on my back grew heavier with each passing step, but I gritted my teeth and kept pace with the others.

The hours dragged on, and as the sun climbed higher in the sky, the heat began to beat down on us mercilessly. Sweat poured down my face, stinging my eyes, and my legs burned from the constant strain. The weight of my pack was now unbearable, digging into my shoulders and forcing me to hunch over just to keep moving.

Beside me, Cedric breathed heavily, his face flushed. Silas stumbled once, catching himself before he hit the ground, his jaw tight with determination. My mouth was dry, my throat parched as the sun baked us. My feet felt like lead, every step more painful than the last. I could feel myself swaying, my vision blurring at the edges as the heat and exhaustion began to take their toll. The urge to stop gnawed at me with every tortuous step, perhaps, no one would notice if I just fell behind. But a voice rang out in my head – fierce; a reminder of why I had left home in the first place.

I can't give up now. If I falter here, how can I ever face what's ahead? How can I ever prove to myself that I'm more than the boy who never left his homestead? How can I ever find my brother?

I glanced around, searching for strength in others' faces, but they too were locked in their own battles—some faltering, others gritting their teeth and pushing through the pain, others falling helplessly.

I forced myself forward, one step after another, together with my comrades. 'We're all struggling,' I thought, 'but maybe that's what makes us soldiers: we keep moving.

"Keep moving!" one of the marshals shouted, walking alongside us, smacking the back of one of the boys who dared to slow down.

I forced myself to keep my head up, focusing on the steady rhythm of my feet hitting the ground. My heart pounded in my chest, my legs trembled beneath the weight of my body. For a moment, I thought I might collapse—my body on the verge of giving out—but then I heard Lord General Kyder's voice ringing out in the distance.

"You think this is hard? This is nothing compared to what awaits you on the battlefield! Only the strong survive, and only those who push beyond their limits will ever know victory!"

Kyder's words sparked something inside me—a fire that pushed me forward, even when every part of my body screamed in protest. I clenched my jaw and kept going, my muscles burning, but my will unbroken. The march seemed to stretch on forever, a never-ending slog through dust and sweat, but eventually, we returned to the camp, our legs heavy and our spirits battered.

We collapsed to the ground, gasping for air as we dropped our packs. My entire body ached, and I felt like I might pass out at any moment. But there was no rest to be had.

"On your feet!" Kyder ordered. "The day is far from over."

I staggered to my feet, my limbs trembling as I followed the others to the training yard. There, wooden dummies and sand-filled pits awaited us, marking the area for hand-to-hand combat training.

We were paired off, and I found myself face-to-face with Garron, a burly recruit who looked more like a blacksmith than anything else. His arms were thick and corded with muscle, his face set in a grimace as he cracked his knuckles, ready for the fight. The sand under my boots shifted as I took a hesitant step forward, my fists clenching at my sides. My heart hammered so loudly I was sure Garron could hear it. Around us, the recruits faced their opponents, their voices hushed with anticipation.

"Hand-to-hand combat is more than brute strength," one of the drill masters called out. "It's about technique. It's about staying calm under pressure. But make no mistake—today, you'll fight like your life depends on it, because one day, it will."

The horn blew and Garron smirked, his gray eyes boring into mine, and before I had time to think, he lunged at me, his fist swinging toward me with brutal force. I didn't think—I couldn't. All I could do was move.

CHAPTER
7

I barely had time to react. He was faster than I expected, dodging to the side as his fist sailed past my head. The next blow caught me square in the chest. Pain rippled through my torso and for a moment, I couldn't breathe.

Stay calm. Stay standing. I told myself as the world tilted and my legs wobbled beneath me. Gasping for air, I tried to steady myself, my fists raised in a defensive stance. Garron came at me again. He feinted to the left before grabbing my arm in a crushing grip and pulling me into a grapple. I struggled against his hold but it was like wrestling with a bear, and before I could break free, I found myself slammed to the ground with a bone-jarring thud. I tasted blood.

"Get up!" the drill master bellowed, his voice like the crack of a whip.

I spat blood and grit on the sand and rolled to my feet, my chest heaving as I faced Garron again. My fists trembled and my feet felt like pudding, but I refused to back down.

I have to prove I'm more than a farmer's son.
I have to prove I belong here.

I darted under his arm and slammed my fist into his ribs. He grunted, a flicker of pain flashing in his eyes. His eyes narrowed as he swung at me, arms flailing, but I dodged the blow, my mind focused on staying on my feet.

He grunted. I heaved.

The fight dragged on, each blow draining more of my strength. My body screamed in protest with every move, but I fought with every ounce of will I had left. By the end, both Garron and I were bruised and exhausted, our faces slick with sweat and dirt but I refused to give up. For a moment, I thought about my village—the fields of wheat swaying in the breeze, the smell of freshly tilled soil. I shall return someday; and I shall return stronger, better than when I left. I must.

"Enough!" the drill master called, signaling the end of the sparring session.

I collapsed to the ground, my breath ragged. I could barely move, every muscle in my body screaming in pain. Sweat and dirt clung to me but I couldn't help a small smile I had survived. The first day was over, and somehow, I had made it through.

***

We were formed into lines, the weight of our shields dragging our arms down as we stood at attention. I shifted under the burden, the strap of my shield cutting into my shoulder. My helmet felt like a furnace on my head, even in the cool morning air.

"Today, you march," Marshal Garrick announced. "Ten miles in full gear. I don't want to see anyone lagging. You'll learn to carry that shield as if it's part of your body. Now move!"

With that, we set off across the uneven terrain surrounding the camp. The earth was soft from the morning dew, but as the sun rose higher, it began to harden beneath our boots. I focused on each step, trying to match the rhythm of the march as we carried our shields before us.

The shield weighed as much as the earth itself, the leather straps rubbing raw spots into my skin. Every time I thought I'd found a comfortable position, another shift in the terrain would send a jolt through my arm, forcing me to readjust. The pack on my back seemed to grow heavier by the minute, and the clinking of swords and armor filled the air around us like a constant reminder of the burden we carried.

Cedric, marching beside me, grunted with effort, sweat already streaking down his face. "How long do you think this will last?" he muttered.

I couldn't answer, my throat too dry to speak. My legs burned with the effort of keeping up, but I forced myself forward. I would not be left behind.

The Marshals kept a close watch on us as we marched, barking orders for the lines to stay tight, for us to keep our shields up. It was a far cry from the simpler, easier marches of the day before. This was warfare practice—every movement meant to prepare us for battle where lives would be on the line.

Hours passed, and by midday, we had covered several miles. My feet felt as if they had been ground down to bone, the straps of my shield biting deeper into my shoulder with every step. Now and then, a recruit would stumble, falling to one knee under the weight of their equipment, only to be yanked back to their feet by a Marshal with a growled threat or sharp order.

"Get up! Lag in battle, and the reaper shall claim you where you fall!!"

Finally, we reached a rest point, where the Marshals allowed us to collapse in the shade of a few trees. The sparse woodland here bore the same ash-grey bark of the trees near my village, though the saplings here were smaller, stunted by the rocky soil of Centralia's central moutainlands. I dropped my shield with a thud, sucking in deep breaths of the cool air as my muscles screamed in protest. Overhead, the wind carried the faint, acrid tang of the iron forges in the villages surrounding Central, where our weapons were being made. I glanced over at Silas, whose face was pale with exhaustion.

"This is worse than I imagined," Silas panted, wiping sweat from his brow. He muttered something about the ease of those days long ago at home where he'd grown up lifting bags of flour instead of marching with shields.

I nodded, too tired to form a proper response. My arms trembled as I removed my helmet, letting the breeze cool my drenched shaggy hair. The weight of my equipment felt like it had doubled in the few hours we had been marching.

But before long, the Marshals were herding us back into formation. "Enough rest!" Marshal Garrick called out. "We march back to camp, and when we return, you'll be learning how to fight with those shields."

The return march was even worse. Every step back to camp was agony. My muscles screamed, and my vision began to blur as the sun rose high in the sky. I could see other recruits struggling just as much, but no one complained—we all knew that falling behind would bring the wrath of the Marshals.

When we finally returned to the camp, we were dead on our feet, but the day's training was far from over.

"Shields up!" Marshal Garrick commanded as soon as we entered the training yard. "You've learned how to carry them. Now you'll learn how to fight with them." Behind him, a towering banner flapped in the wind, the golden Dracoleon of Centralia emblazoned against a dark red field—a reminder of the kingdom we were sworn to protect.

I groaned inwardly but lifted my shield again. But the weight of the shield was nothing compared to the weight of my promise to Ma and Pa. This hellish grind was my only chance to find Eamon. Around me, recruits cursed or gritted their teeth, and the rhythmic clang of distant anvils reminded us all of what this kingdom was built on; sweat, steel, and unyielding will. I braced myself for the next round of punishments; the art of shield combat. We were paired off and instructed how to block, how to strike, and how to form a defensive line. The weight of the shield, which had been burdensome enough during the march, now became an essential tool for survival.

With every clash of wood and metal, I could feel my body reaching its limit. But I pressed on, knowing that this was what I had signed up for. I was no longer a farmer's son from Elsenburg—I was becoming a soldier of Centralia, ready to face whatever awaited me on the battlefield, ready to conquer every obstacle to find my brother.

By the end of the day, I could barely lift my arms. We were sent stumbling back to our tents, every step a reminder of the grueling day behind us. We ate our meager rations in near silence, too exhausted to talk, before collapsing into our bedrolls.

And tomorrow, we knew, would be no easier.

CHAPTER
8

Three Weeks Later.

The sun rose over the training camp, its light now seeming less fierce, almost as if the day itself knew we had earned a reprieve. The air was cool, the light soft as it bathed the sprawling camp in a golden glow. For me, the rhythm of training had become second nature. Gone were the days when my legs trembled after long marches, or my arms burned with the weight of my shield. Now, the routine felt as familiar as working the fields in Elsenburg.

I stood among the other recruits, our ranks tighter and more disciplined than when we had first arrived. Our once-awkward movements had transformed into the confident, precise steps of trained soldiers. My muscles had hardened, my frame stronger than it had ever been. The wooden sword in my hand felt more like an extension of my arm, no longer a foreign object to wield, but a tool I had mastered.

Marshal Garrick, still as imposing as ever, strode down the line of recruits, his sharp gaze inspecting us. He had been relentless in his training, never allowing us a moment's rest, nor letting us falter. Yet in his eyes today, there was a glimmer of something I hadn't seen before—approval.

"You've all come far," Garrick growled, halting before me, his gaze sweeping over me. "Three weeks ago, half of you couldn't even lift your shields. Now you're soldiers—almost."

I stood tall under Garrick's scrutiny, no longer flinching at the Marshal's rough demeanor. I had earned my place here. The blisters on my hands had hardened into callouses, and the once-fresh bruises from combat training had faded into memories of battles fought in the training yard.

Soon, we lined up for a full inspection. Our armor was polished, our shields and swords at the ready. I wore my gear with ease now, no longer weighed down by the heavy chainmail or thick leather straps. My helmet, which had once felt like a cage, now fit snugly atop my head, and my sword rested comfortably at my side.

"Today's a special day," Garrick said, pacing before us. "You're not green anymore. You've survived the drills, the marches, and the combat training. Now it's time to see if you can fight like true soldiers of Centralia."

We murmured among ourselves. There had been rumors circulating for days about a final test, one that would determine if we were ready to join the real ranks of the army.

I exchanged a glance with Silas, who stood beside me in the line, his face calm and his eyes filled with anticipation. We had trained together, fought side by side, and endured everything the Marshals had thrown at us. We were ready.

The training yard was a place I had come to know intimately. Every patch of dirt, every splintered fence post, every scar in the ground left by a fallen recruit was familiar to me now. The once-foreign clamor of swords clashing and orders being barked had become the background music of my life.

Hand-to-hand combat had become second nature. My sword strikes were fluid, my shield blocks were sharp and well-timed. I no longer stumbled when carrying the weight of my armor, and my endurance had grown to match the demands of the long marches. We had learned formation tactics, how to fight as a unit, and how to cover each other's flanks. The lessons drilled into us over countless hours were now instinct.

And yet, for all the progress I had made, I knew this final test would be unlike anything we had faced before.

"Form up!" Garrick's voice snapped us out of our thoughts, and we fell into formation, shields up, swords drawn.

Today would prove whether the past weeks of grueling training had truly prepared us for war.

We gathered in the central yard, our eyes scanning the camp for any sign of what was to come. A line of Marshals stood in front of us, their expressions grim, giving no hint of what we were about to face. Marshal Garrick, towering above the others, stepped forward with his arms folded across his broad chest.

"Listen up!" he bellowed, his voice cutting through the morning air like a blade. You've marched, you've fought, and you've bled, but today will be the hardest thing you've ever done. The Trial of Iron will push you beyond your limits. This is not just a test—it is a culling of the weak"

He let that hang in the air for a moment, the weight of his words sinking in.

"You will face exhaustion, hunger, and fear," he continued. "No breaks, no mercy. Only the strongest will finish."

I felt the tension in my chest tighten. I had grown used to the rigors of training, but this was different. The Marshals rarely spoke in such dire terms, and when they did, it wasn't to scare us—they meant every word.

The trial began with a forced march. Not just any march, but a grueling, unrelenting trek across the rocky mountain that surrounded the camp. Fully armored and carrying all our gear—swords, shields, and heavy packs—we were expected to cover miles of harsh terrain with no breaks. The rocky ground was uneven, making every step feel like a battle against the earth itself. And yet, for all the progress I had made, I knew this final test would be unlike anything we had faced before.

Marshal Garrick's words echoed in my mind: "A soldier who can't march dies on the road. Keep your pace or fall behind!"

The first few hours passed in relative silence, the only sounds being the clinking of armor and the steady tramp of boots. But soon, each step felt like wading through quicksand, the weight on my back more than just steel and leather- it was the burden of every expectation ever placed upon me. What if I fail? The thought struck like a lash, sharper than the piercing sun on my back. Ahead, Cedric grunted, his jaws set.

"You think this is worse than Garrick's obstacle course?" he managed, his voice strained but teasing.

I forced a chuckle. "If I say yes, will you carry my pack?"

His short laugh broke the tension for a moment, but I could see the same doubt flicker in his eyes. We both knew there was no going back, but neither dared voice the fear gnawing at our resolve. As the hours wore on, fatigue set in. The sun climbed higher, burning away the mist and turning the ground beneath our feet into a blistering stretch of stone. Sweat poured down my face, stinging my eyes. My shield felt heavier with each step, my legs burning with the effort of moving forward, each step blurring into the next in an endless rhythm of pain."

Around me, some of the other recruits began to falter. One tripped over a rock and crashed to the ground, his breath coming in ragged gasps. Another dropped his shield, unable to carry it any longer. But the Marshals offered no help, no reprieve. Garrick, marching at the head of the group, didn't even look back.

"Keep moving!" Garrick barked. "A real enemy won't wait for you to catch your breath!"

I clenched my jaw, focusing on my breathing, one step at a time. My feet throbbed, and the weight of my armor felt like it would crush me. But I kept moving, refusing to be one of the men left behind. I had made it too far to fail now.

After what felt like an eternity, we reached a steep incline, a jagged hill that rose sharply in front of us. This was no ordinary portion of the mountain—it was a rock-strewn monster, its surface littered with boulders and jagged outcrops that seemed determined to tear at our feet and drag us down. This would be our next challenge: an uphill climb in full gear.

"Get up there!" Garrick roared. "And don't you dare slow down!"

I gritted my teeth and started the climb. Every step was a plea to the gods to make it stop. Rocks slid beneath my boots as if the hill itself wanted to see me fail. Each step was a battle of will, my legs trembling under the strain.

Ahead of me, some of the recruits had started crawling on all fours, desperate to keep moving, while others slipped and fell, only to be met with the sharp rebukes of the Marshals.

"There's no quitting in war!" one of the Marshals shouted as he grabbed a fallen recruit by the collar and hauled him to his feet. "Get up, or get out!"

My world narrowed to the rocks in front of me. I could barely think, every part of my body focused on the next step, the next push upward. My shield felt like a slab of iron strapped to my arm, and my sword clanged heavily at my side, but I refused to drop it. I had to make it to the top.

When I finally crested the hill, my legs nearly gave out beneath me. I wasn't sure how long we had been climbing, but it felt like hours. The world spun slightly as I steadied myself, forcing my breathing to slow.

But there was no time to rest.

At the top, we were greeted by a wall of wooden dummies lined up in rows, each with shields and wooden swords tied to them. This was the next stage—combat.

"Form up!" Garrick ordered.

We lined up, forming tight ranks, and the commands began. "Shield wall!"

I moved on instinct, raising my shield and locking it with the men beside me. We were tired and battered from the march, but the training had burned these movements into our bones. As the Marshals began attacking the line with blunted weapons, my muscles screamed in protest, but I blocked and countered, holding the formation.

"Push forward! Show me the discipline we've drilled into your bones. Hold that line!" Garrick shouted.

We advanced, step by agonizing step, shields raised, using every ounce of strength to drive our way through the gauntlet. The Marshals didn't let up, raining blows on us from every side, testing our endurance, our focus.

My arms ached from the weight of the shield, but I kept going. The hours dragged on as we repeated the drill again and again—push forward, form ranks, defend, counterattack. We fought against exhaustion and hunger gnawing at our bellies, but we didn't stop.

When the combat drills finally ended, I collapsed onto the ground, gasping for air. The sun had begun to set, casting long shadows over the camp. I was drenched in sweat. My body moved on instinct alone, my mind lost in a fog where time and pain had become indistinguishable. But we weren't finished yet.

The final part of the trial was a night watch. We were ordered to guard the camp perimeter through the night, facing mock ambushes and surprise attacks from the Marshals. Sleep was a distant dream, our minds running on pure instinct. My legs swayed beneath me, and every shadow looked like an enemy. My sword felt like it would slip from my numb fingers.

I could hardly see straight. My vision blurred, and my body barely responded to commands, but I was still standing. As the first rays of light touched the camp, Garrick called us all together. We stood, bearing a newfound resolve. None of us were as we once were. The trial had laid us bare leaving nothing but our will to endure.

When Jarin clasped my shoulder, I flinched, startled by the warmth of the gesture.

"We've done it, my friend," he said, his voice thick with exhaustion. I nodded.

Yes indeed. We had.

"You've made it," Garrick said stepping before us, his voice though still firm was quieter than usual. "Most men would've broken long before this. But not you. Today, you proved yourselves. You're ready for war."

I didn't feel like celebrating. My body ached too much, and my mind was too foggy. But somewhere deep down, a spark of pride flickered. I had survived the Trial of Iron. I had proven myself.

Now, I was a soldier of Centralia.

CHAPTER
9

As twilight broke over the camp, the first light of morning revealed the troops gathered in a semicircle before the imposing figure of Lord General Kyder, the Iron Bear General. His presence stilled the air around him, the scars on his face more prominent and imposing tonight, even in the dim light. Today was the day we would take our Oath of Service, pledging our lives to the empire and its cause.

I stood among my brothers, the members of the Iron Blades Imperial Regiment. My heart throbbed with the thrill of what awaited us, and the dread of what we could endure whirled all around me and coursed through me and the ranks like a living pulse. Jarin and Cedric were at my sides, their faces reflecting the same emotions as mine—a blend of fear, determination, and pride. "Soldiers of Centralia," General Kyder began, his voice loud like thunder, commanding our full attention. "You stand before me today as men who have endured trials and tribulations, training under the watchful eyes of our esteemed Marshals. You have pushed through exhaustion, blood, and sweat to earn your place in this army. Today, you will affirm your commitment to our cause, not just to your comrades, but to the realm itself."

I straightened my posture along with the others, my heart swelling with pride. The weight of Kyder's words settled over us like a mantle of honor. We had given everything—our strength, our tears, and our courage—to reach this point.

"The battles ahead will not be won by strength alone," he said as he paced before us. "The enemy you face is wily, ruthless, and unyielding. We shall fight and win; not for glory, but for our own very lives. You are soldiers now; soldiers of Centralia, and the empire's future rests on your shoulders."

For the first time, I saw the faintest crack in his otherwise stiff demeanor—a fleeting shadow. It chilled me more than any enemy ever could.

He continued, "With this oath, you will bind yourselves to the ideals of bravery, loyalty, and honor. You will fight not just for yourselves, but for every citizen of Centralia who looks to you for protection. You will defend our lands against those who threaten to divide and destroy it."

His words felt like a weight pressing down on my chest. This was more than a mere ceremony; it was a vow—a commitment to my brothers in arms, to my family, my brother. Each word spoken by Kyder seemed to solidify my resolve, welding together every doubt and fear into a hardened sense of purpose.

I looked at Jarin and Cedric, and my heart swelled with the bond we had built through the relentless trials, through shared hardship and triumph. "Repeat after me," Kyder commanded, raising his sword high above his head. "I swear my loyalty to the Emperor of Centralia, to defend the realm against all foes, to uphold the honor of my brothers in arms, and to lay down my life if necessary for the greater good of our Empire."

One by one, we echoed the oath, our voices rising together until they filled the camp like a rallying cry. "I swear!" I shouted, my voice merging with those of my comrades, and in that moment, I felt the collective strength of our unit, as if we were no longer many men but a single force, bound by the same determination.

Kyder lowered his sword, and a satisfied smile crossed his rugged face. "You are now officially soldiers of the Iron Blades Imperial Regiment. May your strength carry you through the battles that lie ahead."

As the ceremony concluded, I felt the tension shift. The excitement of what lay ahead stirred within me, igniting a fire in my chest. We were more than soldiers; we were protectors, bound to carve our name into history.

As the moon climbed higher in the sky, the time for departure arrived. We gathered our belongings and prepared for the march to the Imperial Capital of Central. It was a time of transition, of stepping into the unknown, but with my comrades by my side, I felt an unwavering sense of unity among us.

As I hunched over packing my gear, Cedric nudged me, laughing, "You look like you've swallowed a rock."

I stood straight. "Maybe, I have. What about you? You are too calm."

He shrugged, "Someone has to be." He hefted his pack over one shoulder, and the glint of his armor caught the moonlight. Ready for the march?" He asked his voice light despite the seriousness of the moment. As ready as I'll ever be," I replied, forcing a smile. With our gear packed and our spirits lifted, we fell into formation, our breaths visible in the cool night air. The sound of marching boots echoed against the earth, and the banners of Centralia fluttered proudly in the wind.

***

The road stretched ahead of us, a winding path that would lead us to the edge of the capital. I glanced around at my fellow soldiers, their faces filled with resolve. We had trained together, suffered together, and now, together, we would fight.

As we marched, the landscape began to change, the gentle hills of the training camp giving way to the more rugged terrain. The path was long and arduous, but it only fueled my determination. The Imperial Capital loomed in my mind—the bustling streets, the grand architecture, the soldiers who had come before us.

My thoughts turned to the unknown future that awaited us. The glint of sword and shield, the sound of steel clashing in battle, and the cries of the brave warriors who would fight alongside us in Wintmore. With each step, the reality of our journey sank in.

Hours passed, and the moon began its descent as the sun rose, casting a golden hue over the land. As we reached the crest of a hill, we paused to catch our breath. In the far distance, the silhouettes of the Imperial Capital shined.

My heart raced at the sight. This was it.

We were soon to be woven into something far greater than ourselves.

And so, as the sun rose into the sky, the men of the Iron Blades Imperial Regiment marched forward, our future uncer-tain but our resolve unbreakable. We were soldiers of Centralia, bound by honor and duty, prepared to face whatever challenges awaited us in the bloody lands of Wintmore.

CHAPTER
10

The sun rose over Central as we entered the city gates, our boots clanking on the cobblestones as we marched through the bustling streets. The towering walls and grand structures of the capital rose around us, filled with statues and symbols of Centralia's storied past. This city, with its legacy of warriors and heroes, would be our temporary home before we ventured into the war-torn lands of Wintmore.

As we moved through the city, I marveled at the scale of the place. Towering statues of past generals lined the main thoroughfares, each figure frozen in a pose of strength and valor. One of them, held a massive sword raised to the sky, symbolizing the might of Centralia and its enduring spirit.

"It's more magnificent than I imagined," Jarin whispered, his gaze sweeping over the architecture. "I didn't think anywhere could be this grand."

We passed a series of bustling markets, where merchants shouted over one another, eager to sell their wares. Exotic spices, gleaming weapons, and intricate tapestries were spread out on stalls, creating a tapestry of color and sound. My senses were overwhelmed by the sights and smells, from the sweet aroma of fresh pastries to the rich scent of leather armor hanging from wooden racks.

Finally, we reached the Grand War Hall, a sprawling fortress of stone and iron. Banners bearing the sigil of Centralia—a golden Dracoleon—flapped in the breeze. The War Hall was built like a fortress within a fortress, and I felt a chill of excitement run down my spine as we entered.

Inside the courtyard, we were greeted by a general, a tall man clad in dark armor with a scarred face that spoke of battles hard-fought. He stood beside a knight, he was a formidable figure in his own right.

"I am General Aldric," he announced, his voice carrying through the courtyard. "You are here to serve under my command as we prepare for the campaign in Wintmore. These are the knights you will answer to."

The knight stepped forward.

Sir Gareth of the Iron Guard stepped forward, his sword resting on his shoulder. He was a lean man with a quiet strength, clad in armor etched with intricate designs. "I will be over your division, we are the blood of the regiment the spearhead that will pierce through the enemy's defenses."

After the knight had spoken, General Aldric nodded approvingly. "You will be here in Central for a few days before we depart. Take this time to explore the city and prepare yourselves. Familiarize yourselves with the streets and the people. This city is more than just our capital—it's the heart of our empire, and it's what you'll fight to protect."

Dismissed from the formalities, we wandered back into the city, eager to explore. We meandered through winding alleys that branched off from the main streets, discovering hidden court-yards and ancient buildings draped in ivy. Everywhere we went, we could feel the pulse of Central, its people busy and alive.

"Let's find a tavern," Cedric suggested with a grin on his face. "I've heard The Silver Dragon serves the best ale in the city."

We soon found the tavern, a cheerful haven for travelers tucked away on a quiet street. Inside, we were greeted by the warm glow of a fire and the hearty laughter of patrons. We ordered mugs of ale and settled around a corner table, our voices low as we spoke of the coming days.

"To Central and Elsenburg," Jarin toasted, raising his mug. "And to the battles ahead."

We clicked our mugs heartily, drank to our fill, and ventured back out into the lively streets of Central, determined to make the most of our time in the city. The sky was a brilliant shade of blue, and the sun cast a golden glow over the city's ancient stone buildings. We had heard rumors of the famed markets and the splendor of the Grand Hall, and today, we would see it all for ourselves.

The main marketplace stretched out before us, a labyrinth of stalls and tents that seemed to go on forever. Every corner of the square bustled with activity—merchants hawking exotic wares, children darting between stalls, and travelers from distant lands mingling in the crowd. The sheer variety was overwhelming: stalls filled with rich silks from the south, fragrant spices from the east, and weapons forged by the empire's finest smiths.

"Look at this place!" Jarin said, eyes wide as he scanned the scene. "It feels like the entire world is here."

Cedric grinned, his gaze fixed on a stall selling intricately carved wooden figurines. "It's like a festival. I can see why they call Central the heart of the empire."

I walked slowly, taking it all in. There was a stand where an old woman sold herbal tonics and dried roots, and another where a group of musicians played lively tunes on lutes and drums, their melodies weaving through the air and adding to the market's vibrant atmosphere.

We stopped at a blacksmith's stall, where rows of glinting weapons lay on display. The blacksmith, a burly man with soot-streaked arms, noticed my interest and held up a finely made sword, its hilt adorned with an intricate pattern of leaves.

"See something you like?" the blacksmith asked with a grin.

I picked up the sword, testing its weight. It was beautifully balanced, the blade sharp and gleaming. "It's a fine weapon," I said, running my fingers along the polished edge of the blade. "Forged right here in Central," the blacksmith replied proudly. "Nothing else like it in the world."

We continued to wander, stopping now and then to inspect other stalls. At one, a merchant offered us samples of strange fruits I had never tasted before, their flavors sweet and tart. At another, we watched as a jeweler worked with delicate precision to set a bright red gemstone into a golden ring.

As we explored, we bumped into a group of soldiers we hadn't met before, easily recognizable by the red and gold insignia on their cloaks. Among them was a tall man with sandy blond hair and a warm smile. His armor bore the crest of the Kingdom of Noble, marking him as an ally of the Centralian Empire. He extended a hand and introduced himself with a firm handshake.

"Name's Edric," he said, his accent slightly different from ours. "From the Kingdom of Noble. Thought I'd join you for the upcoming campaign."

I shook his hand, intrigued. "A Noblite? What brings you here?"

Edric's eyes sparkled with a hint of pride. "My blood comes from these lands. My great-grandfather fought for Centralia before Noble became an ally. He moved to Noble after a war, but his heart never left this place. My father always told me stories of the empire. Figured it was time I honored my ancestors by serving alongside their kin."

Jarin looked impressed. "So you're here by choice, not just duty."

Edric nodded. "Aye. Central and Noble are allies, but to me, it's personal. I want to be part of something bigger, something my great-grandfather would be proud of."

We talked as we wandered through the market together, exchanging stories. We spoke of our training and experiences so far. Edric regaled us with tales of Noble's rolling green hills and its massive stone keeps, painting a picture of a land that sounded as grand as Central itself.

As we neared the far end of the market, we reached the steps of the Grand Dracoleon Hall, an awe-inspiring structure that rose like a mountain from the heart of the city. Massive stone columns supported the archways, and intricately carved friezes depicted scenes from the empire's history—battles fought, treaties signed, and heroes celebrated.

Inside, the hall was even more magnificent. The ceiling towered above us, a masterpiece of painted murals and golden inlays. Sunlight filtered through stained-glass windows, casting colorful patterns across the marble floor. The hall was filled with people, nobles, and commoners alike, each pausing to take in the grandeur of the space.

"This place," Cedric breathed, his voice filled with wonder, "it's like something out of a legend."

I nodded, feeling the same sense of awe. The Grand Dracoleon Hall was more than just a building; it was a monument to everything Centralia stood for—a testament to its power, its history, and its enduring spirit.

We walked through the hall, pausing to study the intricate tapestries that lined the walls. Each one told a story, depicting scenes from Centralia's long and storied past. In one, a line of soldiers marched through a snow-covered forest, banners held high as they faced an unseen enemy. In another, showed the great Dracoleon coming down from the heavens onto the battle kneeling before the first emperor.

We reached the center of the hall, where a massive mosaic spread across the floor, depicting the map of Centralia and its surrounding lands. I traced the lines with my eyes, noting the territories that made up the empire.

As we prepared to leave the hall, Edric turned to me, a thoughtful look on his face. "You know, I've always heard tales of Central, but being here—seeing it with my own eyes—it's more than I could have imagined."

I smiled, understanding exactly what he meant. "It feels like the world could start and end in this city."

We walked back out into the sunlight, the weight of the Hall's history resting on our shoulders. We had come to Central as recruits, but standing among its wonders, we felt like a part of something much larger. As we walked back through the market with Edric, laughing and sharing stories, I knew that these were the moments I would carry with me into battle—memories of a city that, to me, now felt like home.

The exploration had been exhilarating, and the sights of Central had left us in awe. Yet, as the day wore on, our excitement began to morph into a mischievous energy, and before long, we were daring each other to explore corners of the city where soldiers were perhaps not so welcome.

As we wandered into a quieter alleyway off the main market, Edric's eyes lit up when he spotted a group of older men playing dice outside a small, weathered inn.

"Fancy a bit of a gamble, lads?" Edric grinned, his eyes glinting with mischief.

I hesitated, but Jarin shrugged. "We've but one chance to explore Central. Why not take it?"

Cedric, always quick to rise to a challenge, raised an eyebrow. "Do we have the coin to risk, though?"

Cedric chuckled, digging into his pouch for the coins. "I'll put a few Emeruls down. Let's see if Lady Luck's on our side today." We approached the dice players, and after a few moments of good-natured banter, we joined the game. At first, our luck seemed promising. With a confident flick of his hand, Edric made a decent win on his first roll, collecting a small handful of coins. Cedric laughed as he won a round himself, his infectious grin widening with each toss of the dice. But soon, the tide turned, and the small pile of coins we'd gathered began to dwindle.

Tension thickened in the alley. One of the older players fixed a glare at Edric. "You lads better know when to quit," he warned, his voice gruff.

Edric, though, seemed unfazed. He leaned in, rolling the dice with a practiced ease, his composure unwavering even as our luck soured. But just as the dice clattered across the ground, a shout rang out.

"Oi! You soldiers don't belong here!" A stout man with a sour expression had spotted us from the inn's doorway, and he didn't look pleased. "Take your trouble back to the barracks!"

My heart raced as the realization hit—we were in over our heads. The dice players scowled, and the older man crossed his arms, his glare turning from Edric to the rest of us.

Cedric grabbed Edric's shoulder, pulling him up from the game. "Time to go, I think."

Jarin nodded, stepping back from the growing scowls of the alley's regulars. "Agreed. Before we wear out our welcome."

Jarin stole some coins and some other trinkets from the table and we bolted, laughing spiritedly as we dashed back toward the main street. I could hear the angry shouts behind them, but I didn't dare look back. We wove through the marketplace, dodging between carts and startled shoppers as we sprinted away from our impromptu gamble.

"This way!" Edric called, leading them down a narrow alley that opened onto a quieter lane. We darted through, only slowing once we'd put several blocks between ourselves and our disgruntled opponents. The four of us leaned against a wall, breathless but laughing like schoolboys caught in the middle of a prank.

Cedric bent double with laughter, clutching his side. "Next time, Edric, remind me not to let you choose our pastimes!"

Edric shrugged, a playful grin on his face. "We got out alright, didn't we? Besides, I almost won us a decent sum before it went south."

I shook my head, laughing despite myself. "Almost isn't good enough when it gets us chased out of town!"

We shared a few more moments of breathless laughter before glancing around, suddenly aware that we were a fair distance from the headquarters—and running late for our evening assembly.

"Come on," I urged, still grinning. "We need to get back to the Grand War Hall before they notice we've been gone for too long."

Without another word, we took off running, winding our way back through the city streets. As we reached the War hall's main gate, the sun was just beginning to dip toward the horizon, casting long shadows across the courtyard.

Breathless but exhilarated, we entered, sharing conspiratorial smiles as we joined the other soldiers who were gathering in the main hall. It had been a risky venture. I looked around at my comrades and knew that these moments—of laughter, trouble, and shared adventure—were as much a part of soldiering as the battles ahead.

Back at the War Hall, we managed to slip into the mess hall just as the evening meal was being served. We filed in with the other soldiers, trying to blend into the crowd as we queued up for our rations. My stomach growled, and the scent of stew and fresh bread was a welcome comfort after our unexpected sprint through Central.

We filled our bowls with the thick, hearty stew and found a quiet corner to sit. Cedric tore into a chunk of bread, smirking as he nudged Edric. "Almost thought we wouldn't make it back," he said.

"Bah," Edric scoffed, taking a spoonful of stew. "Just a bit of fun. And we're here, aren't we? No one's the wiser."

But just as the words left his mouth, I noticed three familiar figures entering the mess hall, stopping to speak with the officer at the door. It was the old men from the dice game, but now they wore the dark robes and insignias of scribes, their faces unmistakable.

"Cedric," I hissed, my eyes widening. "Look."

The old men looked round the room, their eyes sharp and searching. Realization dawned on Cedric and Jarin's faces, and they ducked their heads instinctively, pulling up their hoods as if to make themselves invisible. Jarin looked down, hunching his shoulders as we attempted to blend in with the crowd.

"What are the odds?" Jarin muttered, lowering his head.

"Pretty high, apparently," Edric replied, casting a quick glance around. "We need to disappear. Fast."

"Stay calm," I said. "Let's finish our meal and get out of here before they spot us."

We ate as quickly as we could, huddled together in their corner. I tried to keep my focus on the food, but my gaze kept darting back to the scribes, who were moving slowly through the hall, chatting with the soldiers and taking notes. They seemed intent on their business, but now and then, one of them would glance around, as if searching for someone.

I ducked my head, spooning the last of my stew into my mouth. The others had finished as well, and we nodded to each other, slipping quietly from our seats. We moved carefully through the rows of tables, doing our best to stay out of the scribes' line of sight.

Just as we reached the door, I heard one of the scribes laugh loudly, a familiar, mocking laugh. I glanced back and saw the man lean in close to the officer, pointing vaguely in our direction. Not waiting to find out if we'd been recognized, I tugged Edric by the arm, and the four of us slinked into a side corridor, moving swiftly through the shadows.

We found a narrow alcove near the supply room and pressed ourselves against the wall, holding our breath as footsteps echoed down the hall. The scribes' voices grew louder as they passed by, chuckling over some shared joke, blissfully unaware of the young soldiers just out of sight. We waited until the sound of footsteps faded away, exhaling a sigh of relief.

"That was perilously close," Cedric murmured, running a hand through his hair.

Edric grinned, the tension melting into a chuckle. "Close enough to keep us on our toes. Those old men have more power than they let on."

When we were sure the coast was clear, we slipped out from our hiding spot and made our way back to the bunks. The day's adventures had left us exhausted but buzzing with a sense of excitement. We had faced danger, albeit in the form of irate scribes, and emerged unscathed.

As we lay on our cots, the vigor finally yielding to weariness, I looked over at my friends, grateful for their loyalty and shared sense of mischief. And as the sounds of the bustling Grand War Hall faded into the night, I closed my eyes, letting sleep take me, knowing tomorrow would bring new challenges—and likely, more adventures.

CHAPTER 11

The next morning, we found ourselves in the training yard, assembled with the rest of our troop. The sun had barely risen, and the crisp morning air held a chill that cut through our armor. We stood at attention, awaiting orders from Sir Gareth of the Iron Guard, the commander of our section of the regiment. Sir Gareth was a tall, imposing figure, his armor polished to a mirror-like gleam and his gaze sharp as he regarded the assembled men.

"Today, we focus on formation drills and defensive tactics," he announced, his voice carrying over the yard with ease. "You are the wall that will hold the line. In Wintmore, there will be no room for hesitation or doubt. You will need to move as one, fight as one, and defend as one."

I straightened, feeling pride swell in my chest. Sir Gareth was known for his discipline and mastery of defense, and training under his watchful eye was both an honor and a challenge. We quickly fell into lines, shields in hand, just as he barked at us to form a tight defensive wall.

"Raise your shields!" His voice boomed, as he paced along the line of men. "Keep them level, lock them together—like this." He demonstrated, positioning his own shield in line with mine, forming an impenetrable barrier before letting go. "The strength of your shield wall is only as strong as the man beside you."

I adjusted my shield, feeling the weight of it press against my arm as I locked it with Jarin's to my right and Edric's to my left. We braced ourselves, forming a tight seamless line. Sir Gareth stepped back to observe our form and nodded.

"Good. Now, hold steady and stay low," Sir Gareth continued. "You'll need to absorb the force of an attack without breaking rank."

Sir Gareth grabbed a wooden staff and moved along the line, pushing against our shields with calculated strikes, testing our balance. When he reached me, a firm blow sent a jolt up my arm. But I held steady, gritting my teeth and pushing back with all my strength.

"Not bad," Sir Gareth remarked, moving on to test Cedric and Edric. "But remember, when the enemy strikes, they won't hold back. So, neither should you."

After several rounds of defensive drills, we shifted to offensive maneuvers. Sir Gareth paced along the line. "Watch closely," he commanded, hefting his shield into position.

He crouched slightly, his shoulders widening out, and the edge of his shield locking against the one to his left. "This is your wall," he said, his voice low but deliberate. With a fluid shift forward, the shields moved in unison, seamless as a single, unyielding barrier.

Then, his sword arm snapped forward, the steel gleaming in the dim light. It wasn't a swing—it was a quick, precise thrust that jabbed through an imagined opening before retreating just as quickly. "You strike fast and pull back. Never let the wall break."

He repeated the movement, slower this time, as we followed the arc of his blade and the steady rhythm of his steps. When he finished, he turned, scanning us with an expression that dared any of us to falter. "Now, do it."

I practiced the steps, feeling the strain in my legs as I held my shield high, each step forward a calculated advance. Sir Gareth was relentless, correcting our form and pushing us to improve with each round. The drills were intense, and soon my muscles ached from the effort, but I kept my focus, determined to meet Sir Gareth's standards.

After practicing for what seemed like ages, Sir Gareth called for a rest, and we lowered our shields, breathing heavily. Sir Gareth stood before us, his expression stern but not unkind.

"You've done well for recruits," he said, his gaze sweeping over us. "But remember, this is only the beginning. Wintmore will test you in ways this training yard cannot. Out there, you won't have the luxury of time to adjust your stance or catch your breath. You must be ready for anything."

We stood straight, absorbing the gravity of his words.

"Rest now," Sir Gareth said, gesturing for us to disperse. "We'll resume in an hour with sparring drills. I want to see how well you hold up under pressure."

As we moved to sit in the shade, I exchanged a look with Jarin, who gave me a weary but determined grin. Cedric stretched his arms, rolling his shoulders to ease the stiffness, while Edric took a long drink from his canteen.

"He's tough," Cedric muttered, wiping sweat from his brow. "But I can see why they say he's never lost a defensive line."

We were exhausted but content. As the sun began to dip toward the horizon, Sir Gareth called us together one final time. It was brief. "You've made significant progress today. Carry this energy forward. Dismissed!"

We scattered, each making our way back to the barracks.

Our time in Central was drawing to a close, and we would soon march toward Wintmore. For now, we were content with the day's accomplishments and the bonds we were forging.

After the rigorous training session under Sir Gareth's watchful eye, we were granted some respite, and a rare afternoon of leisure stretched before us. The sun hung low in the sky, casting a warm, golden hue over Central. The city seemed to glow in the evening light, its towers and spires silhouetted against the colorful sky. The atmosphere was light. Soldiers lounged in the courtyard, some mending gear, others engaged in friendly sparring matches or deep in conversations.

Cedric stretched his arms above his head, a mischievous glint in his eye.

"You know," he began, glancing at the group, "we've seen all the main attractions—the Grand Hall, the central market—but I overheard some of the locals talking about a part of the city that's off the beaten path."

Jarin looked up from polishing his sword. "Oh? And where's that?"

Cedric leaned in conspiratorially. "There's a market tucked away in the older part of the city. They say you can find things there that you won't see anywhere else—rare artifacts, forgotten relics, and, if tales are true, a little bit of magic."

Edric raised an eyebrow, interest piqued. "Legends coming to life, is it?"

"Exactly!" Cedric quipped. "We're in the heart of the empire, lads. Seems a shame not to explore it fully before we march off to Wintmore."

I considered this and my curiosity stirred. "It could be worth a look. Besides, we've earned a bit of adventure after all the drills."

Edric nodded. "I've heard whispers about these places back in Noble. They say Central holds secrets even its own citizens have forgotten."

Jarin sheathed his sword, a playful smirk on his face. "Well then, it's settled. A little expedition before dusk?"

Cedric clapped his hands together. "Excellent! Let me grab my cloak. We'll need to blend in—wouldn't want to stand out as soldiers wandering where we maybe shouldn't."

I secured my cloak, the fabric worn but reliable, and ensured my dagger was strapped securely at my side – not that I expected trouble, but it never hurt to be prepared.

We set out from the barracks, weaving through the familiar streets bustling with evening activity. Vendors called out to passersby, touting everything from spiced meats to handcrafted trinkets. Children laughed as they chased one another underfoot, and the melody of a street musician's lute drifted through the air.

"Which way are we headed?" I asked, keeping pace with Cedric.

"East, toward the older districts," Cedric replied, his eyes scanning the surroundings. "We'll pass the Griffin Fountain and then take a left into the narrow streets. From what I've gathered, that's where the usual maps end and the real adventure begins."

Edric chuckled softly. "You seem to have done your diligence, I see."

Cedric shrugged modestly. "Just keeping my ears open."

As we moved further from the central squares, the buildings began to change. The stonework of the city's buildings grew more archaic; ivy clung to walls, and the streets narrowed, paved with uneven cobblestones that echoed with our footsteps.

The city felt different here—quieter, almost contemplative. Lanterns hung from wrought iron hooks, their flames not yet lit, waiting for nightfall.

Jarin broke the silence. "It's hard to believe we're still in the same city. Feels like we've stepped back in time."

"Such is Central," Edric remarked. "Layer upon layer of history. My father used to say that if you listen closely, you can hear the whispers of the past in places like this."

I glanced at the fading inscriptions on a nearby archway, the symbols worn but still intricate. "I wonder what stories these streets could tell."

We continued, eventually reaching the Griffin Fountain as Cedric had described. The stone griffin stood proudly in the center of a small square, water trickling from its beak into a moss-lined basin below. A few locals loitered nearby, casting curious glances at us but offering no challenge.

"Left, here," Cedric instructed, leading us into an even narrower alleyway.

The path sloped gently downward, and the sounds of the bustling city faded, replaced by a quiet hum that hinted at activity just out of sight. The walls here were closer, and the overhanging balconies nearly touched above them, creating a tunnel-like passage that was both intriguing and somewhat suffocating. A thrill ran through me.

"Starting to feel like we're entering another world," Jarin said.

I cocked my head to one side "That's the idea, isn't it?"

The alley opened up slightly, and strains of music reached our ears—a haunting melody played on an unfamiliar instrument. The air grew richer with scents I couldn't quite place—incense, aged wood, and something akin to spices from distant lands.

Cedric paused, turning to face us with a satisfied smile. "Gentlemen, we're almost there."

"How can you tell?" Edric asked, eyeing the shadowed path ahead.

"Call it a hunch," Cedric replied. "And the fact that the map ends right about here."

I chuckled. "So we're venturing beyond even your secret map now?"

"Precisely," Cedric said with a wink. "Isn't that where the real discoveries are made?"

We shared a light-hearted laugh.

"Onward then," I said, taking the lead.

We moved forward, languidly. The alleyway began to show signs of more frequent use - scuff marks on the stones, occasional bits of cloth caught on rough edges, and subtle carvings near doorways that seemed to mark the territory.

As we rounded a bend, voices became discernible—soft conversations, the occasional burst of laughter, and the rhythmic clatter of what sounded like wooden chimes. The glow of torchlight flickered against the walls, casting dancing shadows that beckoned us closer.

"Looks like we've found it," Edric murmured.

I stepped forward and held up a hand, signaling a brief pause. "Before we go any further, perhaps we should agree to stick together. Places like this might not take kindly to strangers wandering."

Jarin nodded. "Agreed. We watch each other's backs."

Cedric's eyes gleamed with excitement. "And keep our wits about us. Who knows what wonders we'll find?"

With a collective nod, we proceeded, stepping into the threshold of the hidden market.

It was a sprawling underground bazaar, illuminated by a web of lanterns hanging from ropes crisscrossing above the warm light casting dancing shadows along aged stone walls. Stalls lined both sides of the winding pathways, each one a kaleidoscope of colors and curiosities. Vendors from distant lands stood behind tables cluttered with items that defied easy description—glimmering crystals that seemed to pulse with inner light, intricate clockwork devices whirring softly, and scrolls penned in languages long forgotten.

"This place is incredible," I whispered, my eyes darting from one fascinating object to another.

Cedric leaned in closer. "Keep your wits about you. Places like this can be... unpredictable."

We moved together, careful not to stray too far from one another. Jarin paused at a stall displaying a collection of masks carved from dark wood, each one bearing a unique expression—some joyful, others haunting.

"Look at this craftsmanship," Jarin remarked, reaching out to touch one of the masks.

"Careful," the stall owner cautioned, his voice raspy. He was a slender man with sharp features and eyes that seemed to see more than what was in front of him. "These masks hold the spirits of their makers. They are not to be handled lightly."

Jarin withdrew his hand, offering an apologetic nod. "My apologies."

Edric was drawn to a table covered with weapons unlike any he had seen—daggers with serpentine blades, swords etched with glowing runes, and bows crafted from materials that shimmered under the lantern light.

A burly vendor with a thick beard watched him appraise the items. "Ah, a man of discerning taste," the vendor said. "Perhaps something here calls to you?"

Edric shook his head. "I'm only looking, thank you."

As we continued deeper into the market, the crowd grew thicker, and the ambiance shifted. Musicians played unfamiliar instruments, their melodies both enchanting and disconcerting. The chatter of various languages created a hum that was both invigorating and disorienting.

I stopped at a modest stall tucked between two larger ones. Unlike the others, this table held only a few items—a small collection of pendants, a weathered book, and a peculiar-looking amulet. Behind the stall sat an old man, his face lined with age and eyes that seemed to peer beyond the present, and shrouded in an aura that held a distant sadness.

"Something draws you here, young soldier," the old man said softly, his gaze meeting mine.

I felt a slight shiver but stepped closer. "I'm merely perusing for now," I replied.

The old man gestured to the items before him. "These are not mere trinkets. Each one has a purpose."

My eyes were drawn to the amulet—a simple piece of dark metal, shaped like a shield with a single, small emerald set in its center. "What's this one?" I asked.

The old man's lips curved into a faint smile. "Ah, the Heartguard. It protects the bearer from harm when courage alone is not enough."

Cedric and the others gathered around, intrigued.

"Sounds like a good luck charm," Edric remarked.

"Perhaps," the old man conceded. "Or perhaps it's something more."

I turned it over in my hands, hesitating. It seemed familiar. Had I seen this emerald piece somewhere before? Or was it merely something similar? Maybe, my mind was playing tricks, conjuring memories that never truly existed.

"How much are you asking for it?"

The old man gazed into my face for a moment, as if searching for something. Then he shook his head slowly. "For you, child, there is no charge. It is a gift."

I exchanged a wary glance with Jarin. "I can't accept that without offering something in return."

The old man reached out and gently closed my hand around the amulet. His fingers were cold, almost chilly. "Payment is not always made in coin. Sometimes, it's enough to know that an item has found its rightful owner."

As the old man's grip tightened, a strange tingling spread from the amulet to me as if it had indeed whispered my name.

CHAPTER 12

A subtle tension hung in the air. I cleared my throat, feeling a sudden strange comfort. "Thank you," I said, unsure of what else to say.

"May it serve you well," the old man replied. His eyes tarried on me for a moment before his gaze became distant once more; as if he had already moved on from our exchange.

As we moved away from the stall, Cedric leaned in. "That was... strange."

"Indeed, it was," I murmured, slipping the amulet into a pouch on my belt. The old man's eyes had seemed mysterious, filled with something I couldn't quite name. Urgency? Desperation? Whatever it was hovered over me like a ghostly whisper I couldn't shake.

Edric glanced back over his shoulder at the bustling crowd. "Old markets like these are full of legends and superstitions," he said. "Maybe he truly believes the amulet will help you."

I laughed at the incredulity of Edric words, but the laughter felt hollow. Perhaps, it was nothing. Perhaps, he just wanted to rid himself of the thing. The weight of the amulet felt almost unnatural, more than just a piece of jewelry.

"Or, maybe it's cursed," Jarin added with a chuckle. I forced a smile, but the anxious knot in my stomach remained. The market had lost its charm. The vibrant energy now felt hollow, the air charged with something I couldn't explain. Every flicker of movement caught my attention, and every misplaced sound pricked at my senses. The sense of being watched settled over me. Was it the crowd? Or was it this amulet? Or just paranoia? I could hear Edric and Jarin speaking, but their words were more like distant echoes.

"We should head back," I said. My voice came out more abrupt than I intended, but with a flippant shrug of their shoulders, they gave their assent and we began to wind our way out of the market. The lanterns flickered above, their lights seemingly dimmer now, as though even they sensed something had happened. The cool night air met us as we stepped into the alleyway, the oppressive atmosphere lifting slightly. Central's familiar noise welcomed us back: laughter from a nearby tavern, the distant clatter of a cart on cobblestones and the warmth of ordinary life.

I kept my hand on the pouch, my fingers brushing the amulet as we walked, its cool surface a reminder that I hadn't just imagined it all.

"Well, that was something," Jarin said, breaking the silence, his voice filled with amusement. I managed a real smile this time.

"Not what you see every day," Edric added, shaking his head.

Cedric, who had been quiet most of the time, turned to me. "Do you think that old man's amulet is really special?"

I shrugged, my hand tightening around the pouch. "It feels significant somehow," I couldn't explain why, but it felt like it was meant to be with me—a thought as reassuring as it was unsettling. We walked on in silence after that, the streetlamps casting long shadows across the cobblestones The city came alive in its own way at night: —music spilled out from open tavern doors, people's laughter mingled with the clinking of mugs, and the air was crisp with the promise of nightfall. I glanced at my comrades, each lost in their thoughts, and wondered what tomorrow would bring. The barracks loomed ahead, its stone walls bathed in torchlight. The clank of armor and the murmurs of soldiers preparing for the night reminded us of our duties. "Let's get some rest," I said. "Tomorrow is another day of training."

***

Back at the barracks, the days blurred together: relentless drills, sparring sessions, and tactical exercises under Sir Gareth's guidance filled every waking moment.

"Discipline and unity are our greatest weapons," Sir Gareth declared during a morning assembly, his voice echoing across the training grounds. "Each of you must be the pillar your brothers can rely upon."

I felt the weight of his words as I practiced formations with my unit. The clanking of armor and the synchronized steps of my comrades echoed around me. Each step, each movement was deliberate, honed for efficiency and strength. I focused on the rhythm, the way our boots hit the dirt in unison and the way our shields locked together seamlessly. There was comfort in the discipline, in knowing that we moved as one.

But there were moments when doubt crept in. Was I strong enough to be that pillar? Could I be the one my brothers relied on when it mattered most? I pushed those thoughts away, forcing myself to focus on the task at hand. There was no room for hesitation or overthinking.

In the evenings, we gathered in the mess hall where conversations and laughter mingled with the crackling of the fire as we ate. One night, as we were finishing our meal, Cedric leaned in, a glint of excitement in his eyes.

"Have you heard the news?"

Edric looked up, curiosity piqued. "What news?"

Cedric lowered his voice conspiratorially. "In a week, we'll be marching a grand parade before the Emperor himself. It's a tradition— before we depart for Wintmore."

I felt a jolt of something—pride, maybe, or anxiety. A parade before the Emperor. It was a chance to show our strength and our readiness. But it was also a test, a moment where all eyes would be on us. "The entire city will be watching,"

The following days saw a shift in our training. We moved from combat drills to perfecting ceremonial formations and maneuvers. Every step had to be perfect, every salute synchronized, every movement a reflection of who we were. Sir Gareth and the other knights drilled us tirelessly on marching in unison, saluting with exact timing, and maintaining an impeccable appearance. Tailors moved through the barracks, adjusting our uniforms to ensure a flawless fit, while armorers polished our breastplates and helmets until they gleamed. The banners bearing the emblems of the empire were unfurled, their colors vibrant against the sky, and the musicians practiced their martial tunes, the rhythm setting a steady pulse that echoed through the barracks.

"Presentation is a reflection of honor," Sir Gareth reminded us time and again, his eyes sharp as he inspected our lines. "You are not just soldiers; you are the embodiment of Centralia's strength and valor."

On the eve of the parade, I checked my gear again, ensuring every buckle was in place, and every seam was straight. "It's hard to believe," Edric mused as we prepared our uniforms, "Marching before the Emperor…"

***

The morning of the parade was clear and crisp. Central buzzed with anticipation, banners fluttering from balconies, and citizens lining the streets. Children perched on their parents' shoulders, waving miniature flags, while elders stood with hands over their hearts, eyes glistening with pride. The drums thundered as we marched down the grand avenue, each step in perfect rhythm. The city was a spectacle of color and sound, and the banners of Centralia fluttered proudly from every rooftop and balcony.

I kept my head forward and tried to keep my expression steady. Beside me, Cedric and Jarin marched in perfect synchronicity, their expressions solemn. The foot soldiers marched at the forefront, their billhooks and spears held steady. Behind us, the armati—the common horse-troops—rode with discipline, their mounts adorned with caparisons of deep crimson, and I could hear the steady clop of hooves behind me. Archers of the king's guard followed, their longbows unstrung but ready, quivers full of feathered arrows expertly fletched. The hobilers—light cavalry—flanked the procession, their horses agile and their riders vigilant.

As we neared the Imperial Palace, the grandeur of its marble spires and intricate carvings struck me anew; carvings depicting the history of Centralia: battles won, alliances forged, and the prosperity of the realm. The plaza was vast, its polished stone glittering like water under the morning sun. Flanking the plaza were colossal statues of former emperors and legendary knights, their stone gazes fixed eternally on the empire they had shaped.

At the far end of the plaza stood the grand dais, draped in rich fabrics of deep red and gold. Upon it sat none other than Emperor Valerius III himself, a figure both imposing and regal. Clad in ornate armor that blended seamlessly with his imperial robes, he wore a crown that caught the light with every subtle movement. He was with big in stature, and his presence seemed to fill the entire space, his gaze—sharp and discerning, taking in every detail as we approached. To his sides stood the High Council and esteemed generals, including General Aldric, General Kyder, and the knights under whom we served. Before the emperor's dais, we halted in unison. The movement was flawless—a testament to the countless hours of drilling that had brought us to this point. Then a moment of stillness enveloped us, until it felt like the entire world was holding its breath.

The command echoed through the ranks: "Kneel!"

In perfect harmony, we lowered ourselves onto one knee, heads bowed in respect. Together, our voices rose in a resounding pledge, "For Centralia, and for the Emperor!"

Emperor Valerius III rose from his throne, commanding our full attention. He stepped forward to the edge of the dais, his gaze sweeping over us. The silence that followed was profound and I held my breath.

"Brave soldiers of Centralia," his voice carried effortlessly across the plaza, rich and authoritative. "Your display of unity and strength fills my heart with pride. You stand here not only as warriors but as the embodiment of our empire's ideals—courage, honor, and unwavering loyalty."

His words buoyed us. I dared a subtle glance upward, and for a fleeting moment, I caught his eyes. They weren't just regal;

there was something there—a regard for us, for what we represented. It made everything we had endured —the countless hours of training and the sacrifices we had made to stand here today—worth it.

"As you march toward Wintmore," the Emperor continued, "carry with you the hopes and prayers of every citizen of Centralia. Your actions will shape the future of our realm."

His words sank in, the reality of our mission pressing down on me. Wintmore—it wasn't just a distant place anymore. The Emperor raised his hand in a gesture of blessing. "Rise, soldiers, and go forth with the knowledge that the spirit of Centralia marches beside you."

As the emperor's speech ended, the crowd erupted into cheers, the once-muted excitement now unleashed in full force.

At the next command, we stood as one, the motion fluid.

Beside me, Cedric's eyes shone. "This is it," he breathed. "We're part of this!"

I nodded and swallowed the lump in my throat. There was a gravity to this moment, an understanding that what lay ahead would shape us, not just as soldiers, but as people. Edric's voice cut through my thoughts, steady and resolute. "For Centralia and the Emperor," he echoed quietly, reaffirming the vow we had just proclaimed.

Jarin gave a subtle smile, glancing between us. "And for one another."

Those words resonated deeply. This wasn't just about duty to the empire—it was about the bonds we had forged, the brotherhood that tied us together. We continued down the avenue, the path leading us toward the city's gates and the journey beyond. The sounds of the celebration gradually faded, replaced by the rhythmic cadence of our march. Yet, the memory of the

Emperor's words and the collective voice of our pledge remained vivid in my mind.

The parade had been more than a ceremony; it was a rite of passage. It was a defining moment that marked the transition from training to reality. We carried not only our weapons and armor but also the essence of Centralia's spirit. The road to Wintmore awaited, and with it, the challenges that would test everything we had sworn to protect.

We were ready, my brothers-in-arms and I.

I fiddled with the amulet that I had tied around my neck, and suddenly, I thought of Eamon.

CHAPTER 13

After the parade, we returned to the barracks with renewed purpose. The exhilaration of the day's events lingered, but there was little time to dwell on it. The reality of our imminent departure to Wintmore had set in, and preparations intensified throughout the Grand War Hall.

The following morning, the barracks buzzed with activity. Quartermasters moved between units, distributing equipment and ensuring that each soldier was adequately supplied. The clatter of armor being adjusted and weapons being inspected filled the air. I spent hours meticulously checking my gear—sharpening my sword, reinforcing the straps of my armor, and ensuring that my shield proudly bore the emblem of Centralia.

In the armory, blacksmiths worked tirelessly to repair and enhance our equipment. The heat from the forges mixed with the crisp autumn air, creating a haze that hung over the smithy. I watched as sparks flew with each strike of the hammer, their rhythm steady and reassuring. There was something almost hypnotic about it.

"Your sword's in good shape," a burly blacksmith with a ready smile commented as he examined the blade I handed over. "But a little extra edge never hurt anyone." With practiced skill, he honed the blade, each movement precise. When he handed it back, the edge gleamed with renewed sharpness.

"Thank you," I replied, genuinely appreciating the craftsmanship. It wasn't just a weapon—it was an extension of myself, something that needed to be ready for whatever lay ahead.

Training sessions resumed, but the focus had shifted. Sir Gareth gathered us on the parade grounds, his demeanor as serious as ever. "Our time here is short," he began, his voice carrying over the assembled soldiers. "We will drill once more on battlefield formations and signals. In Wintmore, communication and discipline will be our lifeblood."

I felt the weight of his words settle over us. Wintmore was no longer some distant idea—it was real, and it was coming fast. We moved through complex maneuvers, honing our ability to react swiftly to commands. The foot soldiers practiced forming defensive lines with the pavises, and shields interlocking to create an impenetrable wall. Archers rehearsed firing volleys over our heads, coordinating their timing to maximize effectiveness without endangering us. I could hear the twang of their bows, the whistle of arrows cutting through the air.

During a sparring exercise, I found myself paired with Edric. We circled each other, weapons at the ready. There was a glint in his eyes that made me grin.

"Let's see if that training from Noble gives you an edge," I teased lightly, trying to ease the tension that had settled in my shoulders.

Edric smirked, his stance shifting slightly. "Be careful what you wish for."

We exchanged blows as we danced around each other, the clash of steel ringing out across the parade grounds. There was a familiarity in our movements—we knew each other's strengths and weaknesses, and we used them to challenge one another. The bout ended in a draw, both of us panting, yet grinning at each other.

"Well fought," Sir Gareth acknowledged. I hadn't realized he'd been observing from nearby. His gaze was stern, but there was a hint of approval there. "Remember, your true strength lies in supporting each other."

As the sun began to set, casting long shadows across the grounds, we were dismissed. Back in the barracks, the mood became somber. Many of the men took the time to write letters home or engage in quiet conversation. There was a sense that we were on the edge of something, and everyone dealt with it in their way.

I sat on my bunk, absently running my thumb over the edge of my shield, when Cedric approached, carrying two mugs of ale. "Figured you could use one," he said, handing it over with a smile.

I grabbed it, feeling the coolness of the mug in my hand. "Here's to the road ahead," I said, lifting it slightly.

We clinked our mugs together. "Hard to believe we'll be leaving Central tomorrow," Cedric mused, his gaze distant for a moment. "This city has been good to us."

"It has," I agreed, taking a sip. The ale was smooth and flowed down my throat, bringing welcome comfort.

"But it's time we put all this preparation to use." The thought of finally leaving was both exhilarating and terrifying. We had trained endlessly for this, and now it was time to prove ourselves.

Jarin joined us, a playful glint in his eye. "I hear they've stocked extra rations for the march—best not be late for the briefing tomorrow," he said with a grin.

I forced out a chuckle. "Trust you to think of food at a time like this."

Edric appeared as well, settling in with the group. His expression was more serious. "Speaking of which, I've been thinking about Wintmore. They say the terrain there is treacherous—dense forests and rocky mountains. We'll need to stay sharp."

Jarin crouched beside me. "It is the cold I dread. Wintmore's a treacherous place," he said, his voice steady, though his eyes flickered like the flames. "Jagged cliffs. blizzards so harsh you can't see your own hand in front of you. A good man can lose himself out there."

I raised an eyebrow, leaning against my bunk. "And a bad man?"

Jarin's lips twitched, almost a smile but not quite. "A bad man we can handle," he said grabbing the hilt of his sword. He paused, his gaze drifting outside. "I've been through Wintmore once before. Years ago."

The way he said it—low, clipped, as though the words carried too much weight—made me glance up.

"And you made it out," Cedric quipped.

Jarin gave a short laugh, but it lacked humor. "Left something behind, though." He gave a harder tug at the hilt of his sword. "Maybe it's still waiting for me."

I watched him for a moment, the easy banter of their usual exchanges absent. I wanted to ask what it was, but something in his expression—a tightness around his jaw, a shadow in his eyes—told me not to push.

Instead, I said, "We'll be in and out before the cliffs even know we're there. We've trained for this. Sir Gareth has seen to that."

Jarin smirked, but the sharp edge of his earlier words clung in the air. "Sure, he has," he said, but the flicker of doubt in his tone persisted with me for the rest of the night.

We spent the rest of the evening sharing stories and recalling moments from our time in Central, every foreboding forgotten.

***

Laughter filled the barracks, mingling with the crackling of the hearth fire. For a while, the weight of what lay ahead seemed lighter, replaced by the warmth of camaraderie. These men were more than comrades—they were brothers, and that bond made all the difference.

The final day in Central dawned clear and cool. There was a stillness in the air as if the city itself was holding its breath. We assembled for one last training session—a ceremonial march through the training grounds. As we stood in formation, I felt a surge of pride. This was what we had trained so hard to achieve.

General Aldric addressed us, his presence commanding respect. "Today, you stand on the threshold of duty," he proclaimed, his voice strong and unwavering. "Your journey to Wintmore will not be easy, but know that you carry the strength of Centralia with you."

The remainder of the day was devoted to final checks. Supply wagons were loaded with provisions, weapons were secured, and horses were tended to by the stable hands. I took it all in as I moved through the bustling camp—the organized chaos that came with preparing for something monumental. It felt surreal, knowing that tomorrow we would leave Central behind, stepping into the unknown.

As evening approached, we gathered for a communal meal in the great hall. Long tables were laden with hearty fare—roasted meats, fresh bread, an abundance of fruits and vegetables. The atmosphere was warm, the room buzzing with conversations. I could feel the energy in the air, the anticipation for what was to come. It was a moment to enjoy the present, to share in each other's company before the road ahead took us into uncertainty.

Toasts were made and voices rose in unison to honor our leaders and the cause we served. I lifted my mug along with the others, my heart swelling with pride. Sir Gareth stood to address us one final time before our departure, his presence commanding our full attention.

"Each of you has shown dedication and growth beyond measure," he said, his gaze steady as he looked at each of us. "Carry that with you into Wintmore. Stand firm, fight with honor, and return with pride."

I found myself holding onto his every word, letting it sink deep into my bones. I looked around the room, at the faces of my comrades, and felt the strength of our unity. We were ready.

Later, I wandered into the tiny temple of Kyrethar nestled within the Grand War Hall, a modest space adorned with symbols of protection and valor. The air inside was calm, a welcome contrast to the busy camp. I lit a candle, offering a silent prayer to the gods for safe passage and the well-being of my friends. The flame flickered, casting dancing shadows across the stone walls and I found myself whispering my hopes—for courage, for strength, for us all to return home. The weight of what lay ahead settled over me, but there was comfort in the act, a sense of peace that I desperately needed.

My thoughts drifted back to home, to Elsenburg, a place that seemed so far away now. I imagined Ma's face and Pa's. I tried to conjure their faces in my mind's eyes, but I couldn't. A lump caught in my throat. The thought of never seeing them again left an ache in my chest.

And then, there was Eamon. He was the only reason I was on this journey. A sudden bout of helplessness shrouded me, with a guilt I couldn't quite bear. My eyes flicked to the candle once more, and I blinked against a sudden sting in my eyes, refusing to let the emotion take root. I couldn't afford to falter now. There was too much at stake. But somewhere deep inside, beneath all my resolve, I couldn't shake the fear. What if this was the last night I ever saw Central? What if it was all for nothing?

That night, as we settled into our sleeping frames, a quiet fell over the barracks. The usual murmurs and rustlings were subdued, each of us lost in our thoughts. I lay awake, staring up at the roof. Now, as night crept over the barracks and the stars began to flicker above, the reality of the journey finally settled into my bones.

I clenched my fists over the amulet —the unexpected gift of the amulet that now hung around my neck—but it didn't erase the cold uncertainty scratching around in my mind. What if I didn't make it back? What if I became another soldier lost to the war, a face forgotten? My breath hitched. The thought of not being there for my family, for Eamon, gnawed at me.

I reached up and touched the amulet again, the metal cool against my skin. Its presence was a small comfort; that there was something beyond the battles ahead. A promise, perhaps, that I wasn't alone. I closed my eyes, allowing myself to drift, knowing that tomorrow would mark the beginning of a new chapter— one that would test everything we had prepared for.

***

At first light, the city of Central stirred with a quiet urgency. I awoke to the sound of distant horns signaling the start of the day, the crisp morning air carrying the mingled scents of dew-covered grass and the faint aroma of burning wood from early cookfires.

We moved with practiced efficiency, our actions hurried yet composed. I swung my legs over the edge of my sleeping rack, quickly donning my underarmor, and the amulet. I wasn't sure why I carried it, but it felt important—before finishing by securing the plates of my breastplate and greaves. The metallic clicks of buckles and clasps echoed softly in our quarters as my comrades did the same. Cedric tightened the straps on his gauntlets, his expression focused, while Jarin methodically sharpened the edge of his sword with a whetstone. The rhythmic scraping sound blended into the morning's symphony.

"Don't forget this," Edric said, tossing my helmet to me with a half-smile. "Wouldn't want you going into battle without that."

I caught it with a nod of thanks, placing it beside my pack. I checked the contents of my satchel: rations, a small flask of water, a spare pair of boots.

Outside, the courtyard buzzed with activity. Soldiers moved in organized clusters, loading supplies onto wagons and ensuring that everything was secured for travel. The clatter of hooves on cobblestone signaled the arrival of the cavalry units, their horses freshly groomed, manes braided to keep them neat during the march. I watched the stable hands hurry about, offering the animals water and feeding and soothing them with gentle pats. I made my way to the armory for a final equipment check. The quartermaster, a grizzled veteran with a keen eye, inspected my gear meticulously. His gaze lingered on my blade, and he ran a finger along the edge.

"Blade's in good condition," he noted. "Make sure it stays that way."

"Yes, sir," I replied, meeting his eyes. There was no room for error. Everything had to be perfect—we couldn't afford anything less.

Passing by the blacksmiths' forge, I watched as sparks flew and the hammering figures worked with a focus that was almost meditative. The heat from the furnaces spilled into the cool morning air, creating a mist that swirled around them. In the stables, the scent of hay and leather greeted me. The horses stood ready, their coats gleaming in the early light. Edric was there, adjusting the saddle on his mount.

"Ready for the long road?" Edric asked, tightening a strap.

"As ready as I'll ever be" I answered, giving the horse an affectionate pat on the neck. "She's a beauty, isn't she?"

"Sturdy and reliable," Edric agreed. "She'll get us where we need to go."

Trumpets sounded, their clear notes cutting through the morning bustle. Officers moved through the ranks, calling out orders and directing soldiers to their positions. I spotted Sir Gareth atop a small rise, his presence commanding as he oversaw the preparations. I regrouped with Cedric and Jarin, the three of us exchanging nods.

"Looks like it's time," Cedric said, adjusting the strap of his shield.

"Let's make sure we don't leave anything behind," Jarin added, hefting his pack onto his shoulders. I cast my gaze upon my belongings, ensuring all was in its rightful place. As the sun fully breached the horizon, the gates of Central began to open.

Massive and ornate, they swung outward with a slow, deliberate grace, revealing the road stretching ahead—a ribbon of dirt and stone winding through the rolling hills and beyond. It was a sight that overwhelmed me—excitement for the journey, trepidation for the unknown, and a deep sense of longing for what we were leaving behind.

***

We arrayed ourselves in columns, our armor gleaming in the sunlight, and banners fluttering in the gentle breeze. The sound of marching feet and the creak of wagon wheels created a steady rhythm, a heartbeat that pulsed through the ranks. I took my place beside my comrades and I felt a pang of nostalgia.

"Hard to believe we're leaving it all behind," I mused aloud, the words escaping before I could stop them.

"But we'll return," Edric said confidently, his voice steady. "And with stories to tell."

His eyes glimmered with certainty, and I found myself nodding. He was right—this wasn't the end. We were leaving, but we would come back stronger, with tales of bravery and bonds forged in the crucible of battle.

A murmur spread through the ranks as General Aldric rode to the front, his steed a magnificent warhorse adorned with ceremonial armor. The sight of him, composed and commanding, filled me with a sense of purpose. He raised his hand, signaling for attention, and silence fell over the assembled troops.

"Soldiers of Centralia!" His voice carried effortlessly over us, rich with authority. "Today we march not just as an army, but as the shield and sword of our empire. Our journey will be long, and challenges await us, but know that the spirit of Centralia marches with us."

A cheer rose, a unified sound that seemed to reverberate through my very bones. The energy of my comrades surged around me, bolstering my resolve. As the command to march echoed through the ranks, a ripple of movement surged forward. I stepped off in unison with the others, the synchronized rhythm of our boots against the cobblestones creating a steady cadence that resonated through the air. The morning sun bathed us in its light, illuminating our armor and weapons, which glinted like a river of steel flowing through the heart of Central.

We advanced along the grand avenue, retracing the path we had taken upon our arrival in the city. The towering edifices of the grand halls rose on either side, their marble columns and intricate carvings standing as testaments to the empire's history and achievements. Banners hung from balconies, their vibrant colors fluttering gently in the breeze. The streets were lined with citizens who had gathered to witness our departure—faces filled with pride, hope, and solemnity. My gaze swept over the familiar sights, each landmark now imbued with deeper meaning. The bustling markets were abuzz with activity, yet a hush fell over the vendors and patrons as we marched by. Shopkeepers stood at their doorways, hands over their hearts or offering respectful nods. The aromas of Centralian spices mingled with the crisp morning air, creating a sensory memory that I knew I would always carry with me. I tried to commit every detail to memory, a piece of home to hold onto.

As we approached the central square, the majestic statue of General Aldrin came into view, his stone figure forever poised in a gesture of valor. The sunlight cast shadows that played across his chiseled features, making him appear almost lifelike. I felt a surge of inspiration as I looked at him, reminded of the legacy my comrades and I were now a part of. We were part of something much bigger than ourselves—a continuation of the ideals and sacrifices that had come before us.

Suddenly, from the corners of my eyes, I spotted the old man from the hidden market. His hood was drawn back. Then, our eyes met, and for a moment, time seemed to slow. He offered a subtle nod, a gesture filled with unspoken understanding. It was as if he knew the journey I was about to undertake, and in that nod, I felt an acknowledgment of the path I had chosen.

A warmth spread through me, my hand instinctively moving to touch the amulet hidden beneath my armor. And in that moment, I knew. I remembered where I had seen the amulet before. It rushed towards me, like a wave of colors, of memories, of a past. It was the last day I spent with Eamon before he left. We had gone deeper into the market at Elsenburg and while I bought meat, he had lingered in a trinket store. I had seen him fiddling with a pendant that looked like the one that now hung around my neck. A bolt shot through my body as figments of what I still did not understand whirled in my mind. A feeling took form in me; that the amulet was somehow, in a way I didn't yet understand, connected to my brother. I darted my eyes to where the old man had stood, but he was gone, disappeared into the bowels of the city streets as suddenly as he had appeared.

"Everything all right?" Cedric asked quietly beside me, noticing my brief distraction.

I nodded, reluctantly tearing my eyes from the crowd. "Yes. I'm...absorbing it all."

And I did. I swallowed the unsettling feeling in my chest and absorbed everything around me—every detail, every sound, every face. This was the last time I'd see Central for a while, maybe longer. Maybe forever. The city, in all its splendor, felt both familiar and suddenly distant. It was as if, by leaving, we were already starting to become part of its history, rather than its present.

The city's grandeur unfolded around us like a piece of cloth. The procession approached the Grand Gate of Central—a monumental archway carved from ancient stone, adorned with elaborate reliefs depicting the founding of the empire and its greatest triumphs. The sight of it never failed to inspire awe. It wasn't just a gate—it was a symbol of everything Centralia stood for, the strength and resilience of our people. It stood as both a protective barrier and a ceremonial passage, its towering presence commanding respect.

As we neared the gate, I could feel the weight of the moment pressing down on us. It stood open now as if baring its mouth to cast us out.

Passing through it would symbolize more than just leaving the city—it was a transition into a new chapter of our lives, one that would test everything we had trained for. The crowds pressed closer here, offering final cheers and waves, throwing flower petals that drifted down like confetti, their bright colors adding touches of beauty to the monochrome of steel and iron. I felt a strange mixture of pride and longing as I looked at the people, their faces filled with hope. They believed in us, and that belief was something I couldn't afford to let down.

I glanced upward at the inscriptions etched into the archway, ancient words invoking protection and victory for those who passed beneath from Kyrethar the god of war. The shadows cast by the gate enveloped us briefly as we moved through, and I felt a chill despite the warmth of the sun. It was like stepping into the unknown, a final severing of the ties that bound us to the safety of home. But as we emerged on the other side, the landscape opened up—a world bathed in sunlight, stretching endlessly toward the horizon. The open road lay ahead, flanked by rolling hills and the distant outline of forests. It was beautiful, in a way that spoke of freedom and possibility.

The sounds of the city faded behind us, replaced by the rhythmic march of boots on earth and the gentle clinking of armor. The air was fresher here, carrying the scents of grass and wildflowers, untamed and alive. I took a deep breath, feeling a swirl of emotions—excitement for the journey ahead, a touch of sadness at leaving home, but above all, a sense of readiness. This was what we had trained for, what we had prepared ourselves to face. I looked around at my comrades—Cedric, Jarin, and Edric—all wearing expressions that mirrored my own sentiments.

"This is it," Jarin said softly. "No turning back now."

"Wouldn't want to even if we could," Edric replied with a faint smile.

I felt the amulet against my chest once more. There were so many questions left unanswered, so many paths we couldn't predict. Yet, with every step forward, my resolve only strengthened. The path to Wintmore would be arduous, but we were prepared. We had to be.

CHAPTER 14

As the spires of Central faded into the distance, the vast expanse of the Centralian plains unfolded before us. The once-towering walls and bustling streets were replaced by rolling hills carpeted in hues of green and gold, swaying gently under the caress of the wind. Soon, the outlines of the city disappeared, swallowed by the horizon. The sky stretched endlessly above, a dome of brilliant blue dotted with the occasional wispy cloud. The initial excitement of departure gradually gave way to the rhythm of the march. Boots pressed into the well-trodden dirt road, creating a steady cadence accompanied by the jingling of armor and the creak of leather straps. I focused on the rhythm, the familiar sound grounding me as the sun climbed higher, its warmth intensifying with every passing moment.

I adjusted the weight of my pack, the straps digging into my shoulders. The amulet beneath my armor shifted slightly, the cool metal pressing against my chest, its presence a constant, comforting weight. The old man's words echoed in my thoughts, but they felt distant now, drowned out by the rhythm of boots on dirt and the jingling of armor. It wasn't the amulet itself that lingered in my mind—it was who it reminded me of. My brother's face flickered in my memory, sharp and vivid, like a blade catching the light.

I forced my gaze to the horizon, trying to focus on anything else but the guilt in my chest. How long had it been since I'd truly thought of him? Days? Weeks? The daily grind of the army had dulled that edge, and the realization hurt my heart.

"Watch your step, Kaelan," Cedric called beside me, his voice snapping me back to the present. I stumbled slightly, catching myself.

"Thanks," I muttered, my cheeks flushed as I straightened up. The amulet shifted again, a silent message I couldn't ignore.

I wasn't sure if I believed in magic or fate, but it felt right, like a part of a riddle I hadn't yet solved.

I glanced at my comrades. Cedric was humming a tune softly, his eyes fixed on the horizon. His voice was barely audible over the noise of the march, but it was enough to lighten the weight in my chest. Jarin was lost in thought, occasionally rolling his shoulders to ease the stiffness. He had that look in his eyes again—the one that said he'd see this through no matter what. And Edric, ever observant, maintained a steady pace, his gaze sweeping across the landscape, thoughtful and alert.

The plains of Centralia were both beautiful and unforgiving. Open fields stretched as far as the eye could see, dotted with clusters of wildflowers and occasional groves of hardy trees. There was a freedom to it, an openness that was both exhilarating and daunting. But the lack of shelter meant we were exposed to the elements, and by midday, the sun was merciless, searing the road and every inch of exposed skin. The heat shimmered in wavering mirages that danced just out of reach, stretching the very air to its limits.

"Didn't think the plains would be this vast," Cedric remarked, wiping beads of sweat from his brow.

"Or this hot," Jarin added, squinting against the sun's blaze.

Edric took a swig from his canteen. "We'll need to ration our water carefully. The next stream isn't for miles."

I already felt the dryness in my throat, moisture sapped from my body with every step. "Keep an eye on each other, don't let the heat steal your focus." I said, my voice a little raspier than usual, "Speak up if you feel faint. It is not just about being tough—it is about making sure we all make it through this together."

We marched on with only the occasional farmhouse, small village in the distant or a herd of grazing animals to break the monotony. Farmers paused in their work to watch our procession pass, some raising a hand in silent salute. I caught the eye of an old man leaning on his pitchfork, his gaze steady as he watched us. I wondered what he saw—hope, pride, or maybe just a group of young men heading into something unknown. I returned his nod, and for a fleeting moment, felt a strange connection.

As the afternoon wore on, conversations dwindled as the strain of the march took its toll. It became about keeping one foot in front of the other, maintaining the pace, and conserving what energy we had left. The officers moved along the ranks, offering words of encouragement. Their voices were a lifeline, something to pull us forward when our bodies wanted to give in.

Sir Gareth rode alongside our unit, his presence steadying. "Keep your heads up," he called out, his voice carrying over the rhythmic march. "Remember, endurance is as much a part of a soldier's strength as skill with a blade." His words grounded me, living entities mingling with the air I breathed, settling in my chest with a tightening promise—what we had to endure and how we would endure it.

My mind wandered, recalling the stories my brother used to tell me about journeys like this—tales of perseverance, of camaraderie forged on the long roads. He would speak of the bonds that were formed during the hardest moments, the friendships that became unbreakable. It was in times like this, he said, that you found out who you truly were. I hoped he was right. I hoped that I'd become someone he could be proud of.

The sun began its descent, casting the plains in a golden glow. Shadows stretched long across the ground, and the oppressive heat finally began to ease into a more comfortable warmth. A cool breeze picked up, rustling the tall grasses and providing a welcome relief. I closed my eyes for a moment, savoring the feeling. It was a fleeting kindness from the gods, but one I was grateful for.

"Thank the heavens," Jarin sighed, his voice breaking the silence. "Thought the sun would melt me into my armor."

Cedric chuckled weakly beside me. "At least we'd have a statue to commemorate you."

Edric grinned, his eyes still bright despite the fatigue. "Come on, it's not that bad. Builds character."

I smiled. Despite the grueling conditions, the shared hardships seemed to strengthen our friendship.

As dusk approached, the order was given to make camp for the night. We moved with practiced efficiency—setting up tents, gathering firewood, and tending to the horses. The campsite sprang to life, a temporary village amidst the open plains.

I helped pitch our tent, driving the stakes into the firm ground. The physical exertion was almost soothing, giving me something tangible to focus on. The scent of stew soon filled the air and lifted everyone's spirits—after a day like today, it was exactly what we needed.

We gathered around a small fire, bowls of hearty stew in hand. The sky above transformed into a canvas of deep purples and oranges before settling into the dark blues of night with stars beginning to emerge like scattered diamonds. I found myself staring upward, feeling a sense of awe at the sheer vastness of it all. Out here, away from the city lights, the sky felt endless.

"Not a bad view," Edric remarked, gazing upward.

"Better than the confines of the barracks," Cedric agreed, a wistful smile on his face. "Though I wouldn't mind a softer bed."

Jarin stretched out, leaning back on his elbows. "You and your creature comforts," he teased, a grin playing on his lips.

We ate in companionable silence for a while, the crackling of the fire providing a soothing backdrop. The weariness of the day's march settled into my bones, bringing a quiet sense of accomplishment. We had made it through another day, each step taking us deeper into the unknown, our goal hovering somewhere beyond the horizon.

Sir Gareth made his rounds, stopping by our group. "Rest well tonight," he advised, his gaze moving from one of us to the next. "Tomorrow will be much the same, and we need everyone at their best."

"Yes, sir," we replied in unison and watched as he moved on, his silhouette blending into the growing darkness. We soon prepared for the night. I was assigned the first watch along with a few others, and I made my way to the perimeter of the camp. The plains at night were a vast expanse of shadows and subtle sounds—the rustling of grass, the distant call of nocturnal creatures, and the gentle whisper of the wind. It was both beautiful and unnerving, the kind of silence that made one feel small.

I stood quietly, my senses attuned to the environment. The cool air was a relief after the day's heat, and the gentle crackle of the campfires behind me provided a comforting backdrop. Shadows danced at the edge of the firelight, their flickering shapes casting elongated figures across the ground.

The sounds of the plains at night were eerily beautiful, showing the wildness that lay beyond the boundaries of our camp. My hand rested instinctively on the hilt of my sword, an act borne out of habit—the ingrained instinct of a soldier. I walked around, the flickering light of our campfires barely holding the darkness at bay. There was something comforting in the ritual of standing watch, the routine of it. And tonight, as I gazed into the darkness, my thoughts wandered. The journey had once again tested me in ways beyond endurance. And between the focus on duty and the bond I'd formed with my comrades—a brotherhood bond—the pang of my brother's disappearance had started to thaw. Another pang of guilt washed over me. My brother, who had now been missing for several months, had once been a constant presence in my mind, his memory a guiding force. Before my army life began, I had thought of him constantly of finding him, of the promises I had made to myself. Now, it felt like the promise had been swallowed by the day-to-day struggle of my present life.

The amulet seemed to pulse with life, an anchor to my brother and a reason why I couldn't falter. I let out a sigh. It had somehow become a desperate hold on my hope for him. I couldn't let myself forget that. Not now. Not ever.

CHAPTER
15

I was lost in thought, as my gaze mindlessly scanned the horizon. Something caught my eye—a faint glimmer of light moving slowly in the distance. I narrowed my eyes, focusing. A series of lights—lanterns swaying gently from tall poles. As they drew nearer, I recognized the unmistakable formation of a caravan. The wagons were adorned with crimson banners bearing the emblem of intertwined gears and arrows—a symbol I knew all too well.

I drew a sharp breath.

"The Crimson Merchant Alliance," I murmured, my heart quickening.

Eamon!

I turned, my heart pounding as I made my way back to the campfire where Edric was resting. I moved carefully, making sure not to disturb the others who were asleep. Reaching Edric, I knelt beside him and gently shook his shoulder, my voice a whisper filled with urgency.

"Edric! Edric!"

Edric blinked awake, rubbing his eyes as he tried to focus.

"I need you to cover my watch for a moment."

"What?" He sat up. "What going on?" he asked quietly, his voice still thick with sleep.

The caravan continued to approach and a rush of urgency hit me. "My brother might be with that caravan," I said, my voice low but urgent. His eyes softened, and he nodded. "Go," he said, pulling himself up. "I'll mind things here."

A sigh of relief escaped my lips. "Thank you, Edric."

I didn't waste another moment. I moved quickly, slipping through the dark, sleeping camp. The night air felt charged, as if it could sense the tension running through me, heightening my senses as I made my way toward the plains. The caravan's lights grew brighter, flickering like fireflies in the deep, endless dark.

What would I say to him? Would he be glad to see me? Or angry that I had left Pa and Ma all by themselves at Elsenburg?

I could see the outlines of the wagons now, the flicker of lantern light illuminating the dust that hung in the night air, the creak of wooden wheels melding with the soft clatter of hooves. The caravan advanced with a measured calm, unhurried in its movement. I stretched my neck, my eyes scanning for any sign of him.

Had he changed, or would he still be the brother I remembered? My stomach knotted at the thought. Did he think of me as much as I had thought of him?

The merchants were dressed in vibrant fabrics that spoke of far-reaching trade and wealth. The guards moved alongside, their eyes roaming the dark plains, alert and ready. I raised a hand in greeting. "Hail, travelers!" I called out, my voice carrying over the quiet rattle of the caravan. I searched each face hoping that a familiar voice would jump from the shadows and say, "Hey, little brother," and then proceed to throw his head back and laugh heartily.

The caravan went quiet. The procession slowed to a halt, the guards shifting almost imperceptibly into defensive positions. Their hands rested on the hilts of their swords, eyes narrowed as they watched me—a lone figure approaching them in the dead of night. I could feel their suspicion, the tension in the air palpable as I moved closer.

An older merchant stepped forward, his gaze cautious but not unfriendly. He was a stout man, his beard neatly trimmed, his eyes marked by the experience of countless journeys. He studied me for a moment before speaking. "What brings a soldier of Centralia out to meet us at this hour?"

I stopped a respectful distance away, trying to catch my breath. The weight of the moment pressed heavily on me, but I forced my voice to remain steady. "I am Kaelan, marching with the Centralian army toward Wintmore," I began, feeling the eyes of the merchants and guards on me. "I noticed your caravan bears the emblem of the Crimson Merchant Alliance. I'm searching for my brother, Eamon, who was a member of your guild. I was hoping he might be traveling with you—or that you might have news of him."

A murmur passed among a few of the merchants, though none of them spoke out. The older merchant stroked his beard, his expression thoughtful. "Eamon, you say? The name is familiar, but we have many members scattered across the land. Our paths haven't crossed with his in recent times."

My heart sank. I took a step forward, but before I could respond, another merchant stepped forward—tall and slender, his features sharp, his eyes keen. "We're headed to the Kingdom of Noble" he offered. "Our route has taken us from the southern ports of Kilnor up through Centralia, but we've not encountered an Eamon along the way."

I shook my head as a dull ache settled in my chest. I couldn't let it end here. I had to know more. I took a deep breath to steady my voice. "I hope you meet him in your travels. Any news you might have would be greatly appreciated. You can send a message through any Centralian soldier, and it shall get to my ears." I said, my gaze shifting from face to face. "It's been months since I've heard from him, and I'm worried."

Then, one of the guards—younger than the others—spoke up. "Do you speak of Eamon... Light brown hair, well kept, and a quick wit?"

My heart surged, hope igniting like a flame. "Yes! That's him!" The words tumbled from my lips, filled with urgency. I stepped forward, my voice trembling with desperation. The guard glanced at the lead merchant, who gave a slight nod. He stepped closer to me, lowering his voice. "I know him."

My face broke into a relieved smile, "You know Eamon! Please, tell me!"

"The last I heard, he was assigned to a caravan heading into Wintmore. That was before the conflict got worse. I haven't heard from him since."

The guard's expression softened, and I saw something flicker in his eyes—respect, maybe even empathy. He extended a hand. "I'm Malik," he said. "I knew Eamon well. We served together on the Wintmore route."

I reached out, grasping his hand tightly as though by holding him, I could somehow, hold onto my brother. "It's a relief to meet someone who knows him," I said, my voice too loud for the quiet night. "Can you tell me anything about where he might be?"

Malik sighed, his gaze drifting back to the caravan before returning to me. There was a heaviness in his eyes that made my stomach clench. "Eamon commanded our Wintmore caravan, always watching the horizon for threats others could not see. When tensions started to rise, and there were whispers of rebel bands causing unrest, he grew concerned. He worried for the safety of our people and the cargo."

He paused. "Eamon decided it was too dangerous for the entire caravan to stay. He sent me back to Centralia to report to the Crimson Merchant Alliance—to warn them, so no more caravans would be sent into a brewing conflict."

I listened, my heart heavy with the weight of each word. "So he stayed behind?" the question came out in a whisper.

Malik nodded, his expression earnest. "He insisted on leading the caravan out of Wintmore himself, making sure that our remaining goods and those who chose to stay were protected. That was the last time I saw him. Word has been scarce since the hostilities intensified."

A surge of pride welled up inside me, tightening my chest. "That sounds like him," I said, wistfully. "Always thinking of others first."

Malik nodded, a small smile touching his lips. "Your brother is a brave man," he said. "If anyone could navigate through that turmoil, it's him."

I took a deep breath, trying to absorb the weight of Malik's words. The news wasn't exactly comforting, but it was something. "Thank you for telling me this," I said, my voice firmer now, "It means much to me to know what happened."

Malik nodded. "Of course," he said, sincerity in his eyes. "I wish I had more recent news. Many of us have been concerned about those who remained in Wintmore."

As we spoke, the lead merchant approached, his expression pensive. "Your brother's actions likely saved many lives," he said, his voice carrying a weight that spoke to the risks my brother had taken. "The alliance wishes we knew where he might be now."

I met his gaze, "I intend to find him—or at least learn of his fate," I replied. "Our army is marching toward Wintmore. Perhaps our paths will cross."

The merchant regarded me thoughtfully, concern etched on his face. "The road ahead is fraught with danger. The rebels and extremists in Wintmore have grown bold, and the conflict between the empires has disrupted many of our usual routes."

His warning weighed on me, but I couldn't let fear stop me. Not now. I straightened, my resolve unshaken. "All the more reason for us to be there," I said firmly. "To restore peace and avenge our crown prince."

Malik stepped closer, placing a hand on my shoulder. "I wish you luck on your journey," he said, his voice filled with emotion. "If you find Eamon, tell him Malik sends his regards."

I nodded, feeling a flicker of warmth. "I will."

The caravan began to stir, the merchants moving about, preparing to continue their journey. The lead merchant offered me a slight bow, his eyes kind despite the uncertainty ahead. "Safe travels, soldier. May the gods favor you."

I returned the gesture, my chest tightening. "And you," I replied. "Thank you for your time and the news you have shared."

As I watched the caravan move away, their lanterns gently fading in the darkness, I felt light. The sense of purpose within me burned brighter. The road ahead would be fraught with dangers, but the image of Eamon—brave and steadfast, putting others before himself—steeled my will. He had always been the one to lead by example, and now it was my turn to follow in his footsteps. Whatever lay ahead, I would find him, or at least find the truth of what had happened to him. And as I stood there, alone in the night, I felt that familiar blend of fear and pride settle within me—a reminder of why I had come this far, and why I couldn't turn back now.

***

I turned and made my way back toward the camp, the stars above guiding my steps. The plains felt a little less overwhelming now as if the weight of my purpose had made the expanse easier to cross. The distant howls of wolves echoed through the night—a reminder of the wildness that both separated and connected us all, of the journey still ahead.

When I reached the perimeter, I spotted Edric, still on watch. His silhouette was framed by the dim glow of the campfire, and he looked up as I approached. "Everything all right?" he asked quietly, his eyes searching mine.

I nodded, though the emotions within me were anything but simple. "I didn't find him," I admitted, my voice carrying both the weight of disappointment and the faintest glimmer of hope. "But I spoke with someone who knows him. Eamon stayed behind in Wintmore to help others escape the rising dangers."

Edric's expression softened, and he offered me a sympathetic smile. "Your brother sounds like a remarkable man," he said, his voice filled with quiet respect.

I looked away for a moment, as tears stung my eyes. Pride, worry, fear—they all churned within me, "He is," I said, my voice steady but tinged with unshed tears and remnants of sadness that felt more powerful than ever. "And I'm more resolved than ever to find him."

Edric nodded, his gaze unwavering. "Then we'll keep an eye out together," he assured me, his words a promise that eased some of the weight on my shoulders. "Now, get some rest. You have a long day ahead."

I managed a watery smile.

"Thank you, Edric," I said sincerely, the words carrying more meaning than I could express at that moment.

I settled into my bedroll. The camp was now quiet, the only sounds were those of sleeping soldiers and the faint crackling of dying embers The encounter tonight had stirred a storm of emotions within me—hope, fear, pride—but most importantly, it had given me something real to hold onto. I knew now that Eamon had been out there, fighting for others, just like I knew I had to fight for him.

As sleep began to take me, I whispered a silent vow to the darkness: I would find Eamon. I owed him that much, and I owed it to myself.

CHAPTER 16

The first light of dawn brushed the horizon its pale shades of pink and orange spreading across the sky, casting a gentle glow over the dew-kissed grasses of the plains. The camp began to stir, the crisp morning air filling with the muted sounds of soldiers rousing from sleep. There were the clanking of armor, the rustling of tents being dismantled, the low murmur of conversation, and the distant calls of men preparing for the march. I blinked away the remnants of sleep, my mind slowly returning to the present. Then the memories of the previous night came flooding back—the encounter with the caravan, the news about Eamon. But I shook it off. I had another duty to fulfill.

I sat up and began packing my belongings with the efficiency of someone who had done this countless times. I rolled my bedroll tightly, secured it to my pack, and started putting on my armor. Each piece felt like a part of me, the weight grounding me in my purpose. I reached for my tunic, my fingers brushing against my chest where the cool metal of the amulet should have been.

My hand met only the fabric of my undershirt.

A flicker of confusion crossed my mind I patted my chest again, more firmly this time, but felt nothing. Frowning, I quickly scanned the area around my bedding, expecting to see the glint of metal somewhere nearby. But there was nothing.

An uneasy feeling lodged itself inside me. I knelt, sifting through my belongings, my hands moving with increasing urgency. I checked every pocket, shook out my blankets, and scanned the ground around me—nothing. The amulet was gone. And with this knowledge, my heart sank into my stomach. The one thing that tied me to Eamon, the one thing that had become my closest ally, was missing. It felt like a bad omen.

I felt the panic creep in, tightening around my chest. How could I have lost it? I never took it off. It wasn't just a piece of metal—it had become a reminder of why I was doing all of this. The thought of losing it was like losing a part of myself.

"Everything all right?" Cedric's voice pulled me from my frantic search. He stood at the entrance of the tent, a half-packed satchel slung over his shoulder, his expression curious.

I took a deep breath to keep my voice steady. "I can't find the amulet," I said, feeling the edge of panic creeping in despite my efforts to stay calm. Cedric's brow furrowed, and he stepped closer. "Are you sure? Maybe it slipped off during the night."

"I never take it off," I snapped. My hands moved faster as I sifted through my things, my frustration growing with each passing moment. "It has to be here somewhere."

I jogged my mind for the last time I felt the reassuring presence against my chest. It was during the march. Could I with certainty say I had not lost it during the long walk to the camp last night? A frustrated sigh escaped my lips.

"Need a hand?" Jarin peeked into the tent.

I looked up at him, my expression betraying the concern I was trying to hide. "Please," I said, grateful for any help I could get.

The three of us tore the small space apart, checking under bedrolls, inside boots, and even among the folds of the tent itself. Each moment that passed deepened the anxiety twisting in my gut. Losing it felt like a sign, a failure I couldn't afford.

But despite our efforts, the amulet remained elusive, as if it had vanished into thin air.

Outside, commands were being shouted as the soldiers prepared to move out. The clatter of gear being loaded, the creak of wagons, and the snorts of horses all blended into a cacophony of sounds that only heightened the pressure building inside me.

"Kaelan, we have to go," Jarin urged gently, his voice cutting through the noise. "We're assembling now."

I stood up slowly, my frustration evident in every movement. My eyes swept over the ground one last time. "I don't understand," I muttered, my voice edged with disbelief. "It was right here."

The tent flap rustled, and Edric appeared, concern etched across his face. He looked from me to the mess of scattered belongings, then back again. "Is everything okay?" he asked, though I could tell he already knew the answer.

My throat felt tight as I forced out the words. "I've lost the amulet," The weight of those words pressed down on me, the loss feeling like a blow I wasn't ready for.

Edric exchanged a glance with Cedric, who had been helping me search. "We'll help you look for it when we set up camp tonight," he said placing his hands on my shoulders. "But we can't stay here any longer."

He was right. We couldn't stay any longer. I took a deep breath, trying to push down the sense of loss and frustration that threatened to swallow me. It felt wrong to leave without it, but I forced a nod, "You're right. Let's go."

I grabbed my pack and slung it over my shoulder, stepping out of the tent and into the morning light. The camp was nearly dismantled, the soldiers falling into formation with practiced efficiency. There was a palpable urgency in the air, the rhythm of the march pressing everyone onward. I felt a pang of helplessness—everything was moving forward, but I was leaving a part of myself behind.

As we joined our unit, I cast one last, resigned glance back at the spot where my tent had stood, with the realization that I might never see the amulet again. A forlorn sadness overwhelmed me. I felt exposed, as if a piece of my armor was missing.

"Keep your spirits up," Cedric said quietly as we fell into step, his shoulder brushing against mine in a gesture of support. His words were meant to reassure me, but the hollow feeling in my chest remained.

I managed a faint smile, more for his sake than mine. "I shall," I replied, though doubt hovered just beneath my words.

***

The command was given, and the column began to move, the soldiers marching forward in unison, leaving the remnants of the campsite behind. I focused on the rhythm of my steps, the weight of my pack, and the warmth of the rising sun on my face. The sun climbed higher, its rays stretching across the plains, signaling the start of another long day.

As we marched on, the landscape began to change around us. The endless plains, with their vast openness, gradually gave way to rolling hills that rose and fell like gentle waves. In the distance, the outline of a dense forest emerged, its towering trees standing like silent sentinels. The canopy above formed a rich, green veil that swayed in rhythm with the breeze, and the air grew cooler, carrying the scent of moss and the crisp aroma of pine. It was a welcome change, yet I was shrouded with uneasiness.

By midday, we had reached the edge of the forest, the vast expanse of greenery stretching out seemingly without end in either direction. Sunlight filtered through the thick leaves, casting dappled shadows on the ground, an ever-shifting mosaic of light and dark that danced beneath our feet. "Stay alert," Sir Gareth commanded, riding alongside the column, his voice firm. "The forest can conceal many things. Keep your formations tight."

I adjusted my grip on my spear, my eyes perusing the surroundings. The loss of the amulet still weighed heavily on my mind, but I couldn't let myself get distracted—not here. The forest was alive with sounds—the rustling of leaves, the distant call of birds, the occasional snap of a twig underfoot. Each noise set my nerves on edge, my senses heightened by the knowledge that danger could be lurking anywhere.

As we moved deeper into the forest, the trees grew denser, their branches intertwining above us to form a natural archway. The path narrowed, forcing us into a single file, and the steady rhythm of our march was muffled by the soft layer of fallen leaves and pine needles beneath our boots. It was a strange, almost eerie quiet.

"Quite the change from the open plains," Cedric quipped over the gentle rustle of the forest.

I nodded, though I kept my focus on the path ahead. The sense of exposure I felt without the amulet was a gnawing presence in the back of my mind.

"I sense we're being watched," Jarin muttered from behind, his gaze darting among the shadows that seemed to move with us.

Edric, a few steps ahead, gave a nod. "Forests, my friend, have a way of playing tricks on the mind. Stay sharp," he advised, his voice low but steady.

The forest was both beautiful and unsettling—sunlight pierced through gaps in the canopy, illuminating patches of wildflowers in vivid colors and clusters of mushrooms growing along fallen logs. The air was rich with the scent of damp earth, the subtle fragrance of blooms that seemed to thrive in the shadows. It was peaceful, almost deceptively so, and that only added to my wariness.

I tried to stay focused, forcing my thoughts to the task at hand—the march, the mission, the need to remain vigilant. But even as I peered through the trees, my thoughts kept drifting back to Eamon, to the amulet, to the promise I had made to find him. It felt as though the forest knew my fears, amplifying them with every creak of a branch, every rustle of leaves. I clenched my jaw, determined not to let my worries get the best of me.

Hours passed as we weaved our way through the dense woodland. The soldiers kept a steady pace, the earlier chatter fading into a focused silence. The undergrowth thickened in places, forcing us to navigate around protruding roots and low-hanging branches. It was slow going, and each step seemed to require more effort as the day wore on.

As afternoon gave way to evening, the forest began to thin, the trees grew sparser, and the terrain inclined upward. A sign that we were approaching the mountains. The sun dipped lower in the sky, casting long shadows across the forest floor and bathing everything in a warm, golden glow. It was beautiful, but it also meant the day was nearly over, and with it, our progress came to a halt.

"Hold here!" came the call from the front ranks, the command echoing back through the column.

We halted in a small clearing, the trees opening up to reveal a sweeping view of the horizon. In the distance, I could see the mountains—their majestic peaks rising, the summits kissed by the last light of the day. The mountains looked both beautiful and formidable, a challenge waiting for us just beyond the forest.

"We'll set up camp here for the night," Sir Gareth announced, his voice carrying over the clearing. "There's fresh water nearby, and this clearing will serve us well."

Relief rippled through the troops as we began the familiar routine of setting up camp. Tents were erected in neat rows, fires crackling to life soon after, their smoke curling lazily up into the canopy. The scent of cooking food began to mix with the crisp forest air, lifting everyone's spirits after the long march. It was a comforting ritual, the sense of community it brought, the warmth of the fire driving away the weariness of the day.

I busied myself with gathering firewood, the physical activity a welcome distraction. Each step through the undergrowth, each branch I gathered, gave me something tangible to focus on, something to anchor myself in the present. I couldn't afford to let my mind wander—not now, not with the challenges ahead.

As I returned to my tent, a sense of exhaustion settled over me, but so did an undeniable sense of accomplishment. We had made progress, and that mattered. "Long day," Cedric remarked, sinking onto a log beside the fire, his voice pulling me from my thoughts.

I sat down next to him, feeling the warmth of the flames on my face. "Indeed," I agreed, my gaze drifting to the mountains beyond the treetops. "The terrain is getting tougher."

Jarin joined us, a wry grin on his face. "At least we'll have the mountains to look forward to," he said sarcastically. "Nothing like a steep climb to start the day."

I couldn't help but smile at his teasing tone, the humor cutting through the tension of the evening. "True enough," I said running my hand over my empty neck feeling naked without the amulet, exposed, vulnerable.

Edric walked over, a chuckle escaping him as he sat down. "Better than trudging through more forests, in my opinion," he added, grinning.

I let out a breath, allowing myself to relax, if only for a moment.

We settled around the campfire as the cooks prepared the evening meal. For marching rations, the food was surprisingly hearty. Bowls of savory stew were handed out, filled with chunks of salted meat and root vegetables preserved for the journey. Freshly baked flatbread accompanied the stew, its warmth and softness a welcome comfort after days of chewing on hard biscuits.

I savored each bite, the rich flavors rejuvenating me after the long march. The warmth of the stew seemed to seep into my bones, easing some of the tension I hadn't realized I was carrying. "Not bad at all," I remarked, dipping my bread into the thick broth. "Almost feels like a home-cooked meal."

Cedric nodded appreciatively beside me. "If this is what we get in the forest, perhaps the mountains will serve us a feast," he said, a hint of humor in his voice.

Jarin laughed, his eyes glinting in the firelight. "At this rate, I might start enjoying these marches."

I chuckled and watched them as they threw words at one other. The glow of the flames cast a gentle light on our faces, the shadows flickering against the dark trees that surrounded us. Conversations flowed easily among the men-at-arms, stories and jokes passed around as we enjoyed the brief respite. It was moments like this that made the hardships of the journey bearable—the shared laughter, the sense of unity that bound us together.

As we finished our meal, I noticed a figure approaching—Sergeant Roderic. He was a stern but fair man, known for his sharp eye and his strategic mind. He stopped near our group, his expression all business.

"Kaelan, Cedric, Jarin, Edric," he called out, his tone brisk and commanding. "Sir Gareth requests your presence at the command tent."

We exchanged curious glances, and the relaxed atmosphere was instantly replaced with a sense of urgency. I wiped my hands on my tunic, nodding at the sergeant. "Yes, Sergeant," I replied, rising to my feet.

The four of us made our way through the camp, weaving between tents and soldiers tending to their equipment. The air was filled with the low murmur of conversation, the occasional clank of armor being adjusted. As we approached the center of the camp, the command tent loomed before us, its entrance flanked by banners bearing the emblem of Centralia. Torches illuminated the area, casting a steady glow that cut through the encroaching darkness. Inside the command tent, Sir Gareth stood over a map spread across a sturdy wooden table, his expression intent as he studied the lines and markers. The flickering candlelight cast shadows on his weathered face, giving him an even more imposing presence. Beside him stood General Aldric in his glory. Seeing both of them there, hunched over the map, only heightened the importance of the moment.

I took a deep breath and stepped forward with my comrades.

"Good evening, lads," Sir Gareth greeted us, his gaze sharp as he looked us over. "We have a task that requires your attention."

General Aldric gave us a nod, his eyes assessing each of us as if measuring our capabilities with his eyes. "We need reliable men for this assignment."

I felt a burst of pride at being considered for the assignment, but also a twinge of apprehension. Sir Gareth pointed to an area west of our current position on the map, his finger resting on the dense woodland that stretched beyond our camp. "Our scouts have reported unusual activity in this sector. Could be bandits, could be something else. We can't afford any surprises."

Edric leaned in, his brow furrowed as he studied the map. "What kind of unusual activity, Sir?" he asked, his voice measured.

Sir Gareth's expression hardened. "Flickering lights, distant sounds—things that don't belong," he replied. "The forest can conceal many threats. We need you to scout the area and report back. Ensure there are no dangers that could hinder our march."

Cedric straightened beside me, his voice steady. "We're ready to depart immediately, Sir Gareth."

General Aldric placed a hand on the table, his gaze locking onto each of us in turn. "Exercise caution," he said, his tone leaving no room for doubt. "The safety of the regiment depends on accurate information."

I nodded firmly. "Understood, Sir."

Sir Gareth's eyes lingered on us for a moment longer before he nodded. "Good. Take what you need and set out at once. Return before dawn with your findings."

As we exited the tent, the weight of the assignment settled on my shoulders. This was our first major assignment of consequence. And we could not afford to falter, not with our brothers relying on us to see it through.

CHAPTER
17

S trange lights, bandits - A perfect night for a stroll." Jarin quipped, adjusting the strap of his sheath, his voice carrying a hint of humor that lightened the strain.

"Better than sitting idle," Edric replied with a faint smile, though I could see the seriousness in his eyes.

We made our way back to our tent and gathered our equipment. I checked my sword and dagger, the cold metal reassuring in my hands. I pulled my cloak tighter around my shoulders as the night's chill settled in, the oppressive darkness outside pressing closer.

"Everyone ready?" Cedric asked, his voice low.

"Ready," we confirmed in unison.

The sounds of the camp began to fade as we moved toward the western edge. The distant murmur of voices and the crackling of campfires slowly gave way to the stillness of the forest. The sentries nodded to us as we passed, their eyes briefly meeting ours. Towering trees enveloped us, their intertwining branches forming a woven canopy that shut out the sky. The air seemed different here—heavier, filled with the scent of damp earth and the quiet rustling of unseen creatures.

"Stay alert," I advised quietly, my voice taut. It wasn't just a warning for them—it was a reminder for myself. The trees loomed like silent watchers, and every shadow seemed to hold a story waiting to be told, or a threat waiting to be revealed.

The moonlight shone through the canopy, casting ghostly shadows on the forest floor. The underbrush rustled beneath our boots, but otherwise, the woods felt unnaturally still – an ominous quiet that pressed in on us. We moved in a loose formation, each of us scanning a different sector as we advanced. It felt as if the woods were holding their breath, waiting for something to happen.

After what felt like an eternity, we paused in a small clearing, the silence almost deafening.

"Did you hear anything?" Edric whispered, his voice barely audible.

I held my breath, my ears straining for any sound. A faint rustle broke the quiet. My pulse quickened as I scanned the shadows, my grip tight on the hilt of my sword. Jarin shook his head. "Nothing," he replied, his eyes scanning the darkness, his hand resting on the hilt of his sword.

Cedric pointed ahead, his eyes narrowing. "There's a faint light that way," he said, his voice barely more than a breath. "Could be what the scouts mentioned."

I followed his gaze, peering into the darkness. Sure enough, there was a dim, flickering glow visible between the trees, distant but unmistakable, like the light of a campfire partially obscured. My stomach tightened at the sight—the unknown waiting for us, the possibility of danger just beyond reach.

"Shh," I raised a finger. "We don't want to announce our presence." The others nodded, and we began to move again, slowly, using the cover of the night. The light grew more distinct, and with it, the faint murmur of voices—muffled, but unmistakably human.

"Bandits," Edric murmured, as his eyes flicked to me.

"Or worse," Cedric added grimly, his grip tightening on his sword, his eyes darting from shadow to shadow.

I signaled for the others to spread out slightly, keeping within sight of each other. The light grew brighter as we moved, and soon the outline of a small encampment came into view. Figures huddled around a fire, their features obscured by cloaks and the flickering shadows cast by the flames. My heart pounded as I studied them, trying to discern anything that might give us a clue as to who they were.

I raised my hand, motioning for everyone to halt. "Quiet," I whispered. The others nodded, their expressions tense but resolute. The risks were clear—if we were discovered, there was no telling how this would end. But we couldn't turn back; we had to find out what was happening here.

Gathering our resolve, we prepared to move closer, to uncover the mystery that awaited us in the depths of the forest. Each step felt heavy, the forest pressing in on us as if it knew we were intruding on something that should remain hidden.

Advancing cautiously, we approached the source of the flickering light. As we drew nearer, the outlines of an old settlement began to emerge from the darkness—a cluster of dilapidated buildings, their forms barely visible through the thick growth of vines and moss. The structures were crumbling, their roofs sagging, and their walls weathered and worn by time. It looked like it had been abandoned for years, perhaps even decades. Yet, there had been light, and that meant someone had been here.

"This doesn't look like a bandit camp," Edric whispered, his eyes scanning the eerie scene before us. His voice held a note of confusion, mirroring my own thoughts.

"This is a ghost town," Jarin murmured, gripping his sword a little tighter.

I furrowed my brow, unease gnawing at me. "But we saw light coming from here," I said, my voice low. "Someone must have been here recently." It didn't make sense. There had been voices, movement—all the signs of life, and yet now we were met with silence and decay.

We moved cautiously through the crumbling buildings, the air thick with the smell of decay, damp wood, and dust that seemed to cling to my skin. Moonlight spilled across the ruins, casting long shadows that seemed to shift and watch us. Every creak of the floorboards and movement in the underbrush set our nerves on edge,

Cedric pointed to a fire pit at the center of the settlement. "Cold ashes," he observed, his voice hushed. "Whoever was here left some time ago. The fire has been dead for hours!"

"We saw light here moments ago, did we not? Where is it?"

A wave of frustration surged within me, mingling with the unease that hadn't left since we first approached the camp. Whoever had been here had slipped away, leaving behind only questions. I clenched my jaw, biting down my urge to flee.

We split up to search the area, staying within sight of one another. I moved carefully, my eyes scanning every corner, every shadow. Edric examined what looked like an old forge, its chimney cracked and cold, the remnants of a life long abandoned. Jarin peeked into a small shack, finding nothing but broken pottery and cobwebs, his expression one of disappointment. Cedric circled around, his eyes sharp, keeping watch for any signs of movement, any hint we weren't alone.

The settlement was silent, the stillness oppressive. I couldn't shake the feeling that we were being watched, that even the forest itself was holding its breath, waiting.

I approached the largest building—a house that, despite its dilapidated state, still stood more intact than the others. The door hung ajar, swaying gently with the breeze. It creaked softly as I pushed it open, the sound echoing in the silence of the abandoned settlement. Inside, the room was filled with shadows, the faint moonlight barely illuminating what remained of a life once lived. A table lay overturned, a chair broken, shelves empty except for a few scattered, forgotten belongings.

Where had the flickers of light we'd seen before come from? What happened to the moving silhouettes we had glimpsed from the woods?

I stepped inside cautiously, each footfall causing the floorboards to groan beneath my weight. Every sense was on high alert, my ears straining to catch any sound that might indicate we weren't alone. The tension in my chest tightened with each step further into the darkness.

Suddenly, a sound cut through the silence—a small clink, like something dropping onto the wooden floor. I froze, my breath catching in my throat, my heart pounding in my ears. My eyes darted toward the source of the noise.

"Show yourself!" I called out, my voice carrying more courage than I felt. The words seemed to vanish into the shadows, swallowed by the emptiness of the room. Only silence answered.

I turned toward the far corner, where the faintest glimmer caught my eye. My pulse quickened as I walked over, each step feeling heavier than the last. Kneeling, I reached into the dust and debris, my fingers brushing against something cool and metallic. I gasped. It was the amulet.

The dark metal gleamed faintly, its surface etched with age and wear, but the emerald at its center caught a shard of light that seemed to pierce straight through me. The amulet I thought was lost forever now, inexplicably, lay in my hands. I stared at it, my mind reeling.

"No," I murmured, my voice trembling with disbelief.

My hand shook as I held it. The amulet fitted perfectly into my palm as though it had always been there. This couldn't be happening. I was certain I hadn't had it since we left the plains. How could it possibly be here, in this abandoned place?

I had searched everywhere, turned over every inch of my belongings, and yet here it was—miles from where I had lost it. I had scoured the plains, torn through every inch of my gear. There was no way this could be here, miles from where I had last seen it. My heart pounded, the confusion swirling into something darker, heavier. I stared at it, the questions gnawing at me. What was I missing?

"Kaelan?" Cedric's voice sliced through the haze of disbelief and confusion called from the doorway, breaking me out of my thoughts. His silhouette appeared against the dim light outside. "Everything alright?"

I turned to face him, the amulet still clutched tightly in my hand. "I... I found it," Cedric stepped inside, his brow furrowed. His gaze fell to my hand, and his expression shifted from curiosity to shock. "Impossible! How did it get here?" he asked, his gaze shifting from me to the amulet, his own confusion mirroring mine.

I shook my head, my thoughts still spinning. "I have no clue," I admitted. My voice wavered, the uncertainty of it all gnawing at me. There was something profoundly unsettling about its presence here, a sensation that set the hairs on the nape of my neck on edge. Edric and Jarin joined us, their faces taut with concern as they stepped into the room. The moment their eyes landed on the amulet, the same shiver of dread that had crept up my spine reflected on their faces. "Are you sure it is the same one?" Jarin asked hesitantly. But he knew the answer with the way he stared at the amulet.

"It's mine," I said firmly, my voice stronger now. "See this…" I traced the scratches on the edges, as I pushed it into his incredulous face, "I would know it anywhere."

"He shifted uncomfortably, "Perhaps, someone found it and …" His voice lacked the confidence it usually carried.

"Why would it end up here? In this place? It doesn't make sense."

Cedric ran a hand through his hair, his eyes darting around the room. "We need to leave," he muttered. "Now."

But I didn't move. My fingers tightened around the amulet, the cool metal biting into my palm. This wasn't just a lost object returned by chance. It was a message. Or a warning.

I slipped the amulet back around my neck, feeling its familiar weight settle against my chest. The sensation was both comforting and unnerving.

"We should report this to Sir Gareth," I said, my voice steady, though my mind was still racing. "Something strange is going on here."

As if in response to my words, a sudden chill swept through the room. The air grew colder, and I could have sworn I heard voices—faint whispers echoing from the very walls around us.

My heart skipped a beat, and I exchanged uneasy glances with the others.

"Did you hear that?" Edric asked, his voice sharp, his hand moving instinctively to the hilt of his sword.

There was something deeply wrong about this place, something that sent a chill coursing down my spine.

"Let's get out of here," Cedric urged, his eyes wide, his voice filled with unease. "I don't like this place."

"No," I replied firmly, my voice cutting through the tension. "We can't report back without understanding what's happened here." Even as I spoke, I wondered if I was making a mistake. I knew the risk, but something had drawn us here, and I could not turn back without answers.

CHAPTER 18

Edric hesitated for a moment, his eyes meeting mine, before nodding. "Kaelan's right," he said, his voice filled with resolve. "Something brought us here, and we need to find out what."

Jarin let out a sigh, his grip on his sword tightening. "Alright," he muttered, his gaze shifting warily around the room. "But let's be quick about it."

We moved deeper into the settlement, our steps echoing in the oppressive silence. A wooden door swayed on loose hinges as a faint breeze whispered through the deserted village. I pushed the door open with slow, deliberate force. The creak of the hinges echoed in the silence, each sound amplified by the terror that gripped us.

The interior was dim, illuminated only by slivers of moonlight filtering through cracks in the walls. The air was thick with a musty odor, mingled with something else—something dank and metallic.

As we moved further into the room, the source of the smell became apparent and I felt my stomach twist. Lying scattered across the floor were several bodies, their lifeless forms partially concealed by the shadows. The corpses were fresh, their skin pale, their eyes vacant, staring into nothingness.

"By the gods," Jarin whispered, his face blanching at the sight. "What happened here?"

I swallowed hard, the tang of fear sharp in my mouth. My eyes darted around the room, my mind racing to process the grim scene. Taking a steadying breath, I approached one of the bodies cautiously, careful not to disturb it. The deceased lay motionless, with dark red tunics adorned with symbols that I didn't recognize.

Edric crouched by one of the bodies, "Gods above, who are they? I've never seen uniforms like this." His face was pale.

"They're not from around here," Cedric muttered, his voice low and tense. "And they didn't die quietly.' He pointed a finger at the throat of one of the dead. "Look at these wounds." We all looked at the clean slash on the dead man's throat, his eyes wide and staring, and his hands clenched into fists.

"Who are they? And who left them here like this?" I asked aloud, my voice croaking with frustration. It made no sense—if there had been a battle, where were the victors? And why had they left these bodies behind?

Jarin's gaze flickered around the room, his knuckles white on his sword's hilt. "Who cares who they are? They're dead, and we're standing here like bait."

I took a steadying breath, trying to push the unease from my mind. "Gareth needs to know what we've found. Now."

My eyes narrowed as I tried to piece together the fragments of a story that refused to reveal itself.

Edric moved toward the walls, his eyes catching on something carved into the wood—strange markings, hastily etched, arcane symbols and phrases in an unfamiliar language. He ran his fingers over them, his expression puzzled. "I've never seen writing like this before."

"We can't keep this to ourselves," I said, my voice sharper than I intended. "Sir Gareth shall have to make the call." There was more happening here than we had realized, something beyond the simple dangers of the forest. "This isn't just an abandoned settlement."

Cedric stood, stepping away from the bodies, his face pale. "Agreed," he said, his voice tight. "Let's get back to camp."

Edric straightened, his expression grim. "We must be careful. If this is what we stumbled into, what else is waiting out there?"

We quietly exited the building, the night air hitting me like a cold slap. The forest around us seemed different—darker, more twisted. The trees loomed taller, their branches reaching out like skeletal arms against the night sky. The wind whispered through the leaves, carrying with it indistinct murmurs that made my skin prickle. I couldn't shake the feeling that the forest itself was watching us, waiting for something.

"Something's out here," Jarin muttered, his hand tightening on his sword.

"Keep moving!" I hissed, clutching at the amulet at my chest.

We moved swiftly, every step careful. The overgrown path felt longer, darker. Shadows flickered at the edges of my vision, and each time I turned to look, there was nothing there. But I knew better than to dismiss it. Something was out there, something that wanted us to know it was watching. The journey back to camp felt longer. It felt like the woods were trying to hold us back, the shadows reaching out, urging us to turn around. I kept my eyes forward, focusing on each step, willing the camp to come into view.

At last, the faint glow of campfires broke through the darkness, bringing with it the familiar sounds of the encampment—men talking, the clanking of armor, the crackling of fires. Relief washed over me as we crossed the perimeter, my shoulders finally loosening as the sense of immediate danger began to fade. We headed directly to the command tent, the glow of lantern light spilling out from beneath the canvas, casting long shadows on the ground. Inside, Sir Gareth was bent over a map with a few other officers, his expression focused. He looked up as we approached, his brow furrowing slightly.

"Back sooner than expected," he said raising his eyebrows as he studied us. "What did you find?"

I took a deep breath. "An abandoned settlement with fresh bodies, Sire," I forced my voice to be steady. "They're not ours, and we couldn't identify their origin. There were signs of a recent battle." The words felt surreal even as I spoke them, the image of the lifeless forms still vivid in my mind.

Sir Gareth's expression hardened, his eyes narrowing. "Did you encounter anyone else?"

"No, Sire," Edric answered, his voice carrying the tension we all felt. "But we felt as though we were being watched. Something isn't right out there." The knight's brow furrowed as he drummed his fingers on the desk, his gaze shifting between each of us. After a moment, he nodded. "You've done well to bring this to my attention," he said, his voice carrying a weight of authority. "I'll increase the watch tonight and send a larger party to investigate at first light."

With a nod of dismissal, he turned back to the officers, his focus shifting back to the maps. We left the tent, the tension between us still palpable. As we made our way back to our own tent, the weight of what we had seen pressed down on me. The images of the bodies, the strange symbols, the feeling of being watched—they all played over and over in my mind, refusing to let go.

We settled into our tent, but sleep was impossible. I lay on my bedroll, staring up at the canvas ceiling, my thoughts a whirlwind of confusion and fear.

The amulet rested against my chest once more, the cool metal a familiar presence, but it brought me no comfort. Instead, it felt like a symbol of the mysteries that seemed to be unfolding around us, mysteries that I couldn't begin to understand. I closed my eyes, trying to force myself to rest, but the unease gnawed at me, refusing to let go.

Whatever lay ahead, one thing was certain: our journey was becoming more perilous than any of us had anticipated, the uncertainty of what we faced weighed heavily on my mind.

***

The following morning, the camp was abuzz with activity. The unsettling discovery of the abandoned settlement had prompted swift action from the leadership. General Aldric had gathered his officers, including Sir Gareth, to discuss the safest route forward. The decision was made to alter our course and move into the mountains, avoiding any potential threats lurking in the depths of the forest. Word spread quickly among the soldiers, and I could see the mixed reactions. Some were visibly relieved to be leaving the ominous woods behind, their fear of the unknown giving way to cautious optimism. Others, however, were wary—the mountains were no easy task, and the challenges ahead would test us in ways the forest hadn't. I understood both perspectives, but there was no time to dwell on it. We had our orders, and we needed to move.

We packed our gear swiftly and efficiently, the routine motions a comforting contrast to the uncertainty of what lay ahead. As the sun climbed higher into the sky, the regiment set out. I adjusted the straps of my pack, feeling the familiar weight of my armor and supplies settle against my shoulders. The amulet rested securely against my chest once more, but its mysterious reappearance continued to puzzle me. Every time I felt it against my skin, my heart contracted, as if I was trying to grasp something beyond my reach. I pushed the thought aside, trying to focus on the trail ahead. I had to keep my wits about me. We all did.

CHAPTER
19

The dense forest gradually began to thin, the towering trees giving way to rocky foothills dotted with hardy shrubs and the occasional twisted pine. The path became steeper, and the air grew colder with each step upward. The mountains loomed ahead, their summits capped with snow and shrouded in wisps of cloud that hinted at an approaching storm. It was hard not to feel small against such a vast, imposing landscape.

"At least the view is improving," Cedric commented, glancing back at the expanse of the forest now spread out below us. His tone was lighthearted, an attempt to lift the mood.

I turned to look, my gaze sweeping over the vast canopy of green that stretched to the horizon. He was right—it was beautiful, in a way that made me feel both awestruck and unsettled. The forest looked almost peaceful from up here, its secrets hidden beneath the canopy, the horrors we had seen now distant memories. "True," Edric agreed, his voice muffled as he pulled his cloak tighter around him. "But it's getting colder by the minute."

Jarin cupped his hands over his mouth, his voice barely audible over the wind. "There's supposed to be an old mining settlement not far from here. Vendett's, I think. The tycoon from Centralia. There might be some shelter there."

"Vendett?" My head perked up as I tried to recall what I had heard of him. "He had mines everywhere, didn't he? If this is one of his, it might still have decent walls to keep the wind out. Let's hope it's more than a pile of rubble." I said, a hint of hope creeping into my voice.

"Anything's better than this," Edric muttered, his eyes scanning the snow-draped mountains ahead.

The thought of having a roof over our heads gave me a renewed sense of determination. We needed to make it there— before the mountains swallowed us in their unforgiving embrace.

The path narrowed as we ascended, forcing the column to adjust our formations. The terrain grew more treacherous with each step, the rocky trail demanding our full attention. Horses were led carefully, their hooves clattering against the uneven stone. The wagons creaked under their loads, the drivers guiding them with practiced skill to avoid the roughest patches. I could feel the tension in the air, every man focused on keeping us moving forward.

Sir Gareth rode along the line, his voice cutting through the wind. "Steady, men. The mountain tests all who dare to cross it, but we are more than equal to the challenge. Keep an eye on the clouds; a storm is brewing." His words were meant to reassure me, but they only made the knot in my stomach tighten. I glanced up, watching the sky darken, thick gray clouds gathering like an ominous curtain above us.

The wind picked up, sharper now, carrying tiny flecks of ice that stung my exposed skin. The first snowflakes began to drift down, and they soon intensified, delicate but foreboding, a reminder of how quickly these mountains could turn against us.

"This could turn into a blizzard," Edric said, his voice edged with concern.

General Aldric conferred with his captains, his expression tense. "How far to the mining settlement?" he asked, his voice barely audible over the howling wind.

A scout stepped forward, his face partially obscured by the hood of his cloak. "Not far, sire. Perhaps an hour's march if we maintain pace."

General Aldric nodded, his decision swift. "Then we press on," he said, his voice filled with authority. "Inform the men." The promise of shelter seemed to ripple through the ranks, a glimmer of hope stirring among the men. It showed the way the weary men straightened, the way they pushed forward, each step filled with purpose. We were close—we just had to hold on a little longer.

***

"There!" Cedric shouted over the howling wind. He pointed ahead, and I followed his finger, squinting through the swirling snow. Through the white haze, I could just make out the outlines of buildings nestled against the mountainside. The old mining settlement stood as a bastion against the elements, its sturdy stone structures appearing almost welcoming despite their age and abandonment. Relief washed over me at the sight. We had made it.

The troops cheered as we approached. The thought of facing a mountain blizzard without shelter had been a grim one, and the weight of that fear seemed to lift as we neared the settlement.

"Form up!" Sir Gareth's voice cut through the wind. "We'll secure the perimeter before settling in. Stay vigilant—abandoned doesn't always mean uninhabited."

We moved with purpose, spreading out to inspect the buildings and surrounding area. Cedric, Jarin, Edric, and I were assigned to check the eastern side of the settlement. As we passed between the structures, I noted the signs of long vacancy: doors hanging ajar, snow drifting in through broken windows, and pathways obscured by drifts. It was eerie, the silence of the place amplified by the oppressive cold.

"Feels like a ghost town," Cedric murmured, his voice muffled by his scarf. There was a haunted quality to the structure. It felt like it was holding its breath as if waiting for something—or someone—to break the silence.

"At least we'll have walls around us tonight," Jarin replied forcing a thin smile to his lips. He gently pushed the splintered doorframe and the wood groaned in protest, barely holding. I nodded, though my chest tightened as I glanced at the snow-dusted floor and the faint, claw-like scratches on the doorframe. Edric's gaze shifted toward the mine entrance—a gaping black hole in the mountainside, framed by heavy, weathered timbers. "Let's hope nothing has taken up residence since it was abandoned," he said, his tone half-joking. The dark mouth of the mine seemed to stare back at us, its gaping maw twisted in a mocking grimace.

I offered no reply, but my eyes scanned the area warily as we moved. The amulet seemed to pulse subtly, warming against my chest. For a moment, I wondered if it was real or just my imagination, but I pushed the thought aside, forcing myself to focus on the task at hand. As the last of the daylight faded, the camp slowly took shape within the settlement. Fires were lit within fireplaces and sheltered areas, their warm glow casting flickering light against the stone walls. The scent of cooking food began to fill the air, mingling with the crisp coldness of the mountain. The murmur of conversations rose as soldiers settled in, sharing food and laughter, the rigid postures from earlier eased. I took a deep breath, letting the warmth of the fire seep into my skin.

Outside, the blizzard intensified, the wind howled like a living thing, rattling the shutters and moaning through the gaps in the old structures. We gathered around the hearth. The firelight flickered across our faces, and I could see the exhaustion in the eyes of my comrades, the lines of worry slowly easing as they warmed themselves. The atmosphere was subdued but grateful. Despite the day's challenges, we had reached a haven for the night, and that was more than we could have hoped for just hours ago.

"Just in time," Edric smirked, rubbing his hands together near the crackling fire inside one of the larger buildings. The flames danced, their warmth a welcome relief from the biting cold that had followed us all day.

I nodded, my gaze shifting to the fire. "Let's hope the storm passes quickly," I said, though I knew there was no telling how long we would be at the mercy of the mountain's fury. We had made it to the shelter, but the thought of being stranded here, surrounded by the blizzard made my stomach twist. As the storm raged outside, the soldiers, in a light-hearted banter, speculated about the history of Vendett's mining operations. Some spoke of hidden treasures left behind, their eyes glinting with curiosity, while others shared superstitions about abandoned mines, hauntings, and sightings. I listened, letting the stories sail over my head as my thoughts kept drifting back to the feeling that had pestered me since our flight from the accursed woods.

"Whatever the case," Sir Gareth announced as he passed by, his voice steady and commanding, "Get some rest. We move out at first light, weather permitting." It was beyond dispute; our time here was temporary. We still had a mission to complete and a journey to continue. I nodded to myself, knowing that rest was what we all needed now, even if sleep felt elusive.

I settled into my bedroll, pulling the blankets snugly about me. I watched the flickering fire cast shadows on the stone walls, the shapes shifting and twisting like ghostly dancers and listened to the roar of the blizzard outside and the muffled chatter of my comrades settling in for the night. I finally closed my eyes, exhaustion pulling me in.

Outside, the blizzard raged on, the old mining settlement standing resilient against the onslaught. The mountains loomed silently, guardians of secrets yet to be revealed. Snow piled against the stone walls, and the wind howled like a chorus of tormented spirits. Inside one of the sturdier buildings, around the fire, the men's voices had grown quieter, stories giving way to snores. I slept fitfully, the wind's wail rattling loose shutters and slipping through cracks in the old stone walls, and the cold still finding its way through layers of blankets and cloaks.

I started to doze off at rest. But each time I began to drift away, some sound—a gust of wind, a groan from the timbers— pulled me back to wakefulness.

"This place doesn't feel right," Jarin muttered from his corner, his voice barely above the crackle of the embers. His words echoed in the silence, heavy and unacknowledged.

"The mountains play tricks on the mind," Cedric finally acknowledged, though his usual levity was absent. "We've shelter for the night—that's all that matters."

I tugged my blanket tighter, trying to ignore the faint creaks of the building settling under the weight of the storm. My eyelids grew heavy, but I couldn't sleep. The fire flickered, dimmed, and flared again, casting sudden, jagged shadows across the room. I startled up, my breath misting in the chill air. A sound—low and guttural, almost inaudible— had drifted through the storm outside. I strained to hear it, my heart thudding painfully in my chest.

The moment passed. The storm swallowed the noise—or perhaps I'd imagined it. I exhaled slowly forcing myself to lie back down.

The storm seemed to relent for a moment, the howling wind dying into an unnatural silence. It was in that stillness that the first scream tore through the night, cutting through the quiet like a knife. A blood-curdling scream that jolted me awake. I shot upright, my heart pounding in my chest as the echoes of the scream were swallowed by the storm raging outside. The cold air bit at my skin, and for a moment, I couldn't tell if I was still dreaming. Another scream pierced the air, sharp and unnatural. I bolted upright, my body stiff with shock. For a moment, I couldn't breathe, my chest constricting as if the cold itself had gripped my lungs. The sound didn't belong here—no human voice should carry such raw, primal terror.

Was it real? My mind clawed for answers, struggling to separate the scream from the howling wind that rattled the shutters. A sickening dread settled in my gut, cold and heavy, and I realized my hands were trembling even as I reached for my blade.

"Gods…" I whispered, my voice barely audible over the storm. The word wasn't a prayer—it was a futile attempt to steady myself, to make sense of what I had just heard.

Cedric's voice cut through the haze, sharp and urgent. "Did you hear that?" His fear was palpable, but there was a steely edge to his tone as he gripped his sword. His eyes darted to the doorway as if expecting the shadows themselves to lunge at us.

A growl rumbled through the air, low and guttural. It wasn't human. Or was it? The sound twisted, rising to a pitch that set my teeth on edge, and for a moment, I was paralyzed.

"Get up!" Cedric bellowed, his voice cracking as he raised his blade. I snapped out of my reverie as the others also scrambled to form a line by the door, our movements sharp and desperate. The firelight flickered faintly, and we strained to discern what was happening outside the door.

Then came the sound of a crash—wood splintering, a scream cut short, and a metallic smell of blood hit me as though the air itself had turned to iron.

Something heavy thudded to the ground just beyond the doorway. My stomach churned as dark, glistening liquid started pooled beneath the frame.

And then it moved—a shadow, crouching, but unnaturally tall, shifting just outside the door. The growl came again, closer this time, accompanied by a wet scrape across the ground.

The air felt heavier, colder, as though the storm itself had seeped into my bones. My fingers tightened around my blade, but they trembled with a helpless, primal fear. Whatever was out there, it was coming.

Before I could move, another scream tore through the night, this time from the eastern part of the settlement, accompanied by the unmistakable sounds of chaos—shouts, growls, the clashes of metal.

Suddenly, the alarm bells began to ring, their frantic clanging echoing through the storm. It was a sound that sent a chill deeper than the cold ever could, a call to arms that meant one thing: we were under attack.

CHAPTER 20

To arms!" Someone shouted from outside "We are under attack!" Their voices were barely audible over the howling wind.

My head whipped from side to side, my fingers trembling as they wrapped around the familiar hilt. Edric and Cedric were already moving out the door, their faces pale but resolute. There was no time for hesitation.

"What in the name of the gods is this?" Jarin exclaimed, fumbling to secure his helmet, his voice tinged with panic.

The door burst open, and a soldier stumbled inside, his eyes wide with terror and feet stained with blood. "Wolves!" he gasped, his breath coming in ragged puffs. "A pack of wolves has entered the camp!"

My mind raced, struggling to make sense of it. Wolves? It defied all reason. Wolves in the mountains weren't unheard of, but this wasn't normal—an unprovoked attack, and in the middle of a blizzard? Something felt off, but there was no time to question it.

"Move! Now!" I commanded, my voice steadier than I felt. There was no time to think, only to act. I led the way to the door, my heart pounding in my ears as we stepped out into the storm.

The wind sliced through the air, stealing my breath, and the snow blurred everything to shadowy silhouettes. The settlement, which had felt like a haven just hours before now echoed with chaos. Screams thundered through the storm, mingling with the snarls of the wolves and the cries of the wounded.

Dark shapes darted between the buildings—large, shadowy figures with glowing eyes and snarling jaws. They moved with an uncanny coordination, targeting isolated soldiers with lethal efficiency. Fear paralyzed me as I took in the scene—four men already lay motionless in the snow, scarlet blood staining the ground around them. The sight made my blood run cold, the reality of the danger we were facing sinking in. Suddenly, the amulet grew warmer against my skin, its heat pulsing in steady waves. As the chaos increased, the heat intensified, radiating from the pendant in a surge, as though it were alive, breathing. And though it was hot against my skin, it had a soothing and comforting feel.

"Over there!" Cedric shouted, pointing to a group of wolves circling a fallen comrade. My gaze followed his gesture, my heart lurching at the sight. We couldn't let this happen—not to our brothers-in-arms.

"Hey!" Jarin shouted back at me, his sword cleaving through a wolf that lunged too close. I tightened my grip on my blade, the chill of sweat on my palms and the hot amulet against my chest. I struck over and over – everything blurred into a frenzy of snarls and shouts. The wolves fell at our feet, snarling, howling, dying. Mindlessly, I slashed, my sword cutting through skin and bones as if it had a mind of its own. The battle raged on; a blur of fur, steel, and blood. Gradually, I sensed a shift. The soldiers around me fought with renewed vigor, pressing the attack. I could see the wolves' hesitation, their yellow eyes flickering with uncertainty before they began to retreat, slipping beyond our perimeter. Their haunting howls echoed in the darkness, fading into the night, and I finally allowed myself a breath.

My chest heaved as I looked around, my gaze sweeping over the camp. It was a mess. Tents had been ripped apart, cabin doors in splinters, supplies were scattered everywhere, and men lay on the ground, some clutching wounds while others were eerily still. Healers rushed to the wounded, their voices urgent but controlled. The scent of blood was heavy in the cold night air.

"Is everyone all right?" I called out, my voice strained. I turned to where I last saw my friends, my heart pounding not just from the exertion but from fear of what I might find.

Cedric gave me a weary smile, wiping away the blood from a shallow cut on his cheek. "A few scratches," he said. "Nothing serious." The relief that washed over me was palpable, though it was quickly tempered by the sight of Edric's grim expression.

Edric shook his head slowly, eyes downcast. "Fourteen men… lost," he murmured, his voice tight. "Wolves don't do this. There's something…Something happened here."

I swallowed, my throat dry as I looked out towards the darkness beyond the camp. I had no answer. Something indeed had happened here. Something was off about the attack, something unnatural— as if the wolves had not acted of their own accord. And there was something in the way I fought – as if I wielded the valor of ten men. It gnawed at me all morning.

Sir Gareth organized patrols and reinforced defenses, his voice carrying over the camp. "We can't afford to be caught off guard again," he declared, his tone leaving no room for argument. "Double the watch and keep weapons at the ready."

I exchanged a glance with Edric, the unease I felt mirrored in his eyes.

"We need to stay alert," Edric said, his expression grim. "There's more at play here than meets the eye." The weight of his words hung heavily between us. As we made our way back to our quarters. The wind howled outside, its sound carrying an almost sinister undertone. I tried to ignore it, focusing on the warmth of the fire. Even the small comfort of shelter felt fragile as if the walls could barely keep the darkness at bay. I lay down, but sleep was elusive, my mind replaying the night's events over and over, my grip tight on the now-cold amulet. Every creak of the building seemed to echo the growls of wolves. Dawn finally broke, a reluctant, pale light filtering through the remnants of the blizzard that had battered the old mining settlement through the night. I stirred from what felt like only moments of sleep, my body stiff and cold. The chill had seeped into everything, and I shivered as I sat up, trying to rub warmth back into my limbs. Around me, my comrades were waking as well, their faces drawn and weary.

"Morning," Edric said quietly, stifling a yawn as he pulled on his coat. "If you can call it that."

"Did you manage any sleep?" I asked, though I already knew the answer from the dark circles under his eyes.

"Not much," he admitted, giving me a tired smile. "Kept thinking one of those monsters would pounce on me while I slept." His words were made to be lighthearted but they made my stomach twist, the memory of those piercing yellow eyes still too fresh.

We gathered our belongings, each movement deliberate. The silence between us could be cut with a knife. A commotion near the center of the camp drew my attention. Soldiers were gathered in a tight cluster, their hushed whispers and concerned murmurs spreading like wildfire. The unease was palpable, and I could feel it gnawing at me.

"What's going on?" Cedric wondered aloud beside me, adjusting his cloak.

We made our way toward the crowd, pushing gently through the throng until we could see what had drawn everyone together. Sir Gareth stood in the center, his expression grave, his gaze fixed on the ground before him. I followed his line of sight, and my breath caught in my throat. Two soldiers lay still, their bodies lifeless. There were no wounds, no signs of struggle—just the cold, stark finality of death. A chill deeper than the winter air ran through me.

"What happened?" I asked a soldier standing nearby, my voice brittle, as if speaking too loudly would shatter the fragile silence.

He shook his head, his face pale and eyes wide with terror. "Found them like this during the morning rounds. No one knows how they died." His words hung in the air, heavy and unsettling. I felt helpless. The thought that something— someone—could kill our men so easily without leaving a trace was terrifying.

Sir Gareth's voice rose above the murmurs, commanding our attention. "We have lost two more brothers under mysterious circumstances," he said, his voice steady "I understand that fear and uncertainty grips us all, but we must remain steadfast." His eyes moved over us as if trying to instill a sense of resolve.

I tried to hold on to that, but it was hard when the unknown loomed so heavily over us.

I noticed General Aldric approaching, his face a mirror of the somberness that seemed to have settled over the entire camp. He and Sir Gareth exchanged a few words, their conversation too clipped and quiet for me to hear, but the grim set of their jaws told me enough. After a moment, General Aldric turned to address us, his eyes blazing.

"Men," he began, his eyes sweeping over the gathered soldiers, "given the events of last night and this morning, we have decided to break camp immediately. Wintmore lies a day and a half's march from here. We will proceed without rest until we reach our destination."

A murmur of surprise and apprehension rippled through the crowd. The thought of marching without rest through the mountains was daunting. My legs ached with the mere thought, but the alternative—staying here was far worse. "Prepare your gear," Sir Gareth ordered, his voice sharp, cutting through any lingering doubts. "We depart within the hour. Stay close, stay vigilant, and look out for one another."

I exchanged a glance with Edric, Cedric, and Jarin. "Looks like we won't get a chance to catch our breath," I said, my voice tinged with resignation.

"Better to move than waiting for whatever's stalking us to strike again," Jarin replied. We hurried back to our quarters, gathering our belongings, and checking and double-checking our equipment. My fingers were numb from the cold, making the straps and buckles difficult to manage, but I forced myself to focus. Around us, the camp was a whirlwind of urgent activity—tents were being struck, supplies packed, and horses readied. The snow made every task harder, but we moved without hesitation, each of us knowing what had to be done. As we prepared to leave, I caught sight of the bodies of our fallen comrades, now covered and placed gently onto a sled. It made my chest tighten, a painful reminder of what we'd lost. It felt wrong to leave them behind, and I was grateful they would be coming with us, even if only in this way. The solemnity of the moment reinforced the urgency of leaving this cursed place behind.

The column formed up, and under General Aldric's command, we set off along the mountain path. The snow was deep in places, the footing treacherous. I could feel the cold biting at my face and hands, and each step was a struggle against the frozen ground. But we pressed on, driven by the need to reach Wintmore, by the hope that there we might find safety.

The sky above was a flat, unbroken gray, offering little comfort or warmth. The wind had finally calmed, but the chill in the air was unrelenting. The landscape stretched out around us, stark and desolate, the jagged peaks rising like monstrous teeth against the horizon. It felt as though the world itself was against us, the cold and the emptiness pressing in on all sides.

Hours passed. Soon, dusk approached, and the light began to fade, but we didn't stop. Torches were lit, their flickering light casting long, dancing shadows along the path. The flames made the darkness seem even deeper, the shadows among the rocks and snow moving in ways that made my skin prickle with unease. But no one spoke of it. We all felt it—the tension, but we kept our eyes forward, our steps steady.

"How much farther?" a soldier behind me murmured, his voice heavy with exhaustion.

"Not sure," another replied. "But we can't be far now." I could hear the weariness in his tone, and it mirrored the way my own body felt—like each step took twice the effort it should.

Sir Gareth rode alongside the column, his presence somehow reassuring amidst the fatigue and cold. "Move men! Move! ," his voice carrying over the sounds of crunching snow and labored breaths. "Every step brings us closer to safety."

The night dragged on. My mind wandered, drifting back to the faces of the men we'd lost. The memory of their lifeless forms haunted me. I clenched my jaw, forcing myself to focus, to keep one foot in front of the other. In the early hours of the morning, a faint glow appeared on the horizon—the first hint of dawn. I blinked against the light, my tired eyes struggling to adjust. The terrain began to slope downward, and I could feel the oppressive chill start to ease, if only slightly. It was a small comfort, but I held onto it.

"There," Edric whispered beside me, pointing ahead. I followed his gaze.

Nestled in the valley below was the outline of a settlement—a Centralian controlled town of Wintmore. Relief flooded through me, a surge of energy that I hadn't thought possible after the long night. I could hear the murmurs of the men around me, their spirits lifting at the sight.

"Almost there," I said, a hint of a smile breaking through my tired face.

As we descended toward the town, the details became clearer. The town was larger than I'd imagined, its walls standing tall against the cold, smoke curling from chimneys, and the faint sounds of life just audible over the wind. It felt like a glimpse of warmth after the long march."

General Aldric called for a halt, his voice cutting through the rising chatter. "Men, we have reached Wintmore. Stand tall—you have endured much to get here." His words brought a subdued cheer from the ranks, a quiet but heartfelt acknowledgment of what we'd accomplished.

As we approached the gates, they opened cautiously, and a small contingent of Centralian guards emerged to meet us. Their eyes were wary, their hands resting on their weapons. I couldn't blame them—after everything we'd been through, I was wary too.

"State your business," the lead guard called out, his gaze sharp as it swept over our ragged column.

General Aldric stepped forward, his posture commanding despite the exhaustion that surely weighed on him as well. "I am General Aldric of the Centralian Army. We've come to fight in the front lines."

The guard studied us for a moment, his eyes lingering on our weary faces and the sled carrying our fallen comrades. Finally, he nodded. "Welcome to the hell that is Wintmore General. We've been expecting you."

As we passed through the gates, I couldn't shake the feeling that our challenges were far from over. Finally, we were in the wintery hell of Wintmore.

CHAPTER 21

The soldiers moved briskly within the walls, unloading wagons filled with supplies and reinforcing defenses in anticipation of the conflicts ahead. I watched them work, swiftly and efficiently. The air was crisp, each breath producing a puff of mist that disappeared almost as quickly as it came. "At last, a moment to rest," Cedric remarked beside me, hoisting his pack over one shoulder as we stepped into the courtyard

Edric chuckled beside us. "Let's hope the beds prove as warm as the welcome,"

A group of stone-faced soldiers led us to a barracks where the warmth from a central hearth welcomed us. Wooden sleeping frames lined the walls, each with a thick woolen blanket folded neatly at the foot. It wasn't luxury, but after days in the biting wind, it felt like it. I claimed a cot next to Edric, dropping my pack onto the floor with a weary sigh before unpacking my belongings and setting aside my sword and shield. I examined my blade for nicks and scratches, making a mental note that it needed tending. My fingers brushed against the amulet beneath my tunic, and I paused. The warmth of the room seemed to fade for a moment, replaced by the cool weight of the metal pressed against my skin, grounding me in a way the warmth couldn't.

Will it finally reveal its secrets?

Does it even have the answers?

Or am I chasing whispers in the dark?

Edric's voice broke through my thoughts. "We should check in with the quartermaster," he said, rubbing his hands together and placing them toward the hearth to keep warm. "I could use some fresh supplies." I nodded.

"Indeed," I replied, managing a tired smile. "I fear my stomach has long since lost memory of the taste of proper food."

The thought of a hot meal made my mouth water. The dry rations we'd been living on were barely enough to keep us going, and the idea of something hearty and warm felt like a small piece of salvation.

Edric grinned, his eyes brightening at the prospect. "Let's not waste any time then." With that, we gathered our things and headed out of the barracks, making our way toward the supply depot, weaving through clusters of soldiers and stacks of crates. The air was filled with the sounds of men calling out orders, the clinking of armor, and the scrape of heavy crates being moved. When we reached the depot, the quartermaster—a stern-faced man with a meticulous demeanor—greeted us with a curt nod.

"Name and station?" he asked, his quill poised over a ledger, not even glancing up.

"Kaelan, Cedric, and Edric of the Iron Blades Regiment," I answered. I was almost asleep on my feet.

The quartermaster gave me no glance. He tapped his quill on the table, his eyes perusing the records before he offered a small nod.

"You're cleared for replenishment. Rations, wound pouches, and winter gear are available. Make sure you're properly equipped—the weather here is savage." His words were delivered in the same clipped, detached tone.

We gathered our allotted supplies—dried meats, hardtack, and fresh canteens. My fingers glided across the thick gloves and additional cloaks they gave us, grateful for each extra layer of clothing. Even so, I wasn't sure when I'd ever feel truly warm again. As we stepped out of the depot, snow began to fall lightly, the flakes drifting lazily from the gray sky. I watched them for a moment, lost in thought.

"It seems the snow is far from done with us" Edric commented, tilting his head upward.

"At least we're not marching in it—for now," Cedric said, a wry smile tugging at his lips.

His humor, even in times like these, was something I had come to rely on, a small anchor that kept us all from slipping into despair.

Back at the barracks, we organized our gear, each of us moving with sluggishness. I sank into a seat by the central hearth letting its warmth seep into my tired muscles. Before long, my gaze wandered to Jarin, who had been unusually quiet since we'd returned. He was sitting on his sleeping frame, a distant look in his eyes that made my startle.

"Everything alright, Jarin?" I tried to keep my tone light.

He blinked, as if coming out of a trance, and looked at me.

"I feel a little unwell," he admitted, his voice lacking its usual jollity. "Though I suspect the weariness is taking its toll upon me."

Edric raised an eyebrow, glancing at him. "You're pale as a ghost."

Jarin forced a weak smile, waving a dismissive hand. "I'll be fine," he insisted, his voice thin, "Just need to sleep it off."

But his eyes betrayed him – they were weary and uncertain and held a quiet plea that he couldn't seem to put into words. I endeavored not to fret, but worry bubbled in my stomach.

Jarin's condition worsened as the evening wore on. He shivered beneath his blanket, his forehead damp with sweat and his breathing shallow.

Cedric placed a hand on his arm. "You're burning up," he said, his eyes wide with concern "This isn't just fatigue, Jarin."

Without a second thought, I rose. "I'm getting the healer," I said, my voice firmer than I felt.

I hurried to the infirmary, my footsteps echoing off the stone walls. Inside, the healer looked up from tending a soldier, his satchel of herbs close at hand.

"Can I help you?" He asked. His face looked weary, like one who had not rested well for a long time.

"It's my friend," I blurted out in a flutter. "He's running a high fever and looks unwell."

The healer didn't hesitate. He nodded, gathering his supplies. "Take me to him."

I turned on my heel, leading him back through the winding halls, my anxiety growing with each step. At the barracks, Jarin was lying down, his condition unchanged. His face was flushed, his breathing labored. The healer knelt beside him, pressing his fingers lightly to Jarin's wrist, counting the beats, then tilted his neck and peered into his eyes. His steps were slow and measured. I watched him closely, my hands clenched into fists.

"He's showing signs of mountain fever." The healer finally stood up, putting tiny vials and bottles back into his little box,

"Not uncommon for those unaccustomed to these elevations and climates."

"Is it serious?" Edric asked stepping closer, his voice muffled. The healer nodded gravely. "It can be if not treated promptly. He needs rest and proper care. We'll move him to the infirmary at once where we can monitor his progress."

Jarin tried to protest, his voice jagged and raspy. "I can remain here... there's no need to burden you."

"That is no matter, Jarin," I said firmly, stepping closer to him. "Your well-being takes precedence above all else right now. We'll see you well." He argued no further. We helped the healer move him to the infirmary, settling him into a bed near the warmth of a brazier. I could see the relief in his eyes as he finally relaxed, the heat offering some comfort. The healer worked swiftly, preparing a tonic from various herbs, explaining that it would help reduce the fever and strengthen his body's defenses. I watched every movement, wishing there was more I could do.

"Will he recover soon?" Cedric whispered, terror in his eyes.

The healer gave a small, reassuring smile. "With luck and rest, he should improve in a few days. But the next twenty-four hours are crucial." I swallowed hard, nodding in understanding.

As we left the infirmary, the snow fell heavier, the wind cutting through the narrow passages of the fort.

"Now is not the time for any of us to endure more hardship. Things are hard enough as it stands." Edric remarked, frustration in his tone. My gaze drifted to the barracks where Jarin lay.

"He shall recover. I'm certain of it." My words felt hollow, more like a plea than a certainty.

We made our way back to the barracks, our hearts dampened by the unease that settled over us like a heavy blanket

***

We sat on my sleeping cot, our hands clasped morosely before us as a suffocating silence pressed heavily upon us. In those few months, Jarin had become more than the shepherd I'd scarcely known in Elsenburg—he had become my friend, my comrade, and a brother in this far land. Never had I seen him falter, nor shown such frailty as now.

"Do you think the others fare any better?" Cedric asked, breaking the silence. His voice was quiet, almost as if he didn't want to disturb the fragile calm that had fallen over us. He glanced around at the weary faces of our fellow soldiers, his eyes filled with uncertainty.

I took a deep breath. "Hard to say," I answered honestly. "But we have to stay focused. The battles lie not only beyond there." I gestured beyond the walls of the fort, where the snow-covered wilderness stretched endlessly. "They rage in here too." I tapped a hand to my chest, trying to convey what I couldn't put into words. The fears, the doubts, the exhaustion—a battle we had to face, one that didn't end when we put down our swords.

The snow continued to fall, each flake adding to the thick blanket that already covered the fort. It muffled the sounds around us, turning everything into a hushed, almost dreamlike state. Soldiers huddled around hearths, their faces illuminated by the flickering light of the fires. Murmured conversations and scattered laughter filled the space. For the three of us, there were no words. We huddled together as our hearts gingerly carried our unspoken fears.

CHAPTER
22

The following morning, we were summoned to the central courtyard by General Aldric. Despite the early hour, we assembled promptly, our breath forming a mist in the frigid air.

The sky above was a pale gray, the sun struggling to break through the thick blanket of clouds that hung overhead. It was as if the world itself held its breath, waiting for whatever was to come next. General Aldric stood atop a raised platform, his imposing figure wrapped in heavy furs over his armor. His eyes swept over us, each man standing at attention

"Men of Centralia," General Aldric began, his voice carrying clearly. I stood among my comrades and listened as his words echoed across the assembled soldiers. "We have come to Wintmore not only to face an enemy on the battlefield but also to confront the harshness of this land itself. The cold here is as much our adversary as any foe with a sword."

He paused, letting the weight of his words sink in. I could feel the truth in them—how our strength seemed to drain away, how every movement became just a little harder "To ensure our success," he continued, "we must become accustomed to these conditions. From this day forward, we shall train outside for half the day, regardless of the weather. Embrace the cold; let it strengthen you rather than weaken you. Use it to forge your resolve."

A murmur ran through the ranks as the men exchanged glances—some resigned, others grim. We all knew the wisdom in his words. Not that it made it easier.

Sir Gareth stepped forward, his expression unyielding. "Training schedules shall be adjusted henceforth," he announced. "We will focus on drills that not only sharpen your combat skills but also harden your endurance against the elements. I am not blind to the toll this weather has taken - that some of you have fallen gravely ill. Such frailty is to be expected when the wind cuts to the bone. Yet, while we offer prayers for their quick recovery, let's not forget the truth; a soldier who can fight in any condition is a soldier who can prevail."

I exchanged glances with Edric and Cedric. None of us cared for spending half the day training in the bitter cold, when we could be with Jarin. But we gathered in the courtyard once more, forming ranks as the officers issued commands. The first exercises were grueling, focusing on physical conditioning: running laps around the fort's perimeter, performing calisthenics, and engaging in mock skirmishes. My breath came in ragged bursts, but I pushed myself forward, feeling the burn in my muscles and the sting of the cold against my skin.

"The winter's breath cannot catch you if you stay ahead of it!" Sir Gareth bellowed. His words pushed us forward. We couldn't let the elements break us.

Sweat trickled down my back despite the frigid temperature as I parried Edric's thrust during our sparring session. The wooden practice swords clacked sharply, the sound echoing off the stone walls around us.

"You're getting slow," I teased Edric, sidestepping his next attack with a grin.

"Maybe I'm just giving you a chance," he shot back, a grin spreading across his face.

Nearby, Cedric practiced archery, his fingers stiff as he notched arrows and released them toward distant targets. I could see him adjusting his aim, compensating for the gusts of wind that threatened to throw off his shots. But Cedric was nothing if not persistent, each shot a testament to his focus and skill.

After what felt like hours, the officers finally called for a break. We gathered around the large braziers set up around the courtyard and I held my hands over the flames, feeling the sting of the heat as the blood returned to my fingers.

"Not so bad, once you get used to it," one of the soldiers commented, rubbing his hands together, a small smile on his face.

"Speak for yourself," another muttered, his teeth chattering. "I can't feel my ears." I chuckled at that, the shared misery somehow lightening the burden.

As we resumed our drills, the sky began to clear. A weak sunbeam broke through the clouds, casting a faint glow over the courtyard. It wasn't much, but it was enough to lift our spirits, By midday, General Aldric called for the training to conclude. "You've done well," he said, his voice loud and marked with pride. "Rest now, eat, and recover your strength. We'll continue tomorrow." I had made it through the morning, and I knew I could do it again.

***

Back in the barracks, I had only Jarin in my mind. I swiftly shed my outer layers, hanging them near the hearth to dry.

"Any news on Jarin?" I asked Cedric. He was reclined on the bench polishing his dagger.

Cedric shook his head, his expression grim. "I spoke with the healer earlier. His fever hasn't broken yet, but he's hopeful." I don't know whether it was the way he said it, but my heart skipped a beat. "He'd be fine," I said a little too loudly and stalked to my sleeping corner to keep my gear.

Cedric collapsed on his seat. "He'd hate missing out on all this fun," he said wryly, gesturing to the barracks around us. It was the kind of challenge Jarin would have thrived on, and not stuck in the infirmary.

I managed a thin smile. "We shall fill him in when he's well again,"

The rest of the day passed slowly, the hours blurring into each other as we tried to keep ourselves busy. We parried at the courtyard and tended to our equipment. My sword needed sharpening, and I found a strange comfort in the repetitive motion, the scrape of the whetstone against the blade. We shared stories, trying to keep our minds occupied, the sound of laughter occasionally breaking through the tension. Later, we made our way to the fort's mess hall, where a hearty meal of stew and fresh bread awaited us.

As evening settled in, I felt the need to step outside, to clear my head. The sky had cleared, and stars beginning to emerge against the deepening blue. I closed my eyes and let my hand find its way to the amulet beneath my tunic and thoughts of my brother surfaced unbidden—I wondered where Eamon could be; if he was enduring similar hardships; if he was safe; if he was in an infirmary somewhere sick, wounded, dying. I quickly brushed off the thoughts. A pang of longing struck me, sharp and sudden.

"We'll find each other," I whispered into the night, a vow carried away by the gentle breeze. I had to believe that, just as I had to trust Jarin would recover. It was the only way to survive in a place like this.

***

The next morning, I was adjusting my gear when Edric approached, his expression grave, with something in his eyes that made my stomach drop.

"Kaelan, you need to come to the infirmary," he said quietly, his voice lacking its usual lightness. "It's Jarin."

Without a word, I followed him through the bustling corridors, the murmurs of other soldiers fading into the background. Cedric stood beside Jarin's bed, arms crossed tightly over his chest, his chest heaving. I swallowed hard as I took in the sight before me. Jarin lay there, motionless, his skin pale and clammy, a sheen of sweat glistening on his forehead. His breathing was shallow, each inhale a visible struggle.

Seeing him like this frightened me, and I cast a questioning look at the healer who had weariness burrowed in his brow.

"He doesn't look well."

He approached us, wiping his hands on a piece of cloth, tiredness evident in his demeanor "I'm afraid his condition has worsened overnight." His voice was soft as if suffering under the weight of his impotency. "The mountain fever has taken a stronger hold, I'm afraid."

A chill that had nothing to do with the cold outside seeped into my bones and a sense of helplessness settled over me. "Is there anything more you can do?"

The healer sighed, "We've administered all the concoctions available to us here."

"Is he... Is he going to live?" Cedric's voice trembled as he spoke, his question hanging in the air like a fragile hope.

The healer looked at us, his gaze gentle and sad. "It's difficult to say," he replied quietly. "The next few hours are critical. If his fever doesn't break soon…"

The gravity of the situation settled over us like a heavy blanket, suffocating in its weight.

I pulled a stool closer to Jarin's bedside and sat down, taking his hand in mine. It was unsettlingly cold to the touch, and I squeezed it gently, willing some of my warmth to reach him.

"Jarin," I whispered. "We're here with you. You're strong—you can fight this." My throat felt tight, and I fought to keep my emotions in check.

A faint flicker of movement passed under Jarin's eyelids, his lips parting slightly as if he were trying to respond. No sound came out, but it was enough to give me a glimmer of hope. Edric placed a reassuring hand on my shoulder, his grip firm and steady. "He knows we're here," he said, "That must count for something."

Time stretched on, each moment feeling like an eternity as we kept vigil by Jarin's side. The sounds of the fort faded away, replaced by the rhythmic ticking of a clock and the soft crackle of the fire. I watched Jarin's face, searching for any sign of improvement, my heart aching with every shallow breath he took. Cedric paced nearby with a coiled restlessness I had not seen in him before. His gaze occasionally drifted to the window where the snow swirled outside, his lips taut.

Suddenly, Edric spoke, breaking the silence. "Remember when Jarin challenged Sir Gareth to an archery contest?" he said, a weak smile creeping to the corner of his lips.

I managed a small chuckle. "He was so sure he'd win. Ended up missing the target completely on the first shot."

"But he insisted on a rematch," Cedric added, pausing his restless pacing. "And didn't stop until he actually beat him."

"Well, until Sir Gareth let him win, more likely." Edric said. We laughed, and for a fleeting moment, the air softened as if the memory had blown some hope into the stifling silence.

But Jarin let out a bout of cough and the moment shattered. We watched him anxiously as he drew in a painful breath, his face contorting with discomfort. My smile faded, and I intertwined my fingers with his. The healer moved to check his temperature again, his expression unreadable.

"His fever is rising," the healer said softly, his voice tinged with regret. "But we're doing everything we can to keep him comfortable."

I suddenly felt a surge of desperation. "Is there no medicine, no treatment we haven't tried?"

The healer shook his head, his eyes filled with sympathy. "Without specific herbs that we don't have here, there's little else we can administer," he replied, his tone heavy. "A messenger has been sent to a nearby town, but with the weather as it is..."

I turned my gaze back to Jarin and watched his face, pale and gaunt. Fear and helplessness washed over me in waves.

"Stay strong, Jarin," I whispered, my voice trembling. "You will pull through." I squeezed his hand gently, willing him to open his eyes. But he lay there, groaning with each labored breathing, to fight just a little longer.

Hours passed. Soldiers came and went from the infirmary, their voices hushed. But Edric, Cedric, and I remained by Jarin's side. The healer brought warm compresses, doing what he could to ease Jarin's pain. But he laid there groaning with each jagged breath, as his body burned with fever. It was agony to watch, but we couldn't move a step.

As night fell, the flickering light of the hearth cast long shadows across the room, the warmth barely enough to chase away the chill in my bones. I could hear the faint whistle of the wind outside, like a melancholic wail.

Edric cleared his throat, his voice thick with emotion.

"Remember how he always talked about wanting to see the ocean? Said he'd never seen so much water in one place." His eyes were fixed on Jarin, his expression somber. Cedric sighed, his eyes glistening in the dim light. "He convinced us to go together after the campaign. Made us promise we'd take him there." His voice broke slightly, and he quickly looked away and swallowed.

I gripped Jarin's hand more tightly, my own emotions threatening to overwhelm me. "And we will. We will all go together, just like we promised."

The healer approached once more, a jar of poultice in his hands. "Yes. You should speak to him," he advised. "Let him know you're here. It may provide some comfort."

We gathered closer, each of us taking a moment to share our words—memories of past adventures, and dreams for the future. I leaned in, my voice soft but full of conviction. "You're not alone, Jarin. We're here with you. Hold on a little longer. We've faced so much together, and we'll see this through too." My voice finally broke and I bent my head and cried.

By morning, Jarin had made a turn for the worse. The light of dawn filtered through the infirmary windows and bathed him in a dim glow. His face was white and his fingers had taken a bluish hue. The only sign that he was alive was the faint rise and fall of his chest.

I leaned in closer, my voice breaking as I spoke. "Please, Jarin," I murmured. "Fight."

We sat, slouched in weariness, as sorrow seeped into my heart, filling it to the brim. The healer stood a short distance away, his hands folded solemnly as if waiting for something to happen.

Jarin's eyelids fluttered open briefly, his gaze unfocused and searching. His eyes, once bright and full of mischief, now held a quiet resignation. He mustered a weak, crooked smile—an echo of the boy who'd once laughed at our endless teasing.

"Looks like... I might not find what I was looking for," he rasped. It was faint, like leaves brushing against the cobblestones, and I leaned closer and rubbed his hand. "Don't say that, Jarin," I replied, my voice a croak. "We'll all find it. Together. You must hold on a little longer."

Jarin's gaze softened, lingering on each of us as if memorizing our faces, and my heart clenched painfully.

"Thank you, brothers... for everything," he whispered, the effort costing him more than I wanted to admit. "Look after each other."

Edric swallowed, his voice breaking as he spoke. "We will, Jarin. We promise. But you're going to pull through this. You have to."

A peaceful expression settled over Jarin's face, and he took a slow breath. "It's all right," he murmured. "I've made my peace. Just... remember me."

Cedric reached out, gripping Jarin's other hand gently. "Jarin. Jarin..."

Jarin's hand in mine grew slack. His chest rose once—then fell in a shallow, shuddering breath. And then... nothing. His body relaxed and his eyes drifted closed.

The air seemed to shift at that moment and the faint crackle of the hearth faded into an unbearable stillness. I sat frozen, my hand still wrapped around his. A faint warmth lingered in his fingers, but it faded fast, slipping away like the last embers of a dying fire. The room felt colder, as though the heat had been sucked out with his final breath.

"Jarin?" My voice cracked. It hung in the silence, unanswered.

I stared at his face, my heart aching. Edric's hand fell on my shoulder, his grip trembling. I couldn't bring myself to look at him. Cedric knelt beside the bed and his shoulders shook with silent sobs. The healer stepped forward, his movements deliberate, as though unwilling to disturb the fragile peace that had settled over the room, and slowly lowered himself beside us, joining in our mourning.

I couldn't stop staring at Jarin's face, searching for any sign of life, any flicker of eyelids, any movement of his fingers His features were serene, the remnant of a smile still etched on his lips, as though he had simply drifted off to sleep.

Time felt suspended, each moment dragging like an eternity. The faint whistle of the wind beyond the infirmary seemed softer now, mournful, as though the earth itself grieved with us.

Cedric finally broke the silence, his voice raw and unsteady. "We'll never forget you, Jarin," he whispered. "You'll always be with us." His hand reached out to brush Jarin's hair back from his forehead. Tears welled in my eyes again, and I let them fall,

"Goodbye, my friend," I murmured, my voice trembling "You fought hard."

The healer placed a comforting hand on my shoulder. His rheumy eyes were filled with sympathy. "I'm sorry," he said, his words sincere and heavy. "He fought bravely."

Edric turned away, wiping his eyes with the back of his hand, his shoulders trembling. Cedric stood motionless, his gaze fixed on Jarin's in disbelief. None of us wanted to move. We stayed with him as though our stay around his bed might change what had happened. But Jarin was gone, only his memory remained—etched into the very fabric of our lives, a reminder of everything we had fought for and everything we had lost.

CHAPTER 23

The world outside seemed unchanged, the fort alive with activity, as if it had not borne witness to the tragedy that had befallen us. We buried Jarin in the cold, hard earth. For a moment, we stood there shovels in our hands, our breaths mingling with the frosty air. We finally turned and slowly made our way back toward the barracks the weight of his loss pressing heavily on us. No one spoke. Our steps were silent, heavy with grief. Cedric had his head bowed and swiped angrily at the tears that betrayed him. Edric's face was taut, his jaw set, as he walked on stoically.

A sharp voice broke through the stillness.

"Kaelan, Edric, Cedric,"

A messenger hurried toward us, his breath visible in the cold frigid air; his eyes softened as he took in our somber expressions.

"General Aldric requires your presence in the command tent at once."

We exchanged weary glances. None of us were ready for whatever new challenge lay ahead, but refusal wasn't an option. We followed him through the maze of tents and structures, my legs feeling heavier with every step.

Inside the command tent, General Aldric and Sir Gareth stood hunched over a large map spread across a wooden table, their brows furrowed in concentration and their fingers tracing lines and symbols as they spoke in hushed tones. Several other officers stood nearby, their faces grim, their postures stiff with urgency.

General Aldric straightened as we entered, his eyes sweeping over us. "You have my condolences," he said, his gaze softening for a brief moment as he took in our somber expressions. "Jarin's loss is a heavy blow, not just to you but to us all." I swallowed hard and nodded. "Thank you, sire." It felt inadequate — the exchange between us—like an inadequate acknowledgment of the boulder of grief that weighed on my heart, but I forced myself to keep my shoulders straight, and my face impassive. The general straightened, His gaze sharpened, and his tone shifted, "We have received troubling reports from the Imperial High Command. There's word from the scouts that a Wintmorian garrison is fortifying its position here, roughly two days' march from our current location. If they're allowed to strengthen further, they'll sever our supply lines and force a retreat."

He pointed to a spot on the map, marked with symbols. I stepped closer, my eyes tracing the lines and symbols, trying to focus on the task at hand. "Our mission is to advance toward this garrison and engage the enemy forces. Disrupting their operations is crucial to gaining the upper hand in this region."

Sir Gareth stepped forward, his expression as determined as ever. "Our purpose is clear. We advance at dawn and strike swiftly. There's no room for error."

I leaned over the map, taking in the terrain. Forests and rivers dotted the path to the garrison—natural obstacles that could work for or against us. I took a deep breath, trying to steady myself, and spoke up. "What role shall we play, sire?" I needed something concrete, something to focus on amidst the chaos inside me.

General Aldric's eyes met mine, his voice steady. "You and your band will be part of the vanguard." His eyes rested on my face as if he had reposed all his trust in us.

Edric nodded sharply. "We're ready, sire."

"Very well," General Aldric concluded, his eyes sweeping over us. "Dismissed. Use the remainder of the day to ready yourselves and your brothers. And remember—this battle could turn the tide in our favor. Stay focused."

As we left the tent, Cedric who had been quiet took a deep breath beside me and placed his hand on my back. "Jarin would have told us to stop brooding and get to work," he said quietly,

I nodded, swallowing hard against the lump in my throat. "Then let's make sure his memory isn't wasted. We fight not just for Centralia, but for him as well,"

Edric placed a hand on each of our shoulders, his grip firm. "Let's make sure his sacrifice wasn't in vain,"

Jarin's sacrifice wouldn't be forgotten, and it would fuel us in the battles to come.

***

News of the upcoming battle had spread quickly, and I could see it in the eyes of the soldiers around us—the disquiet, the tenacity, and the understanding that what lay ahead could change everything.

I polished my armor, the rhythmic motion of the cloth against metal almost meditative. With steady strokes of the whetstone, I sharpened my sword, each scrape a reminder of battles fought—and those yet to come. Supplies were inventoried, and every item was scrutinized and inspected to ensure we were ready for what lay ahead.

As evening fell, I found myself standing outside, my gaze drifting toward the distant mountains shrouded in twilight. The cold air stung my cheeks, but I scarcely noticed it. My thoughts were filled with Jarin—his laughter, his stubbornness, the way he always managed to lighten even the darkest moments. We would march into battle and he would not be there to fight by my side.

I reached for the amulet around my neck, feeling its cool surface against my palm. I closed my eyes, took a deep breath, and whispered, "For Centralia, for Jarin, and for those who stand beside me." That night, sleep came fitfully. Dreams of Jarin haunted me, his laughter echoing in the void between memory and loss.

By dawn, I was ready—or as ready as I could be.

***

The morning air was crisp, the sky, a pale blue as the sun began to rise, casting a soft light over the snow-covered landscape. We gathered in the courtyard, alert and ready for the task ahead.

"Our target is two days' march ahead," Sir Gareth called out as he rode along the lines, his voice carrying above the sound of clinking armor, "Fight not only for Centralia but for those we've lost. Let their memory drive you forward." His words struck a chord, and I glanced at Cedric and Edric. We exchanged silent nods, a shared determination in our eyes. General Aldric stood atop a small rise. "We must move swiftly and strike decisively. Stay vigilant; the enemy is cunning and will not hesitate to exploit any weakness." His words were crisp and to the point, and soon enough, we set out.

The crunch of our boots on the snow created a steady rhythm as we departed the fort. I kept my gaze ahead, the vast expanse of white stretching out before us, broken only by clusters of evergreen trees, their branches heavy with snow. A pale gray sky loomed above, the kind that promised no reprieve from the cold. The first day of marching was arduous, the cold unrelenting, seeping into my bones and gnawing relentlessly. Still, I pushed forward, step after step. I wasn't the only one struggling—I could see it in the faces of the men around me—but no one complained. We all knew what was at stake.

As evening approached, the officers selected a place to make camp—a shallow valley sheltered by rocky outcrops. Tents rose quickly and fires crackled to life, a welcome sight in the gathering darkness.

I joined Edric and Cedric around a modest fire, feeling the warmth slowly seep into my frozen limbs. For a while, we simply sat, staring into the fire as though its flicker could chase away more than the cold.

"Feels strange without Jarin," Cedric said eventually, his voice low. He didn't look up, his eyes locked on the flames.

I swallowed, the familiar ache rising in my chest. "He'd have told us this cold was nothing compared to winters back home," I could almost hear him, teasing us for sitting so quietly, urging us to smile despite everything. I forced a thin smile, though it felt brittle.

Edric poked at the fire with a stick, his jaw softening. "He would have kept us talking."

I gazed upward at the emerging stars, feeling the cold night settle around us. "We'll honor him by completing our task," I said quietly, my breath misting in the air. "It's what he would have wanted." The others nodded, their faces solemn in the firelight.

My sleep was shallow that night, I drifted in and out of fleeting dreams, haunted by images of home and Eamon and Jarin's laughter echoing like a ghost.

CHAPTER 24

The second day brought more challenges. The terrain became rugged, the snow deeper and the path less defined. Each step felt heavier, the chill seeping into my bones despite my efforts to keep moving. The officers urged caution; we all knew we were entering contested territory. Scouts were sent ahead, slipping into the distance like shadows, their task to survey the land and warn us of any sign of the enemy.

By midday, we reached the edge of a dense forest—a wall of snow-laden trees and undergrowth stretching across our path. General Aldric decided we would go through it. The alternative would have been to skirt around the forest, adding days to our journey, a risk we couldn't afford. The men hesitated for a moment, glancing at the darkened treeline, but then we moved forward, plunging into the labyrinth of trees.

The deeper we ventured, the more uneasy I felt. The usual sounds of the forest—birds, rustling branches—were absent. It was too quiet, and the silence suffocated me, each crunch of snow beneath my feet echoing like a warning. The shadows between the trees seemed to shift, playing tricks on my eyes, and I tightened my grip on my weapon, my knuckles whitening under the leather gloves.

I felt the green heat from my amulet before I saw any danger. It pulsed with urgency—alive, insistent—but it didn't scald me. A warning. I gasped as the realization struck and darted my eyes around, searching for the danger I knew was lurking. Suddenly, a sharp horn shattered the stillness—the signal from one of our scouts. Tension rippled through the ranks as the column came to an abrupt halt. But I was ready. I steadied my breath, fingers tightening around the hilt of my blade, every muscle taut, waiting for the next move.

Sir Gareth's voice rang out, "Prepare for engagement!" He drew his sword, and the metallic rasp was echoed by hundreds around. My pulse quickened, and my eyes darted from shadow to shadow. Subtle movements caught my attention—figures slipping between the trunks, barely visible, their forms blending with the dim light of the forest. Without warning, a volley of arrows descended upon us, the air filled with the sudden hiss of missiles. "Shields up!" someone shouted, and I raised mine just in time, the impact rattling my arm. The world narrowed to the chaos around me—the clatter of arrows against shields, the cries of men, the thudding of boots on snow as we scrambled for cover. Our archers responded swiftly, loosing arrows toward the unseen enemy, the shafts disappearing into the gloom of the forest.

"Wintmorian scouts!" Edric's voice cut through the noise, shouting from somewhere to my right. "They're trying to slow us down!"

They emerged from the shadows — the Wintmorians—with arrows, daggers, and heavy axes, they moved like apparitions, blending seamlessly with the trunks and brush of the landscape. They looked half-clad, their coverings stitched together from scraps of leather and roughspun cloth, frayed at the edges, and riddled with patched tears. Their faces were rigid with fury, marred by ugly, jagged scars, or perhaps, strange markings, drawn into their cheeks and foreheads. The lines were crude and uneven, as though marked in haste or in anger.

I found myself in the middle of the chaos as they engaged us in close combat. The clash of steel echoed through the forest. Every muscle in my body wound tight as I took in my surroundings.

"Push them back!" Sir Gareth's voice rang out above the ruckus. "We must break through!" His command drove through the fog of battle, giving me a direction to channel the fire raging in my veins.

The once serene forest erupted into a battleground. The blanket of snow that had covered the ground was now marred by footprints and blood, the serenity shattered by the violence of conflict. The air was thick with the clamor of clashing steel, the twang of bowstrings, and the cries of men locked in battle. Shadows flickered among the trees, the muted overcast light only adding to the eeriness of the scene.

My fingers wrapped around the hilt, my knuckles pulsating in readiness. My lungs burned with each gulp of frigid air, my breaths quick and shallow. Ahead of me, a Wintmorian scout emerged from behind a snow-laden pine, his eyes narrowing beneath the rim of a battered helm adorned with a strip of fur. A jolt shot through my chest as blood roared in my ears as I locked eyes with him.

The scout lunged at me with surprising speed, his axe swinging in a deadly arc toward my midsection. I sidestepped just in time, feeling the rush of air as the blade whistled past my armor.

I turned the movement into an attack of my own, bringing my sword up in a swift upward slash aimed at his exposed side.

He twisted his body, deflecting my blow with the haft of his axe. The clash of metal rang out, reverberating through my arm, and we circled each other, wary and tense, the screams of men and the sharp acrid smell of blood hanging heavy in the air. His eyes locked on mine, and I could see the predator's gleam in them—he was testing me, looking for a weakness. Around us, the battle raged on. I caught a glimpse of Edric, his shield raised as he fought off two assailants, his spear jabbing out to keep them at bay. Cedric was further back, moving with a fluid grace firing arrow after arrow from his bow, each shot finding its mark with deadly precision. We were all scattered, but we were holding our own.

The scout feinted to the left, then attacked from the right, his axe coming down in a brutal overhead chop. I barely managed to raise my shield in time, the impact jarring my entire frame and forcing me to stagger back. A sharp ache seared up my arm, spreading like wildfire to my shoulder but I held firm, gritting my teeth against the force of it.

"Look around you, boy," the scout snarled, his strange accent thick with disdain. "The earth here drinks blood – and yours is the next."

I didn't reply. I couldn't afford to waste my breath on words. I focused on his stance—the way his left foot was positioned slightly ahead, his weight uneven. Feigning a stumble, I drew him in, letting him think he had me on the ropes. He took the bait, surging forward with confidence.

At the last moment, I pivoted on my back foot, swinging my sword in a low arc. The blade sliced through the leather of his boot, biting into flesh. He yelped, his leg giving way beneath him, and I seized the advantage. I stepped forward, delivering a swift strike to his weapon arm, feeling the edge of my sword cut deep. The axe fell from his hand, landing with a soft thud in the snow.

"Yield," I commanded, my sword leveled at his throat. My chest heaved as I looked into his eyes hoping he would surrender. But instead, his eyes flashed with defiance, and he spat out his final words, "I'll never yield to your ugly Centralian blood."

I didn't hesitate. I slashed my blade across his throat, and he crumpled to the ground, the light fading from his eyes. I swallowed the bile that rose to my throat and turned away. Moving through the fray with precision, I cut them down, scantily clad skirmishers with scarred faces, their armor no match for the sharpness of my blade. A sudden movement caught my eye. Another Wintmorian leaped from the underbrush and landed before me. He towered above me, his muscles rippling through the frayed ends of his fabric. His eyes were cold and merciless, peering at me like twin daggers. His gauntlets, almost as large as shields, clenched around a massive dagger, the blade gleaming with malice. For a few moments, we stared at each other, and then, a wry smile crept to the corners of his mouth as he approached me with deliberate slowness.

"I knew it was you!" his said his face ugly and filled with rage.

"What?"

"You have the nerve, to show your face again after what happened at Briarwick."

His voice was scratchy, like one with a bad cold.

"Briarwick? What are you saying?"

"Do not be coy with me Eamon!" he snarled and circled me like prey, "You changed your hair to be darker and shaved your beard, but I know that face. The same face that watched us burn? The one that betrayed our secrets to the enemy! We have control of Briarwick. It's still a wasteland, the underbelly of Wintmore, but it's ours. Your plans did not work for long." He flashed brown, decayed teeth.

My brow furrowed in confusion. *Eamon?*

Around me, cries of battle seemed like a disturbance, whirling my head as I tried to make sense of his words. I had never met with the Wintmorians soldiers nor had anything to do with his likes. It didn't make sense he was talking about Eamon? My brother?

"I'm not Eamon," my voice quaked, "Eamon is my brother. Tell me where he is! Where is my brother…?"

"Your brother?" he spat. "Whatever lies you need to sleep at night, spy."

"I am not Eamon…"

"You shall answer for Briarwick…"

He charged at me from the side, with the dagger raised, his eyes set with murderous intent. Time seemed to slow. Confusion clouded my mind and I knew I couldn't raise my shield in time. I braced myself, preparing for the impact.

Then, an arrow zipped past, so close it stirred the hair by my ear, and found its mark in the attacker's neck. The Wintmorian stumbled, the dagger slipping from his grasp as he fell into the snow. I exhaled sharply and glanced back.

Cedric stood there, lowering his bow, a grim smile on his face. "Watch out, brother," he called out, his voice carrying a note of relief.

"He knew Eamon. He knew Eamon," I muttered under my breath, but Cedric had already turned away, sending another arrow whistling through the air toward its mark.

I got on my knees and pulled the Wintmorian until he was resting his back on the bark of a tree.

"When was the last time you saw Eamon? Is he still in Briarwick?" His unfocused eyes lolled back as blood trailed from his mouth. He jerked, and then he was still.

I shook him hard as if to wrench him back from death.

"Is my brother safe? Is Eamon alive?"

Only silence answered.

I looked around dazed. The clash of steel and the cries of the wounded blended with the thunder of hooves and the hiss of arrows. I stumbled over a broken shield, my breath shallow as I turned in every direction, searching for clarity amidst the chaos. Had Eamon been in Wintmore all these months as a spy? Faces blurred—friend and foe alike—and the canopy of trees and brushes spun with relentless, dizzying intensity. My thoughts were tangled and my pulse pounded in my head. Like the forge fire, the green heat burned in my chest, and every sound seemed to be Eamon's, calling my name, yet I couldn't tell where to turn. It was as if the very air conspired to disorient me.

"Kaelan! Behind you!" I heard Edric's voice, sharp and urgent, cutting through the maze in my mind.

Instinct took over. I spun just in time to see a Wintmorian bearing down on me, a heavy mace raised above his head. There was no time to think—I raised my shield and the mace came down with a bone-rattling crash, splintering the wood and sending a tremor up my arm. The force of it nearly knocked me off my feet, and my shoulder throbbed under the blow. The jolt reverberated through my frame as I fought to stay upright.

The Wintmorian's eyes were locked on mine, a cruel smile tugging at his lips. I swung my sword in a wide, defensive arc. He dodged easily, his mace already swinging around for another strike. I ducked, feeling the rush of air as the weapon whistled just above my head. There was no time to think, only to act. I stepped forward, slipping inside his guard, and drove my shoulder into his chest with all the force I could muster.

We collided heavily, and the impact sent a jolt through my body. I used the force to thrust my sword upward, aiming for the vulnerable spot I'd glimpsed beneath his arm. The blade found its mark, piercing the seam of his armor, my blade streaming with crimson and I could feel his heartbeat through the blade. For a fleeting moment, surprise flashed across the man's face, his eyes wide with disbelief. Then he stumbled back, his body going limp as he crumpled to the ground.

I dragged air into my lungs, each breath cutting like icy daggers. Then, I took a moment to survey the battlefield. The Centralian soldiers pressed the attack, forcing the Wintmorian scouts to retreat. I could see Sir Gareth riding through the chaos, his sword flashing as he directed our troops, his voice carrying above the noise.

"Regroup! Hold the line!" he commanded.

I pushed forward, joining Edric and Cedric. They were both still in the thick of it—Edric with his spear, using it to keep the enemy at bay, and Cedric switching deftly between his bow and short sword, depending on what the moment demanded. I felt a surge of relief at seeing them both still standing, still fighting.

"Are you injured?" Edric asked as he glanced my way, his eyes taking in the damage to my shield and the blood staining my side.

"Just bruised," I assured him, though I could already feel the aches settling in, promising to make themselves known later.

A horn sounded from within the forest—a long, low note that seemed to reverberate through the trees. It was a signal to retreat. The Wintmorian scouts began to pull back, slipping away into the shadows of the forest with practiced ease. A few archers loosed arrows to cover their withdrawal, but it was a half-hearted effort, more for show than with any real intent. I longed to follow them, to inquire about my brother, but I knew it would be of no use.

"Don't pursue!" Sir Gareth's voice cut through the air as if he had read my mind. "Maintain formation!"

We held our ground, weapons ready, watching as the Wintmorians disappeared into the treeline. The forest seemed to grow quiet again, the sudden absence of battle almost disorienting. All I could hear was the labored breathing of the men around me, the distant cawing of crows drawn by the scent of blood, and the throbbing of my own beating heart.

What have you done, Eamon?

***

"Is it over?" Cedric asked, his voice cautious, his eyes sweeping through the trees for any sign of movement.

"For now," Edric replied, though he didn't lower his guard. None of us did. Sir Gareth approached his expression stern but with a hint of approval in his eyes. "Well fought," he said, his gaze passing over each of us. "They sought to delay us, but we've held firm."

I nodded, wiping the sweat and melted snow from my brow. "They were determined," I said, my voice rough from exertion. I tried to put Eamon out of my mind and face the present, "These weren't just scouts, sir—they fought like seasoned warriors."

"Agreed," Sir Gareth said, a frown tugging at his brow. "Which means they know we're coming and are preparing."

My mind drifted again. Eamon, a spy? And for our Army? What happened with the Crimson Merchants? With all the talk of trade. Just trade. And I had believed him. Ma and Pa had believed him too. Now, I was left to piece it all together from fragments of different stories, chasing shadows while he risked his life doing gods-know-what!

And yet. I couldn't shake the pride bubbling beneath the anger. Eamon, the dreamer, the reckless fool, taking on a risk like this. By gods! It was deadly and foolish. But it meant something. He meant something to this war!

Still, anxious thoughts twisted my guts. Was he still in Wintmore? If they found him…I couldn't let my mind go there.

I watched as the men regrouped, and took a moment to inspect my damaged shield. The wood was splintered, barely holding together, but it would still serve its purpose. I adjusted the straps, flexing my fingers to get some feeling back into them. The heat had seeped out of the amulet, and I could feel the pendant, cool once more, dangling around my neck.

"Here," Cedric said, appearing at my side and handing me a flask. "It's not much, but it'll help."

I accepted it gratefully, taking a swig of the strong liquor. It burned its way down, spreading warmth through my chest, and I let out a breath. "Thank you, my friend. Im in your debt," I said, handing it back to him.

He waved his hands dismissively, "It's just a flask, Kaelan, not a treasure chest."

"For saving my life out there."

"Well, someone has to keep your stubborn neck intact, right? Can't have you running off to meet death before I get to annoy you a little longer, can I?"

I grinned, but I knew it didn't quite reach my eyes.

"That Wintmorian. He knew Eamon."

"He did? How so?"

I didn't know how much I should say when I knew so little. Eric approached. He was nearby, cleaning his spear. Now, he came closer, his eyes darting around the forest as he worked. "They'll be waiting for us now," he said, his tone thoughtful. "We should expect a tougher fight ahead."

"We must get ready. We have come this far." I replied, meeting his gaze.

"Are you well? You look like what death vomited."

"I'm fine. Come, let's go. "

We resumed our formation, moving cautiously through the remainder of the forest. Scouts were sent ahead in greater numbers, and flanking units spread out to watch for any sign of ambush. Each rustle of the wind and each shadow between the trees seemed like a threat. We were on our way to the Wintmorian fortress. If I got to the fortress…when I got to the fortress, I would find a way to enter the heart of Briarwick, find Eamon, and take him home.

***

We finally emerged from the treeline, the landscape opened into rolling hills blanketed in snow. My breath caught in my throat as my eyes lifted to the sight before us. In the distance, the Wintmorian garrison loomed—a fortress of stone perched atop a rocky outcrop, its flags bearing the enemy's emblem fluttering defiantly in the wind.

CHAPTER 25

The stronghold was imposing, its high walls and towers standing like sentinels, commanding a view of the surrounding terrain. Smoke rose from within, a sign that a sizable force waited for us behind those walls; and the fortress itself seemed to taunt us with its defiance.

"This won't be easy," Cedric said beside me, his gaze fixed on the fortress, "No," I agreed, my eyes narrowing as I studied the stone walls. "But we know what's at stake." I gazed at him, my voice firm. "And we fight for more than just ourselves."

I fight for Centralia.

I fight for Eamon.

I fight for Ma and Pa.

I fight for my brothers, and for Jarin.

As we set up camp under the looming shadow of the fortress, the silent night carried with it the distant sound of drums from within the enemy walls. The rhythmic beat seemed as if the enemy was issuing a challenge, daring us to come and face them. I clenched my jaw, the sound echoing in my ears. Dusk settled over the snow-covered hills, the light fading into a deep, chilling blue as the Centralian army made camp within sight of the Wintmorian garrison.

The fortress loomed in the distance, its stone walls bathed in the orange glow of torches and braziers. The air was crisp and biting, each breath forming a fleeting cloud before disappearing into the darkness. Around me, the sounds of hammers and saws echoed softly as the soldiers worked diligently, preparing for the battle to come.

I stood on a small rise overlooking the camp and surveyed the organized chaos below: tents being erected, supply wagons being unloaded, and soldiers tending to their equipment. The atmosphere was tense; the men's faces showed it, and their movements, urgent yet purposeful, reflected it in every action.

"Deep in thought?" Edric's voice pulled me back from my reverie. He approached in slow, deliberate strides as he came to stand beside me.

I nodded, my gaze fixed on the distant fortress. Its walls loomed over the landscape. "That garrison won't be easy to take," I said quietly.

"True," Edric agreed, following my line of sight "But we've faced challenges before."

A faint smile curled my lips. He was right—we'd endured trials that would have broken lesser souls. Cedric joined us, carrying a quiver of arrows slung over his shoulder.

"The officers are gathering for a war council," he said, his voice breaking through the tension. "Sir Gareth asked us to attend."

I raised an eyebrow, a flicker of surprise crossing my face. "Us? I thought such meetings were meant for those of higher rank."

"Seems they value our prowess after that skirmish," Cedric replied with a slight smile. There was a hint of pride in his voice, and I couldn't help but feel a swell of it myself. "Come on, we'd best not keep them waiting."

We made our way to the central command tent, its entrance guarded by two sentries who nodded respectfully as we passed. The robust heat from a brazier kept the tent warm. The atmosphere was thick with suspense. The officers gathered around a large table, their eyes focused on the detailed map spread across it.

General Aldric stood at the head of the table. Around him were several principal officers, including Sir Gareth and Captain Maren. A warmth spread through me, and I walked taller with pride as I went to join the men. "Gentlemen," General Aldric began, "Our scouts have returned with news of the enemy's defenses." He gestured to the map, where markers indicated the garrison's layout. "The fortress is well-fortified, with towering walls and few means of entry. Their gates are strengthened, and engines of war line the battlements. However, their numbers are fewer than ours, and we hold the advantage of swift progress."

Captain Maren stepped forward, his finger tracing a path on the map. "Their weakest point is here," he pointed to the eastern wall. "It's less defended, for they deem the steep terrain impassable. With a skilled company, we could scale it and strike from within, catching them unawares." I narrowed my eyes as I studied the map. The eastern wall towered into the sky, its slippery stones jagged and weathered by time.

"A perilous venture," Sir Gareth remarked, "but one that could turn the tide in our favor should it be carried out with precision."

I exchanged glances with Edric and Cedric. We had faced danger before, and this was no different. Before I could say a word, Edric stepped forward. "We volunteer for the task."

The room fell silent, all eyes turning to us. General Aldric studied us for a moment, his gaze weighing our words. "Your bravery is noted," he said finally, "but this task requires meticulous preparation and capable hands."

I stepped forward, though I felt my pulse quicken. "With respect, sir, we've traversed difficult terrain before and have proven our worth. Allow us the opportunity to contribute in a meaningful way."

The general considered my words. The gravity of the decision enveloped everyone, and I held my breath, waiting. Finally, he nodded. "Very well. Sir Gareth, gather a group of our most capable soldiers. Kaelan, Edric, Cedric—you will be part of this band."

"Thank you, sir," we replied in unison.

"Now, to the broader strategy," General Aldric continued, his gaze sweeping over the assembled officers. "While the assault party infiltrates the eastern wall, our main forces will mount a frontal assault to draw their focus. Archers will provide covering fire, targeting their engines and defenders on the walls. Siege weapons are being prepared to breach the gates should the need arise."

Captain Maren stepped forward, his expression severe. "Timing will be critical," he said, pointing to the map. "The warriors must be arrayed by first light. Once we receive a signal—a flare from within the fortress—we will commence the frontal assault."

The chamber hummed with final preparations as tasks were assigned, maps unfurled, and fallback strategies established.

When the council was adjourned, Edric, Cedric, and I conferred with Sir Gareth to deliberate on the details of our tasks. I could see the concern in Sir Gareth's eyes, though his voice was steady as he addressed us.

"You'll move under the cover of darkness," he said more than once. "Silence and stealth are paramount. The climb will be treacherous—ice and snow will make your footing uncertain."

He handed each of us hooks and coils of sturdy rope. "Take these to ascend the wall. Once inside, your charge is to see that the gate workings are undone, and open the fortress to our forces."

Cedric examined the equipment, his brow furrowed. "What about enemy sentinels within the fortress?" he asked.

"There will be some," Sir Gareth acknowledged, his gaze shifting to Cedric. "But their numbers should be limited on that side. Avoid engagement if possible. Speed is your ally."

Edric nodded, his jaw set. "Understood, sir. We won't let you down."

Sir Gareth's eyes softened slightly, and he placed a hand on my shoulder. "I have faith in you all," he said quietly. "Return safely." His words sounded like a warning, or perhaps, a plea.

I checked my gear meticulously—my sword was sharp, my armor secure, and every strap and buckle was in place. I checked my amulet. It was cool on my chest; I knew it had followed me to this battle, a silent companion in my journey. I wondered whether it could direct my path to the road that led to Eamon; whether it could protect Eamon as it had protected me.

"Ready?" Edric's voice cut through my thoughts, and I looked up to see him adjusting his cloak, making sure it would blend with the shadows.

I nodded, taking a deep breath. "Ready."

We joined the rest of the assault party—a group of ten seasoned soldiers known for their agility and composure under pressure. I knew most of them, I had sat with them round a hearth and drunk gourds of ale, while they laughed and told loud stories. Now, their faces were grim, eyes focused as they moved with quiet precision. We set out from the camp, moving silently across the snowy landscape. The night was moonless and the stars had hidden behind a thick veil of clouds, shrouding us in darkness.

Ahead, the fortress loomed, a looming figure outlined faintly against the sky. The torches along the battlements cast a slight glow that barely reached the ground below. Their flickering light seemed like a warning not to approach.

We crouched closer, grateful for the darkness. We stopped at the base of the eastern wall and looked up at the daunting height before us. The wall loomed above, slick with ice and almost covered in snow. My stomach clenched at the sight—it looked more difficult than I'd anticipated. "Remember, no noise," Marcus, our leader, whispered. He was a quiet man, his voice barely audible over the wind. "We climb single file. Secure your holds and test every step."

"Yes, Sir."

One by one, we launched our grappling hooks. The soft clink of metal against stone seemed impossibly loud in the silence of the night. I watched as my hook found purchase, the claws gripping the stone tightly. I gave the rope a testing tug, feeling it hold firm. It was time.

I started my ascent, feeling the strain in my muscles almost immediately as I pulled myself upward. My boots searched for footholds on the uneven surface, each step a careful, deliberate movement. The wind picked up, a frigid gust that threatened to unbalance me, and I pressed myself closer to the wall, focusing on my breathing—steady, controlled. One step at a time, I told myself. Keep moving.

About halfway up, I heard a soft noise below me—a muffled curse. I glanced down just as Cedric slipped, the foothold he'd trusted crumbling beneath him. The rope jerked violently as he scrambled, his hands clutching for anything to stop the fall. I froze, gripping the rope like a lifeline, my pulse thundering in my ears. His legs flailed about for a few precious moments, then, he suddenly got a foothold and hoisted himself up on another sleek stone.

"You all right?" I mouthed, my eyes locking with his.

Cedric grunted, his knuckles white as he clung to the rope. I waited until I saw him steady himself before continuing the climb, my heart still hammering in my chest.

Reaching the battlements, Marcus quickly peeked over the edge, his eyes scanning for any sign of movement. After a tense moment, he signaled us to join him. I hauled myself over the top and dropped onto the stone. We moved swiftly and silently, dropping down into the shadows of an inner courtyard.

The sounds of the fortress at night were minimal—a few guards chatting near a fire, the distant clatter of cookware from the kitchens, and the ever-present howl of the wind. The atmosphere was tense, every noise amplified in the stillness. We split into smaller groups to cover more ground. Edric, Cedric, and I moved toward the gate mechanism, sticking close to the walls and avoiding open spaces. The structure was unfamiliar but navigable, with corridors and archways leading us closer to our objective.

As we turned a corner, we bumped into a lone guard patrolling the area. My heart leaped into my throat as the guard's eyes widened, his mouth opening to shout an alarm. It was but a moment. Before he could make a sound, Edric clamped his hand down over the guard's mouth with the swiftness of an eagle clamping on prey. Without hesitation, I stepped forward and delivered a swift blow to the back of his head. The guard went limp, and we caught him before he could fall too heavily.

We dragged the unconscious guard into a dark alcove, working quickly to bind and gag him.

"That was too close," Cedric whispered, his eyes searching the darkness for any other threats.

"Shhh," I cautioned, and he gave a little nod. We reached the gatehouse, a sturdy building that housed the devices controlling the fortress's main gate. Two guards stood at the entrance, their weapons at their sides, unaware of our presence. Marcus joined us, his eyes assessing the situation. He gestured for two of our archers to ready their bows.

I watched as they drew their arrows, the pressure palpable. The arrows flew, and the guards collapsed without a sound, their bodies crumpling to the ground. Moving quickly, we entered the gatehouse. The air inside was heavy with the scent of oil and metal, gears and levers dominating the space—the heart of the fortress's defenses. Another guard was there, his nose buried in a ledger, oblivious to our presence until it was too late. He looked up, his eyes widening in shock, but before he could react, Marcus was on him, silencing him swiftly.

"Secure the area," Marcus ordered. "Kaelan, you and Cedric handle the mechanism. Edric, watch the corridor."

I stealthily moved to the controls, and my heart pounded as I examined the array of gears and levers. "Disengage the locking pins and release the counterweights," My voice didn't sound like mine, but. Cedric nodded, his eyes meeting mine for a brief moment before we set to our task.

The levers were heavy, each one resisting our efforts, but we pushed on. The machinery groaned in protest, the metal grinding against itself, but slowly, it began to move. I could feel the vibrations under my hands as the gears turned, and the distant rumbling echoing through the walls, signaling that the gates were opening. My heart lifted—it was working.

"Give the signal," Marcus said, his eyes flicking to one of the soldiers. The man needed no more words. He immediately drew his bow and fired a flare arrow into the sky. It burst into a bright red bloom, illuminating the night briefly before fading into darkness.

Outside the fortress, I knew General Aldric saw the flare. I could almost picture him giving the command. "Advance!" The Centralian forces would move forward, siege engines rolling, archers readying their bows.

The frontal assault had begun.

CHAPTER 26

The alarms blared.

The defenders had realized the gates were compromised, and chaos erupted around us as soldiers scrambled to respond. Marcus's eyes met mine. "Time to go," he declared.

We dispersed, each of us seeking to sow confusion and chaos wherever we could. I set fires to supply carts, the flames licking hungrily at the wood and sending thick smoke billowing into the air. I could hear Edric and Cedric nearby, cutting bowstrings, their blades slicing through the taut cords with swift efficiency. The sound of horses whinnying filled the air as we opened the pens, the animals bolting into the courtyards, causing more disarray.

I turned a corner and came to an abrupt halt. A Wintmorian soldier stood there, his eyes narrowing as he saw me. Before I could think, he lunged. His sword arced toward my chest in a blur. I barely raised my blade in time, the clash of steel jolting through my bones. Sparks flew. A breathless moment of silence followed as we regarded each other, my amulet burning hot on my chest.

Then, chaos. His strikes came fast—one, two, three—each forcing me to retreat, each testing the strength in my arms. My parry faltered. The next blow grazed my shoulder. Pain flared in me sharp and hot. I gritted my teeth and struck back, mindlessly slashing upward in a desperate arc.

He staggered. Blood seeped through the gap in his armor, dark and spreading. His sword slipped from his grasp, dropping unceremoniously to the ground. He gasped and crumpled to the ground as his blood pooled around him.

I exhaled heavily, wiping my blade against my tunic. I cast my gaze around and rejoined Edric and Cedric. We moved together, fighting our way toward the main courtyard. The gates were now fully open, and Centralian troops poured in, the clash of battle echoing throughout the fortress. Sir Gareth led the contingent, his sword held high.

"Press forward! Secure the battlements!" he commanded, his voice cutting through the clamor of battle like a clarion call. The Centralian soldiers surged ahead, their spirits ignited by the force of our initial success.

The fortress courtyard had become a maelstrom of combat, shadows flickering under the blaze of torches and the pale light of dawn creeping over the horizon. I found myself at the forefront of the charge, my heart pounding in rhythm with the thundering footsteps around me. The amulet blazed, guiding my hands, propelling me forward, guiding my war dance.

The Wintmorian defenders regrouped, rallying atop the stone stairways that led to the battlements. I could see them gathering, their archers already positioned along the ramparts, unleashing arrows into the chaos below. The deadly shafts whistled through the air, and I heard the cry of a soldier beside me.

He gasped and fell to the ground, an arrow jutting from his shoulder, his face twisted in pain.

"Shields up," I shouted, my voice hoarse and raspy. I raised my own shield, creating a protective barrier, and others followed my lead. We moved together, advancing toward the staircases, our shields forming a makeshift wall. The constant drumbeat of arrows thudded against our shields, but we held firm. Sounds of arrows thudding against the wood was a constant drumbeat.

Edric moved beside me, his spear poised and ready. "We need to take out those archers, or we'll be pinned down!" he yelled over the din of battle.

I glanced back. "Cedric, can you provide cover?"

Cedric, a few paces behind us, nodded without hesitation. He nocked an arrow to his bow, his eyes narrowing in concentration. He drew the string back to his cheek, his movements flawless. I watched as he released, the arrow arcing gracefully through the air. It found its mark in one of the enemy archers, who toppled backward out of sight.

"One less to worry about," Cedric remarked, already reaching for another arrow.

"Go on!" Sir Gareth's voice rang out. I saw him slice through an opposing soldier's defense with practiced ease, the man's sword clattering to the ground as he stumbled. Sir Gareth pressed on, not missing a beat, his presence rallying those around him.

We reached the base of the stairs, and Edric and I led the ascent. The stone steps were slick with ice and scattered debris, each foothold dangerous. As we climbed, a Wintmorian defender lunged toward us, wielding a halberd with a wickedly curved blade. I raised my sword just in time, parrying the initial strike. The defender was strong, his stance wide and grounded, his eyes locked on mine.

Edric thrust his spear toward the man's midsection, forcing him to pivot and momentarily lose his balance. Seizing the opportunity, I stepped inside his guard, my body moving on instinct. With a swift upward slash, I caught him under the arm where his armor was weakest. He groaned, his weapon slipping from his grasp as he fell onto the steps.

"Keep moving," I urged, aware of the press of soldiers behind us, the urgency of our mission driving me forward.

We emerged onto the battlements—a narrow walkway atop the fortress walls, lined with crenellations that provided both cover and a vantage point. The view from this height was dizzying; the fortress grounds sprawled below, a conflict with pockets of skirmishes erupting like sparks from a fire.

Wintmorian archers repositioned, some drawing swords as the close-quarters fight reached them. I barely had time to take in the scene before a trio of enemy soldiers advanced toward us, their eyes steely with fury. The leader, a broad-shouldered man, wielded a longsword, its blade catching the gleam of torchlight. Without hesitation, he charged, his weapon coming down in a powerful overhead strike aimed at me.

I sidestepped, feeling the rush of air as the sword grazed past my shoulder. The closeness of it made my heart skip a beat, but I countered with a horizontal slash aimed at his midriff. He parried deftly, sparks flying as our blades met. We exchanged a rapid series of blows—thrust, parry, feint, riposte—our footwork a deadly dance atop the battlements. Each clash of steel sent a shock up my arms, the strain beginning to wear on me.

Beside me, Edric was engaged with the other two soldiers. He deflected a thrust with the shaft of his spear, then spun it with precision, delivering a swift strike to one man's knee. The soldier buckled, and Edric followed with a precise jab to incapacitate him. The remaining opponent pressed Edric hard, their weapons clashing in a fierce exchange of blows.

My duel intensified, the Wintmorian before me proving to be a skilled opponent. He matched me strike for strike, his eyes cold and focused. He feinted to the left, then lunged to the right, the tip of his blade aiming for my side. I saw the move coming, and I pivoted sharply, his sword slicing through empty air.

Seizing the moment, I drove forward with my shoulder, catching him off guard. The impact forced him backward, his back colliding with the parapet. I didn't hesitate. I brought my sword up, the point resting just beneath his chin.

"Yield," I commanded, my voice firm, my sword point unwavering beneath his chin. His eyes flickered momentarily with defiance, his jaw clenched, but the realization of his precarious position sank in. Slowly, he nodded, lowering his weapon, the tension in his body easing. I took a step back, keeping my gaze locked on him, ready for any sudden movements. He hesitated, then started to run, his eyes never leaving mine until he disappeared into the chaos of the battlements.

I turned, searching for Edric. He was just a few paces away, dispatching the last of his opponents. His spear jabbed into the man's side, and from where I stood, I slashed at him with my sword, sending him toppling to the ground. Edric's breathing was heavy but controlled, and he gave me a terse nod.

"Thanks," he said, his voice rough. "I had it under control, but backup is always appreciated." Before I could respond, an explosion shattered the air sending us staggering. I caught myself against the cold stone, my ears ringing from the blast. We looked toward the source. It was a section of the fortress wall where Centralian soldiers had detonated barrels of gunpowder. Stones tumbled down in a cloud of dust and debris, and I watched as our soldiers poured through the breach, their battle cries rising above the cacophony.

"Reinforcements are in," I observed, feeling a surge of hope amidst the chaos. "We need to secure the towers."

Just then, Cedric appeared, having ascended another staircase. He moved with the quiet grace that seemed second nature to him, his eyes sharp and focused. "Archers are still targeting our men from the northern tower," he reported. "We need to take it out."

I agreed.

We navigated the battlements, ducking under stray arrows and leaping over fallen stones and debris. The northern tower loomed ahead—a cylindrical structure with narrow windows and a conical roof. It seemed to rise endlessly against the darkened sky, with the torches flickering along its height casting long shadows. As we approached the entrance, a portly Wintmorian sergeant stepped into our path, flanked by two guards.

"You'll go no further!" the sergeant bellowed, swinging a hefty mace with surprising agility for a man of his size.

I met the sergeant's charge, and our weapons clashed with a resonant force. He was strong, far stronger than I'd anticipated, and each swing of his mace threatened to shatter my defenses. I focused on my footing, dodging his heavy blows, and looking for any sign of weakness, any opening I could exploit.

Beside me, Edric and Cedric engaged the two guards. I could hear the grunts of effort and the clash of steel. Edric parried a sword thrust, his spear spinning in his hands before he delivered a swift kick that sent his opponent reeling. Cedric moved in close, his dagger flashing as he slashed at the guard's arm, disarming him.

The sergeant pressed his attack, his mace a blur as he swung it with deadly intent. I backed up, my feet slipping slightly on the icy stones. The edge of the battlement was just behind me, and my heart lurched as I felt the void at my back. With a fierce overhead swing, the sergeant aimed to end it decisively. I dropped to one knee, the mace whistling past my head and smashing into the stone merlon behind me, chipping off fragments that sprayed around us.

Seizing the opportunity, I lunged forward from my crouched position. My shoulder connected with the sergeant's midsection, and the force of it unbalanced him. He stumbled. I rose swiftly, bringing my sword down in a precise strike to the back of his knee. He roared in pain as he fell to one leg, his voice echoing across the battlements.

"You're tenacious, I'll grant you that," he growled, his face twisted in pain as he tried to rise again.

"It's over," I stated, my sword poised at his throat. My breath came in ragged bursts, my arms trembling with the effort of holding my blade steady.

The sergeant's eyes flickered with a mix of anger and resignation. He exhaled sharply, the fight leaving him. "Do what you must," he spat, his voice filled with bitterness.

I hesitated for a heartbeat, then struck him on the temple with the pommel of my sword, watching as his eyes rolled back and he slumped to the ground, unconscious. "No need for unnecessary bloodshed," I muttered under my breath, stepping back.

With the entrance clear, we rushed into the tower. The spiral staircase was dimly lit by flickering torches, their shadows dancing on the worn walls. Above, shouted commands, the scuffle of boots, and the snap of bowstrings echoed down the narrow shaft.

"Quickly, before they realize we're here," Cedric urged, his voice tight with urgency.

We ascended the stairs, our boots pounding against the stone steps. My heart raced and the cold air searing my lungs as we climbed. At the top, we burst into the chamber where several Wintmorian archers were positioned at narrow windows, their backs to us as they fired on the Centralian forces below. This was our moment.

We charged in, and the archers turned, their faces twisting in surprise, their hands reaching for daggers as close combat became inevitable. I closed the distance to the nearest archer, striking swiftly. My sword struck his wrist, sending his weapon flying. He stumbled back, his eyes wide with fear and shock.

Edric engaged another archer to my right, their blades clashing in the confined space of the tower. The archer was nimble, darting, and weaving, but Edric's strength and reach gave him the edge. He pressed the attack, his strikes measured and powerful until a well-placed blow knocked the weapon from the archer's hand. The man raised his hands in surrender, resignation clouding his eyes.

Cedric, even in these close quarters, favored his bow. He nocked an arrow with practiced ease, drawing and loosing it in one fluid motion. The arrow flew true, finding its mark in the shoulder of an archer who had aimed at me. The man cried out and fell over. I shot Cedric a grateful look, nodding in silent thanks.

"Secure them," I ordered. We moved quickly, binding the captives with strips of cloth torn from banners that adorned the room. The Wintmorian captives glared at us, but there was no fight left in their eyes.

With the tower under our control, Cedric strode to one of the narrow windows, his gaze sweeping over the tumult below. "Let's turn the tables," he said, drawing an arrow with grim satisfaction. One by one, his arrows flew, each shot precise and deliberate. I watched as each arrow disrupted the enemy formations, providing cover for our Centralian troops advancing through the fortress grounds. The sight of our soldiers pushing forward filled me with hope. We were turning the tide.

Edric and I stood beside Cedric, scanning the battlefield from our elevated vantage point. The fortress seethed with a tangled, erratic motion —soldiers clashing in the courtyards, siege engines battering the gates and flags changing hands as positions were overrun. The sounds of battle—the cries of men, the clash of steel, the dull thud of battering rams—filled the air, a cacophony of war that seemed almost surreal from this height. For a fleeting moment, I thought I saw Eamon, with his wild red hair and long arms. I squinted and peered into the maze of soldiers below, but the moment was gone.

"Look there," Edric said, pointing toward the central keep. I followed his gaze and saw a concentrated group of Wintmorian soldiers forming a defensive line at the entrance to the keep. They were determined to hold their ground, their stance defiant even as the battle raged around them. At the forefront of our forces, I saw Sir Gareth, his sword flashing as he led the charge. His presence was unmistakable.

"We can't stay up here while our comrades bleed below," I said, my voice charged with fervent energy We descended the tower with haste, our footsteps echoing off the stone as we navigated the battlements to reach the courtyard below. The wind whipped at my face, the cold biting into my skin, but I barely felt it. My focus was on the battle ahead, on the clash that awaited us at the keep's entrance.

As we neared, the sound of combat grew louder. I gripped my sword as we moved into the fray. The Wintmorians were making their stand but we were determined to break them.

The clash at the keep's entrance was fierce, bodies pressing against each other in a desperate struggle.

I plunged in, parrying a strike from a Wintmorian swordsman. His face was set, his eyes hardened by desperation. We exchanged blow after blow, the clash of our swords lost in the chaos that surrounded us. My heart pounded in my chest, each strike sending vibrations up my arm, but I pushed through, my focus narrowed to this one opponent.

The swordsman feinted high, then swept low, his intent betrayed by a shift in his stance. I sidestepped and countered, driving him back. He staggered, his face contorting in pain, and I knew this was my chance. I pressed the advantage, stepping forward and delivering a calculated strike that knocked the sword from his grasp striking him in his chest.

Nearby, Edric and Cedric fought side by side, Edric's spear kept opponents at bay with measured precision, while Cedric darted in and out, striking with deadly accuracy. I marveled at the way they moved as if they were one.

Suddenly, a commotion drew my attention to Sir Gareth cutting a line through the Wintmorian line with unmatched skill. He confronted their captain—a tall man with a scar running across his cheek, his eyes reflecting both fatigue and unflinching will.

"Stand down," Sir Gareth demanded, his voice carrying a weight that seemed to still the chaos around us. "Your forces are defeated."

The captain shook his head, a grim smile on his lips. "We may fall, but we will not yield."

Their duel began. Each strike was deliberate, each parry a testament to their skill. The surrounding soldiers paused, their attention drawn to the gravity of the confrontation. I watched intently, every muscle in my body tensed, ready to intervene if necessary. The exchange was swift and brutal, their swords clashing with a ferocity that spoke of the stakes at hand.

Sir Gareth moved with precision, his strikes calculated, his footwork flawless. The Wintmorian captain was a worthy opponent, his defense formidable, but I could see the exhaustion in his movements. They circled each other, their swords a blur of steel, until finally, Sir Gareth saw his opening. With a deft maneuver, he disarmed the captain, the man's sword clattering to the ground.

Breathing heavily, the captain met Sir Gareth's gaze, his chest heaving. "Finish it," he uttered, his voice laced with resignation.

Sir Gareth lowered his sword slightly, his eyes softening. "There is honor in surrender," he said. "Your men need not perish needlessly."

A moment of silence hung between them, the clamor of battle fading into the background as we all held our breath. I watched the captain, his gaze sweeping across the battlefield, taking in the sight of his forces—dwindling, broken, their position untenable. The lines on his face deepened, and with a heavy sigh, he signaled to his remaining soldiers,

"Lay down your arms, men. We have done all we can."

CHAPTER
27

The sun rose early, its golden light spilling over the snowy landscape, and a new sense of calm seemed to settle over the fortress. Its rays illuminated the stone walls, the banners, and the faces of the soldiers who stood—victorious, yet weary. General Aldric moved to the steps of the keep and stood before us.

"Brave soldiers of Centralia," he began, his voice cutting through the cold morning air. "Through your courage and unwavering commitment, we have secured a vital stronghold. This fortress stands now as a testament to our resolve and a beacon of hope in these harsh lands."

A rousing cheer followed, the men buoyed by the general's words.

"Let us honor those who fell today," he continued, "Their sacrifice will not be forgotten. We press on, not just for victory, but for peace."

I looked toward the horizon, where the first rays of sunlight kissed the distant peaks. The light touched me, and the warmth of the amulet against my chest stirred with a quiet heat that felt like home.

We had swiftly secured the prisoners and tended the wounded. Flags bearing Centralia's emblem were raised atop the keep, the deep red and gold fluttering proudly in the wind.

The sounds of the celebration slowly faded as the night wore on. I stood on the keep and watched the morning approach. The soldiers laughed, clapping each other on the back, but I felt distant from it all. They were all lost in the moment, basking in the relief of the battle's end, yet I couldn't shake the feeling that something was amiss. This victory, hard-earned and costly, should have been enough to lift me. But it wasn't. A weight pressed on my chest refusing to ease.

I thought of what lay ahead. There would be no time for rest, no time to savor the triumph. By tomorrow, we'd take stock of our losses, tend to the wounded, and prepare for the next battle. In that moment, the future felt both distant and unbearably close.

Why had I done all this? To find Eamon, the responsibility to protect my family—it all seemed heavier with each passing day. And yet, I couldn't shake the nagging thought that perhaps, in my attempt to preserve what was, I had lost myself in the process. How much of what I did was truly my choice, and how much was driven by duty? Was I just playing a part, or was there something I truly desired beyond the battlefield?

"We did it," Edric said appearing beside me, his gaze following mine.

I smiled. "Aye, we did." The words felt almost surreal as if I needed to say them aloud to truly believe it.

"What's next for us?"

Finding for my brother.

"We rebuild, we fortify, and we prepare," I replied, aloud. "The battles may continue, but so will we."

Cedric nodded, his eyes thoughtful. "And perhaps along the way, we'll find answers to the questions we've carried with us." He cast me a knowing look as if he had read my mind.

I smiled and right there and then, I decided to search for Eamon as soon as it was safe. The decision brought a rare sense of peace.

***

The fortress was ours, and the atmosphere shifted as the fervor of battle gave way to the diligent efforts of securing our hard-won prize. Soldiers moved methodically through the stronghold, attending to their tasks with a renewed sense of purpose. The sun now hung higher in the sky, its warmth melting the lingering frost and casting a golden glow upon the stone walls. Though there was a sense of calm, a moment to breathe, work still remained. I joined a group tasked with reinforcing the main gate. The massive wooden doors had taken a beating during the siege and required immediate attention. Alongside carpenters and engineers, I helped to lift heavy beams into place. My muscles ached from the strain, but the collective effort and the shared determination of everyone around me were invigorating.

"Steady there," called out Master Holt, the keeper of the forge, his voice carrying over the clatter of tools. "We need this secured before nightfall."

"Almost there," I replied, adjusting my grip on the beam. I pushed through, feeling the weight settle into place with a satisfying thud. The beam fit snugly against the iron brackets, and I allowed myself a small smile of satisfaction.

Nearby, Edric attended to the supply stores. He moved fast, his voice ringing out as he directed the soldiers around him.

"Make sure the perishables are moved to the cellar," he instructed, his tone firm but encouraging. "And keep the poultices and healing supplies at hand. We need to be prepared for anything."

I caught his eye, and he gave me a nod. We were building something, contributing to something greater than ourselves.

Cedric, with his sharp eyes and steady hand, had been assigned to the watchtower. From that vantage point, he could survey the landscape for any signs of enemy movement. He was at ease up there, his gaze sweeping over the snow-covered hills that seemed less ominous under the daylight. Knowing he was keeping watch brought comfort.

As the day progressed, it began to feel less like a conquered territory and more like a new home. The men worked tirelessly—repairing, fortifying, and organizing. In the central courtyard, Sir Gareth coordinated patrols and set schedules for the watch rotations. While repairs continued, he reminded us that vigilance must not falter. Success might be ours, he said, but we couldn't afford to let our guard down.

By late afternoon, the bulk of the urgent tasks had been completed. The fortress's defenses were shored up, the wounded had been tended to, and the prisoners were secured in a manner befitting honorable treatment. I took a moment to catch my breath. Leaning against the newly reinforced gate, exhaustion settled into my bones. But there was also pride—pride in what we had accomplished and in the men around me.

General Aldric gathered the troops once more,

"Men of Centralia," he began, his sharp eyes missing nothing. "Your efforts today have been exemplary. Not only have you proven yourselves on the battlefield, but your dedication to fortifying this stronghold speaks volumes of your commitment."

General Aldric paused, as a satisfying smile softened his features. "In recognition of your hard work and to honor those who fought bravely, we shall hold a feast tonight. Let it serve as a celebration of our victory and a moment to reflect on the challenges we've overcome."

A cheer rose from the assembled soldiers. The prospect of a hearty meal felt like a gift and lifted everyone's spirit. The weariness of the day eased, replaced by a sense of anticipation. As dusk approached, preparations for the feast began in earnest. The kitchens were alive with activity, with cooks and assistants bustling to prepare an array of dishes. The enticing aromas of roasted meats, freshly baked bread, and spiced stews filed the fortress, brightening even the darkest corridors. It was as if the fortress itself was being transformed, the harshness of the stone walls softened by the warmth of what was to come.

Long tables were set up in the great hall, adorned with candles. The once formidable space, designed for strategy and governance, was now transformed into a place of fellowship. The flickering candlelight reflected off the stone walls, making the hall seem almost magical, a stark contrast to the battlefield it had been just hours before.

I washed and changed into a clean tunic, grateful for the small comfort. The water was cool and refreshing, washing away the grime and strain of the day. I carefully placed the amulet back around my neck and wore my clothes over it. At the great hall, I was greeted by the sight of my fellow soldiers already gathering. Laughter and conversations filled the air. The atmosphere was one of joy and relief—a collective exhale after the tension of recent days. I couldn't help but smile as I looked around, seeing the faces of those who had stood beside me, who had fought and bled for this moment.

"Over here!" Edric's voice called out, and I saw him waving me over to a table where Cedric and several others were seated with him. I made my way through the crowd, weaving between tables and chairs until I reached them.

Then, a tankard of ale was pressed into my hand before I even had a chance to sit down. "To our hard-fought glory!" one of the men toasted, raising his drink high, his voice full of exuberance.

"To Centralia!" we all echoed, the clinking of tankards punctuating the cheer. I took a long drink, the cool ale washing over my tongue, its bitter taste a welcome change from the dryness of the day. It was a simple thing, but it felt like a rare gift—to sit here, to drink, to laugh with friends.

Platters of food were piled high—succulent roast boar glazed with honey and herbs, bowls brimming with root vegetables seasoned to perfection, and baskets overflowing with crusty loaves of bread. There were even treats of dried fruits and cheeses, rare luxuries in these harsh lands. I felt my stomach growl, the sight and smell of the food making me realize just how hungry I was.

I tore a piece of bread from the basket, the crust crackling under my fingers, and dipped it into a bowl of stew. The flavors were rich, and the warmth spread through me as I ate. Around me, the men talked and laughed, their voices filling the hall with life and energy. Edric leaned forward, his eyes alight, as he mimed a sweeping sword strike recounting the clash with bold gestures and grand embellishments. Cedric smirked, and made a wry remark that sent the table into fits of laughter. For a moment, I allowed myself to let go of the weight I carried. The memories of the fallen, the elusiveness of my brother, the uncertainty of what lay ahead—they were still there. But tonight, I chose to focus on the here and now; on the faces of my friends, on the warmth of the hall, on the taste of the food, and on the sound of laughter. This was what we fought for—these moments of peace, however fleeting.

As I looked around the hall, at the men who had become my brothers, a sense of belonging that went beyond words enveloped me. We had faced the darkness together, and tonight, we celebrated that we had come through it.

As we ate, stories bounced off the walls, laughter erupted frequently, and it was as though the struggles and fears of the battle had become fuel for our joy, each story a testament to what we had faced together.

"Do you remember the look on that guard's face when the gate swung open?" Edric recounted, his grin wide and infectious. "He couldn't decide whether to fight or flee!"

Cedric chuckled, shaking his head. "I thought Kaelan here was going to single-handedly take the battlements before we even got there."

I shook my head modestly, feeling the heat rise to my cheeks. "How could I when I had good company?" We all laughed.

Sir Gareth made his rounds through the hall, stopping by tables to share a word or two with the men. When he reached our group, he placed a firm hand on my shoulder, his eyes meeting mine with a look of genuine respect. "You performed admirably today, Kaelan. Your leadership did not go unnoticed."

"Thank you, sir." Pride swelled in my chest. It was rare for Sir Gareth to offer praise. I nodded, hoping the gratitude I felt showed in my eyes.

As the evening wore on, General Aldric stood at the head of the hall, raising his hands for attention. Gradually, the room quieted, all eyes turning toward him. The energy in the hall shifted, a collective anticipation filling the space.

He lifted his goblet high. "To the fallen—we honor their memory. To the living—we cherish their fellowship. And to Centralia—may our homeland know peace and prosperity."

"To Centralia!" we all echoed, our voices strong and heartfelt, reverberating off the stone walls. I raised my goblet. This was why we fought—for our homeland, for each other, for the hope that one day, peace might be more than just a fleeting dream.

CHAPTER 28

S oon, music filled the air as a few soldiers produced instruments—a lute, a flute, and a drum. They played lively tunes that set feet tapping and inspired some to dance. The melodies were traditional Centralian songs and impromptu creations that captured the mood of the evening—joyous, hopeful, and relieved. I found myself relaxing in a way I hadn't for weeks. The weight of the campaign, the loss of Jarin, and the constant vigilance seemed, for a moment, to ease.

Edric nudged me, his eyes gleaming with mischief. "Kaelan, you look like you could use a dance. Or maybe a song?"

I laughed, shaking my head. "I'll leave the singing to you, Edric. We don't want to scare off the musicians."

He grinned, raising his tankard. "A wise choice." His good-natured teasing made me laugh, and I realized how long it had been since I felt this lighthearted. As the music continued, I joined in when a familiar song was sung, our voices mingling with the melody, the words a comforting reminder of home.

As the laughter around the table ebbed, one of the soldiers who had led us, Marcus, leaned forward, his eyes sparkling.

"You know, I've been thinking. It's funny, isn't it? How we have spent a while dodging arrows, burying friends, and drinking gods-knows-what in this gods-forsaken place just to keep warm. And now, we are here toasting and drinking as if this whole madness is behind us. As if we have forgotten those who didn't make it." He belched loudly and swallowed the remainder of the contents of his tankard. "As if we have suddenly become invincible."

The room grew quiet as the soldiers exchanged uneasy glances. Marcus didn't speak much, but when he had several flasks of ale, his tongue loosened. Edric raised his tankard, his expression half amused, half wry. "Well, Marcus. If you've got a better way to celebrate, I'd love to hear that."

Marcus chuckled, his face flushed. "Oh, I am not complaining. I'm just wondering if the gods are watching and having a good laugh at our expense. All the cheering and laughter over a war we'll probably get sent back to before our drinks have settled in our bellies."

Cedric snorted and shook his head.

"Don't give the gods ideas yet. The last thing we need is those folks betting on who gets to see Tvaron first."

I drained the contents of my tankard and dropped it on the table a little harder than I intended. "If they do, at least, we have given them a good show, and Tvaron is just the guider of souls he may even feel bad for us!"

Laughter rippled through the table, this time with an air of defiance. The type that came not from free-flowing joy but sheer stubbornness of will, clawing back at the absurdity of it all.

I suddenly felt stifled. Needing a moment to myself, I stood and made my way outside onto a balcony overlooking the courtyard. The night sky stretched above me, clear and endless, stars sparkling like diamonds against the velvet darkness. The chill in the air was refreshing, and I took a deep breath, filling my lungs. It felt good to be alone for a moment, to let the cool air clear my mind.

From there, I heard scattered laughter and conversation. As the night wore on, the conversations around the table turned more introspective. Talks of home, of lovers left behind, of hopes for the future. The laughter quieted, replaced by a deeper, more reflective mood. I listened, my own thoughts drifting as I stared into the starry night.

Footsteps approached, and I turned to see Cedric joining me. He leaned against the stone railing, his eyes on the sky. "Needed some fresh air?"

"Just collecting my thoughts," I replied, my gaze drifting across the courtyard below. "It's been quite a day."

"That it has," Cedric agreed, leaning against the stone railing beside me. The cool night air surrounded us. "Jarin would have enjoyed tonight."

I nodded, and my lips moved in a bittersweet smile. "He would have been the soul of the merriment," I said, my voice softening. We stood in comfortable silence for a moment, each of us lost in our memories. "What comes next for you?" Cedric asked, breaking the silence, his voice gentle. "After all this, I mean."

I took a deep breath, considering his question. "I'll go back home with Eamon, I can't face Ma without him," I said, my gaze turning toward the horizon. "The last I heard, he was here in Wintmore. With the fortress secured, maybe I'll finally have the chance to continue my search." The thought of Eamon was always there, a constant pull at the edge of my thoughts, a reminder of what I still had to do.

Cedric nodded, his expression sincere. "I hope you find him, Kaelan. If there's anything I can do to help, you have only to ask."

"Thank you," I replied, my heart swelling with gratitude. "Your support means a lot." It wasn't just words—having Cedric by my side, knowing he would be there if I needed him, made all the difference.

We rejoined the festivities, the warmth of the hall wrapping around us like a comforting embrace. The music had softened, but the laughter and chatter continued. I finally let myself get lost in it. It wasn't often that we had moments like this.

As fatigue began to take hold, the great hall gradually emptied. The soldiers retired to their quarters, their faces content, their steps slower as exhaustion finally caught up to them. I took it all in—the flickering candlelight, the warmth, the sense of peace that had settled over the fortress.

When I finally lay down in my cot, the sounds of the fortress settling for the night surrounded me—the snores, the soft murmur of voices, the distant clink of metal and the crackling of a dying fire. And for the first time in what felt like forever, I allowed myself to rest fully. The warmth of the celebration lingered, and as my eyes closed, I felt a sense of peace wash over me. For once, my dreams were devoid of nightmares.

***

The days that followed were marked by a tranquility that had been absent for much of our campaign. The fortress, once a bastion of enemy strength, had become a haven for us. The harsh winter landscape outside contrasted sharply with the warmth that flourished within these stone walls. It felt like a different world, one where we could finally catch our breath.

Each morning, I awoke to the soft glow of dawn filtering through the small window near my sleeping chambers. The air was crisp, but it no longer carried the weight of impending conflict. I joined my comrades in the common hall, where the aroma of fresh bread and hearty porridge greeted us. Conversations rose and ebbed, their lighthearted chatter filled with mirth and the sharing of stories both old and new.

"Did you hear about Thom's misadventure with the kitchen maid?" Edric teased one morning, his eyes twinkling mischievously.

I grinned, shaking my head. "I imagine it didn't end well for him."

Cedric chuckled, his eyes gleaming with amusement. "Oh, she set him straight, all right. Chased him out with a ladle!"

Laughter erupted around the long wooden table, the banters turning into little fights that ended before they started. Training continued, but it was different now. Less about preparation for imminent battle, and more about honing our skills, maintaining discipline, and finding our footing again. Sword drills were conducted in the courtyard under the watery winter sun, the clanging of metal on metal a familiar and almost comforting sound. Archery practice took place along the battlements, with targets set against the backdrop of distant snow-capped peaks. There was something almost serene about it, the rhythmic pull of the bowstring, and the steady focus on the target.

I often found myself atop the walls, gazing out over the vast expanse of white that stretched to the horizon. The snow-covered terrain seemed almost peaceful, undisturbed except for the occasional flurry of wind that sent sparkling crystals swirling into the air. There was a sense of contentment within me, mingled with a strange restlessness. The stillness was welcome, yet a part of me longed for movement, for purpose beyond the fortress walls.

One of such afternoons, I joined a group tasked with exploring the nearby woods to gather additional firewood and scout for any signs of movement. The forest was serene, the tall evergreens standing like silent guardians, their branches heavy with snow. The only sounds were the crunch of snow beneath our boots and the distant call of a lone bird, echoing through the quiet.

"It's hard to believe we were fighting for our lives not long ago," Edric remarked thoughtfully, hefting an axe over his shoulder as we walked.

"Peace can feel unfamiliar after so much conflict," I agreed, glancing at the towering trees around us. "But it's a welcome change."

We paused beside a frozen stream, the ice glistening under the slanting rays of sunlight. Cedric knelt to examine tracks leading toward the trees, his eyes narrowing as he studied them. "Deer," he noted, looking up at us. "Perhaps we can supplement our rations with some fresh game."

The idea was met with enthusiasm, and soon we were tracking the elusive animals through the woods. By the time we returned to the fortress, we had enough venison to provide a feast that rivaled our earlier celebration. Evenings were spent around the hearth, where stories flowed as freely as the ale. Tales of home, dreams for the future, and reflections on our journey fostered a deeper sense of unity among us. It was during these times that I felt the weight of everything we had endured slowly easing, replaced by something warmer—something like hope.

"What's the first thing you'll do when we return home?" a young soldier named Oswald asked the group one night, his eyes bright with curiosity.

The question was not unfamiliar, but it yanked me from my seat again and threw me upside down. Home!

What's home?

Or where?

Is it a place?

Or the people I carry in the tight chambers of my heart?

Edric replied thoughtfully, his gaze distant. "Help with the harvest and enjoy a meal that isn't cooked over a campfire. And maybe, finally fix the barn roof. It's been falling apart since last spring and I had been promising my Mama that I'd do it before the rains." He shrugged, "Well, things got in the way." He laughed, a sudden burst of mirth that didn't quite ring true. But I envied him for the simplicity of his aspirations, and the ease with which he spoke of them.

I patted his shoulders. "She'd be glad to have you back, barn roof or not." He chuckled lightheartedly, "I guess Cedric has no barn roofs to mend."

Cedric smiled wistfully, his eyes softening. "I plan to sit by the sea of noble and watch the ships come and go. I'll sit on the rocks, and feel the salt wind on my face. Maybe, I'll build a little shack, and live out my days listening to the waves. The sea doesn't ask anything of you. It just…is. There's something calming about the ebb and flow of the tides. It reminds me that life goes on, no matter what."

I nodded, though my thoughts wandered. I knew what they expected me to say. That I'd return to our farm with Eamon. That I'd find him, wherever this damned war had thrown him. It was true, but the burden of it felt particularly heavy on my chest tonight. So, I hid my pain behind my tankard and said nothing.

But, finding him was my goal, my promise—everything else would come after.

CHAPTER
29

The days passed in a comfortable rhythm. Maintenance of the fortress continued, but without the urgency that had driven us before. Repairs were made to the outer walls, and the storerooms were well-stocked against the winter's demands. Scouts reported no signs of enemy activity, and messages from Centralian command praised our success but offered no fresh orders or counsel for the days to come. It was a time of rest, of rebuilding, yet beneath the surface a subtle tension seemed to crawl towards us with each passing day.

Sir Gareth's gaze lingered on the distant horizon during his inspections, and his brow furrowed as if he were searching for something beyond the snow-covered peaks. I heard it in the hushed conversations that ceased whenever anyone else approached. It was as if the very air carried a whispered warning. One evening, I sought out Sir Gareth myself, in the war room where maps and dispatches were spread across a large table. The room was dim, lit only by the flickering glow of a few lanterns. Sir Gareth stood with his back to the door, his hands clasped behind him as he stared intently at a chart marked with various symbols and annotations.

"Sir Gareth," I greeted him with a bow, stepping into the room. He turned, offering me a faint smile.

"Of course, Kaelan," he said, his voice warm but tired. "What brings you here?"

I took a step closer, choosing my words carefully. "I couldn't help but notice a change in the atmosphere," I began. "Is there something we should be preparing for?"

Sir Gareth regarded me thoughtfully for a long moment, then nodded. "Perceptive as always," he said, his tone appreciative. "While we haven't received any clear word or news yet, there are indications that Wintmore is regrouping. Our scouts have noted increased activity in regions we thought were abandoned."

I nodded slowly. The unease I'd felt solidified into something more tangible. "So this calm may be temporary."

"Indeed," Sir Gareth affirmed, his gaze steady. "It's wise to remain vigilant. Complacency can be as dangerous as any enemy."

"Should we begin additional preparations?" I asked, my mind already turning over the possible steps we could take. "Adjust our patrols, reinforce defenses?"

Sir Gareth gave a slight nod, his gaze never wavering from the maps spread across the table. "I've already instructed the officers to take precautionary measures," he said. "But I don't wish to alarm the men unnecessarily. Morale is high, and that is something we cannot afford to lose."

"Understood," I replied. "I'll make sure my men stay sharp without raising undue concern."

"Thank you, Kaelan."

As I left the war room, I couldn't shake the unease that had taken hold of me. The fortress, with all its strength suddenly felt vulnerable—a solitary outpost in a vast and unpredictable landscape. I tried to push the thought aside and do what I could. Later that night, as I sat near the hearth with Edric and Cedric, I shared my concerns. The fire crackled softly, casting dancing shadows across the walls, and for a moment, I hesitated. But these were my brothers, the ones I trusted most.

"I spoke with Sir Gareth," I said, my voice low enough that only they could hear. "He believes Wintmore may be mobilizing again."

Edric sighed, his expression turning serious. "I suppose it was only a matter of time before they responded," he said, his brow furrowing.

"We can't let our guard down," Cedric added, his eyes reflecting the flickering firelight. "But we also shouldn't let fear overshadow the present. We've earned this peace, however fleeting it might be."

I nodded, their words resonating with something deep within me. "You're right," I agreed. "Still, we should be prepared."

In the following days, subtle changes were made throughout the fortress. Watchmen grew more vigilant, venturing farther afield. Training sessions took on a slightly sharper edge, the emphasis on readiness and discipline. The officers maintained an air of calm authority, careful not to let the undercurrent of foreboding become overt. But the soldiers—they all sensed the shift. It was in the way we held our weapons, the way we watched the horizon, alert for any sign of movement.

One morning, I found myself atop the battlements, watching the sunrise. The sky was painted in hues of pink and gold, the kind of beauty that made everything else seem distant, almost unreal. I felt a presence beside me and turned to see General Aldric, his cloak billowing gently in the breeze.

"It's a beautiful sight," the general commented, his gaze fixed on the horizon.

"Yes, sir," I replied, my eyes following his. "Hard to imagine anything amiss on a morning like this."

General Aldric nodded slowly, his expression thoughtful. "Nature has a way of masking turmoil with serenity," he mused. "But we must look beyond appearances."

I hesitated for a moment before speaking. "I hear an attack is imminent?"

The general was silent, his eyes never leaving the horizon. "The word that has come to us suggests that Wintmore cannot afford to let this fortress remain in our hands unchallenged," he finally said. "They will act—it's only a question of when and how."

"We'll be ready," I assured him, my voice steady despite the unease swirling in my chest.

General Aldric turned then, meeting my gaze. "I have no doubt," he said, "Your dedication is commendable, Kaelan. The men look up to you."

"Thank you, sir," He placed a hand on my shoulder, his grip firm. "Stay vigilant. And remember, sometimes the greatest battles are fought not with swords, but with patience and resilience."

I watched as he departed, his figure retreating down the stone steps. His words echoed in my mind. The calm we were experiencing was both a blessing and a test; a blessing and a curse.

That evening, as the soldiers gathered for their meal, a subtle restlessness hung in the air. Conversations were stilted, eyes glanced more frequently toward the doors, and ears seemed attuned to sounds beyond the walls.

Edric raised his cup, his voice breaking through the murmurs of the hall. "To the days of peace we've enjoyed," he toasted, his eyes meeting mine across the table. "May they bolster us for whatever comes next."

We all raised our cups in unison. "Hear, hear," voices echoed around the hall, the sentiment heartfelt.

I looked around the room. Whatever storm lay on the horizon, we would face it together, fortified by the bonds we had forged and the victories we had achieved. It wasn't just words—there was a weight to the promise we made to one another. These men were my brothers, and I could count on them as much as they could count on me.

Retiring to my cot that night, I felt strange. The fortress was quiet, but the silence seemed to hum with expectation. I lay awake for a while, listening to the faint sounds of the night—the distant howl of the wind as it swept over the snow-laden peaks, the creak of timber settling within the ancient stone walls, the muffled footsteps of the night watch patrolling the ramparts. It was a comforting rhythm.

The fire in the hearth had dwindled to embers, casting a faint orange glow that flickered across the rough-hewn beams above. I pulled the blanket up to my chin as my thoughts drifted—to home, to the family I had left behind, to Eamon and where he might be. Sleep came restlessly, filled with fleeting dreams of home and battles fought. I saw Jarin's face, his laughter echoing faintly, and then the image shifted, replaced by the looming uncertainty of what lay ahead. It was as though my mind couldn't quite let go of the worry, even in sleep.

The darkness outside was profound, the moon obscured by thick clouds that blanketed the sky. The fortress stood like a solitary sentinel amidst the vast expanse of white, its towers piercing the night. All seemed calm, yet beneath the surface, something dark and restless simmered waiting to strike. It was a fragile calm. And I knew—deep down—that it wouldn't last forever.

CHAPTER 30

I stood in a wheat field that stretched endlessly into the horizon. It was startlingly bright as if the sky was painted in streaks of white and yellow, a scene so achingly familiar that my chest ached with longing. I saw everything through a haze of bright light and squinted as I tried to bring it into focus. I saw Ma first. Her laughter floated through the air, clear and sharp as a bell. She gathered her frock around her as she bent to gather wheat in her apron. She wore the blue floral frock that Pa had bought her last spring. The wrinkles around her eyes had disappeared, and she looked like a young girl again. Pa stood nearby, his hands resting on the haft of a scythe, watching Ma with a rare softness in his eyes.

Eamon was there too, in a shroud of light, perched atop a fence post, whistling a cheerful tune as he tossed a coin into the air. It spun, catching the sunlight, then vanished into shadow.

"Eamon!" I called out, emotion bubbling in my chest.

But Eamon didn't answer. Instead, he turned his head, and my heart sank. My brother's face was a blur, his features shifting like smoke in the wind. The field began to dim, and the sunlight rolled down the horizon, obscured by thick, dark clouds. A cold wind swept through, carrying with it the scent of iron and damp earth.

I blinked, and the field was gone. I now stood in the middle of Wintmore, I was in a city I didn't recognize its streets winding, vines crawling up the buildings like snakes. The walls were damp, streaked with moss and blood, and the air was thick with the stench of rot. Ma's laughter was replaced by her cries, her voice echoing from somewhere deep within. I turned around, searching for her, but I couldn't see her.

"Kaelan!"

It was Eamon's voice this time, distant and desperate.

I ran, my boots splashing through shallow pools of water or maybe blood. Shadows twisted and reached for him, as I stumbled now through a dense woods—large trees and underbrush. Then I fell, tumbling through narrow tunnels that closed in around me, and the cries grew louder, more frantic.

"Kaelan!"

Finally, I stumbled into an open chamber and shuddered. A figure stood in the center, cloaked in darkness. It held something in its hands— my amulet, glittering in green light. I cupped my hands over my eyes to discern who or what the figure was, and it jerked its face towards me.

I awoke before I could see its face, my body drenched in sweat. I still clutched my amulet tightly in my hand, holding on as if to dear life. My neck ached, and I tried to crack it, to no avail. Around me, men slept. And everywhere was silent save for the soft snores of sleeping soldiers.

I lay down again, but sleep eluded me. The dream's weight pressed on my chest like a boulder. I made an instant decision. I must enter into the bowels of Wintmore and cut my brother out of its grasp.

***

I would have gone with Cedric or perhaps Edric, and it would have been easier. But it would be unfair to endanger my friends for my personal motives. The men talked about the squalid and dangerous alleys of Briarwick. "You can buy even the emperor's underpants in those streets," they said.

So, I got up while the world still slept. The sun was still peeking timidly from the horizon, its pale rays struggling to pierce through the mist in the air, and made up my mind to seek my brother. And find him.

***

I was fast. My hands moved in quick motions as my heart hammered in my chest. I tugged the hood lower over my face feeling the weight of the coarse wool scratch against my cheeks. The fabric smelled of sweat and damp hay, and something else I couldn't identify. It hung just a little too loose on my shoulders, but it served its purpose. A Centralian soldier would never make it far in Wintmore's underbelly without getting a gift of a dagger to his chest, or someone forgetting a knife in his belly. So I'd bartered for this threadbare cloak with a half-empty flask of ale and a reluctant promise not to ask questions about its previous owner.

I walked with measured steps, neither too fast nor too slow. The streets were dark and shadowy, with alleys snaking between crumbling stone walls streaked with soot. Briarwick was nothing like Elsenburg. The air here was thick with forge smoke and the stench of unwashed bodies, almost a wasteland.

The people moved like phantoms—hooded figures slipping in and out of side doors, sneaking looks at outsiders from beneath their brows, and hushed conversations cut short when a stranger approached. I kept my steps even and my head low as I approached a cluster of men huddled around a burning barrel.

"I'm looking for someone," I said. I tried not to seem as grim as I felt, my voice taking on a gaily and cheerful tone, "Young man. Light brown hair. Amber eyes. Name's Eamon. You've seen him around?"

The men exchanged glances. One of them, his face half-hidden beneath a greasy cap, gave a low chuckle. "Ain't no 'Eamon' here," he said, his tone mocking. "If he's smart, he's long gone. If he ain't, he's under the ground."

I clenched my fists beneath the cloak but kept my tone steady. "He was headed for the Crimson Merchant Alliance. They're here, aren't they?"

The man's laughter dried up like snow melting on a summer day. "Best forget you said that," he muttered, shoving his gloved hands deep into his cloak. The other men shuffled uncomfortably, suddenly more interested in the flames than in what I was saying.

I walked on, frustration coiling tighter in my belly. With every step, I grew reckless with disappointment, asking everyone I saw. Yet, every question was met with shrugs or hostility. The boy who'd dreamed of adventure, of seeing the world, had vanished into the depths of Wintmore as though he'd never existed. Was he truly a spy for the Centralian army? Had his cover been blown? Was he still alive?

I was halfway down another shadowed alley when I heard,

"Nice cloak." A voice drawled behind me, light and teasing.

I spun around, my hands instinctively dropping to the dagger at my belt. A girl leaned against the brick wall, one boot crossed lazily over the other. She looked about my age or maybe a year older, with sun-kissed skin with freckles all over and a tumble of chestnut wavy curled hair spilling out from beneath a tattered hat. Her eyes as light as the sky, sharp and glinting like polished steel, danced with mischief.

"Who are you?" I demanded, my grip tightening on the dagger. I had never fought a girl before.

"Depends," she said, pushing off the wall and sauntering closer. "Who's asking?" She cast a quick, appraising glance over me, her gaze loitered on the ill-fitting cloak. "Let me guess. You're some miller's son playing the hero? Or maybe a runaway noble looking for adventure?"

"I'm looking for my brother," I said, ignoring her jibe. Her brows lifted in mock surprise.

"A brother, is it? How sweet. And here I thought you were just another soldier on the hunt for something… less noble." I stiffened. "I'm not a soldier."

"Of course, you're not," she said, her tone dripping with sarcasm. "And I'm the Queen of Wintmore." She circled me now, her steps light and deliberate. I caught a glimpse of the dagger tucked into her belt, its handle worn from use. A scavenger, then. Or something worse.

"You know something about the Crimson Merchant Alliance?" I asked, my patience fraying at the ends.

"Maybe," she said, flashing a sly grin. "But tidings are not given freely, you know. Especially not here."

"What's your price?"

She tilted her head, as though considering me for the first time. "Oh, I don't know yet," she said. "You're intriguing enough to keep me curious for now. But I'll think of something."

I hesitated, studying her carefully. She bounced, like a ball of light; sharp and unpredictable, the kind of person who could just as easily lead me into a trap as guide me to the answers I sought. But something about her—her audacity, her vibrant energy—struck a chord I couldn't quite name.

"Do you have a name?" I asked, finally.

"Do you?" she shot back, her grin widening.

"Kaelan."

"Kaelan," she repeated, rolling the name around on her tongue like she was tasting it, teasing me. I ignored her, my heart beating fast against my chest. I didn't know whether my trembling was because of my anxiety or because of what I saw in her eyes.

"Alright, Kaelan. You can call me Lilah. For now."

She extended a hand. Her fingers were covered in soot. I hesitated, then clasped it briefly. It was warm.

"Let's see if we can find your brother, shall we?" she said, turning on her heel and striding down the alley. "Try to keep up."

"What do you care? Why must I follow you?"

But I followed her, my heart pounding with a mix of wariness and something else—something he hadn't felt in a long time. Hope. She weaved through the labyrinth of streets, deep into the heart of the city's darkest alleys, where the air was heavy with the stench of decay and the light of the city's higher streets didn't dare reach. The alleys grew narrower, the walls streaked with grime and claw marks from rats bold enough to fight for scraps.

I kept my hand on my dagger as we moved. I didn't trust Lilah, but I needed her. I watched her, hidden under piles of dirty clothes, fast on her feet, and unaware—or perhaps indifferent— to how beautiful she was. And yet, for all her sharp words and the occasional smirk she threw over her shoulder, she hadn't betrayed me. Yet.

"Are you sure about this?" I asked, my voice low, trying to hide my uneasiness.

Lilah glanced back, her dark eyes gleaming even in the dimness. "I won't take you to just anyone," she said. "But him? He knows things. Everyone owes him something, which means he's got ears everywhere. If your brother's here, he'll know."

We wove through more smelly alleys and muddy puddles before we stopped at a door that looked more like a splintering piece of driftwood hammered into a rotting frame. Lilah knocked three times, a rhythm that seemed too deliberate to be random.

The door creaked open just enough for a single eye to peer out.

"Lilah," a voice rasped. It was old, broken like the edge of a whetstone worn too thin. "What's this stray animal you've dragged into my home?"

"Business," Lilah said. She unceremoniously pushed the door open and strode in, leaving me to follow.

Inside, the room was dark save for the soft glow of a single lantern hanging from the ceiling. The man who stood before me was stooped, his body wrapped in layers of patched cloth. His face was obscured by shadows, but his hands—gnarled and calloused—rested on a cane that looked more like a weapon than a support.

"Name's Jareth," the man said, his voice scraping like gravel. "And you… you're not from around here."

I stepped forward, ignoring the way the man's eyes seemed to measure me, dissect me. "I'm looking for my brother," I said. "Eamon. Tall, light brown hair, amber eyes, scar on his cheek. He was supposed to be traveling with the Crimson Merchant Alliance."

Jareth tilted his head, considering. Then he laughed—a low, guttural sound that made my stomach twist.

"Everyone comes to me for something," Jareth said, leaning on his cane. "But answers aren't free, Centralian. What've you got to trade?"

I hesitated. My fingers brushed the coin pouches at my belt, heavy with the last of my savings. I didn't like this man or trust him, but what choice did I have? I unhooked one of the pouches and tossed it onto the table before him.

Jareth picked it up with deliberate slowness, weighing it in his hand before pouring the coins into his palm. He counted them out loud, each clink of metal against metal jarring.

"Generous," Jareth said finally, tucking the coins away. "All right, soldier. Here's what I know. Your brother's alive. Foolhardy, like all young men, but alive. He skulked around whispering secrets to the enemy. Bold, if you ask me." My heart constricted. If this stranger in the most squalid city in Wintmore knew my brother was a spy, how could my poor brother protect himself— or his life?

"My brother is no spy." The words tumbled out of my mouth even though I was unsure of the verity or falsity of it.

"So you say." He placed the coins back in the pouch and put it under his cloak.

"Where is he?" I demanded, my voice sharp.

"Patience," Jareth said with a smirk. "You'll see him. He's at the old mill near the river. You show up here tomorrow, just before sunrise, and I'll take you to him. But don't come alone. They won't trust you otherwise."

"Who are 'they?'"

"The ones who'll open the door."

He spoke in parables, but my relief was like a tide crashing over me, sweeping away the doubt that had clung to me for days. I now had a time. A place.

Eamon was alive.

But as I turned to leave, Jareth's laughter followed me.

"You've got hope now, Centralian," Jareth called after me, his voice mocking, "But hope's a heavy load to carry through these streets. Watch your back."

Without another word, I stepped into the streets and headed for the barracks. I stopped in the middle of the narrow alley, my hand instinctively going to my belt. Nothing. Empty. The realization hit me like a cold splash of water on my face.

My remaining coin pouch, the last of my savings, was gone. Not just that—my dagger, the small elephant carving Eamon had given me when we were boys, even the little brass clasp I used to fasten my odorous cloak—all of it had vanished.

I spun around in shock and my eyes met Lilah's, who lingered behind me audaciously, her arms crossed and an infuriatingly casual grin plastered across her face.

Fury crawled up from my toes.

"You!" I growled, "You robbed me."

She tilted her head, mock innocence shining in her dark eyes. "Me?" she said, a hand fluttering to her chest. "I didn't lay a finger on you, soldier boy. If you lost something, maybe you just weren't paying enough attention."

I stepped closer, my fists clenching. "You took me to him knowing this would happen. You and that old man—you're in it together!"

Lilah didn't flinch. Instead, she gave me a lopsided smile, sharp and unrepentant. "Of course, we are," she said. "You think Jareth gives out favors for free? Or that I lead people to him out of the goodness of my heart? Please."

My jaw tightened, but before I could speak, she held up a hand.

"Look," she said, her voice softer now, though the sharp edge never quite left her tone. "You came here for answers, didn't you? And now you have them. Your brother's alive. You know where to find him. That's more than most people leave Jareth's door with."

I wanted to argue. But I stopped myself. Cedric would have known what to say to this irreverent girl, and how to say it. But she was right.

The coin, the dagger, the carving—they were gone, but so was the weight of not knowing. For months, I'd been wondering about my brother's fate, grasping at shadows. Now I had something real.

I let out a breath, my shoulders sagging as the anger drained from me. "You could've just asked for more coin," I muttered at last.

Lilah laughed; a light, carefree sound that felt out of place in the dank alley. "Oh, and miss this look on your face? Never."

I shook my head, half in disbelief, half in reluctant amusement. "You're impossible."

"And you're stubborn," she shot back, turning on her heel. "Come on. Let's get moving. Without that fine dagger of yours, you need some protection if you want to stay alive long enough to see Eamon."

I glared at her, but she only smirked, her light eyes dancing. By the time we reached the edge of the slums, I was smiling despite everything. The thought of Eamon, alive and waiting for me, burned brighter than my anger with the pretty thief and her haggard accomplice.

Eamon was alive. And I would see him again.

CHAPTER
31

I awoke abruptly to the sharp blast of a horn that shattered the pre-dawn stillness. My heart pounded as I bolted upright, the echoes of the horn mingling with the sudden clamor of voices raised in alarm. "To the walls! The enemy approaches!" A voice bellowed from outside, urgency lacing every word.

I threw off my blankets and scrambled to my feet, my mind a tangle of thoughts. I was supposed to leave this morning to fetch Eamon. Cedric and Edric had agreed to accompany me, yet I had been anxious through the night and had hardly caught a wink of sleep. The cold air bit against my skin. My breath puffed out in misty clouds as I fumbled in the dim light, grabbing my tunic and hastily pulling it over my head. Eamon would be waiting for me, I thought frantically. I needed to find a way to get to him. Mindlessly, I put on my armor. The familiar weight of chainmail settled onto my shoulders with practiced ease. My fingers moved deftly, buckling straps and securing plates. The amulet hung against my chest, taunting me with its weight.

Around me, the barracks erupted. Soldiers leaped from their sleeping frames, their expressions shifting from confusion to alertness. The wooden floorboards trembled under the collective rush of boots as men hurried to arm themselves. Edric appeared beside me, his eyes sharp.

"The Wintmorians," Edric stated tersely as he fastened his armor. "They've come sooner than we expected."

"Seems the storm has broken," I replied, strapping my sword belt around my waist. "Are the others alerted?"

"Yes," he answered. "What about your brother? What are we supposed to do?"

"I don't know." I was crestfallen, but I wouldn't think of it now. "Where is Cedric?"

"At the eastern wall," Edric informed me, his voice steady. "He'd meet us there."

I nodded, grabbing my shield. The polished metal felt like an extension of myself. The cacophony outside intensified—shouts of orders, the clang of weapons, the distant rumble of movement beyond the walls.

We rushed out into the courtyard, the frigid air stinging my face and filling my lungs with each sharp breath. Torches blazed along the battlements, their flames whipped by the biting wind. Snowflakes began to fall, sparse at first, then increasing in density—a swirling curtain that added to the surreal atmosphere.

Sir Gareth stood near the main gate. "Archers to the ramparts! Infantry, form up below!" His eyes blazed. "If they want this fortress, they'll have to take it from our dead cold hands! Move, men!"

Edric and I pushed through the throng, ascending the stone steps that led to the outer wall. The stones were slick with frost, each step requiring caution even in our haste. At the top, we were met with a sight both awe-inspiring and ominous.

The plain before the fortress stretched out like a vast, white canvas, but it was now marred by the dark shapes of the approaching Wintmorian army. Torches dotted their ranks like malevolent stars, illuminating the gleam of armor and the points of spears. The sound of drums drifted across the distance—a steady, rhythmic pounding that resonated like the heartbeat of some great beast. My heart clenched at the thoughts of Eamon. He was still out there. But now, with the enemy already at our gates, every delay, every moment wasted, felt like a nail in his coffin. Was he safe? Or had he fallen in the bloody path of the Wintmorians? Had I compromised his life? Was he in danger because of me? The weight of my promise hung heavier than the armor on my shoulders. Every step felt like it might be the one that either saved him or sealed his fate.

"They've brought siege engines," a soldier close by remarked grimly, pointing toward massive silhouettes being maneuvered into position. Trebuchets and battering rams, their wooden frames reinforced with iron, loomed against the backdrop of the dim horizon.

Cedric appeared beside us, his bow already in his hands. He looked out over the enemy formations, his eyes narrowing. "The world has gone mad. How are we to reach your brother in this chaos?"

"Let's fight today's battle," I replied. "We shall find a way."

"They're wasting no time," he observed, his voice calm but edged with tension. "Looks like they intend to overwhelm us with sheer force."

"Then we'll make them pay for every inch," I declared. I turned to the soldiers gathered along the wall, my voice rising in sudden anger. "Archers, prepare your arrows! Wait for the command!"

Men moved into position, the tension tangible in the air. Quivers were filled, and bowstrings were tested. The archers stood in a line, silhouetted against the fiery glow of torches. Each one of them knew what was at stake, and it showed in their eyes—We must protect what was ours.

Below, the infantry formed ranks, shields interlocked, and spears at the ready. The murmur of prayers mingled with the final clatter of armor being secured. Healers and runners darted between units, conveying messages and dispensing final ministration. General Aldric rode along the inner perimeter, his horse's breath steaming in the cold air. "Stand firm!" he called out, his voice carrying with authority. "Today, we show them the strength of Centralia! Remember what you fight for—your homes, your families, your brothers beside you!"

A cheer rose, defiant and echoing against the stone walls. I felt a surge of strength solidify within me. There was no room for hesitation now. I glanced at Edric and Cedric, their expressions mirroring my own. We had faced countless trials together—the battles, the hardships, the losses. This would be no different. We would fight, and we would win. Together.

With each passing moment, the Wintmorian drums grew louder, pounding like a heartbeat, The ground seemed to tremble beneath us, vibrating under the weight of their march. Snow continued to fall, each flake catching the torchlight, creating an eerie, ethereal glow over the impending battlefield.

"Steady!" Sir Gareth's voice rang out. "Hold your fire until they are within range!"

Time seemed to stretch, each moment etched with clarity. I could make out the individual figures of the enemy now—their armor adorned with the white and blue sigils of Wintmore, their faces shadowed beneath their helms. Among their ranks were divisions of heavy infantry, archers, and cavalry, a well-organized force intent on reclaiming what we had taken. My hands trembled, but I kept my focus, refusing to let fear take hold.

Suddenly, the drums ceased. The air became still save for the whisper of the wind and the soft whistle of snow. My grip tightened on my shield, my muscles coiled and ready.

Then, a horn sounded—a deep, resonant note that signaled the commencement of the assault. The Wintmorian front lines surged forward, shields raised, voices raised in a battle cry that tore through the morning air.

"Archers—loose!" I shouted, echoing the command relayed by the officers.

A volley of arrows soared upward, darkening the sky like a flock of deadly birds. They arced gracefully before descending upon the advancing enemy. Cries erupted as men fell, the initial impact staggering but not halting their momentum. The sight of the arrows finding their mark filled me with bitter triumph—we were making them pay for every step they took.

"Prepare for the next volley!" Cedric called out, already fitting another arrow to his bow. His movements were fluid, honed by constant practice. I could see the focus in his eyes, the steadiness of his hands. It was in moments like this that I realized just how much we had all grown—how far we had come.

The enemy's archers responded in kind, their arrows slicing through the air toward the fortress walls. I raised my shield instinctively. The sharp thuds of projectiles striking stone and wood echoed around us. A soldier nearby grunted as an arrow found its mark, collapsing to the walkway beside me.

"Chirurgeon!" Edric yelled for the healers, his voice urgent as he dragged the wounded man to safety. Siege engines rumbled forward, teams of oxen straining to pull the massive constructs through the snow. Crews worked tirelessly to position them within range, the trebuchets loaded with heavy stones and incendiary materials. The sight of those monstrous machines sent a chill down my spine—they were here to break us, to tear us down bit by bit and bring our walls crumbling down.

"They're targeting the walls!" a panicked voice warned behind me.

"Keep firing!" I urged, my voice rising above the din. "We must disrupt their advance!"

A fresh wave of arrows sliced through the air, their deadly hiss mingling with the screams of dying men. Beneath the rain of arrows, the infantry stood resolute, eyes fixed ahead, muscles taut, gripping their weapons with white-knuckled determination as the enemy surged closer.

The first of the siege projectiles hurtled toward the fortress, a massive stone crashing into the outer wall with a resounding impact. The structure shuddered but held firm. Flames erupted where incendiaries landed, casting a harsh glow over the battlefield. The shock of the impact reverberated through my body but there was no time to dwell on it.

"Fire teams, extinguish those flames!" Sir Gareth ordered, pointing to where soldiers were already moving with buckets and sand.

I shivered as I took in the scene. The Wintmorians were well-prepared and determined. This would be a grueling defense.

"Kaelan!" Cedric's voice called out. "Look there!"

I followed his gaze, my eyes narrowing as I spotted a contingent of enemy soldiers breaking off from the main force. They were moving toward a less fortified section of the wall—the eastern side, where the terrain was rougher and the defenses weaker.

"They are using our strategy against us," I realized, panicked. "We need to reinforce that position."

"I'll alert the commander," Edric said, already turning to move.

"Come on," I said to Cedric, quickening my pace. "We can't let them breach the wall."

We descended the steps swiftly, moving through the chaos of the courtyard. Soldiers hurried in all directions. The clash of metal, the shouts of orders, the cries of the wounded—it was a cacophony that filled every corner of my mind.

At the eastern wall, I rallied a group of defenders, my voice steady despite the chaos. "Form up along this section! Archers, take positions above. Infantry, prepare to repel any climbers!"

The men moved into action. It was moments like these—when every moment mattered, when we stood on the edge of disaster—that showed the true strength of our men. We were intertwined in our fate and we did what had to be done.

I ascended to a vantage point, looking for the enemy's maneuver. The Wintmorians were setting scaling ladders, their soldiers beginning to ascend with alarming speed. My stomach twisted, the sight of them like a dark wave threatening to crash over us.

"Push those ladders back!" I shouted. "Use pikes and poles!"

The first enemy soldier reached the top, his face alight with fierce intent. I met him with a swift strike, my blade cutting through the air and knocking him back. Another took his place almost immediately, but Cedric's arrow found its mark, sending him tumbling down.

Below, more ladders were being raised, a relentless tide of attackers that seemed endless. They were like ants swarming over a fallen carcass, determined and unyielding in their advance. We fought valiantly, but the sheer numbers threatened to overwhelm us.

"Hold the line!" I yelled, parrying a thrust and countering with a decisive blow. My sword connected with the Wintmorian attacker's armor. The enemy soldier staggered back, but there was no time to breathe—another took his place, a relentless tide pressing against us.

The eastern wall had become a fierce battleground. My muscles ached, my body pushed itself to its limits, but there was no room for weakness.

Cedric stood atop the parapet, raining arrow after arrow into the mass of enemies below. His fingers were numb from the cold, but he ignored the sting, his focus unbroken.

"They're not letting up!" he called out.

I glanced upward, my eyes meeting his. "Keep them off us as long as you can!" I replied, narrowly dodging a spear thrust aimed at my side. I retaliated swiftly, my blade finding its mark on the attacker's side. The Wintmorian soldier fell, but two more immediately stepped forward to take his place. It felt like trying to hold back a flood with nothing but my bare hands.

Below, the enemy had succeeded in securing several ladders, and their soldiers swarmed upward, relentless and overwhelming. Despite our efforts to push the ladders away, the sheer number of attackers made it impossible to repel them all. The Wintmorians were single-minded, their coordinated assaults testing every weakness in our defenses.

Edric fought beside me, his spear a blur as he fended off attackers, his breath coming in harsh gasps. "We need more hands!" he shouted, his voice hoarse. "We can't hold much longer!"

Edric was right. We were being pushed back, step by step, our line thinning as men fell around us. A glance along the wall revealed scenes of brutal combat—soldiers grappling hand-to-hand, locked in desperate struggles that often ended with one or both plummeting from the heights. The snow beneath us was stained crimson, with men scattered across the ground, motionless. It was hard to take it all in, but there was no time for despair—only survival.

"Fall back to the inner wall!" Sir Gareth's voice echoed across the ramparts. "Regroup and hold the courtyard!"

The order was relayed down the line, and I signaled to my men. "You heard him! Move back carefully—don't turn your backs!"

We began a fighting retreat, stepping backward while maintaining a defensive front. The Wintmorians pressed their advantage, sensing the shift in momentum. Their shouts and jeers rang out, each step we took back seeming to fuel their confidence. Arrows continued to rain down, and the enemy's siege engines hurled stones that smashed into the fortress's outer defenses, sending shards of stone and clouds of dust into the air.

Reaching the stairway, I directed the remaining defenders downward. As we made our way down, a massive explosion shook the ground beneath us. My heart jumped into my mouth as I saw what had happened—a section of the eastern wall had been breached. The enemy had set off charges at its base, creating a gaping hole through which their forces began pouring like a dark, unrelenting wave.

"They've broken through!" Cedric shouted, his face stark as he joined us at the foot of the stairs.

"To the courtyard!" I ordered, my voice hoarse from shouting. "We make our stand there!"

The inner courtyard was a flurry of activity. Chirurgeons tended to the wounded as best they could amidst the turmoil. Officers barked orders, as they attempted to organize a coherent defense. The fortress's defenders formed a shield wall, bracing themselves for the onslaught about to hit. The air was thick with fear. General Aldric rode to the forefront, his armor gleaming despite the soot and grime. He raised his sword, his voice ringing out above the chaos. "We hold them here! For Centralia! For our fallen comrades!"

A ragged cheer rose, but the exhaustion was evident. But we'd fight—I would not give up. Not until Eamon was safe. Not until Centralia stood victorious.

CHAPTER 32

The Wintmorians poured into the courtyard, their battle cries chilling, like the howling of wolves. The clash was immediate and brutal. My sword met the strikes of foes on all sides. It was chaos—a blur of movement, the screams of the wounded, the clash of steel on steel.

A Wintmorian axeman charged at me, his weapon raised high. I sidestepped the initial swing, feeling the rush of air as the axe narrowly missed my head. I countered with a swift slash across his unprotected flank. He grimaced, pain flashing across his face. Then, he delivered a powerful backhanded blow that I barely deflected with my shield. I stumbled backward, my feet struggling to find purchase on the blood-slick ground.

Before I could recover, another enemy soldier lunged at me, a dagger glinting in his grasp. I barely had time to react, my breath catching in my throat. But then Edric was there. He stepped between me and the dagger, thrusting his spear into the attacker's path. "Keep fighting!" he shouted, his voice steady even as the blade glanced off his armor. Relief surged through me—only to be cut short as a third foe struck Edric from behind with a mace, the blow landing squarely between his shoulders, the impact denting his armor and jolting through his frame.

"Edric!" I cried out, my heart lurching in my chest as I saw him fall to one knee, pain etched across his face.

"I'm—I'm all right," Edric gasped, struggling to stand, his voice strained with the effort.

I moved to cover him, deflecting a sword strike aimed at his exposed side. The Wintmorian in front of me pressed the attack, his eyes cold. I parried and riposted, but fatigue was slowing me down, my movements heavier. The enemy sensed my weakness and pushed harder, each strike coming faster than the last.

Suddenly, an arrow whistled past my ear, embedding itself in my attacker's chest. He faltered, his weapon slipping from his grasp as he collapsed to the ground. I glanced back to see Cedric lowering his bow, a flood of relief crossing his features before he nocked another arrow. "My thanks." He nodded and veered towards the left flank.

From the corners of my eyes, Edric charged forward toward a Wintmorian wielding a bloody sword, his shield held high. Cedric loosed another arrow, striking down an axeman closing in on Edric from behind. Edric finished off the assailant and immediately turned the other way, focusing on a mace-wielding giant.

"You're welcome, Edric!" Cedric called out, smirking despite the sweat streaking his face. Edric shot him a look, his shield slamming against another opponent's sword. "Less talking, Cedric!" "Don't worry," Cedric quipped, nocking another arrow with practiced ease. "I'll save your hide as many times as it takes. Just try not to make it a full-time job."

"Focus on the fight, Cedric! No time for jokes."

"If I stop joking, Edric, I am already dead."

I cast them an exasperated look, "Focus!"

The enemy pressed on without a pause, and we could not afford a single moment of distraction We would hold. We had to hold.

But all around me, our soldiers fell. The defensive line wavered as gaps were torn open, and wounded men cried out. The number of the fallen grew with each passing moment. The Wintmorians advanced steadily, their ranks moving in disciplined unison, like an unstoppable tide.

Sir Gareth fought valiantly, rallying those near him. "Do not yield! Hold your ground!" he urged. But even his indomitable spirit couldn't stem the tide that was pushing us back, step by agonizing step.

A massive Wintmorian soldier wielding a war hammer broke through our line, swinging his weapon with devastating force. My mouth fell open in horror as I watched him strike down two Centralians with a single sweep, their armor crumpling under the brute force of his blows. The sight filled me with both rage and fear—he had to be stopped.

"We have to take him down!" I shouted to Edric and Cedric, my voice raw with desperation.

The three of us moved to intercept, but before we could engage, the ground trembled beneath our feet as another explosion rocked the fortress. A fireball erupted near the western gate, sending debris raining around us. Panic rippled through us as we realized we were under attack from multiple fronts, our defenses collapsing.

"Fallback to the keep!" General Aldric's voice rang out. His order cut through the chaos, and we knew we had no choice.

Chaos ensued as soldiers scrambled toward the inner sanctum. The wounded were borne or steadied as best we could, but many were left behind in the crush—a reality that tore at my heart. The battle was slipping away from us, and the fortress that had once been our refuge was now a death trap.

We slashed our way toward the keep's entrance, the path obstructed by skirmishes and fleeing comrades. Every step was a struggle, the sounds of battle echoing off the stone walls—a cacophony of clashing weapons, desperate shouts, and the relentless drumming of the enemy's advance. I could feel the exhaustion in my bones, but there was no time to stop, no time to breathe.

Reaching the steps of the keep, I turned, and what I saw made my heart sink. The courtyard was overrun. Wintmorian banners were being raised amidst the fray, their colors stark against the smoke-filled sky. The snow had been turned to slush, dark, and streaked with the lifeblood of countless fallen warriors. "We can't hold them here," Edric yelled. "What are our orders?"

I looked to Sir Gareth, who was already organizing the remaining defenders at the entrance. His lips were tight, yet there was no hesitation. "We make our stand inside," he declared. "We buy as much time as we can."

"For what?" Cedric asked, loosing another arrow into the oncoming horde, muttering, "It's like shooting at the sea—no end to them." His hands were steady despite the tremor in his voice.

Sir Gareth's gaze hardened. "To grant us even the slimmest hope of survival."

We retreated into the keep, barricading the doors behind us. The great hall, which had moments ago been a place of feasting and camaraderie, had become our final bastion. Soldiers hurried to overturn tables and stack debris to fortify our position. The wounded were laid along the walls, and healers tended to them with dwindling supplies.

I looked around, my eyes scanning the faces of those around me—exhausted, wounded, but not defeated. There was a fire in their eyes, a resolve that echoed in my own heart. "We need to hold as long as possible," I said to those nearby. "Every moment counts."

The sound of the battering rams on the doors reverberated through the hall, each impact sending a shudder through the wooden barrier. The wood splintered under the assault, cracks beginning to appear, widening with each blow. Men exchanged glances, their faces pale but resolute, gripping their weapons as if the steel alone could hold back the death that loomed before them.

"Remember why we fight," General Aldric boomed across the hall, looking each of us in the eyes. "For Centralia, for our loved ones, for each other. Let that give you strength."

This was it. The final stand.

"Ready yourselves!" I shouted, as the doors burst open, the force of the impact sending splinters flying. The enemy flooded in, and the clash was immediate. I met the first attacker head-on, our blades locking with a screech of metal. I could feel the tremor of fatigue in my limbs, the weight of every moment spent fighting, but I pushed it aside, focusing solely on the battle in front of me. There was no room for doubt, no room for fear. Only survival.

Around me, our soldiers fought with the ferocity of cornered lions, but I could feel the inevitability of our situation. Our numbers were too few, and our strength too greatly diminished. And every blow I delivered felt like it took twice the effort.

Still, we fought on, unwilling to yield or surrender the last shred of hope we had.

A sudden cry drew my attention, and I turned just in time to see General Aldric fall, a Wintmorian blade piercing his armor. He dropped to his knees, defiant, eyes locking with the attacker as the fatal blow struck his head. The general collapsed, lifeless, to the ground. I froze, and for a moment, my legs were paralyzed with shock. General Aldric had been our rock, our anchor in the storm. His death shattered our resolve like a stone breaking the surface of still water. A wave of hopelessness engulfed me, but I forced it back. I was fighting for my life. The men shrank with horror as if they had lost all the will to continue. Our general was gone. I stepped forward and yelled.

"For General Aldric! For each other!" My amulet burned as hot as the anger in my chest. "This hall will not fall while we yet draw breath! Let them find only steel and fury here!"

I rallied the men. I couldn't let the men see me falter, nor could I let them falter. Not now.

Yet, one by one, all around me, my comrades fell until only a handful of us remained, standing against the overwhelming force that surrounded us. Mindlessly, blindly, I slashed and struck. If the sun sank over us today, let it be said we fought with all our strength. Let those who tell our tale say that we left nothing behind and that we fought to the very last man.

"Kaelan!" Edric's voice called out over the chaos, drawing my gaze. Blood streamed from a wound on his forehead, his eyes wide. "We can't hold them!"

He was right. Yet, surrender wasn't an option I could accept. We had come too far. We had sacrificed too much.

The enemy closed in, their ranks tightening around us. A Wintmorian officer stepped forward, his armor dark and imposing. "Lay down your arms," he demanded, his eyes dancing with mockery. "Your lives will be spared."

I glowered at the officer, my grip tightening on my sword. "We will not yield," I said firmly, with the last of my strength.

CHAPTER 33

The officer's eyes narrowed, his lips curling in disdain. "Then you choose death," he said coldly, signaling his men to advance. The Wintmorian soldiers tightened their grips on their weapons, poised to deliver the final blow. I braced myself, every muscle taut. Time seemed to slow as the enemy closed in, each heartbeat pounding like a drum in my ears.

Suddenly, a distant horn pierced the tumult—a deep, resonant note that cut through the chaos like a clarion call. I drew a sharp intake of breath. The sound was unmistakable, its tone carrying the distinct melody of the Centralian Army. The Wintmorian officer hesitated, a flicker of uncertainty crossing his stern visage.

Another horn blast followed, closer this time, accompanied by the rhythmic thudding of drums and the rising clamor of an approaching force. It was a resplendent sound. The very walls of the fortress vibrated with the intensity. Confusion rippled through the Wintmorian ranks, their advance faltering as they glanced toward the source of the disturbance.

My eyes widened. "Reinforcements!" I exclaimed, "It's General Kyder—the Iron Bear has arrived!"

Edric's face lit up. "General Kyder?"

The great doors of the keep burst open behind us, and a contingent of fresh Centralian soldiers flooded in, their armor gleaming and weapons ready. At their head rode General Kyder himself, a towering figure clad in dark steel, a fearsome helm adorned with stylized bear motifs concealing his features except for his bloodthirsty eyes.

"Forward!" General Kyder bellowed. "Drive them out! Show no mercy to those who threaten our soldiers!"

"To arms!" I shouted to my comrades, a newfound energy filling my voice. "Push them back! Help has come!"

Emboldened, we rallied. A renewed battle cry erupted from our throats as we pressed against the Wintmorians, catching them off guard. Their confidence wavered and their formation unraveled under the unexpected counterattack. The impact was immediate. The Wintmorians, caught between our reinvigorated defenders and the overwhelming force of the reinforcements, began to falter. I seized the opportunity, darting forward to confront the Wintmorian officer who had just threatened our demise.

Our swords met with a resounding clash, sparks flying as steel struck steel. His eyes blazed with frustration, and I could see the doubt now creeping into his resolve, "You should have surrendered," the officer spat, his strikes growing increasingly desperate as he tried to fend me off.

"Fate had other plans," I retorted, pressing my advantage. My sword moved with precision, each swing testing his defenses, each step driving him back. Around us, the Centralian soldiers swept through the Wintmorians like a vengeful wind.

Edric and Cedric fought together, carving a path through the enemy ranks toward the courtyard. I caught glimpses of them through the chaos—Edric's spear a blur as he struck down attackers, Cedric's arrows finding their marks with deadly accuracy.

"To the courtyard!" Sir Gareth's voice cut through the cacophony, commanding our forces. His sword arced downward, felling an opponent with a decisive strike. "We can trap them there!"

The Wintmorian soldiers began a hasty retreat, trying to regroup outside. I broke away from my duel, my eyes sweeping across the battlefield. The tide had irrevocably turned in our favor. "They're falling back!" I called out, my voice raw with effort. "Don't let them escape!"

The Centralian forces pursued, driving the enemy through the corridors and out into the open expanse of the courtyard. General Kyder directed his troops with precision. His words coming at us like pebbles. "Archers, take the walls! Cut off their escape routes! Infantry, form a perimeter!"

The Centralian archers ascended to the battlements, arrows drawn and ready. They aimed at any Wintmorian who dared to flee. Our infantry units spread out, forming a solid ring around the courtyard, trapping the remaining enemy soldiers The Wintmorian officer realized the dire situation. His men were surrounded, their numbers dwindling rapidly. He rallied them for a final stand, his voice hoarse but still commanding. "Hold your ground! We fight to the last!"

Edric, Cedric, and I advanced toward the center of the courtyard, joining Sir Gareth and General Kyder.

"Let's finish this," Sir Gareth declared, his eyes as hard as steel.

The two powerful leaders exchanged brief nods, and I felt like singing. We closed in, tightening the noose around the Wintmorians. They were soon exhausted and outnumbered, crumbling under our relentless assault.

Soon, I was face to face once more with the Wintmorian office and immediately dismantled his defense.

"Your fight is over," I said between strikes. "Spare your men further loss. We keep our word."

He hesitated, his aggression faltering for just a moment. "What do you know of honor?" he retorted, though his voice lacked conviction, the fire in his eyes dimming.

"Senseless death serves no one," I replied, my gaze unwavering. "Lay down your arms."

General Kyder immediately approached. His armor gleamed in the pale morning light "Your position is hopeless," he stated, his tone leaving no room for argument. "Order your men to surrender, and they will be treated fairly, we have already taken briarwick."

The Wintmorian officer glanced around—the remnants of his forces were being subdued, weapons discarded in the face of overwhelming odds. His shoulders sagged, "Very well," he conceded, lowering his sword. "We yield."

A collective sigh rippled through the courtyard as weapons were lowered, and the immediate threat dissipated. We moved swiftly to disarm the Wintmorians and secure the area. Healers began attending to the wounded on both sides, the groans of the injured mingling with the hushed murmurs of relief. General Kyder regarded the captured officer with a steady gaze. "You have fought bravely. Your cooperation now will ensure the well-being of your men."

The officer met his eyes evenly. "I will hold you to that promise."

Finally, it was over. I looked around the courtyard—the cost of the battle was evident everywhere I turned. The fallen lay where they had fought, and the wounded sprawled in their battered bodies groaning in agony.

Edric approached. There was a poultice pressed against the cut above his brow. "We did it," he said quietly, his voice barely audible over the sounds of the aftermath. "It's like a dream."

Cedric joined us, his quiver nearly empty, and the weariness in his eyes evident. "Thanks to The Iron Bear," he remarked, nodding toward the imposing figure conferring with his officers. I nodded in agreement. But suddenly, emotions overwhelmed me and before I could think, I found myself embracing them both. "I'm glad we're still standing. I wouldn't have wanted it any other way.'"

***

We spent the next hours aiding the healers and the chirurgeons, comforting the wounded, and helping to fortify the damaged sections of the fortress. I was almost falling over with exhaustion, but we had to keep moving. There was no time to rest. Not yet.

Sir Gareth approached us as we worked, a rare smile softening his usually stern features. "Well fought, all of you. Your actions held the line until reinforcements could arrive. You have my respect."

"Thank you, sire," we replied in unison, the words carrying the weight of our shared relief and pride.

Soon, General Kyder joined us. Up close, I saw the lines etched into his face—a testament to years of warfare—and the sharp intelligence in his eyes. "Your names?" the general inquired, his voice clipped.

"Kaelan of Elsenburg, sir," I replied, standing a little straighter.

"Edric of Windermere in Noble."

"Cedric of Elsenburg, at your service."

The general regarded us thoughtfully. "I've heard of your valor. Centralia needs soldiers like you—resourceful and steadfast. You've grown since you were recruits."

"We're honored, General Kyder."

He glanced toward the keep, his expression turning serious. "This fortress stands because of your efforts. But the war is far from over. We must remain vigilant."

"General," Sir Gareth interjected, "we've captured a high-ranking Wintmorian officer. He may possess information of great import."

Kyder nodded, his eyes narrowing in thought. "Indeed. See to it that he is treated fairly. We will question him once the situation here is under control."

"Perhaps we can gain insight into their plans and prevent further bloodshed," I said.

"That's the aim," the general affirmed, his tone carrying a note of reassurance. "Now, tend to your wounds and rest while you can. There is much to be done."

As the leaders departed to organize the aftermath, I turned to Edric and Cedric, "Let's check on the others,"

And together, we moved through the courtyard, helping those we could.

The sun climbed slowly higher until it was sitting in the middle of the sky overlooking the battered fortress, which though scarred, remained a bastion of Centralian resilience. It stood as a testament to our ruggedness, and I took solace in knowing we had held our ground.

CHAPTER
34

Later, as evening approached, we gathered in the mess hall. The mood was subdued, thick with the weight of loss. I battled not just with the loss of my comrades, I battled with my impotence. I had snuck out to find my brother and failed woefully.

Eamon.

He remained central in my thoughts, louder than the sounds of battle, louder than the cries of the wounded or the clash of steel. I'd promised to save him, to pull him out of Briarwick's cursed streets. But that was before the ambush; before the Witmorian blades carved up our ranks like scythes through grass and left the fort crawling with death.

"I can't go," I groaned under my breath. It was only a few hours after the fight and other men were resting, others nursing their wounds. Sneaking out felt traitorous, but my words tasted like betrayal to my family.

Lorric, the cobbler's son from back in Elsenburg I hadn't noticed him before, he was an archer, had leaned against the wall beside me, arms crossed. His eyes were dark and thoughtful. "You'd be a fool to go after him. Eamon's got his own choices to make, Kaelan. You can't save everyone. Marcus died today. I couldn't save him."

My jaw tightened. Marcus was one of our best he had helped us take the fort. He had fallen to a Wintmorian's spear to his back.

"I'm sorry," I said. He didn't reply. Instead, he shook his head.

"But Eamon is not just anyone, Lorric," I said, suddenly bereft, "He's my only brother."

Lorric's voice softened almost reluctantly, "And if you die chasing after him? Who's left to tell him you cared?" The question hit harder than I expected.

Who, indeed?

I couldn't bring myself to answer. Instead, I stared at the floor, trying to push the feeling of betrayal out of my chest.

"We have suffered so much loss today," Lorric continued, his tone sad, "Don't risk your life for that which you cannot mend."

But I went, regardless.

Edric, ever faithful friend, had gone with me. Cedric stayed back in case he needed to tell a lie about our whereabouts.

The streets of Briarwick were dead. Everyone was gone; the thieves, gamblers, the beggars, and the lost souls who once filled the alleys were gone. It was eerily silent save for the occasional clatter of loose shutters, and the howling of the wind. It was as if the city itself had given up on itself.

Jareth's house was just as empty. The furniture was over-turned with the faint scent of stale ale in the air. It looked as though someone had left in a hurry.

"Empty," Edric muttered, kicking a broken chair aside.

I looked around. "Lilah. She was meant to be here too."

"She's not," Edric replied, "Let's not linger. If Jareth is not here, we have no cause to stay."

I hesitated. There was something Jareth had said, something about where Eamon could be, about not coming alone. He'd warned me that if I did, 'they' wouldn't let me meet him, whoever 'they' were.

The sound of footsteps outside the door jolted me out of my thoughts. With one swift movement, I flung the door open with my sword raised. A figure stood by the threshold, and in one instant, he turned and fled. It was a boy, no older than ten, darting through the alleys with the ease of a person born in it. We pursued him, the boy's footfalls echoing in the empty street. With a swift motion, I grabbed his arm and pressed him against the cold stone wall. He whimpered. He could be older than I thought, but he was as thin as a reed and covered in grime.

"Don't hurt me, sires," he begged, his voice trembling.

"We mean you no harm," Edric replied calmly, his eyes narrowed, "Just tell us where to find old Jareth."

The boy's eyes went wide. "I don't know. By the gods, I don't know."

I pressed harder.

"What of Lilah? She was to meet us here."

"Lilah, the thief? I had not seen her since all of this." He waved his hands around the soulless street.

I released my grip and he bolted, disappearing down the alley. I stood there, still, for a moment, while my heart and my head warred with each other.

Edric laid a comforting hand on my shoulder, "We can't stay here, Kaelan. It is dangerous."

I shook my head. I couldn't go back to the fort without finding Eamon. But something gnawed at me, something Jareth had said. It was about where Eamon would be. The words echoed in my mind, clearer now.

I started running in the other direction. Edric was puzzled. "Where are you going to, Kaelan?"

I turned to him, breathless. "I know where Eamon is."

"Where…?"

"He's at the old mill near the river."

My heart swelled. The air hummed with possibility. If Jareth had spoken the truth, Eamon would be there, though not alone. I wasn't worried. If I had endured the battle with the Wintmorians, whoever was with Eamon wouldn't stand a chance.

We arrived by the mill, breathless. No one was there. No sign of anyone having been there at all. And my heart sank into my stomach.

I sat back in the mess hall now, staring at the table in front of me. Frustration coiled within me, squeezing the air from my lungs. The weight of what I'd lost, what I had failed to do, pressed down on me until it felt like I couldn't breathe. Every choice I had made seemed wrong, every moment I had hesitated, a betrayal. I had left my home, my parents, and now, the fort and my duty behind in search of my brother, but now all I had were empty arms and a pang of aching guilt that threatened to swallow me whole.

****

Edric, Cedric, and I shared a quiet meal. There was no idle chatter, no easy banter. My thoughts drifted, heavy with the weight of my fruitless journey to find Eamon; the dead end that stood before me as stark and unforgiving as a stone wall. It felt selfish, this consuming worry for him when so many others had fallen—especially General Aldric, whose loss weighed heavily on us all. Yet, despite the grief that hung thick in the air, it was the fear for Eamon's life that gripped my heart most fiercely, an agonizing ache I could not rid myself of.

Edric raised his cup, his expression softening. "To those we've lost, and to the hope that we may find a path to peace."

Cedric raised his. "To Eamon and Kaelan. That they may find what they seek."

I raised my goblet in acknowledgment, but I couldn't say a word.

***

Later that night, I found myself drawn to the battlements, I stood alone, staring out over the quiet expanse. The world seemed almost peaceful now, a far cry from the chaos of battle that had raged just a turn of the sun ago.

Sir Gareth approached silently, joining me at the wall. He stood there for a moment before speaking. "A long day," he remarked, his voice carrying a note of exhaustion.

"One I won't soon forget," I agreed, my gaze distant.

"You acquitted yourself well," Sir Gareth said, and I turned to see a rare smile softening his stern features. "General Kyder was impressed."

I shrugged. The praise felt somewhat misplaced. "We all did our part," I replied. Sir Gareth nodded, his eyes thoughtful. I wondered if he knew what I had done.

"True. But leadership comes naturally to some. Have you considered pursuing a command position?"

The question caught me off guard. I blinked and turned until I was facing him. He meant every word. "Well, I hadn't thought much beyond the immediate," I admitted. My mind had been so focused on surviving, on protecting those I loved, that I hadn't allowed myself to consider what might come after. "Think about it," Sir Gareth encouraged. "Centralia needs leaders for the days ahead. People like you, who care for their comrades and stand firm in the face of adversity."

I swallowed, the weight of his words settling on me. "I will."

We stood in silence for a time, the chill of the night air biting at my skin. Despite what had happened, the fortress still stood. A modest victory, yes. But one that carried great meaning. For it felt like a sign. That even in the face of all that was wrong, there was still hope that all could be made right.

"Rest well," Sir Gareth said eventually, his voice low. "Tomorrow brings new challenges."

"Goodnight, Sir Gareth," I replied, watching as he turned and made his way back down the steps.

I lingered for a few more moments, before deciding I had punished myself enough and went to sleep.

CHAPTER 35

I woke up the following morning with a clear, unburdened, mind. The air was crisp, carrying the scents of pine and faint traces of smoke from the previous day's battle. Soldiers moved about the courtyard with a purposeful calm, tending to repairs, sharpening weapons, and sharing quiet conversations that belied the intensity of recent events.

I stood atop the eastern wall, gazing out over the rolling mountains now blanketed in a pristine layer of snow. The landscape was a stark contrast to the turmoil that had so recently engulfed it. For a moment, I allowed myself to believe in that peace—and better mornings.

Edric and Cedric joined me, their footsteps crunching softly as they approached.

"Hard to believe what happened here," Edric mused, leaning against the cold stone. "It's almost as if the land itself has forgotten."

"Nature has a way of cleansing itself," Cedric replied thoughtfully, his gaze sweeping over the snowy landscape. "Perhaps we could learn from that."

I nodded, my eyes still fixed on the horizon. "The scars remain, though. Even if unseen."

Before I could delve further into reflection, a young messenger approached, his breath visible in the chilly air. "Sirs, Sir Gareth and General Kyder request your presence in the command tent."

"Thank you," I replied. "We'll be there shortly."

As the messenger departed, Edric raised his eyebrows at me. "I wonder what this is about."

"There is but one way to find out," I said as I turned to descend the stairs. The command tent was situated near the center of the fortress, a large structure reinforced to withstand the elements. As we entered, the warmth from a brazier washed over us, and the rich aroma of spiced tea filled the air. "Young men," Sir Gareth greeted us with a nod. "Thank you for coming promptly."

"You summoned us, sir," I replied.

General Kyder stepped forward, his gaze assessing each of us in turn. "Your performance during the defense of this fortress was exemplary. Your leadership and bravery were instrumental in holding the line until reinforcements arrived."

"We were merely doing our duty," Cedric said modestly.

"Your humility does you credit," Kyder acknowledged. "But it is important to recognize and reward such qualities."

Sir Gareth exchanged a glance with the General before addressing us. "As you know, the recent battle has led to significant changes in our command structure. General Aldric's untimely death has left a vacancy that must be filled without delay."

We bowed our heads as a moment of sorrow washed over us. "After careful consideration," Sir Gareth continued, "I have been appointed as the new general of this regiment."

"Congratulations, sir," we said earnestly.

"Thank you," Sir Gareth replied. "However, this advancement means that my previous position must now be filled."

General Kyder folded his arms across his chest, his gaze steady. "We require capable individuals to step into leadership roles, especially in times such as these. Sir Gareth and I have discussed the matter, and we believe that you three are well-suited to take on greater responsibilities."

I exchanged a surprised look with Edric and Cedric. "What would you have us do?" I asked, my heart pounding slightly at the prospect.

"Until a new Knight of Centralia can be assigned to this regiment," Sir Gareth explained, "we would like you to stand in as acting officers. Your familiarity with the men and the respect you've earned will ensure a smooth transition."

Edric raised an eyebrow, a hint of incredulity in his expression. "That's quite an honor."

"It is also a significant responsibility," Kyder added, his voice firm but encouraging. "One that I believe you are prepared to undertake."

Cedric nodded thoughtfully, his usual levity replaced by solemn resolve. "We accept, sir. We'll do our utmost to serve effectively."

I took a deep breath, the weight of the moment settling on my shoulders. "We won't let you down, sir."

"Excellent," Sir Gareth said with a faint smile, the tension in his posture easing slightly. "There will be official briefings later today to acquaint you with your new duties."

General Kyder's expression grew more contemplative, his gaze locking onto mine. "There is another matter to discuss, specifically with you, Kaelan."

I straightened, "Yes, General?"

Kyder regarded me steadily, his eyes assessing. "Your actions have not gone unnoticed by the higher echelons of our command. Your leadership qualities, strategic insight, and courage under fire are attributes we seek in the Imperial Iron Regiment."

"The Imperial Iron Regiment?" I repeated, surprised. My mind raced at the mention of the prestigious unit.

Edric's eyes widened as he looked at me. "That's the elite, isn't it?"

"Indeed," Kyder confirmed. "The Iron Regiment is comprised of the finest soldiers in Centralia, tasked with critical missions that require exceptional skill and resolve."

"I'm honored, General. What are you proposing?"

"I'm offering you a position within the Imperial Iron Regiment," Kyder stated plainly. "You would join my command, receive refined training, and undertake tasks crucial to the safeguard of the realm."

Cedric clapped a hand on my shoulder, "That's an incredible opportunity, Kaelan," his voice filled with admiration.

"It is," Kyder agreed, nodding. "However, it is not a decision to be made lightly. Your current regiment needs strong leaders, especially now. Staying here as acting officers could also greatly benefit your comrades."

Sir Gareth interjected gently, his gaze warm. "Ultimately, the choice is yours, Kaelan. Whether you decide to remain with us or join the Iron Regiment, your contributions will be invaluable."

My mind raced, emotions swirling. The prospect of joining the elite forces was both thrilling and daunting. It would offer new challenges and the chance to make a significant impact on the outcome of this war. Yet, my loyalty to my friends and the men I had fought alongside, weighed heavily in my considerations. The bonds we had formed—the shared hardships, the moments of victory and loss—they were not easily set aside.

I took a deep breath, trying to steady my thoughts. "May I have some time to think it over?"

"Of course," Kyder replied his tone calm and laced with quiet understanding. "This is not a decision to be rushed. Take the day to reflect. We will reconvene tomorrow morning."

"Thank you, General," I said, giving him a quick bow.

The three of us stepped out into the brisk afternoon air. We walked in contemplative silence for a few moments, and then Edric finally spoke.

"That's quite the crossroads you've come to," he remarked, his voice thoughtful.

"Indeed."

Cedric glanced at me, his brow furrowed in thought. "What will you do, Kaelan?"

I rubbed the back of my neck. "Truth be told, I don't know," I admitted "To join the imperial Iron Regiment is a rare honor, yet leaving our regiment now feels…wrong."

The thought of leaving nagged at me, like a loose thread in the fabric of a cherished banner. Was it the bond I'd forged with my men, or was it Eamon? Had it always been about Eamon? Was my real reason for wanting to stay because of him? Because he was still here somewhere and I had to find him? His dream of leaving home had always seemed so starkly at odds with my own desire for roots and stability. If I left now, would I become no better than him, chasing ambitions too grand for my reach and leaving everyone else behind?

"Our brothers hold you in high regard," Edric whispered, echoing my thoughts, "Your leadership would be of great asset here. We have endured much together—it would not be the same without you."

Cedric leaned in, "But we can't disregard the weight of what you could achieve in the Iron Regiment. There, you could do much more good. You'd be in a position to take on missions that could change the course of this war."

I rubbed my temple. Each argument seemed to balance the other, and my thoughts remained a tangled mess. We reached the training grounds, where soldiers were engaging in drills under the watchful eyes of their sergeants, and I regarded the men. It was more than just a regiment; it was a family, forged through hardship and perseverance.

Edric placed a reassuring hand on my arm, his voice firm. "Whatever path you choose, Kaelan, it shall be the right one. You'll make a fine soldier, wherever you may be."

Cedric nodded in agreement, his expression softening. "Absolutely. Whether you stay or go, that won't change."

We spent the rest of the day weighing the merits of each choice, yet no decision was reached."

***

Before I slept that night, I sought solitude atop one of the watchtowers. Stars flickered faintly against the indigo sky, their light stark against the biting cold. The chill sharpened my thoughts, a clarity I desperately needed. It seemed that in the quiet of the night, I might find the answer I was searching for.

Footsteps approached, and I turned to see General Kyder ascending the steps. He joined me at the parapet, his gaze fixed on the distant mountains, the peaks just barely visible in the fading light.

"Beautiful view," Kyder commented softly, his voice almost lost to the wind.

"It is," I agreed, my eyes following the line of the horizon.

The general nodded, his expression contemplative. "Have you given thought to the choice before you?"

"I have," I replied, a sigh escaping. "But I admit, I'm still uncertain."

"It's understandable," Kyder said. "There's no wrong decision, Kaelan—only what you feel is right for you."

I hesitated for a moment, then asked, "May I ask, General, why did you choose me for this offer?"

Kyder was still for a while, his eyes contemplating the distant mountains. "I've observed many soldiers over the years," he began. "Few possess the combination of skill, intellect, and integrity that you demonstrate. You lead not just with strength, but with empathy. The Iron Regiment requires leaders who can inspire others, and who can make difficult decisions when the time comes, even at great personal cost. I see that in you."

I felt a burst of pride and this softened the load in my heart. Suddenly, though it felt out of place, the words were at the tip of my tongue—to speak of Eamon, of our childhood in Elsenburg, of Ma and Pa, and the farm we once called home. I could have spoken of how adrift I sometimes felt, drifting farther from both home and my brother. Yet, I knew he would not understand. And it would be bold to think I could share such matters with my superior. I heaved a sigh.

"I am grateful for your confidence in me, sir. It means more than words can express."

"Regardless of your decision, know that my offer stands," Kyder affirmed "And that I respect your dedication to your brothers. Loyalty like yours is rare, and it shouldn't be taken lightly."

"Thank you, Lord General. He placed a reassuring hand on my shoulder. "Take the night to reflect, Kaelan. Trust your instincts. They haven't led you wrong yet."

He turned at once and descended the steps. I remained on the tower, staring out into the vastness of the night. I closed my eyes, took a deep breath, and felt the cold wind against my face. Whatever path I chose, would ripple through the lives of those around me. In the stillness of the night, while I deliberated long and hard, one thought burned clear: I couldn't afford doubt. Not now.

CHAPTER 36

"I have reached a decision."

My friends looked at me searchingly, as if holding their breath.

"I'm going to stay with the regiment. This is where I belong—for now, at least."

Cedric thumped my back as his face broke into a wide grin. "We're glad to hear it. The men will be relieved, and so are we."

"Thank you," I said, my voice thick with emotion. Edric shook my hand enthusiastically. "You made the right call, Kaelan. The regiment needs you—we need you."

"And who else is going to keep you two out of trouble?" I added with a laugh, the burden finally easing from my shoulders.

Cedric chuckled, shaking his head. "Well, someone has to keep us from doing anything too reckless."

"Ready to face the generals?" Edric asked.

I took a deep breath and we entered the command tent together. Inside, General Kyder and Sir Gareth sat hunched together in a deep conversation. They looked up as we approached.

"Kaelan, Edric, Cedric," Sir Gareth acknowledged, nodding in our direction. "Good morning."

"Good morning, sirs," General Kyder's gaze settled on me, his expression unreadable. "Have you reached a decision regarding my offer, Kaelan?"

I met his eyes. "Yes, General Kyder. I've decided to stay with the regiment. My comrades need me here, and I feel my duties lie alongside them at this time."

Eamon needs me.

A moment of silence followed as Kyder studied me, his eyes searching my face. Then, a faint smile touched his lips, and he nodded. "Your loyalty is commendable, Kaelan. Such dedication to one's fellows is a quality that never goes unnoticed."

Sir Gareth nodded in agreement. "Your choice reflects well on your character, Kaelan. The regiment will greatly benefit from your continued leadership."

"Thank you, sirs," I said, "I hope to serve Centralia to the best of my abilities, here or wherever I'm needed."

"Very well," General Kyder said, "We have much to discuss regarding your new responsibilities."

He gestured toward the drawings on the table. "Scouts have identified a critical opportunity. The Wintmorian forces are relying heavily on a supply line that runs through the town of Evenshire. Severing this provision routes could greatly weaken their efforts in the region."

Sir Gareth leaned over the map, his gloved finger gliding along a faint trail winding northeast. "Two days' march," he said as he paused at a marked point labeled Evenshire, It's a small town, but strategically located. The enemy uses it as a transit point for provisions, weapons, and reinforcements."

General Kyder turned back to Sir Gareth. "I am assigning you and your regiment the task of advancing to Evenshire and severing this supply line. It's imperative that we act swiftly and decisively."

"Understood, Lord General," Sir Gareth affirmed, his expression determined. "We will make the necessary preparations immediately."

Kyder's eyes then turned to me. "Kaelan, as the commanding officer, you and your comrades bear great responsibility in this charge. Your knowledge of the men and the lay of the land will serve us well."

The meeting adjourned and we exited the tent. Word spread quickly, and soldiers prepared for the impending march.

Edric clapped me on the back, a grin spreading across his face. "Looks like we're heading out again."

Cedric approached me with a clipboard, his expression focused. "I've taken stock of the headcount and gear. We're fully stocked, though we might need additional rations if we expect delays."

"Good work," I said, looking at the notes he handed me. "Let's requisition the extra supplies just in case. Evenshire might not have resources we can use."

Edric joined us, adjusting the strap of his pack as he approached. "The men are eager to move out. Morale is high, especially knowing you'll be leading them."

As midday approached, Sir Gareth called a briefing for the officers. We gathered in a smaller tent, where a detailed map of the route to Evenshire was displayed across the table. I leaned over the map, taking in the terrain, the landmarks, and the potential threats.

"Attention," Sir Gareth began, "Our mission is straightforward in concept but will require precision in execution. We will march northeast, maintaining a steady but cautious pace. Scouts will be sent ahead to monitor for enemy patrols."

He pointed to various landmarks along the route, his finger tracing the path we would take. "There are natural choke points here and here, which we must secure to prevent ambushes. Once we reach Evenshire, we'll assess the enemy's presence and devise a plan to disrupt or destroy the supply line."

I studied the map closely, frowning at the unknowns. "Do we have any knowledge of the town's defenses or the number of enemy forces stationed there?"

Sir Gareth shook his head slightly. "Limited. Our reports suggest that the Wintmorian presence is moderate, with their efforts largely devoted to provisioning rather than battle. However, we must be prepared for resistance."

Edric tapped a spot on the map, his eyes narrowing in thought. "There's a forested area west of Evenshire. It could provide cover for our approach."

"Good observation," Sir Gareth acknowledged, nodding. "We'll factor that into our strategy."

The council continued, with tasks apportioned and contingencies deliberated. Each officer left with a clear understanding of their role and the mission's objectives. The tension in the tent could be cut by a blade, but there was also a sense of determination—a readiness to face whatever lay ahead.

By late afternoon, the regiment was assembled at the fortress gates. Soldiers stood in orderly ranks and waited for orders. The sun hung low in the sky, casting long shadows across the snow-covered ground. I took a moment to take in the sight of the men, their faces set with resolve. This was it—another step toward weakening the enemy.

Sir Gareth rode to the front of the formation, his horse stamping impatiently in the cold. He addressed the men with a voice that carried across the courtyard. "Soldiers of Centralia, today we embark on a mission critical to the success of our campaign. The enemy relies on the supplies flowing through Evenshire. We will cut that lifeline and weaken their hold on these lands, while Lord General Kyder will be moving westward to try to cut off more supplies."

A cheer rose from the ranks, the sound echoing off the stone walls of the fortress. The men stood taller, their faces alight with determination, and their fists clenched at their sides as the air seemed to hum with the rising fervor. The banners of Centralia fluttered boldly in the crisp air, their vibrant colors a stark contrast against the snow-blanketed landscape. We were ready—a unified force prepared to face whatever challenges lay ahead.

As the cheer subsided, a deep horn sounded—a resonant call that signaled the commencement of our march. And we were on our way again.

CHAPTER
37

I took my place at the forefront of my men, flanked by Edric and Cedric. I glanced over my shoulder at the men under my command—faces both familiar and new, each reflecting a shared dream. "Tread carefully," I advised, my voice steady despite the anticipation thrumming in my veins. "We shall be moving through dense forests and we need to be alert."

Edric adjusted his grip on his spear. "We've been through worse," he remarked with a grin. "But a little caution never hurts."

Cedric tightened the strap of his quiver and looked at the road ahead. "Scouts reported clear paths so far, but the Wintmorians are cunning. Best to expect the unexpected."

Sir Gareth rode at the front, his broad shoulders stiff with purpose. Sharp, calculating eyes swept over the landscape with the precision of someone who had seen too many battles. He rarely spoke of himself—no whispers of a family, a home, or a lover. Yet the way he led us, tireless and deliberate, suggested a loyalty to something far beyond duty. I often wondered what ghosts followed him, and what whispers lay buried beneath the steel in his gaze.

"Forward march!" his voice rang out, sharp and distilled. I was thankful that it was he who led us, guiding us through this trial with a steady hand and a companionate heart.

The gates groaned open, revealing the wilderness beyond. We moved out in disciplined columns, the crunch of snow underfoot marking our progress. The pale blue sky and shimmering frost framed the snowy trees, standing like sentinels along the path. As we entered the forest, the world grew quieter, the subtle rustling of leaves and the occasional snap of a twig replacing the noise of open ground.

"Remember your training," I said, my voice low but firm. "Report anything unusual."

The soldiers moved with practiced ease, adjusting their formation to navigate the narrower trails. Light filtered through the canopy, illuminating patches of ground where small animals scurried away from the marching troops

The forest was beautiful, but it held its perils.

Edric gestured toward faint tracks in the snow. "Deer. At least there's a game around."

Cedric smirked, "Let's hope the Wintmorians haven't scared them all off, A fresh meal would be nice."

We maintained a steady pace, the silence punctuated by brief exchanges and the distant calls of birds. Scouts moved ahead and along the flanks, their keen eyes searching for any signs of the enemy. So far, all reports indicated that the way was clear, but I had learned that the forest's beauty was deceptive, and I knew better than to let my guard down.

As midday approached, Sir Gareth signaled for a brief halt. The soldiers took the opportunity to rest and drink water. I sat with Edric and Cedric near a fallen log, grateful for a moment to stretch my legs.

"How are the men holding up?" I asked as they settled for a short rest.

"Spirits are high," Edric replied, taking a swig from his canteen. "A few are grumbling about the cold, but nothing serious."

Cedric stretched his arms above his head, his bow resting against the log. "No signs of Wintmorian activity. Either they've pulled back, or they're hiding well."

"Let's not get complacent," I cautioned, "We should reach the outskirts of Evenshire by tomorrow evening if we keep this pace."

The horn signaled the end of the rest period and we moved out once more. The terrain grew more challenging as we progressed, with roots and uneven ground hidden beneath the snow. But the men stayed in formation.

As the afternoon began to wane, the forest started to change. The trees grew taller and more closely spaced, their branches intertwining overhead to create a tunnel-like effect. The light took on a golden hue and long shadows danced with the movement of the troops.

I felt a subtle shift in the air. I turned to Edric, keeping my voice low. "This area feels different," I remarked. "Stay alert."

Moments later, a scout emerged from the shadows, approaching Sir Gareth with a swift stride. The exchange between them was brief, but I could see the urgency in the scout's expression. Sir Gareth raised his hand, signaling for the column to halt.

We all stopped, the air charged with anticipation. My hand moved instinctively to the hilt of my sword, as we waited.

Scouts have spotted an abandoned campsite ahead," Sir Gareth announced to the officers. "No immediate signs of the enemy, but we're proceeding with caution."

We advanced slowly, the crunch of snow beneath our boots loud in the forest's heavy silence. When the remains of the campsite came into view—a circle of stones where a fire once burned, scattered footprints now obscured by snow, and broken branches from a hasty departure—a chill crept over me. Cedric crouched, studying the ground. "Too heavy for hunters," he murmured, "Likely a small group of soldiers."

"Perhaps Wintmorian scouts," Edric suggested.

Sir Gareth signaled for us to gather. "Double the watch tonight," he ordered, his eyes roaming the trees. If the enemy was near, we needed to be prepared. As dusk began to settle, we found a defensible location to make camp—a clearing surrounded by dense thickets with a slight elevation that offered a good vantage point. We moved quickly, setting up tents and posting guards at strategic points around the perimeter.

I gathered my men around me. "Get some rest while you can," I advised, my eyes meeting each of theirs. "We'll take the second watch. Stay in pairs and keep your weapons close."

The soldiers nodded, dispersing to their assigned areas. Edric and Cedric stayed with me as we reviewed the map by the dim light of a lantern. The flickering light made the lines on the map dance, but I tried to focus, tracing a path with my finger.

"Evenshire is just beyond this forest," I noted "If the Wintmorians are operating in the area, we'll likely encounter them soon."

"Do we have any idea of their numbers?" Edric asked, his gaze shifting between me and Cedric.

"Scouts suggest it's a moderate force," Cedric replied, his tone thoughtful. "Enough to defend the supply line but not an overwhelming presence."

I leaned back, my mind alive with possibilities. "We must devise a plan befitting the task at hand. A frontal assault might be costly. Perhaps we can devise a means to disrupt their operations without confrontation."

Sir Gareth joined us then, his face illuminated by the flickering lantern light. "I've been considering the same," he said, nodding. "Sabotage, perhaps—" I looked at the map again, the lines and markings blurring slightly as I thought. "We could send small teams to target key points—bridges, storehouses, messenger routes. Hit them where it hurts."

"Agreed," Sir Gareth said. "We'll finalize the plan tomorrow after gathering more information."

The night deepened around us. The temperature dropped and a light snow began to fall, its flakes settled gently on our tents and cloaks.

When my turn for watch came, I moved along the perimeter, the cold biting at my face and hands. The forest seemed endless, shadows stretching between the trees, but nothing stirred beyond our camp. I kept my senses sharp, listening for anything hinting at danger. The night remained quiet, almost deceptively so.

When my shift ended, I returned to my tent. Edric was already asleep, his breathing steady, while Cedric was scribbling notes in a small journal.

"Anything interesting?" I asked softly, not wanting to disturb the quiet.

Cedric looked up, a small smile on his lips. "Just my thoughts," he said, closing the book gently. "It helps me remember what matters."

I nodded, settling into my bedroll. "Get some rest. Tomorrow will be a long day," I murmured, feeling exhaustion tugging at me.

The night was uneventful and morning came swiftly, the gray light of dawn filtering through the canopy above. We broke camp efficiently, the soldiers refreshed and ready, their faces set with renewed strength.

***

As we resumed our march, the forest began to thin. The trees became sparser, and patches of open land appeared more frequently. By midday, we reached a ridge that offered a sweeping view of the valley below.

Evenshire lay ahead—a modest town nestled beside a frozen river, and its streets dotted with figures moving about. From this distance, it seemed peaceful, but its strategic importance was clear.

Sir Gareth called for a halt. "We'll position ourselves here, hidden among the trees," he instructed. "Scouts will gather detailed information on the town's defenses and any enemy activity."

Our band was assigned to assist. We established a concealed position among the rocks and sparse trees, using spyglasses to survey Evenshire.

"There's movement near that warehouse," Cedric observed. "Could be a storehouse."

"Look there," Edric pointed. "Wintmorian banners. They've set up a presence."

As we discussed plans and strategies, the horn sounded softly in the distance—a signal for the bands to regroup.

"It's time," I said, straightening my back and facing them. "We have our mission."

The officers and scouts gathered around us nodded in agreement. The vantage point overlooking Evenshire provided us with valuable insights into the town's layout and the positions of the Wintmorian forces. Smoke from the chimneys curled lazily into the sky, masking the true nature of the activities below.

Sir Gareth unrolled a detailed map of the area on a makeshift table fashioned from a flat rock. "Our objective is to disrupt the storehouse located here," he said, pointing to a cluster of buildings near the river's edge. "A direct assault would alert the entire garrison, so we'll employ a more subtle approach."

I leaned in, studying the map intently. "A small, fast-moving unit could infiltrate the depot and set charges to destroy the supplies. If we time it right, the chaos should allow us to withdraw before they organize a response."

"Precisely," Sir Gareth agreed. He turned to Edric. "Edric, I'd like you to lead the assault team. Your experience with covert operations will be invaluable."

Edric straightened, "I won't let you down, sir."

I glanced at Edric. "You'll have our support. We'll position ourselves here," I pointed to a wooded area northwest of the town, "ready to provide backup if anything goes wrong."

Cedric added, "Our archers can cover your retreat and create additional distractions if needed."

Sir Gareth nodded approvingly. "Good. Remember, the primary goal is to destroy the storehouse and withdraw with minimal engagement. We don't want to become embroiled in a prolonged fight."

With that, we finalized the plan, and the officers dispersed to brief their respective units. The sun dipped lower in the sky, casting long shadows across the snowy landscape. As twilight approached, we made our final preparations.

CHAPTER
38

A few hours later, under the cloak of darkness, Edric's team assembled at the edge of the forest. Dressed in muted colors and equipped with light gear, they blended seamlessly into the surroundings. I watched as Edric moved quietly among them, ensuring each man understood his role.

From my position with the backup force, I watched as the small group melted into the night.

"Signalers in position?" I asked Cedric, who stood beside me, scanning the town with a spyglass.

"Yes," Cedric confirmed. "If anything goes awry, we'll know immediately."

The minutes stretched into an hour as we waited, the silence disturbing. My fingers hovered over the hilt of my sword, clenching and unclenching as I imagined Edric and his men fighting to complete the mission. I kept my gaze fixed on the cluster of buildings identified as the supply depot. A few lanterns flickered near the entrance, and occasional silhouettes moved against the light. Then, it came; a faint glow followed by the muffled thud we had been waiting for. My breath caught. The signal. Cedric leaned closer,

"They've made entry."

For a brief moment, hope sparked in my chest, "Stay ready," I said, rather unnecessarily, "If all goes well, they'll be back shortly."

We watched in silence for a moment.

But the next sound shattered that fragile hope—a sharp crack echoed through the stillness, followed by an explosion. The depot erupted into an inferno, orange light spilling across the night like a bleeding wound. Shouts of alarm broke the quiet as Wintmorian soldiers scrambled to respond.

"Damn it!" Cedric hissed beside me, his gaze fixed on the blaze.

I swept my eyes over the area for any sign of Edric's team. Smoke churned, obscuring the depot, and the chaotic movements of the enemy troops made it difficult to discern friend from foe.

"Do you see them?" I asked, my voice betraying the crack of a rising panic.

Cedric shook his head, frustration flashing in his eyes. "No, the smoke's too thick.

The realization came sharp and cold. Something had gone wrong. I clenched my jaw, forcing myself to think. The seconds stretched unbearably, and I could no longer ignore the nagging thought that time was running out. My fists tightened at my sides, and a low growl escaped me.

The horn blast shattered the night, cutting through the chaos like a clarion call for survival. My men sprang into action, breaking from the treeline as the world erupted into motion around me.

"We can't wait any longer," I turned to the horn-bearer. My voice was harder now, edged with urgency. "Sound the call. We're going in."

"Archers, provide cover!" I commanded, my voice ringing with determination. "Infantry, follow me!"

Cedric notched an arrow beside me, his gaze steely as he looked toward the town. "Let's bring them home,"

The Centralian archers fired toward the enemy positions, arrows cutting through the cold night air, sowing confusion and providing a window for us to move. I led the charge, my sword drawn as we navigated the uneven terrain between the forest and the town. We approached the outskirts of Evenshire swiftly, using the shadows to our advantage. We encountered pockets of resistance—Wintmorian soldiers attempting to regroup amidst the chaos.

"Push through!" I deflected an enemy spear with a quick riposte and sent my opponent reeling. Behind me, my men engaged the enemy headlong. The clash of steel rang out as the two forces met, the sounds of battle blending with the roar of the fire. Cedric and the archers provided support from the rooftops and alleyways, their arrows finding marks with lethal precision, giving us the cover we needed.

I reached the last known location of Edric's team. The heat from the fire had grown intense, the flames roaring and sending sparks into the night sky. Sweat trickled down my back and the acrid smoke stung my eyes.

"Edric!" I called out. The smoke burned my throat, each breath a struggle as I strained to hear any response. "Edric! Can you hear me?"

A figure emerged from the swirling smoke—a Centralian soldier, stumbling toward us. He was coughing and spluttering, his face streaked with soot, clutching a wound on his arm. I rushed at once to help him.

"We walked straight into their trap," the soldier gasped, his voice barely audible. "False supply crates—rigged to shoot jagged spikes —scattered us before we could regroup. They knew we were coming, sir." My heart sank, a wave of cold fear washing over me. "Where's Edric? Where are the others?" I demanded, my grip on his shoulder tighter than I intended.

"Scattered," he managed, deflated. "Some were captured... Edric was still fighting when I last saw him."

The news sliced through my heart like a blade. It was my fault. Edric had volunteered because I'd asked him to, because of his deep-rooted loyalty. The thought clawed at me, sharp and relentless. I forced myself to stand straight, to appear strong for my men.

"We have to find them." I teetered on the edges of fury and desperation. Cedric appeared at my side, his expression grave as he took in the situation. "The Wintmorians are regrouping," he warned. "We need to act fast."

My mind raced. The mission had taken a dire turn, and every moment was precious. I forced myself to take a deep breath, to think. "Form defensive positions here," I ordered, my voice carrying over the noise. "We hold this ground while we search for our men."

Our soldiers moved swiftly, establishing a perimeter amidst the narrow, winding streets. "Split into teams," I instructed. "Search every building, every alley. Look for our comrades and any Wintmorian forces. We won't leave anyone behind."

The soldiers fanned out. The urgency pressed heavily on all of us. The element of surprise was gone, and we knew the enemy was fully aware of our presence. Time was running out.

I led a group deeper into the heart of the town, attacking the enemies as we advanced. The cries of panicked townsfolk echoed off the stone walls and mingled with the shouts of Wintmorian officers rallying their troops. I had to find Edric—I had to bring him back. Turning a corner, I froze. A shadowed line of prisoners shuffled forward under the watch of enemy soldiers. My chest tightened when I spotted him—Edric, hands bound, his head bowed under the weight of exhaustion and pain. Even in the dim firelight, the wicked bruise on his cheek was unmistakable. My stomach churned. I had failed him.

CHAPTER 39

E dric!" I shouted, my knees almost buckling.
His head snapped up, surprise and relief flashing across his face, but before he could respond, his eyes widened. "Kaelan! Watch out!"

The Wintmorian guards reacted instantly, drawing their weapons. There was no time to think. "Engage!" I commanded, and we rushed forward, weapons drawn. The clash was immediate, the narrow space making every movement urgent, every strike a matter of survival.

Anger fueled me, and the need to reach Edric consumed me—I couldn't lose him, not now.

Above us, Cedric appeared on a rooftop, loosing arrows with deadly precision. Edric seized the chance, elbowing the guard behind him. The man's grip loosened, and one of our soldiers quickly moved in, cutting Edric's bonds. He wasted no time, grabbing a fallen sword and falling into step beside me.

"Just another day in the chaos," Edric remarked, a weary grin tugging at his lips as he joined the fight.

Relief flooded me. "You always have to make things interesting, don't you?" He laughed and fell in line and together, we fought, our movements coordinated side by side.

Within moments, we had overpowered the remaining guards. The prisoners—both Centralian soldiers and a few townsfolk—were freed, and we armed them where we could. The need for haste was sharper now. We had to move.

I glanced around as the sounds of approaching soldiers grew louder. "The enemy will be upon us any minute."

"Agreed. They've got more forces heading this way. Our undertaking is compromised."

We began a deliberate withdrawal, moving swiftly through the winding streets back toward our lines. Cedric signaled the archers to cover our retreat, their arrows flying to deter any pursuing forces.

I joined the main group, my eyes darting between the soldiers around me. "We have who we can. We need to extract now," I called out, Sir Gareth's voice cut through the chaos as he arrived with reinforcements. "Fall back to the forest! We'll regroup there!" he commanded, his presence a reassuring anchor amidst the disorder.

We withdrew with practiced haste, covering each other. The Wintmorians, still disoriented by the attack and the raging fire, were slow to pursue, giving us the precious moments we needed. Reaching the relative safety of the trees, I finally allowed myself a breath. The soldiers around me were doing the same, their faces illuminated by the glow of Evenshire's burning depot, the flames lighting up the sky behind us. The Wintmorian shouts faded, swallowed by the night and the dense forest.

✳✳✳

The battle was over, but the air still trembled with the chaos of combat. We had escaped the melee but still felt entangled in it as if it had left its imprint in our bones. The soldiers settled into their defensive positions, but I continued to ruminate all that had happened just a few hours ago, how I had come close to losing Edric. I turned to Edric, the knot of worry in my chest finally loosening. "Are you alright?" My voice was hoarse from shouting.

Edric gave a weary smile, "A few scrapes, nothing serious," he said, his gaze turning back toward the direction of the Wintmorian storerooms. "We walked right into a trap, Kaelan. They must have anticipated our move."

I let my eyes drift to the soldiers around me—some tending to wounds, others murmuring low, exhausted words to one another. There was no triumph here, not yet. We had won a battle, but the war loomed larger than ever.

Cedric joined us, his expression grim. The concern etched on his face mirrored my own. "We need to rethink our approach," he said, deepening my sense of foreboding. "They've clearly strengthened their defenses."

Before I could respond, Sir Gareth approached, his face set in a serious expression. "This was more than just a simple supply storeroom. The Wintmorians were prepared for an attack."

"We need to inform command," I replied, my voice steady despite the turmoil inside me. "This situation is more complex than we realized."

"Agreed," Sir Gareth said, his gaze sweeping over the men, assessing their condition. "For now, we set up a defensive position and tend to the wounded. We'll plan our next move come morning."

The soldiers settled into the makeshift camp, and I tried to rest. The mission hadn't gone as planned—we'd lost men, and the enemy had been ready for us. But we'd managed to rescue our comrades and gather vital information. For now, that would have to be enough.

I found myself gazing back toward Evenshire. The fires were still visible against the dark sky. The orange glow illuminated the town's silhouette, and the crackling of burning wood and the distant sounds of chaos were an aftermath of what had unfolded moments before. The undertaking had turned into a harrowing ordeal, revealing the enemy's cunning and preparedness. Murmurs of concern spread among the men, but not for long. We couldn't afford to let this setback crush us.

Once everyone had reached a safe distance from the immediate danger, Sir Gareth gathered the officers and key soldiers around a makeshift campfire. The flickering flames cast a glow on our weary faces as he peered into our faces one by one.

"Listen," Sir Gareth began, "We've faced unexpected challenges tonight, but we managed to rescue our comrades and gather crucial information. However, we can't afford to let the Wintmorians regroup and strengthen their hold on Evenshire."

I nodded. We weren't done yet—not by a long shot.

"We have a narrow window of opportunity," Gareth continued. "If we strike now, while their forces are still disoriented and recovering from the recent attack, we can cripple their supply lines and disrupt their operations significantly."

The idea of a decisive strike sounded like a good plan, rekindling the fire that had driven us to take on this mission in the first place. I clenched my fist, nodding to myself.

"We need to act swiftly and decisively," Gareth said, his voice as unwavering as ever. "The longer we wait, the more time the

Wintmorians have to reinforce and strategize. Our scouts suggest that their command structure is vulnerable at the moment. This is our chance to deliver a crippling blow."

Beside me, Edric, despite nursing his wounds, stood ready. "What's the plan, sir?" he asked.

"We'll form two main groups. One will lead the charge directly into Evenshire, targeting key infrastructure and command centers to sow chaos and disrupt their communications. The other group will flank from the north, cutting off any potential reinforcements and securing our rear."

Cedric nodded thoughtfully. "It's a bold move, but with the element of surprise still on our side, it could be our best shot at turning the tide in our favor."

"Gather your men and prepare for deployment. We'll need every ounce of strength and strategy to make this work."

The soldiers dispersed to their assigned roles. The air was thick with anticipation as the regiment began to mobilize, the sounds of footsteps and hushed commands filling the stillness of the night. I took a moment to confer with Sir Gareth, finalizing the last details of the assault. Maps were reviewed again, routes were confirmed, and provisions were made for the unexpected. As dawn approached, we began to march, the ground crunching beneath our boots as we moved toward the dense forest that bordered Evenshire. The horn sounded again, its powerful blast signaling the commencement of our assault. We quickened our pace and marched with determination.

The dense forest loomed ahead with shadowy depths and the faintest trace of something almost imperceptible, but unsettling. Trees stood tall and close-knit, their branches intertwined to form a natural barrier against the morning light. We plunged into the foliage, moving swiftly yet cautiously through the underbrush. The sounds of rustling leaves and snapping twigs were masked by our disciplined march, each step calculated to maintain stealth and cohesion.

I led the main contingent, my eyes roaming the surroundings for any signs of enemy sentries. Edric and Cedric flanked me. We were relieved that, at least, we were doing something.

After what felt like an eternity of silent advancement, we emerged into a clearing just outside Evenshire. The town lay before us, and the streets were lit by scattered lanterns, their flickering flames casting eerie shadows on the snow-covered ground.

"The quarries are marked here," Sir Gareth indicated a cluster of warehouses and supply depots near the river's edge. "This is where their supplies are stored."

I nodded, formulating the plan in my mind. "Edric, lead the charge on the west side. Cedric, your archers provide cover from the rooftops. I'll coordinate the flanking maneuvers."

An uneasy silence settled with us. The tension was palpable, each of us aware that the next few moments could decide the fate of Evenshire.

CHAPTER
40

O n my signal," I whispered, my gaze fixed on the town. "Now!"

With synchronized movement, the regiment launched their assault. Edric and his spear-wielding warriors surged forward, moving swiftly to breach the western defenses. The sound of their advance was muffled by the dense forest, but the impact of their force was immediate. With a deafening roar, they smashed through the wooden barricades, steel meeting wood with violent force. I moved to the side, overseeing the flanking units. "Cedric, open fire!" I commanded.

From their elevated positions on the rooftops, the archers loosed a barrage of arrows into the enemy ranks. The Wintmorians, caught off guard by the simultaneous assault from multiple directions, struggled to maintain their formation. Screams and shouts filled the air as soldiers fell, their armor dented and weapons shattered.

"Push forward!" I urged, my sword slicing through the chaos. We moved methodically, securing each building and storeroom with strategic precision. Inside the warehouses, smoke and flames engulfed the supply stores as controlled explosions detonated, ensuring that no valuable resources remained intact.

The Wintmorians, now fully aware of the assault, regrouped and counterattacked with renewed vigor.

As the battle raged on, the tide began to turn in our favor. The disciplined assaults from multiple fronts overwhelmed the Wintmorians, whose numbers dwindled under the relentless pressure. The archers maintained a steady flow of arrows, while the infantry pressed forward, securing strategic points within the town.

Sir Gareth moved through the battlefield with his formidable presence, directing troops and ensuring that every sector was held. "Centralia's forces are holding steady," Sir Gareth reported, his voice carrying authority. "We need to keep the pressure up. Push them back and fortify our defenses."

I nodded, my mind focused on the objective. "We need to eliminate any remaining resistance. Evenshire can't be used as a foothold for further Wintmorian operations."

With the main storerooms destroyed and the enemy forces fragmented, the remaining Wintmorian soldiers were forced into disarray. Our soldiers advanced confidently, reclaiming each street and building with swift efficiency. The combined efforts of the regiment, under Sir Gareth's leadership, ensured that no corner of Evenshire remained untouched by our assault.

I led a group of soldiers through the central square, where the last of the Wintmorian resistance was concentrated. The sounds of battle began to subside, replaced by the crackling of fires and the distant cries of the wounded. Smoke hung heavy in the air.

***

The town of Evenshire was finally ours, yet the weight of victory settled heavily on my shoulders. As the regiment moved through the streets, securing our foothold, I watched the wounded, both friend and foe and felt the quiet ache of what we had lost. The cost of triumph was far steeper than I had imagined. The once-bustling supply storehouses were now charred remnants, their purpose as lifelines for the Wintmorians permanently severed. The once-pristine town of Evenshire now lay in ruins. As we moved through the streets, I passed the old smithy where I had once watched children play. The sounds of laughter were replaced by the crackling of fires and the groans of the wounded. Was this the price of freedom? Was it worth it? Victory, they called it, but all I could see was a quiet devastation. A heaviness choked me—the cost of a victory paid in blood.

Sir Gareth approached me, a satisfied smile on his face. "Well done, Kaelan. Your leadership was instrumental in this victory. "You've done well, Kaelan," Sir Gareth's voice softened slightly as if acknowledging more than just the battle. I. shook my head modestly. "Everyone fought bravely, sir" I replied, glancing around at the soldiers still moving with purpose despite their fatigue.

"We are all defending our homeland. Remember, victory here is just a moment in the long war. Your leadership... It carries the weight of many. Don't forget that."

"Thank you, sir."

As the dust settled and the fires burned low, the regiment began the process of fortifying Evenshire against any potential future assaults. Chirurgeons and healers worked tirelessly to tend to the wounded, while craftsmen assessed the damage to the town's infrastructure.

I took a moment to stand with my friends, looking out over the reclaimed town. The first light of dawn began to break, casting a hopeful glow over the horizon. "We did it," Edric said quietly, a mixture of relief and pride in his voice.

"Yes," I agreed, placing a hand on his shoulder. "But our work isn't done. We need to stay vigilant and continue to push back the enemy." The fatigue I felt was undeniable, but I knew there was no time to rest completely. There was always more to do, more to fight for.

Cedric nodded, his gaze fixed on the horizon. "Evenshire is just the beginning. We have more battles to fight, but today we take one step closer to securing peace for Centralia."

Sir Gareth addressed the assembled soldiers, his voice carrying a tone of both gratitude and determination. "Today, we have achieved a significant victory. Evenshire stands as a testament to our strength and unity. But remember, the war is not over. The Wintmorians will regroup, and we must be prepared to meet them head-on."

He paused, allowing his words to sink in. I could see the doggedness in the soldiers around me, their determination solidifying with each word. "Rest now, but remain ready. Our mission continues, and together, we will ensure that Centralia prevails."

As the regiment settled into the rhythm of victory, I felt a renewed sense of purpose, knowing that the choices I had made, and the sacrifices we had endured, were paving the way for a brighter future. Under the watchful eyes of Sir Gareth, we stood ready to face whatever challenges awaited us, our spirits unbroken and our resolve unwavering.

The following night, the soldiers gathered in the mess hall, sharing stories of valor and moments of levity to lift our spirits.

I sat with Edric and Cedric, reflecting on the day's events. "We need to inform the command about the status of Evenshire and the current Wintmorian operations," I said thoughtfully, my mind already turning to the next steps.

"Agreed," Edric replied, his eyes tired but still sharp. "Sir Gareth is already planning our next moves. We need to stay ahead of them."

Cedric added, "There's a strategic advantage we can exploit with this victory. Cutting off their supply lines here gives us leverage in the larger conflict."

"What's our next target?" I asked, eager to continue our push against the Wintmorians. The victory at Evenshire had ignited a fire within me, and I could feel the same determination mirrored in the soldiers around us.

Sir Gareth reviewed the maps, his finger tracing a route. "Our sources indicate that their main supply route runs through Brackenridge. If we can intercept and disrupt their operations there, we can significantly weaken their forces in the region."

I nodded, my thoughts on what came next. Brackenridge was more than a target—it was the turning point, the key to weakening our enemy's grip on the region. If we took it, we would carve a path through their supply lines, making their efforts untenable. The cost of this victory had been high, and though the spoils of battle lay before us, there was no illusion of ease ahead. The burden of command, of seeing the conflict through to its bitter end, pressed upon my shoulders.

"Yes, sir. It is a strategic location."

"Exactly," Sir Gareth affirmed. "We'll need to mobilize quickly."

With the orders given, the regiment swiftly prepared to move out from Evenshire. I watched as the soldiers gathered their gear, tightened their armor, and shouldered their weapons. As the sun dipped below the horizon, long shadows stretched over the reclaimed town. With a renewed resolve, we set off toward our next objective: Brackenridge.

CHAPTER 41

The first day of the march was hard.

We traveled through dense woodlands and over snow-laden hills, the ground uneven and treacherous beneath our boots. The cold wind whipped at our faces, carrying the scent of pine and the distant echoes of wildlife. We maintained a steady pace, our footsteps crunching rhythmically in the snow. Fatigue from our recent battle wrapped itself around my shoulders, yet, the demands of our charge pushed me onward.

I walked to the front of my regiment, focusing on the path ahead. Beside me, Edric and Cedric kept watchful eyes too. We all knew the risks. But we also knew the stakes. "At least the snow's letting up," Edric commented, glancing at the sky. His voice held a note of optimism, even if it was just a small one.

"Finally," Cedric quipped, brushing snow off his shoulder. "Another hour of that and I would have qualified as a walking snowdrift."

There was scattered laughter, and the men became quiet again. The terrain gradually changed as we moved deeper into the forest; thicker trees, vibrant foliage, and twisted branches. The weather finally eased and the soldiers relaxed, but I couldn't.

My amulet felt warm to the touch all through the day and made me slightly uneasy. Sir Gareth called for a brief halt, allowing the men to catch their breath and check their gear. I took the opportunity to huddle with Edric and Cedric, sharing a flask of water and exchanging quiet words of encouragement.

"Feels like the calm before the storm," Edric murmured, his eyes scanning the woods around us. "Too quiet."

Cedric took a deep gulp from the flask. "Looks like a good day to me."

I heaved a sigh. "We keep moving forward," I replied firmly. "No point in dwelling on what might be. Let's stay focused on what we can control." I knew that fear and doubt could spread like wildfire if we let them. It was my duty to keep us all focused, to keep us pressing onward no matter what.

We resumed our march, moving with practiced precision through the dense forest. The regiment was a well-oiled machine, each soldier knowing his role and place within the formation. I kept my senses sharp, alert to any sign of movement or sound that might indicate an ambush. The tension in the air was almost suffocating, but it also kept us alert.

Several hours later, as the sky began to darken, we reached a small clearing surrounded by towering pines. Sir Gareth raised a hand, signaling the troops to halt.

As soon as he announced we would camp for the night, the men moved swiftly, setting up a cautious camp with low-burning fires. The faint glow of embers and the smell of roasting rations brought a fleeting sense of comfort amid the tension of the dusk.

We settled in for the evening   and I found myself beside Edric and Cedric, our backs against a fallen log. The night was eerily silent. The only sounds were the crackling of the fire and the occasional murmur of conversation among the troops. "It's strange, being out here like this," Cedric said, his gaze fixed on the flames. Edric nodded, his eyes distant. "I said it before, didn't I?"

I smiled, at their banter and reached for my amulet again. It was still warm, neither blazing hot nor cold, and I wondered what it could mean. I shook the thought out of my mind and replied, "But each step we take brings us closer to peace for Centralia. That's what keeps me going."

Cedric poked at the fire, sending a shower of sparks into the cold night air. "Have you ever wondered," he murmured, his voice quieter, "how greatly things have changed over the years? And what shall it be when all this is done? Shall we ever…return to the way of things as they once were?"

Nobody answered. We sat in silence listening to the fire crackling softly in the darkness. I glanced at my friends, the flickering light casting shadows on their faces. We had all changed so much since this war began. The innocence we had once known was long gone, replaced by the hardened exterior that only came from facing death time and again.

"Whatever happens," I said quietly after what seemed like ages, "we shall see it through to the end." My words were more like a promise to myself. No matter what awaited us, I would look out for my comrades. We were bound with something other than just this war.

***

The next morning, we awoke to a sky painted in shades of pink and orange, the sun cresting over the horizon with a promise of fair weather. We broke camp quickly, and before long, we were back on the move, winding our way through the dense forest.

I walked to the front of my men, my gaze focused on the path ahead. I could feel the anticipation building among the men. Brackenridge lay just ahead, and a rising sense of anticipation quickened our steps.   As the sun began its descent, the outlines of Brackenridge finally appeared in the distance. The town was nestled between two hills, its stone walls rising against the backdrop of the surrounding forest. My pulse quickened as we approached, the reality of the impending battle settling heavily upon me.

"Here we go," Cedric muttered, tightening his grip on his bow. I glanced at Edric, his face set, his jaw clenched. "Let's make this count."

The regiment came to a halt at the edge of the forest, just beyond the town's line of sight. Sir Gareth called us together around a makeshift table where a map had been spread out on a flat rock.

"We'll approach from three sides," Sir Gareth instructed, his finger tracing the routes on the map. "The main force will advance from the east, drawing their attention. Meanwhile, the archers will take up positions on the hills to the north and south, providing cover and targeting their defenses."

I scrutinized the map, nodding as I absorbed the details. "And what about the storerooms?" I asked. "If we can disrupt those, we'll weaken their ability to fight back."

"Precisely," Sir Gareth agreed, his gaze meeting mine with a look of confidence that filled me with resolve. Then, he said, "Kaelan, I want you to lead a detachment to the western edge of the town. Take out their supply lines and clear a path for the rest of us."

I nodded.

"We'll get it done, sir."

With the final orders given, the soldiers dispersed, taking up their positions around the town. The tension was palpable, every man acutely aware of the task at hand. As we waited for the signal to advance, I took a deep breath to steady my nerves. This was it—another moment where the outcome of our actions would shape the future of Centralia. The cold air filled my lungs, while the warm glow of my amulet pulsed steadily. It had become part of me; something I had learned to ignore, focusing instead on the task before me.

***

The horn sounded, and we charged forward, emerging from the trees and descending upon Brackenridge with the force of a wave. I led my detachment along the western edge, skirting the line of sight as we moved swiftly toward the storerooms. The snow crunched beneath our boots, muffling the sounds of our approach until we reached the outskirts of the town.

As we entered the first narrow street, the tension tightened. The tall, shadowed buildings seemed to close in, their silence oppressive. I signaled for a pause. I assessed the area, taking in every detail—the distant clamor from the eastern front where the main force had already begun their assault, the faint lantern, lights flickering on doorways, and the muted commands of Wintmorian soldiers ahead. My pulse throbbed, but I forced myself to steady my breath.

My men fanned out, moving with practiced precision, weapons at the ready. Suddenly, a shout echoed from a nearby alley, followed by the pounding of hurried footsteps. I turned just in time to see a group of Wintmorian soldiers rushing toward us, their blades gleaming in the weak sunlight filtering through the clouds.

"Hold your ground!" I commanded, raising my sword. My men formed a tight line, shields forward as the Wintmorians crashed into us. It was here that everything turned on its head.

CHAPTER
42

The first clash was swift. A blade aced towards my side and I twisted, parrying the strike with a powerful slash that forced my opponent back. Moments earlier, my hands had darted to the amulet on my chest, its warmth was like a fire that burned in my heart. My movements were fluid, each strike deliberate, meant to overwhelm rather than merely fend off. Beside me, Edric let out a guttural roar as he thrust his spear into the chest of an oncoming soldier, pinning him into the snow.

The alleyway became a cacophony of grunts and shouts, I ducked beneath a swinging blade, driving my shoulder into the attacker's chest and forcing him back. The Wintmorian stumbled, and I seized the moment, driving my sword into his armor, feeling the give as the blade struck true.

"Keep pushing!" I urged, my voice steady even as chaos surged around us. Cedric stood on a nearby rooftop, his bow drawn and arrow notched. With astonishing ease, Cedric released the arrow, sending it straight into the throat of a Wintmorian soldier who had tried to flank us. I nodded—Cedric's aim was always true, and his presence above gave us an edge.

My eyes darted back to the street, where more Wintmorians were regrouping from the side roads. They had numbers, but I held my ground. I swung my blade in a wide arc, forcing a group of soldiers back as I carved a path through the throng. The fear of failure nibbled at the edge of my thoughts, but I refused to let it take hold. To my left, Edric was locked in a fierce exchange with a towering Wintmorian wielding a massive axe. The man swung with brutal force, the blade cleaving through the air with a deadly whistle. Edric sidestepped the blow, driving his spear into the man's unprotected side. The Wintmorian let out a strangled cry, dropping to his knees as Edric delivered a final thrust. I could see the exhaustion in Edric's eyes, yet he continued to slash and break bones in his wake.

"Kaelan, more coming from the east!" Cedric called out, his voice shrill.

I looked up to another wave of Wintmorian soldiers approaching from the eastern road, their faces set. I signaled for my men to tighten their formation, preparing for the renewed assault. We had come too far to let them push us back now.

"Hold the line!" I shouted, my voice carrying over the chaos. "We fight for Centralia, for our people!"

As the Wintmorians closed in, a fierce rush coursed through my veins, quickening my breath and sharpening my every sense. The day blurred into blood and steel, skirmishes fought in the snow and mud. Men fell, faceless and nameless, their cries echoing long after the fighting ceased. Each victory came at a cost—a dwindling force, a heavier heart. It was as though the gods themselves had lent their fire to my spirit, each heartbeat pounding like the toll of a war drum, steady and unrelenting. The narrow streets had become a battlefield, each alleyway and corner a point of conflict as our forces clashed amidst the snow and blood-streaked cobblestones. The coppery scent of blood mingled with the cold, crisp air and the roar of the main assault echoed through the town, distant yet ever-present.

Sir Gareth led the eastern attack, and he fought as if he had no other purpose in life but to cut down the enemies. I knew we had to break through here—we had to sever the enemy's supply lines and cut off any chance of reinforcements reaching them. I raised my voice, calling out to my men.

"Hold steady! We push forward together!"

Our soldiers answered with a fierce cry, their voices echoing off the stone walls, and their spirits ignited as we advanced deeper into Brackenridge. The streets rang with the sounds of battle, the clash of steel, and the cries of the wounded mingling in a symphony of chaos. I moved with my men, meeting each new wave of Wintmorian soldiers with unyielding force.

Ahead, the enemy regrouped quickly, forming a line of defense just beyond a series of overturned carts and hastily constructed barricades. I scanned their ranks, noting the hardened expressions on their faces. These were not mere recruits—these were seasoned fighters, determined to protect their stronghold at any cost.

"Archers!" I shouted, turning to Cedric. He and the other archers took their positions along the edge of the nearby rooftops, their bows drawn tight as they released arrows in rapid succession. I watched as the projectiles rained down on the Wintmorians, striking armor, flesh, and shields alike. Some soldiers crumpled where they stood, arrows protruding from their bodies, while others scrambled for cover, huddling behind their makeshift defenses.

Taking advantage of the disruption, I led my men forward, weaving through the narrow alleyways that skirted the main road. The ground was treacherous—slick with mud, blood, and fresh snow—but we moved swiftly, gaining ground with every step. The clash of steel on steel echoed around us as we reached the barricades, plunging into close-quarters combat.

I cut them down as they came. I didn't hesitate. Somewhere behind me, someone pleaded for mercy, and another called out for his mama. The sounds were a blur. There was no room for hesitation here—only survival.

Nearby, Edric met an assailant with a swift thrust, the spear tip catching the man just below the chin. The soldier's head snapped back, blood spurting from the wound as he staggered and fell. Edric wasted no time, turning to face another, and driving his spear into the man's side, the force of the blow sending him to the ground, his screams lost in the cacophony.

My attention was pulled to a new threat. A large group of Wintmorian soldiers was attempting to flank us from a side street. I saw the danger—if they succeeded, they could overwhelm our line.

"Cedric, cover the left!" I called out, my voice strained. Cedric nodded and turned, but I hesitated. My eyes followed his as he disappeared into the chaos. He responded without hesitation, pivoting smoothly to unleash a volley of arrows that forced the approaching soldiers back. His arrows struck true, and I watched as the Wintmorians fell, their bodies crumpling in the snow.

"Got it!" Cedric shouted, a grin breaking through the tension on his face. I pushed through the chaotic melee, rallying my men as we advanced. The snow beneath my feet was churned into crimson slush, a treacherous slickness that almost cost me my footing. One of the Wintmorian captains bellowed orders as he attempted to rally his troops and reinforce the barricades.

Our eyes locked for a moment. He knew as well as I did that this line was crucial—if we broke through here, the rest of the town would fall.

I motioned to Edric, to follow me. Together, we charged toward the captain, our boots pounding against the blood-streaked cobblestones. They moved to intercept us, but we cut through them, our swords flashing as we carved a path toward the man shouting commands. I felt the resistance as my blade struck armor and flesh. Warm blood sprayed on my face. My eyes did not leave the captain until I was close. And he met our assault head-on, his sword flashing in a flurry of swift, precise strikes. I barely had time to react, raising my blade to block his attack. He was strong, and he fought with the desperation of a man who knew everything was on the line.

He swung low, aiming to take out my legs and knock me off balance. I leaped back, my heart pounding as I narrowly avoided the blade. He grinned; a predator circling prey, and I knew he was toying with me. The cold air burned in my lungs, and for a moment, all I could hear was the rush of blood in my ears. Edric seized the opening, stepping in with a brutal thrust of his spear. The captain twisted, deflecting the blow, but it left him vulnerable. My blade found its mark, going through his throat. He fell, gargling curses. Almost immediately, the Wintmorian ranks faltered. I staggered, gasping for breath.

"Press them!" I yelled to my men, my voice raw from the effort. As I blocked another swing, for the umpteenth time, a fleeting thought pierced through my resolve: What if we failed? What if I led them all to their deaths?

But the gods still favored us. The barricade began to crumble beneath our assault. The makeshift defenses gave way as we overwhelmed the dwindling defenders. Their line broke, scattering in disarray as they tried to regroup further down the street. I moved swiftly, signaling my men to hold their position as we caught our breath and prepared for the next wave. My heart hammered in my chest and my body ached from the strain. I wiped the sweat from my brow, my eyes scanning the battlefield. The Wintmorians were fierce fighters, but I could see the cracks in their resolve. Their defenses were faltering, their lines unraveling with each push.

Edric joined me, breathing heavily, blood streaking across his armor. "They're on the ropes, Kaelan," he said, his voice filled with hope. "A few more pushes and we'll have them."

I nodded, my gaze fixed on the retreating enemy forces. "We keep pressing," I said. "We can't let them regroup. We need to end this here."

Cedric appeared beside us, his bow still drawn. His face was smeared with soot, but his eyes were sharp and determined. "We've got archers covering the rooftops and streets," he said, his voice steady. "Let's drive them out of here."

I felt a surge of strenght as we rallied our men, pushing forward through the smoke-filled streets of Brackenridge. The clash of steel, the crackle of flames, and the shouts of men filled the air, creating a chaotic symphony that pressed upon my senses. We were close now—I could feel it. One more push and we could take the town.

But the Wintmorians, desperate and defiant, began setting fire to their own buildings in a last-ditch effort to halt our advance. The flames spread quickly, leaping from roof to roof, and consuming the wooden structures with frightening speed. Thick black smoke billowed into the sky, making it hard to see and even harder to breathe.

"Stay close!" I shouted to my men, but my voice was barely audible over the roar of the fire. The heat was oppressive, the smoke stinging my eyes as we advanced. I could see Cedric moving ahead, determined to find a vantage point. He raised his bow, covering the retreat of some of our soldiers as they fell back from a particularly vicious pocket of resistance.

And then, out of the smoke, a Wintmorian soldier emerged, his spear poised to strike. My heart lurched as I realized he was heading straight for Cedric.

"Cedric!" I screamed, but it was too late. The Wintmorian lunged, the spear driving forward with brutal precision. Cedric turned just in time to see it, his eyes widening in shock as the blade pierced through his side. He let out a strangled gasp, his bow slipping from his grasp as he fell to his knees.

"No!" I shouted, my voice breaking. Rage and fear surged through me. I stumbled toward him, cutting down the soldiers that stood in my path. Blood splattered across my face, the warmth only fueling my fury as I swung my blade with everything I had. Slowly, the roar of battle blurred and faded into a dull hum. My brother and friend lay sprawled on the ground, his face pale against a blood-soaked snow. And with each ragged breath, his lifeblood drained from him. I dropped to the ground beside him, my hands trembling as I reached out to support his collapsing form.

"Cedric!" My voice cracked as my hands hovered over the wound, uselessly.

"Stay with me, Cedric. Do not leave me now, I beg you!"

His eyes flickered open, their usual spark dim. He coughed; a wet rattling sound that was bent out of shape. "Looks like…I won't make it to the feast tomorrow."

"Don't say that!"

"Kaelan..." Cedric wheezed, His bloodied hand reached out, trembling. And I grabbed it feeling the chill that was creeping into his skin.

"Do not dare, Cedric!" The voice that came out of me was so strange I couldn't recognize it as mine. "Don't you leave me, Cedric! We're getting out of this together. You promised."

Cedric's lips twitched, his strength fading. "Fight for the both … of us," he murmured. His gaze softened, and for a moment, the chaos around us didn't matter. "And watch your back...you reckless bastard."

"No," my grip tightened as if sheer force could anchor Cedric to this world. "You're not done yet. You've got more tales to tell. More years to live. Don't—"

My heart wrenched. The memory of Cedric's laughter suddenly swept through me, unbidden but vivid. He always had a way of making even the darkest days seem brighter—a talent I envied. And now, here he was, crumpled in the snow, that irreverent grin of his gone.

Cedric gasped, his eyes unfocused, his breathing shallow. "I—I thought... we'd make it."

His gaze met mine one last time, and a faint, wistful smile touched his lips. "It was... an honor." Blood spurted from his mouth.

His eyes fluttered shut, and his body went still.

And then, just like that, he was gone. The light left his eyes, and his body went limp in my arms. The spark that had been my friend, my comrade, extinguished in an instant.

My heart cracked and then imploded. I sat frozen, my hands still clasping Cedric's, the warmth already leeching away. I had lost men before. Comrades, friends, by gods! I had lost Jarin. But this—this was different. This was Cedric, the man who had stood beside me through every bloody trial, who had laughed in the face of death and dared me to do the same.

A scream built in my throat, raw and feral, but I swallowed it down. Not here. Not now. I carefully laid Cedric's body down and closed his eyes with shaky fingers, my jaw clenched so tightly it ached.

"I'll watch my back," I whispered, my voice a rasp. "But you should've stayed to do it yourself, you fool."

Slowly, I rose, my sword unsteady in my grip. I stood over Cedric's body, my hands sticky and cold. I should've done more. I should have saved him this once as he had saved me several times. I should have retreated when we had the chance. But none of that mattered now. Cedric was gone. The man who'd once called me 'the most stubborn ass' in Elsenburg was gone. The friend who could talk me down from my rages with a grin and a joke. The soldier who had followed my every command without hesitation, not because of duty, but because of trust. And I —I had failed him.

What kind of leader let this happen? What kind of friend? What now?

What was I doing here? How had it come to this? Why did I stand amidst this chaos, this sea of blood and steel? The answer should have been simple; to fight, to protect, to endure. But a whisper tugged at the edges of my mind, curling around my resolve, threatening to unravel it. Was it pride that still kept us here? Or duty? Or was it my refusal to admit that the battle was being lost? But what kind of leader abandoned his duty when hope still lingered? I clenched my fists, the weight of grief and guilt pressing down.

Questions tormented me, threatening to hollow me out from the inside. I wanted to stay here, to drown in the weight of it all. To scream until the world cracked apart like my heart just had. But I couldn't.

Because they were watching.

Somewhere out there, my men were watching. They were still fighting, still holding the line because they believed in me. They didn't see the doubt seeping into the cracks and crevices of my broken heart. If they did, the entire fragile crucible holding them together would crumble.

"Damn you, Cedric," I whispered hoarsely. "Why did you leave me to carry this alone?"

There was no room for doubt now.

I would stay and fight.

For Cedric.

His sacrifice demanded more than grief. It demanded blood. And though the weight of his death would linger—would always linger—I would carry it like a shell for as long as I lived.

I cast one last glance at my fallen friend, my chest tight with words I had never had the chance to say.

"Rest now," I murmured. "I'll finish this."

Then I turned toward the fray, my shadow stretching long behind me, as though Cedric was still there, walking with me one last time.

***

But it seemed the universe had something different in mind. I drew my sword, the blade heavy in my hand, and turned back to the battle, my vision narrowing on the enemy lines. The clash of steel echoed. I parried another strike, but even through the frenzy, something felt wrong.

The air was thick with dust, then grew as a low groan beneath my feet, like the sound of a beast waking. I stole a glance toward the Frostspire Hall. The beams sagged precariously, deep cracks spidering across the stone walls where the Wintmore catapults had struck earlier. Loose rubble skittered down grazing my shoulders as I twisted back into the fight.

"Focus!" I snarled at myself, shaking it off. The building could hold a little longer. It had to.

Another warrior barreled towards me with his axe raised above his head. I met him mid-swing, driving him back. My world narrowed to the edge of my blade, the sting of sweat and blood in my eyes, and the roar of men dying around me.

Then, I heard it again; louder this time; a groan that seemed to vibrate through the stone itself.

"Kaelan, move!" someone shouted, but the words were lost in a sudden, terrible crack. My opponent froze, his eyes darting towards the building, mouth agape. For a heartbeat, everything was as still as a dream.

Then, the structure gave way, collapsing in a cascade of burning beams and debris. Beams splintered and fell like giant spears, scraping my skin. Around me, men screamed; some crushed at once, others trapped beneath the weight of centuries-old stone.

"No!" I gasped, too late to stop it. Too late to save them or myself.

Everything surged forward in a blinding deafening rush of stone. Heat and destruction. It groaned one final time like a dying beast before collapsing in a thunderous roar that drowned out everything else. I raised my arms in a futile attempt to shield myself as the weight of the building came down, slamming me to the ground and pinning me beneath the wreckage. The impact knocked the breath from my lungs, and pain erupted through my body, immediate and blinding. My vision blurred, the world fading to a hazy swirl of smoke and ash as I felt consciousness slipping away.

The sounds of battle grew distant, muffled as if I were underwater. I could hear the shouts of my brothers, their voices fading as they were forced to retreat from the fires engulfing the city. Someone called my name—I was sure of it—but the sound was swallowed by the roar of the flames. A face loomed over me. I tried to focus. I forced myself to focus.

"Eamon?"

It blurred into shadows and surfaced again. A white flowing tunic …perhaps gold. I wondered if it was an apparition or a dream.

"Eamon!"

I couldn't hear my voice.

Pain pierced through me like a thousand blades, and I felt myself drifting, my body heavy and limp.

Then, there was darkness.

9 798999 263320